Also by Michael Palmer

OATH OF OFFICE

MICHAEL PALMER

St. Martin's Paperbacks

Excerpt from *Seeds of Deception* used by permission of the author, Jeffrey M. Smith.

This is a work of fiction. All of the characters, organizations, and events portrayed in this novel are either products of the author's imagination or are used fictitiously.

OATH OF OFFICE

For information address St. Martin's Press, 175 Fifth Avenue, New York, NY 10010.

Library of Congress Catalog Card Number: 2011035934

ISBN: 978-0-312-58754-3

Printed in the United States of America

St. Martin's Press hardcover edition / February 2012
St. Martin's Paperbacks edition / January 2013

St. Martin's Paperbacks are published by St. Martin's Press, 175 Fifth Avenue, New York, NY 10010.

10 9 8 7 6 5 4 3 2 1

To Aunt Shirley Rabinowitz, and in loving memory of Aunt Bea

and

To Robin for her laughter, loyalty, and love

ACKNOWLEDGMENTS

Once again, my deepest gratitude goes to Jennifer Enderlin, my remarkable editor at St. Martin's Press, as well as the rest of the gang at SMP, especially Matthew Shear, Sally Richardson, Matt Baldacci, and Rachel Ekstrom.

As with all of my books, agents Meg Ruley, Jane Berkey, and Peggy Gordijn of the Jane Rotrosen Agency have been guiding lights.

When my research needed more, I was lucky to have advice from author Jeffrey M. Smith, Dr. James Gerber, agronomist Aaron J. Lorenz, railroad man Michael Sypulsky, geologist Dan Delea, neurologist Dr. David Grass, author Daniel Palmer, USFS diplomat Matthew Palmer, scholar Luke Palmer, and chef Bill Collins.

And finally, extra-special thanks to ER doc Catherine B. Cuotalow, M.D., Ph.D.

A scientist knew of a species of Arctic flounder that was resistant to freezing in cold temperatures. He wanted his tomatoes to resist cold temperatures so they wouldn't die in frost. The scientist didn't have to wait for the unlikely event of the fish mating with the tomato. Instead, he figured out which gene in the fish keeps it from freezing and then inserted that gene into the tomato's DNA. The anti-freeze gene has never ever, ever existed before in a tomato. But now it's in the scientist's tomatoes and all their future offspring.

Jeffrey M. Smith,
Seeds of Deception

PROLOGUE

I'm finished.

I can't believe this has happened again. I just blew up at one of my patients. The last time, when I screamed at Calvin Summers for continuing to smoke despite a massive heart attack, my medical license was suspended for six months, and I had to go away for treatment. The board of medicine said there was no excuse for that kind of behavior from a doctor, no matter how pure my motives.

Now it's Roberta Jennings. She just stormed out, shouting at me that she was not going to tolerate that kind of abuse, and that she was going to contact the board as soon as she got home. My office staff heard her. The patients in the waiting room heard her.

What am I going to do?

I'm alone. On the wall, beautifully matted and framed by Carolyn, is the signed Hippocratic oath—my oath of office, pledging kindness and compassion to all my patients.

What in the hell have I done?

Jennings's tires just screeched on the pavement as she sped out of the parking lot. I can picture her at the wheel, her face all flushed and angry.

The door to the hallway is closed. I can't simply sit here like a lamb waiting to be dragged to the slaughter, especially when I didn't do anything that wrong. I love my patients, but there's not a chance in the world the board of medicine would understand that. They won't care that Roberta Jennings is eating herself to death.

Hypertension . . . type 2 diabetes . . . ankle edema . . . varicose veins . . . arthritic knees . . . hiatal hernia . . . carbon dioxide narcosis . . .

They won't know how many times I begged her to change—how many diets, how many referrals, how many discussions. They won't see that I had every right to scream at her the way I did. They won't care that I have been at work for hours, seeing my patients in the hospital, which no other docs even do, attending medical rounds, doing paperwork. I haven't even had lunch. I have to do something to save myself—to save my career.

I gaze at two pictures of my family on the corner of my desk. My favorite is the one taken in springtime— Carolyn and our three daughters, huddled together on our front porch swing. The girls are raven-haired beauties, just like their mother. The milkman's kids, I'd often half joke, because they didn't look much like me. The other picture is of Chloe, my youngest. I know I'm not supposed to have a favorite child, so it feels horrible to admit to myself that I do.

Must do something.

Everything I've worked so hard for is in danger. My

breathing is coming hard—shallow and more rapid. It's like I'm trying to suck in molasses. I know exactly what's going on inside me. Chemical signals from the amygdala area of my brain are instructing my heart to beat faster. Adrenaline is being pumped into my bloodstream like rocket fuel.

Witnesses.

Everyone out there is a witness to what happened. They will all be called before the board. That would be the end. A lamb to the slaughter. I must do something to prevent them. I don't remember unlocking my desk drawer and bringing out my pistol. It's still in the locked box I put it in when Joe Perry's office was held up last year.

Now, it's here in my hand.

I release the safety. Everyone out there in the waiting room will testify as to what they heard. And that's all it will take to finish me off. Nobody cares about my patients the way that I do.

Can't believe this happened. . . . What choices do I have? How else can I save my career . . . my family?

People heard. It would be their word against mine. He said/they said. The board would never pull a doctor's license on a flimsy claim like that—especially one as dedicated to his patients as I am. Or would they?

Must do what's fair.

No witnesses.

I open my office door and step out into the hallway. The fluorescent overhead lights are hurting my eyes. With the pistol hanging at my side, I head down the corridor into our newly furnished patient waiting area.

My heart is pounding against my sternum. Blood is churning in my ears. The room has begun to spin.

I wish there were another way.

Two women are in the waiting area—Margaret Dempsey and Allison Roundtree. They both look restless, disturbed by what they heard. I wonder if they were talking about just leaving—deserting my practice and transferring their records to another doctor—probably to my partner, Carl.

Sunlight in the foyer is illuminating dust motes circling in the air. Small details, yet so clear. I double-check that I've got two additional clips tucked inside the pocket of my white coat.

"No witnesses!" I cry out.

Ashley is sitting behind the reception counter, looking distressed. The new nurse, Crystal, is behind her. Ashley is thirty. Two kids. Her glasses hang over her breasts, suspended by a gold lanyard that sparkles against her tight-fitting black sweater.

Details.

There is no other way. I need to protect my career.

For a moment I feel uncertain . . . confused. Then my resolve returns. Must act before they see the gun.

I raise it in front of me.

I'm doing this for us, Carolyn. It's the only way to save the children—to save you and our way of life. Any doctor threatened like I am would handle things the same way. The first shot explodes in my ears. The gun recoils. I fire again and again and again. There is blood everywhere.

Glass shatters.

Ashley looks up at me wide-eyed.

I shoot her in the forehead. She flies backwards and lands on top of Crystal. I feel calm now. In control. I'm a doctor, and I always will be. I begged her to lose weight. I had every right to yell at her. In fact, I didn't even really yell—just raised my voice a little. I walk with determination back down the hallway and turn toward our tiny kitchen. Teresa and Camille are there. They were undoubtedly discussing what to do about me when they heard the shots. Now they are on their feet, screaming.

"No witnesses!" I shout again and again. "No witnesses!"

My office manager tries to speak, but I can't make out what she's saying. My finger tightens, then loosens, then tightens again. The pistol spits fire. Teresa is hit in the throat, Camille in the chest. The women crumble like rag dolls. Camille tries to get up. A shot to the back of her head settles her down. I replace the clip.

Almost done.

Back to the hall. Carl Franklin is in his office. He may not have heard what went on with Roberta, but maybe he did. Carl was never much of a doctor to begin with. He'll probably be ecstatic when they pull my license and tell him to take over my patients because I'm never going to be allowed to be a doctor again.

His office door swings open just as I arrive. Two feet separate us. I can smell his fear. For a moment, I hesitate. I can't get my brain around things. My thoughts are without focus. Is he going to be a witness or isn't he?

"John, what in the hell—?" Carl cries.

I empty the entire clip into his chest and face. His blood splatters over me. Fragments of his bone cut into my skin. I want to tell him it's all Roberta Jennings's fault, but it's too late. I slump against the wall, breathing heavily. They never would have understood. They never would have cared how much being a doctor meant to me.

All at once, I stop.

My God, I've done something very bad. Now the board of medicine will be hard-pressed to let me keep my license at all. I've made a terrible mess of everything. I replace the clip a final time. Then I close my eyes and press the muzzle of the gun to the side of my temple. I picture Chloe in my mind. I'm going to miss her most of all.

Wondering how it all unraveled so quickly, I pull the trigger.

CHAPTER 1

One hour down. Three hours to go.

The afternoon was turning out just as Lou had hoped it would. Enough traffic through the ER to keep things from being boring for Emily, but nothing that would leave her with a lifetime of nightmares and therapy bills. Not that the teen wouldn't be able to handle just about anything that came down the pike. But in an inner city emergency room—even a small satellite facility like the Eisenhower Memorial Hospital Annex—the pike, on occasion, might be carrying violence of the highest order.

"Okay, Em, Mr. Schultz is being a perfect patient. Ten stitches and not a peep out of him. Two more and we'll get him bandaged, up, and home."

"Thank you, Doc," the man beneath the saucer-shaped light said in a raspy voice that could have cut stone. "I didn't feel a thing. Your dad does great work, miss."

"Thank you. I know," Emily replied. "He loves sewing my jeans when they tear, and he was always stitching up my stuffed animals, even when they weren't ripped."

"My son's school has Take Your Kid to Work Day, just like yours," Schultz said, "but I'm a roofer. Three stories up with the wind blowing doesn't seem like a great place for a nine-year-old, so Marky went to the nursing home with my wife and helped her put the trays together. What does your mom do, miss?"

"My name's Emily, Mr. Schultz," she reminded him. "Emily Welcome. My mom's a psychologist. Mostly couples therapy. She didn't think her patients would enjoy having her thirteen-year-old kid sitting in on their sessions."

"I can see why she might feel that way."

"But for a second choice," Lou said, tying off the final stitch, "I believe Mom might have chosen to send Emily up on the roof with you, rather than into this place."

In fact, the first argument he and Renee had gotten into in months was about her belief that there had to be a rule against bringing a doctor's family member into an emergency room—even one with only three nurses, a licensed nurse's aide, an armed security guard, a receptionist, one ER resident, and one board-certified emergency specialist. The Annex essentially served as a walk-in center to reduce the volume of the massive mother ship, just six blocks away.

"Let me send her into the office with Steve," Renee had pleaded.

"Steve's not her father. I am. Besides, how interesting could it be for her to hang out surrounded by a bunch of starched shirts and musty law tomes? I can hear her now reporting to her class: 'I spent my day with my mother's new husband, Steve, watching him making piles of money off a bunch of unfortunates who are suing a bunch of other unfortunates.' Or you might as well send her to my brother's office. Graham does even better at making money than Steve. Plus it might actually give him something to talk to me about besides my lack of a 401(k)."

Even though Lou had ultimately won that round, he had to admit that as usual, Renee had a point, and he had told her so when he apologized for sounding like a jerk. For whatever reason, he had been feeling sorry for himself on the day the forms were due back to the Carlisle School. And despite some misgivings of his own about exposing Em to the raw underbelly of D.C., he had decided to turn Take Your Kid to Work Day into Little Bighorn.

Two hours and thirty-five minutes to go.

So far, so good.

Despite a steady stream of patients, Gerhard Schultz was about as challenging a trauma case as the Eisenhower Annex typically saw. Lou missed the action in the main ER, but in his past life, he had squirreled away enough action points to star in a video game. For now, part-time shifts at the old Annex would do just fine.

Not surprisingly, the patients and the staff loved Emily to pieces. There was a grace and composure surrounding her that won people over almost as quickly as did her dark, unassuming beauty. Thirteen going on thirty. People loved to say that about their kids—especially their daughters. But the old saw, though true in Emily's case, invariably brought Lou a pang. It was hard not to believe that in many ways he had robbed those seventeen years from her.

"Okay, Mr. Schultz," he said, "one of the nurses will be in to dress your arm in just a few minutes. No work until next Monday. If you need a note, the nurse will put one together and I'll sign it. Last tetanus shot?"

"A year or so ago. I . . . um . . . tend to bump into sharp things."

"Sharp, *rusty* things," Lou corrected. "We'll give you a wound-care sheet."

"Your dad's a good man," the roofer said again. "I been around a lot of doctors. I can tell."

"I've been around a lot of fathers, and I can tell, too," Emily said.

Lou wouldn't have been surprised if her smile had healed Schultz's nasty gash then and there, in addition to curing any illness that might have been lurking inside him.

Looking utterly perfect in her sky blue scrubs, she walked back to the doctor's lounge, shoulder to shoulder with her father.

"Well, that was fun," she said when he had settled her in on the sofa, around a cup of hot chocolate from the Keurig machine.

"You think you might like to be a doctor?" Lou asked, remembering that he could have answered that question in the affirmative when he was four.

"I suppose anything's possible. You and Mom are certainly good role models."

"She's a terrific shrink."

"It's hard for you, isn't it."

"What's hard?" Lou asked, knowing perfectly well what she was talking about.

"The divorce."

"It wasn't what I wanted, if that's what you mean."

"People get remarried to their exes. It happens on TV all the time."

"Em, Mom *is* remarried. You got that, bucko? Add me to the mix, and you get a sitcom that would compete with *Modern Family*."

Emily chewed on her lip and picked at a fingernail. "I'm glad you won out and brought me in with you today," she said finally.

"I didn't win anything. It's Take Your Kid to Work Day, and you're my kid. You always were, and you always will be."

Lou crossed to the door and glanced over at the two new arrivals in the waiting room—a Latina woman and the extremely ancient man he assumed was her father. The fellow's color was poor, and he was working for each breath.

"Check an oh-two sat on him, Roz," he said to the nurse, "and have Gordon start going over him right away."

"Thanks. I'm glad you feel that way," Emily was saying. "What would you say if I told you I was losing interest in school?"

Lou narrowly missed spraying out his coffee. "You're, like, tops in your class. You get all A's."

"I'm looking out the window and daydreaming a lot. That can't be anyone's idea of an education."

"You don't go to school to get an education."

Emily immediately perked up. "What do you mean?"

"Call it Welcome's Law. You go to school for the degree. Anything you learn while you're there is gravy."

Her eyes were sparkling now. "Go on."

"Every single day that you manage to stay in school translates into ten thousand people in the world that you won't have to take BS from in your life. The more degrees you have, the fewer little, small-minded people there will be who have big power over you. I stayed in school long enough to get an M.D. degree. Now, nobody can boss me around."

"What about Dr. Filstrup at the Physician Wellness Office?"

Lou groaned. In terms of insight and verbal sparring, Emily was her mother's daughter.

So much for Welcome's Law.

Lou's affiliation with the PWO went back nine years—to the day when his medical license was suspended for self-prescribing amphetamines. He had always been a heavier-than-average drinker, but speed, which he took to handle the sleep-deprivation of working two moonlighting jobs, quickly brought him to his knees. Enter the PWO, an organization devoted to helping doctors with mental illness, physical illness, substance abuse, and behavioral problems. The PWO director arranged for an immediate admission to a rehab facility in Georgia, and kept in close contact with Lou's caseworkers and counselors until his discharge six months later. After that, a PWO monitor met with him weekly, then monthly, and supervised his recovery and urine screens for alcohol and other drugs of abuse.

After a spotless year, his license was restored and he returned to work at Eisenhower Memorial. Three years after that, he was hired as the second of two PWO monitors. For the next year, things went perfectly. Then Walter Filstrup was brought in by the PWO board to head up the program.

"You know, bucko," Lou said to his daughter, "sometimes you're too smart for your own good."

Although he seldom went out of his way to discuss his job frustrations with his child, neither was Lou ever one to measure his words. And the kid was a sponge.

"All right," he said. "Consider my current position with PWO the exception that proves the law. Now, let's get out there and see some patients. You ready to stay in school?"

Emily cocked her head thoughtfully. "For the moment," she said.

"That's all I can ask for. So, let's not fall behind. In the ER business, you never know when something's going to come out of left field and slam you against the wall."

CHAPTER 2

With a nurse, the licensed nurse's aide, and the resident busy with the old man in one of the back examining rooms, Lou handled an ear infection in a toddler, an upper respiratory virus in an elderly woman, and a cracked finger bone in a fifteen-year-old high school shortstop, who was dangerously close to losing an entire limb if he didn't stop leering at the doctor's daughter.

Sixty minutes to go.

It may have been a case of doing the right thing for the wrong reason, but Take Your Kid to Work Day was proving to be a total success.

The nurse clinician, a newlywed named Barbara Waldman, appeared behind a wheelchair at the door to the treatment room. The man in the chair was someone Lou knew well—a sixty-two-year-old who lived in various doorways near the Annex.

"Desmond!" Lou exclaimed, helping the man onto the examining table and out of his tattered air force jacket. "That gang again?"

Desmond Carter dabbed at his bleeding nostrils with a rag and nodded.

For most of the homeless in the area, being beaten for sport by any of several gangs who roamed the neighborhood was routine. Usually, though, the attacks occurred at night. Desmond, though black, was known for playing Irish tunes on a battered pennywhistle. When the music business was slow, he cashed in bottles. A Vietnam vet, he was rail thin, but with eyes that never betrayed the hardship of his life. Today, his face was swollen and bruised, with a split lip and the bloody nose. His oily trousers were shredded at the knees, revealing deep abrasions. One shoe was missing.

"Good to see you, Dr. Lou," Desmond said.

"Sorry this keeps happening, my friend. Want us to send for the police?"

"Ain't worth it. Just some bandages and fix my nose if it's broken. How you been?"

"Doing fine."

"Still at the gym?"

"When I have time. A little sparring, some training when one of the up-and-comers asks for it. Listen, we got to get you undressed and cleaned up. Then we'll check you over and get an X-ray of your nose and any other part that needs it. Desmond, that gorgeous young woman over there is my daughter, Emily. She's here helping us out for the day."

"Ms. Emily," Desmond said, nodding and managing a weak, toothless grin. "It's fine with me if you want to stay."

Lou considered the situation and shook his head.

"Yeah," Emily said. "You walk around your apartment all the time in your boxers."

Had Barbara Waldman been chewing gum, she would have swallowed it.

"You have your hands full with that one, Dr. Welcome," she managed.

"Listen, Em," Lou said, "I don't think so. Why don't you wait in the lounge until we get Desmond taken care of."

He missed his daughter's glare as she left the room.

Nurse and doc gently stripped the vet down and helped him into a pair of disposable scrub pants and a johnny. He had absorbed a pounding, but it was hardly the first time. His abdominal wall was a road map of scars—the result of wounds, Lou had learned, that had led to two Purple Hearts.

Lou clenched his jaw. He had encountered more than enough violence and depravity to have developed something of an immunity, but in truth, he knew he would never be inured—especially when the victim was a guy like Desmond Carter.

He was preparing to examine the man when he heard the soft clearing of a throat from the doorway. Emily was standing there, hands on her hips, looking incredibly like her mother.

"Dad, you know how much I hate being treated like a baby," she said. "I've seen street people before and black people, and even hurt people. It's okay for me to watch—I promise you. You're not protecting me from anything."

Lou looked up at the ceiling and then the wall—anyplace but at his daughter's wonderful face. He had been outmatched by her from the day she was born. Besides, exposing her to Desmond Carter this way seemed right. Still, it was probably something he should discuss with Renee. He envisioned his ex after the fact, arms folded, tapping her foot in exasperation, and heard her reminding him that she did, in fact, have a cell phone.

Better to ask forgiveness than permission, he decided.

"Barbara, does Desmond have a record of an HIV test?"

"Negative test drawn here four months ago," she said.

"Em, you can come in," he heard himself say. "But stand over there by the wall. Barbara, how about getting her into double gloves and a gown. Might as well give her a face shield as well."

Swimming in her gown and looking like a teenager from outer space, Emily inched forward and watched as Lou packed both Desmond's nostrils and explained what he was searching for in each segment of his physical exam. He could see her eyes widen at the man's scars.

"Desmond, are you sure about no police?" Lou asked.

"Next time, maybe. I got a caseworker. I'll tell her."

Sure.

"Barbara," Lou said, turning to the nurse, "how about ordering a chest film and nasal bones? Maybe get a

CBC as well. Then we'll do whatever we have to, to fix that schnoz."

"Okay. Then I'm going to stop in the back and see if Gordo and Roz are all right with that poor old man. I think they're going to transfer him."

"No problem," Lou said.

Moments later, the receptionist appeared at the doorway.

"Dr. Welcome, there's a Dr. Filstrup on the line for you—he says it's urgent."

Lou suppressed a smile.

An urgent call from Walter Filstrup. That had to be an absolute first. He probably wanted Lou to pick up some tuna on his way home and drop it off at the office.

Largely because of the documented strength of his recovery, and the way he related to clients, Lou was well regarded by the PWO board. But he was hardly ready to take over as director. And the truth was, there were few beside Filstrup who seemed interested in the job.

From day one, he and Filstrup were like a cobra and a mongoose—actually, more like a cobra and a *baby* goose. The wellness office was a small one as physician health programs went, leaving the opinionated, bombastic therapist with only a couple of minions to boss around . . . chief among them, Lou.

"Em," Lou said, "Barbara will be right back. Linda, please patch Dr. Filstrup over to the doctors' lounge. I'll talk to him there."

The phone was ringing as Lou entered the lounge.

"Welcome? It's me."

Lou cringed at the sound of his boss's voice. "I'm a little busy right—"

"Welcome, listen. You've really blown it this time."

"I left the seat up in the office men's room?"

"You're not funny. In fact, you're never funny."

"Walter, what is this all about?"

"It's about your darling client, John Meacham, the man whose license you single-handedly got restored."

"He's a terrific guy and a terrific doc. I had coffee with him the day before yesterday. He's doing fine."

"Well, today he shot seven people to death in his office and then turned the gun on himself."

Lou sank onto the arm of the worn leather sofa, unable to take in a breath. "If you're messing with me, Walter," he managed finally, "I swear, I'm going to hang you by your thumbs."

"Turn on the news. Any news."

"You sure it's our client?"

"*Your* client. In case you forget, I never thought he was too tightly wrapped, and I told you that on more than one occasion. I kept pushing to get rid of that touchy-feely social worker therapist you were using, and to get him to a psychiatrist. But no."

"Walter, stop it! This isn't the time. Tell me again. John killed seven people in his office and then killed himself?"

"Not exactly. They're all dead. He isn't."

"Where did they take him?"

"DeLand Regional."

"As soon as I can get relief here, I'm going out there. I can't believe this."

"Believe it. And believe something else, too. All those supporters you have on the board may not be so supporting after this."

Rather than make a disastrous situation even worse, Lou set down the receiver. Surprised when his legs held him up, he stepped numbly into the hallway, headed back to Emily. Ahead of him, facing into the treatment room, her arms folded severely across her chest, her magnificent profile as motionless as marble, was Renee.

Lou moved in next to her. Barbara Waldman had clearly not yet returned, and Emily was alone in the room with Desmond Carter. She had moved to the man's bedside and was holding his hand.

Renee's disapproving expression would live forever in the Take Your Kid to Work hall of fame.

At that moment, Emily looked up. "Mom!" she cried with unbridled glee. "Guess what? I'm going to be a doctor!"

CHAPTER 3

The First Lady of the United States, Darlene Mallory, snapped her flip phone closed and glanced over her shoulder at her chief of staff, seated directly behind her. That look was more than enough for Kim Hajjar to know what had transpired.

"He's not coming, is he," Kim said, leaning forward and whispering in Darlene's ear.

"No, he's not. Try to look happy."

"You mean as opposed to looking like I want to wring your husband's presidential neck?"

Strictly for any paparazzi who might be watching, Darlene forced a smile and nodded. "I'm getting tired of this, Kim."

"I know, hon, I know."

"Last week he announced his intention to begin his reelection campaign."

"No surprise to anyone."

"Except me. He never even spoke to me about it."

Kim hugged her friend. It had been six years since

she had agreed to join her former Kansas State room-mate, then Senator Martin Mallory's wife, in Washington. During that time, the two women had grown closer than ever. The press cared little about First Lady appointments, but what coverage they devoted to Hajjar never failed to mention that she was the first Lebanese White House chief of staff, and that she was a former beauty queen. They seldom touched on her master's degree in sociology. With cameras watching Darlene's every move, having an aide with whom she could communicate almost telepathically had proved invaluable.

"Well, I suppose I'd better push on with this," Darlene said, sighing.

"Does Martin know how much press is here covering this event?"

"I believe that's why he's not coming. The kids are going to be so disappointed. The director says they've worked really hard on their song."

"I'll schedule them to sing at the Rose Garden next week when you and Martin are welcoming the President of Ireland."

"Do you think Martin will be upset if we do that?"

"I don't think he'll care. In fact, he may blow off President Callaghan the way he did these kids. The position sounds important, but in Ireland it's largely ceremonial. Still, Callaghan being a woman, Martin may not want to withstand the flak of standing her up."

Darlene smiled even though her insides were knotted up. "What would I do without you, Hajjar? Put yourself in for a raise."

"That's just what I need to do. I can see the headlines

NOW: ECONOMY DESCENDING DEEPER INTO DUMPER. FIRST LADY CELEBRATES BY RAISING STAFF PAY."

"Okay, no raise. I'll think of something, though. . . . Well, the director's got a what-are-we-waiting-for expression. I suppose I need to move on."

"You'll be great as usual."

Darlene stood, smoothed her skirt, and gave the press corps her A smile. She had chosen a baby blue suit for the ribbon-cutting ceremony, which was in celebration of the grand opening of D.C.'s new Boys & Girls Club. The suit had cost $120 at Macy's, and it sold out from every department store the first day she had worn it in public. Thanks largely to Kim's tutelage, she now knew what colors best flattered her fair complexion, light brown hair, and hazel eyes.

Her brief speech would focus on her two favorite topics—raising her daughter, Lisa, now a sophomore at Yale, and working as first a pediatrician and then the president's wife to improve the nutrition of all citizens of the world, especially children.

Unlike some First Ladies who embraced the guilty pleasure of fashion, Darlene did not, and whenever the cameras weren't rolling, she favored the dungarees and plaid work shirts that were the mainstay of her wardrobe at K State.

"Once a farmer, always a farmer," she had been oft quoted regarding her background as a wheat farmer's daughter.

To the left of the two rows of folding chairs where they were sitting, a broad blue ribbon stretched diagonally across the glass doors of the gleaming new building fluttered gently in the breeze. The Young People's Chorus stood off to one side on metal risers, waiting patiently to sing their song, "The Face of the Waters." Kim had researched the piece and passed on the information that it was about creation. It was a fitting anthem, thought Darlene, considering that once again, she needed to create an explanation for President Mallory's absence. Politics aside, his recently unpredictable behavior concerned her the way it would any loving and devoted wife.

Martin's nosedive in the popularity polls was one of the most historic drops in presidential history. But before the economy tanked, he had touted this particular Boys & Girls Club as a symbol of America's renewed community spirit, and a shining example of the effectiveness of his controversial domestic spending policies. Now, with the country's fortunes in free fall, the costly modern steel and glass structure might well become a symbol of his administration's fiscal excesses.

Darlene crossed to the lectern and spoke to the crowd of several hundred. "I'm afraid I have just received a call from my husband. He is tied up in an emergency meeting and regrettably will not be able to attend this magnificent grand opening. However, he is making arrangements for the Young People's—"

"Is he scared to show his face in public?"

Through the glare of the afternoon sun, Darlene could not see the face of the man heckling her, but he was certainly close by. Too close. Kim must have sensed Darlene's concern, because she immediately went into attack mode and began scouring the crowd for the potentially dangerous protester. The large Secret Service contingent did the same.

Meanwhile, Darlene continued with her address. "The president wanted me to let you know—"

The heckler wasn't finished. "What's next?" he called out. "Will our tax dollars buy a new football stadium for the Skins?"

By this time, Kim had spotted the man and alerted Secret Service agents to his location. The agents acted quickly to cull the protester from the crowd. Darlene was used to hecklers, although their numbers seemed to be increasing at every one of her appearances. It made her sad that the outburst may have eclipsed the real story of the day, which was the children. Perhaps it would turn out for the best that the president had chosen to stay home.

Immersed in a forest of angry pickets, most of the anti-Mallory protesters that day were kept at bay behind a sawhorse barrier set up across the parking lot. Darlene estimated their number might be half as many as those attending the ceremony. In addition, signs with unflattering epithets for the president and his administration were nailed to nearly every tree in the area.

The kids were getting a serious lesson in civics, American style.

Undeterred, Darlene smiled and was about to start speaking again when she felt a tiny tap on her right arm. She looked down into the wide, tear-filled eyes of a boy, no more than seven or eight. The child was dressed splendidly in a green and blue striped tie and V-neck pullover sweater.

"Please," he said. "I promised my mommy and daddy the president would be here. Please."

Darlene laid a hand on his tiny shoulder and swallowed at the orange-sized lump in her throat. Kim immediately sized up the situation and led the child back to his parents.

"Listen," Kim said when she had returned. "How about if I cover for you and you try again to get him down here? It's only, like, a five-minute drive, and the motorcade is probably still standing by."

Darlene smiled at her friend. "Did you just read my mind?"

"No, I read your eyes—probably the easiest thing I'll have to do all day."

"Do you need my talking points?"

"Darlene, I might not spend my free time dissecting every global conflict like some First Lady that I know, but trust me, I could give this speech in my sleep. For now, I'll just stall them—maybe do a little soft-shoe."

Darlene stepped back to the microphone, introduced Kim, and then excused herself from the platform stage. A few feet away, she stopped at a relatively secluded area and, with Secret Service agents keeping close watch, called her husband for the second time.

"Darlene, what is it? Is everything all right?" Martin sounded genuinely worried, probably fearing that the protesters had turned violent.

"Everything here is fine, Marty," Darlene said. "In fact, it's better than fine. It's really something special, except you're not here and you should be."

"Is that why you're calling me?"

Darlene heard the anger in her husband's voice. He had never had much of a temper, but lately outbursts to one degree or another had been coming more and more frequently. At the podium, Kim was entertaining the crowd with stock humorous stories about Darlene's college days.

"Look, I know you're concerned about the polls, honey," Darlene said to Martin, "but you need to stand up for what you believe. Polls don't mean a thing. Polls didn't get you reelected; people did. And these people care about you."

Martin breathed heavily into the phone. "Darlene, what the hell is wrong with you! Are you blind?"

Darlene's pulse accelerated the way it did in the moments before they fought. She felt defensive and was surprised at how quickly her husband had angered. "Please don't speak to me that way, Martin," she said in a harsh whisper.

"Agent Siliphant radioed me. I know how many protesters are there. Do you think I want to come just to get shouted down by an angry mob? Do you know what my approval rating is right now? Do you?"

"Marty . . . I . . ."

"Thirty-eight! Down in less than a year from sixty."

"Please, Martin. Do this for the children."

"You better have made a good excuse for why it is I'm not there, Darlene. I don't want to hear on the news tonight that President Mallory is a coward, or doesn't give a shit about needy kids. That club wouldn't exist except for my initiative."

There was a click and the line went dead. Darlene

stood shaking, breathing deeply to calm herself. At the podium, the mayor had taken over and was regaling the crowd with a story about his childhood on the harrowing streets of D.C.

Kim appeared by her side. "Let me guess," she said. "It didn't go well."

Darlene's hands were still shaking. "I'm really worried about him," she said. "It was never like Martin to behave this way. He's never run from a fight in his life. What do you think we should do?"

Kim answered with an impish grin. "I say once we're done here, we've got two choices for what we should do next."

"And those would be?"

"Either we go shopping, or we go get a drink."

CHAPTER 4

Fighting to control his speed and to maintain at least a modicum of concentration, Lou made the thirty-mile drive from D.C. to DeLand Regional in forty minutes. He hadn't bothered to change out of his scrubs.

Over the years, like most people with a television, he had sat riveted to the set countless times, watching reports of pathetic souls who had, for whatever reason, lost it and gone postal—murdering at random. In most cases, the explanation for the carnage remained a mystery, cloaked in the catchall of *crazy*. After a short stay as the lead, the stories inevitably slipped from the news. The killers who didn't take their own lives, or weren't shot to bits by the police, vanished to prison someplace, or into an asylum. To everyone aside from their shattered families, and the shattered families of their victims, the memory of them vanished like April snow.

Lou could not recall the name of even one of the killers, no matter how many lives they had taken. But

this killer was different. This killer was John Meacham—
for nearly four years, his client, and more recently, his
friend.

Flipping the tuner on the radio of his Toyota, he
checked in on a series of stations. The story was front
and center on many of them, and a bulletin on most of
the rest. Within fifteen minutes, there was nothing new,
and Lou settled back on 103.5 FM, the all-news station.

". . . Meacham, a fifty-two-year-old internal medicine specialist, had been practicing in Kings Ridge
for three years. His partner, sixty-two-year-old Carl
Franklin, was one of the seven victims. At this moment,
Meacham is listed in critical condition at DeLand Regional Hospital. Police speculate that the recoil of his
pistol jerked his shot off line enough to keep it from
being immediately fatal.

"They report that all seven victims were pronounced
dead at the scene of the carnage, Meacham's medical
office on Steward Street in the Kings Ridge Medical
Park. Only one of the victims, a female, whose name is
still being withheld, survived long enough to say anything to authorities. A source in the department has told
reporters that all she said before she died was 'No witnesses.' "

No witnesses.

Lou shrugged and shook his head. Seven dead and
one life hanging by a strand.

No witnesses.

What in the hell does that mean?

Emily had gone home with Renee, and the chief of

the ER department at Eisenhower had rushed over to finish out Lou's shift. The severe weather, which had been on and off stormy all day, was on again—fog, wind, and a chilly, pelting rain.

From what Lou knew, Kings Ridge, population maybe ten or fifteen thousand, was a bedroom community for D.C., surrounded by expansive farms, mostly corn. He had driven through it a couple of times, and remembered the downtown as being fairly affluent and well maintained, with a quaint village green, coffee shops, and restaurants spaced along on the main street.

DeLand Regional, a few miles west of the town, was a level-two trauma center, which meant that orthopedics, neurosurgery, and plastics were covered, although not necessarily in house all the time. According to the news, John Meacham had survived a gunshot wound to the right temple. Under usual circumstances, patients with such an injury would have been transported by chopper to the nearest level-one facility, in this case, Eisenhower Memorial itself. Perhaps a neurosurgeon was available at DeLand, Lou speculated, and didn't want to lose a juicy case. Or perhaps the weather was too chancy.

Poor goddamn Meacham.

What in the hell happened out there?

John Meacham was tightly wound, but not *this* tightly wound. In fact, he had a better-than-decent recovery program, and had mellowed considerably. Word was bound to get out that he had been attending Alcoholics Anonymous meetings for four years, and a few hundred alcoholics and drug addicts in need of the program would decide that they were better off going it on their own.

Any excuse in a storm.

Meacham was one of the first docs Lou had been assigned after he went to work part-time as the assistant to the director of Physician Wellness. A father of three, and a history buff, the internist was a lifelong Virginian, working in D.C. at the time. He played bluegrass on several instruments and could take his motorcycle apart and put it back together. The only two drawbacks in his life were his temper and alcohol. The day he exploded at one of his patients for continuing to smoke following a coronary, Meacham admitted to Lou that he had a ferocious hangover after drinking the night before. The result of his outburst was a report by his patient to the board, a six-month suspension, and a referral to the PWO.

Lou ordered an immediate psych evaluation and sent Meacham away for a month of rehab and anger management. As soon as he was discharged home, Lou signed him to a legally binding monitoring agreement—random urine testing twice weekly, regular psychological therapy, frequent face-to-face sessions with Lou, and involvement with AA.

What could go wrong?

Much to his chagrin and that of his dentist, Sid Moskowitz, Lou was a teeth clencher and grinder. Moskowitz had been pushing forever for some kind of mouth guard, but even in the ring, Lou could barely handle an appliance jamming up against his gag centers like two stalks of rubber celery. He could kick the grinding habit, he insisted, even as Moskowitz was totaling up the cost of the crowns he would soon be installing. He could kick the habit just as he had kicked the drugs.

But not today.

With the wipers slapping steadily, Lou turned into the crowded physician parking lot of DeLand Regional. Four cruisers, strobes flashing, were parked near the ER entrance. Twenty-five yards away was a phalanx of sound trucks. Lou estimated that the glass and redbrick three-story hospital had a capacity of somewhere between 150 and 200 beds. It had a decent reputation from what little he knew, although he had no firsthand experience with the place.

Before he made it to the elevator and up to the second-floor ICU, Lou's credentials were checked three times. There were two uniformed cops—a woman and a man—posted outside the unit, and another man, a broad-shouldered African American in plainclothes, whom Lou guessed might regularly rehearse his air of authority in front of a mirror.

"No one's allowed in there," the man said, performing a heavy-lidded inspection of the new arrival.

"I'm a doctor."

"So's the guy in there who just killed seven people."

"Nice comeback. How about if I said I was a close friend of his?"

"ID?"

Lou passed over his driver's license and wallet-sized medical license. "Neither of these says I'm a close friend of his. I left that one at home."

"I can be a wise-ass because I'm in charge," the detective said. "You can't, because you're not. And the head nurse left word that no one is to be let in until she says so. They're going after the bullet in your close friend's head."

"They're what!"

Incredulous that they were going after the bullet in the ICU and not the operating room, Lou stared across at the man, who looked perfectly serious. *Not possible*, Lou was thinking. Even in the most ragtag level-two trauma center imaginable, no one would be fishing for a bullet while inside the ICU. Generally, what remained of the slug were fragments, and more often than not, the brain trauma caused by trying to remove them wasn't worth the benefits. But no matter what, any procedure, whether an exploration or a decompression maneuver to reduce swelling, would be performed in the operating room.

"Going after the bullet," Lou said. "Of course. Just like they do all the time in the movies. Usually, that's when I snatch up my popcorn and leave."

"Too gross?"

"Too absurd."

The remark appeared to have sailed over the cop's head. "What kind of doc are you, anyway?" he asked.

"Emergency. I work at Eisenhower Memorial in the city. Who's going after the bullet?"

"I have no idea. I don't live around here. I'm state police. We were called in to take over for the locals."

Lou was about to grill the man for information when the glass doors to the unit glided apart and a trim, olive-complexioned woman in scrubs emerged. Tension was etched across her face. It took only a second for Lou to recognize her.

"Sara!"

Sara Turnbull and he went way back—almost to the beginning of Lou's residency, when he was razor sharp, thrilled to be having his dreams come true, and enthusiastic as the Energizer Bunny—back to before his father's financial implosion, and Lou's subsequent moonlighting jobs, and the extra shifts, and the utter exhaustion; back to before the unstoppable downward spiral and the amphetamines, and the visits from the drug-enforcement people.

"God, am I glad to see you," Turnbull said. "When they called from downstairs to say you were on the way up, I nearly jumped through the phone. They're killing him in there, Lou. I don't care what he's done, it's not our job to judge."

CHAPTER 5

"Okay if I go in there, Officer?"

"Sorry to give you a hard time," the cop said. "It looks like you have a boxer's knuckle, there. I'm not used to seeing doctors with boxer's knuckles."

"I work in a really tough ER," Lou replied.

Sara Turnbull was a crackerjack nurse—as smart and intuitive as she was compassionate. There was a time when Lou could have added *passionate* to her list of attributes, but those times were long past. The last he had heard from her was a get-well card forwarded to him in rehab.

"How long have you been working here?" Lou asked as they joined the crowd milling in the gleaming ICU.

"Just four months. My husband's a nurse on med/surg. We have a one-year-old son. It's not Eisenhower, but it's a decent-enough place—at least it was. This is a mess, Lou. An absolute mess. I'm charge nurse today, and I can't follow some of the things that are happening."

"Like someone blindly jamming a hemostat into a patient's brain, fishing for a bullet?"

"Exactly. That's Dr. Prichap. As far as I know, he's a decent-enough neurosurgeon, but I've never seen anyone do that."

"It may be a while before you see anyone do it again," Lou said. "What else?"

"Dr. Meacham is going downhill fast, but no one seems all that alarmed. Do you know him?"

"For a few years. We've actually gotten to know one another pretty well. This came right out of the blue. I can't believe he did it."

"He's over there in three. Dr. Schwartz, the intensivist, has been in and out, but mostly it's been Dr. Prichap. It looks as if things have quieted down now. Prichap may have given up hunting for the bullet."

"I hope so," Lou said, almost to himself.

Lou followed Sara into the cubicle, which was crowded to near overflowing with nurses, radiology, lab, and respiratory techs, what appeared to be a resident, and a short, copper-skinned man—probably from India. ANTHAR S. PRICHAP, M.D. was stitched in blue over the breast pocket of his lab coat. Although he wore scrubs beneath his white coat, it appeared that he had performed surgery just as he was. Next to Prichap was a tray with bloody sponges and instruments piled on it.

No bullet.

On the bed, barely visible in the crowd, was John Meacham. His trachea had been intubated through his mouth, and he was being ventilated mechanically by a state-of-the-art machine that occupied most of the space the crush of bodies did not. A tall man—six feet or so—Meacham looked lost, almost diminutive. He appeared to be unconscious. His eyes were taped shut, and his head had been shaved on the right side. The bullet hole, just above his right ear, seemed to have been widened. On the wall view-box were anterior–posterior and lateral skull films showing a deeply embedded slug, fragmented into one small and two larger pieces, none of which were easily accessible to the entrance wound itself.

Dr. Schwartz, the hospital-employed intensivist, was apparently off with other patients. Why hang around for a plain old everyday gunshot wound to the head?

Lou introduced himself to Prichap, and received an uninterested nod in return. No handshake. Then, without a word, the neurosurgeon drifted into the background as Lou conducted a quick visual scan of Meacham. What he saw immediately disturbed him. There were two intravenous lines—one inserted in the elbow crux of Meacham's left arm, and the other at the wrist of the right. The line at the elbow was barely running, despite a blood pressure reading on the monitor screen that demanded fluids and pressor medications—eighty over forty. Surrounding the spot where the catheter had been inserted was a large swelling. The line was infiltrated, and rather than pouring life-supporting fluid into the circulatory system, it was pooling fluid in the tissues.

Careless, dangerous medicine.

"Sara, that needs to be replaced," he said, pointedly ignoring Prichap, who, at that moment, was looking rather pleased with himself for whatever reason.

The Sara Turnbull he remembered would never have

allowed a critically traumatized patient to have only one working IV. Perhaps in the chaos, she simply had not noticed. In seconds, she was taking down the dressing and preparing to replace the IV line—this time at the wrist.

Lou glanced up again at the perilously low blood pressure reading, which had dropped from a systolic of eighty to seventy-four. Unless the cause could be identified and reversed, John Meacham was heading out. Quickly, Lou began mentally ticking through the possibilities. It took only a few seconds to connect with the right one.

Stunned at what he was seeing, Lou worked his stethoscope into place and listened to Meacham's chest. There were no breath sounds on the right side. The exam was not really necessary. All the information he needed was visible in the distension of the jugular veins along the sides of the man's neck, the slight bowing of the trachea toward the left, the persistently low oxygen saturation, and the asymmetrical hyperexpansion of the right chest.

A tension pneumothorax—collapse of the right lung due to a tear, probably caused by excess pressure from the ventilator. Air was being forced by the vent through the ruptured lung and into the chest cavity. The midline structures including the heart, esophagus, aorta, and other great vessels were being pushed to the left. The absence of breath sounds on the right merely confirmed the diagnosis.

Lou noted that the vent pressure was dangerously high and turned it down. From beside the machine, the respiratory tech—a tall, pencil-necked man in his late twenties—stood smiling at him blandly.

Did you do this on purpose? Lou wanted to shout. *Did you?*

"Everyone, please, listen to me," he called out, louder than he'd intended. The commotion immediately stopped. "I'm Dr. Lou Welcome from the ER at Eisenhower Memorial. This man has a rapidly expanding tension pneumothorax. We need to dart his chest immediately to get the air out of there. Then we'll get a chest tube in. I need an IV angiocath in a number sixteen or fourteen needle. Quickly, please."

Missing from the emergency, except in himself, was any sense of tension and urgency. Lou wondered if anyone in the room really cared whether John Meacham made it or not. It would not be hard to understand if they didn't, even though, as Sara had said, it should never be a caregiver's role to pass judgment on any patient.

This was as bad as it could get. . . . Poor bastard. . . . Poor victims.

What in the hell happened?

A large-bore needle with a plastic catheter running through it was brought on an instrument tray, along with latex gloves, a large syringe, surgical sponges, some surgical snaps, and several culture tubes.

Blood pressure, seventy over thirty. Oxygen saturation, 60 percent. Color worsening.

Moving rapidly, Lou gloved and swabbed some Betadine antiseptic below Meacham's collarbone on the right side. Then he set the plastic catheter aside and attached the needle to a 20 cc syringe. His movements were careful and considered, but almost automatic, like a boxer throwing a right-left-right combination.

To Lou's left, behind the crowd, he could see the neurosurgeon, Prichap, gazing almost placidly out the glass wall of the cubicle. No apparent concern, no offer to help out.

The needle thrust was where the right second rib space was intersected by an imaginary line between the middle of the collarbone and the nipple. Gripping the syringe tightly, Lou forced the needle against the top of the third rib, and then drove it to the hilt, over the bone and into Meacham's chest. The jet of air, under great force, actually blew the plunger out of the syringe. Lou twisted the syringe from the hub of the needle, set it on the tray, slid the catheter into Meacham's chest, then quickly sutured it to the skin. Air continued to hiss out as the collapsed lung struggled to reexpand.

Blood pressure, eighty over fifty. Color slightly improved. O_2 sat, seventy-two.

"Chest tube kit, please," Lou said firmly.

"Here you go, Doctor," Turnbull said, replacing the used steel tray with a fresh one and opening the setup used to insert a much larger tube.

Lou glanced over and realized that the blown IV had been replaced by one that was running smoothly. The emergency was beginning to feel more normal. Despite some improvement, however, Meacham was still in big trouble. In case he was not in a coma, Lou anesthetized an area of skin over the fifth rib, two inches below the catheter. Then, using a scalpel, he opened a slit through skin and muscle, grasped the end of the chest tube with a heavy clamp, and drove it into the space between the still-deflated lung and the inside of the chest wall. Given the relatively minor trauma of most of the patients in the Eisenhower Memorial Annex, this was, he realized, the first time he had inserted a chest tube since before he was sent away.

Just like riding a bike.

A suture to hold the tube in place, connection to a water-seal container to keep air from being sucked back into the chest cavity, and the deal was done.

Pressure, still eighty over fifty. O_2 sat, seventy-nine. Not good.

Lou knew that all he had accomplished was bringing John Meacham back to a man with a bullet hole in his head.

"Nice job," Turnbull whispered, squeezing Lou's elbow.

"Thanks, although I suspect the barn door might be closed shut by now. I don't know who I should go ballistic at first—the respiratory tech, the IV nurse, or that Prichap guy."

"I haven't had much experience with him, but like I said, I've never heard anything bad."

"Well, you have now. How about I take a few deep breaths in the interest of reestablishing my serenity, and speak to him."

"There's a small nurses' lounge out there to the right. Tell me when, and I'll bring him there for you."

"Provided you can get his attention away from the painting on that wall out there."

Lou checked Meacham over again. Not much change.

He tried to imagine what it was like to pull out a gun and shoot to kill someone. It just didn't register. The usual motives—greed, hatred, anger—simply didn't apply. Only crazy.

He headed down the hallway to the nurses' lounge. Two minutes later, Dr. Prichap entered. Once again, he didn't bother shaking Lou's hand. The neurosurgeon, like others in his specialty Lou had dealt with over the years, exuded arrogance. Lou flashed on his four-week rotation holding instruments on the neurosurgery service in medical school.

"Never forget, son," the chief had told him during one seemingly endless procedure, "that's brain you're sucking on."

Just in case, Lou introduced himself again.

Prichap looked as if he could not care less. "The nurse said you wanted to see me," he said.

"I've known Dr. Meacham for a number of years. Just wanted to get your take on what might have happened to him."

"He lost his mind. That is what happened. He lost his mind and killed seven people."

"I suppose. . . . Is this the only hospital you're on the staff of?"

"I am in a five-person group. We cover six or seven hospitals."

"And you've not encountered behavior like Dr. Meacham's in any of those hospitals?"

"Not that I'm aware of. What specialty are you?"

"ER. I work in the ER at Eisenhower."

"I see."

Feeling the surgeon losing interest, Lou decided on a frontal assault. "Tell me, Dr. Prichap, what were you hoping to accomplish by fishing out that bullet?"

Lou fully expected the man to erupt, or at least to storm out of the lounge. Instead, Prichap turned his head and gazed out the window, much as he had in the ICU.

"I . . . do not . . . suppose it . . . would . . . have accomplished . . . anything," he said distantly.

"But if it—"

The surgeon snapped out of his reverie as if he had been jabbed by a cattle prod. "Well, good to meet you, Doctor," he said, turning toward the door.

As he did so, he nearly collided with Sara Turnbull.

"Dr. Prichap, Dr. Welcome," she said breathlessly, "come quickly, please, Dr. Meacham's arrested."

Lou bolted past the neurosurgeon and out the door. DeLand Regional had community support and a reputation for giving good care. Yet the respiratory tech had overinflated Meacham's lungs, the infusion nurse had badly blown a line, and the neurosurgeon was acting like the doctor/barber in a Saturday Western. Even usually reliable Sara Turnbull had failed to notice a malfunctioning IV.

What in the hell was going on?

CHAPTER 6

Bar None was three blocks from the Capitol. The up-
scale lounge served unusual cocktails that seemed to
appeal to congressional aides more than to their stodg-
ier, older bosses. At this hour, it was as safe a place as
any for Darlene and Kim to escape to for a drink. They
waited outside under an awning while a team of Secret
Service agents checked out the interior.

With them on the sidewalk was Victor Ochoa, a tall
veteran agent with salt-and-pepper hair and dark, narrow eyes that appeared to be on constant alert. He
stood a respectful distance from the two women until
sudden static from his radio announced a transmission.

"Cobra here," he said.

"All clear for Buttercup and Wildcat, Cobra," a
woman's voice replied.

"Buttercup and Wildcat," Ochoa echoed.

By tradition, the three members of the First Family
each carried a radio code name beginning with the same
letter. The president, Bronco, had chosen *B* for them.
Darlene had adopted the name of her heroine from the

novel and movie *The Princess Bride,* and Lisa, now twenty-one and a totally independent sophomore at Yale, chose Bullfighter. Kim, to no one's surprise, had gone with the Kansas State mascot.

"Safe in there for a drink, Victor?" Darlene asked.

"So long as you keep away from the Fireball Gimlets, you'll be fine."

The agent escorted them. The space was dimly lit and modestly filled. A jukebox in one corner of the bar played alternative rock songs at a volume that permitted conversation without shouting.

Darlene smiled up at Ochoa and patted him on the arm. "I'm guessing you'd like us to sit over there," she said, pointing to an empty booth that was closest to the emergency exit.

"I knew you'd eventually get the hang of this, Madam First Lady," Ochoa said.

"Victor, it's Darlene. Please. I'd rather you call me Princess Buttercup than Madam First Lady, and you're wrong. I don't think I'll ever fully get the hang of this role."

Ochoa laughed warmly. "Our guide to protocol is thicker than the D.C. phone book. No excessive familiarity, including no first names, even though you're about the most down-to-earth, approachable First Lady I've worked with. Tell you what—I'll be saying *ma'am* and thinking *Darlene.* How's that?"

"That'll be fine. What does your protocol guide say about my going grocery shopping without an advance team clearing the cereal aisle first?"

"It says that isn't going to happen . . . ma'am."

Darlene followed Ochoa, Kim, and another agent beyond the bar, smiling and shaking hands with surprised patrons as she passed by. Then she asked Ochoa for two vodka tonics and settled into the booth, sitting directly across from her friend.

"I'll be the second to admit the constant attention gets tiresome," Kim said. "But at least after shopping, we won't have to lug any of our purchases back home."

"That is a plus. Alas, it was one thing when Martin had an approval rating of sixty percent. Now we're in free fall. The depression or recession, or whatever it is, has seen to it that even shopping is unpleasant for me. Imagine what it must be like for those poor folks who suddenly don't have a job."

Moments later, Ochoa materialized from within the crowd, carrying two tall vodka tonics, each garnished with a crescent of lemon. The women clinked glasses more out of habit than over anything to celebrate.

"I wonder if Victor had to sample our drinks before he brought them over," Kim said.

Darlene took a sip of hers, which she quickly followed with a much longer swallow. The sting of Martin's behavior abated some.

"How did you know this is what I needed?" Darlene asked.

"Honey, it doesn't take Sigmund Freud to figure out that you're stressed out. Look at those circles under your eyes. You've got a social schedule that would exhaust a rhinoceros. On top of that, you're working every spare moment trying to change the eating habits of three hundred million Americans, while keeping the fragile ego of their president appropriately stroked. Sometimes, I don't think you realize just how much you've taken on."

"Well, maybe it's time I put my agenda on a diet."

Kim took a healthy swallow and set her glass firmly on the table. "Nonsense," she said. "Just because the president of the United States acts like your work is irrelevant doesn't make it so. You just have to pace yourself better, that's all—a little more shopping, a little more spa time, a few more vacations, an extra hour at the gym. Sweetheart, you're changing things out there. You've read the reports. You're like the pediatrician to the nation, and people are starting to pay attention to your message."

"Sure, they're starting to listen, but change is coming very slowly. And if we don't get reelected, any chance of making much of a difference will be gone."

"Meal by meal, isn't that your war cry? Keep pushing, Dar. Just don't push yourself over a cliff. Blow off steam when the pressure gets too intense, and for God's sake, don't let that galoot you're married to get away with not giving you or your cause the respect you deserve."

Darlene clinked Kim's glass with more enthusiasm. "You know, Hajjar, I think you'd make someone a great chief of staff. Are you looking for a job?"

"Depends," Kim answered, her rich brown eyes gleaming playfully. "Will I have to keep reminding you how terrific you are?"

"Absolutely," Darlene said.

"Well, then, count me in."

Just then, Ochoa came over to their table, leaned down, and spoke softly in Darlene's ear. "Madam First Lady, Russell Evans is upstairs in the private party room. He asked if you two would be willing to join him for a drink."

Darlene took a hard swallow of her V&T against the tightness that had developed in her chest. She flashed Kim a surprised look.

Evans, former Secretary of Agriculture, had been one of her husband's first cabinet appointments. His resignation, in disgrace, had been responsible for at least some of the drop in Martin's numbers. The scandal had been especially hard on Darlene. She and Evans went back to their childhood years in the Kansas plains town of Dubuque, where their farming families were neighbors even though they lived several miles apart. In fact, Martin had first met Evans through her, not long after the three of them started at Kansas State, and often used him as an adviser during his climb up the political mountain.

"Russ Evans is upstairs," Darlene whispered.

"Goodness."

"He wants to speak with us."

"You okay with that?"

"Are you?"

"Part of me still thinks he was set up, if that's what you mean."

"I feel the same way," Darlene said, "but so far, the way the facts are stacking up, things look pretty bad. Still, he never was anything other than helpful to me. Victor, we'd be happy to speak with him."

CHAPTER 7

Agents moved quickly to escort Darlene and Kim to the front of the bar. The tightness in Darlene's chest refused to abate. Meeting with Evans like this would be juicy fodder for the paparazzi.

Darlene had heard rumors that Evans was going to plead guilty to statutory rape charges in connection to a motel rendezvous with a teenage prostitute. When the news broke, Darlene had sent him a supportive note expressing her hope that an explanation would come clear for the episode, and urging him to put his faith in the justice system. Perhaps, she wondered, he had been unable to take her words to heart, and wanted to position himself for a presidential pardon.

Not only had their lifelong friendship endured, but she had taken a med school elective course in farming and nutrition that he taught. Years later, she was the one to suggest that Martin consider appointing Evans— then an instructor in farming economics—as Secretary of Agriculture. Martin subsequently stood by their friend despite a fair amount of opposition in Congress.

Darlene and Kim followed the agents through a doorway to a narrow stairwell that ascended to the balcony level. At the end of another hallway, they came to a padded vinyl door.

"We've already checked the room. It's safe to go in," Ochoa said.

Darlene pushed open the door and allowed Kim to enter first. Evans was alone, seated at a low table in the center of a dimly lit, cavelike room. The paneled walls were painted black, and the mood lighting cast deep shadows across Evans's round face. During the months since Darlene had last seen him, he seemed to have aged years. He stood up somewhat clumsily as the women entered, and Darlene wondered if he might have been drinking. He was a large, usually cheery man with thinning light brown hair, and at this moment, he exuded gloom.

"Darlene. Kim. Thanks for coming up," he said, extending his meaty hand. "It's good to see you."

"Good to see you, too, Russ," Darlene said, giving him a quick hug in lieu of his proffered handshake. "You look as if you're holding up okay."

Evans replied with his trademark deep baritone laugh. "I've gained fifteen pounds and am rapidly losing what little hair I had left," he said. "But I'll accept the compliment anyway."

Darlene's apprehension was replaced with a heavy sadness at seeing the man looking so beaten. Evans had eschewed life on his family's farm in exchange for a master's degree and a faculty position at an agricultural college. Before the scandal hit, she had enjoyed meetings in his office, surrounded by framed photographs of America's farmland.

"Agent Ochoa said you wanted to speak with me. Is it about your case?"

"Please. Have a seat." Evans pushed closer to the table. "I was at your event today."

"You were?" Kim asked. "I didn't see you there."

Again, that laugh, but this time there was an undisguised tinge of bitterness. "Well, I kept to the background," Evans said. "Not that it matters."

"How so?" asked Darlene.

"I guess I'm still surprised how little anyone recognizes the guy who, for two years, was ninth in the presidential succession order. Once you're not a player in this town, well, you're not a player—except, of course, to the press corps. Now, those guys still have no problem recognizing me. Scandal sells papers. This morning, though, they were too focused on you to notice me. Everyone knew the president had blown off the event. Not even an appearance by Farmer Pornpone, as the tabloids are calling me, could pull their attention away."

Darlene reached across the table and cupped Evans's hands in her own. "You know you have supporters out there, Russ. Not everyone believes the charges against you."

Evans managed a pale smile of appreciation. "Nice of you to say, Darlene. Unfortunately, whoever paid off the girl gave her enough to keep her lies coming, to say nothing of the impact of the box of kiddie porn that investigators found in the back of my closet."

"Sorry if I'm out of place," Kim said, "but what were you doing in that hotel room? We've heard all kinds of rumors and—"

Evans held up his hand. "No, don't be sorry and don't you worry about it," he said. "My lawyer asked me to keep my side of the story away from the press until he heard what the U.S. Attorney had against me. Now that we know they're calling off the prosecution because they can't find the woman who filed the complaint, I'll tell anybody who'll listen—not that it will help get my job back. You see, my son, Derek, has been in trouble since his teens. Drugs and such. I haven't spoken to him in nearly three years until I got this anonymous phone call telling me he was holed up at a motel just outside of D.C., and that he was in some sort of trouble. I think you know that Derek's mother and I have been divorced for some time. I decided not to tell her about the call until I knew what was going on.

"I got to the motel as fast as I could and knocked on room twenty-four as the caller had instructed. The door opened up and I found myself alone in a hotel room with a very young, and very naked girl. A hidden camera on a tripod recorded everything. She literally threw herself at me, pushed me backwards onto the bed, and kissed me several times before I could throw her aside.

"I knew it was a setup and a very volatile situation. I probably should have called the police right then and there, but instead, I ran and called my attorney. I had no idea there was a camera hidden in the room. Later I found out the room was registered in a bogus name the day before, and the clerk who was on the desk at the time told the police it probably was me. The girl said she had done business with me before, and that I liked to have her undress me. But this was the first time I had asked to have the camera there. When the police looked at the film cartridge, the part showing me shoving her off and running away was conveniently missing."

"What about the box of photos in your closet?"

Evans could only shrug and shake his head.

"Sure sounds like a setup to me," Kim said after a moment's pause.

"Even if they drop the charges, I've lost." Evans's voice broke, and for the first time he seemed close to tears.

"Martin was very reluctant to accept your resignation, Russ. You know that, don't you?"

"I know what you've told me, Darlene. And I thank you for that."

"I don't get it," Kim said. "You were the secretary of *agriculture*. Don't take this the wrong way, but I don't see why anyone would go after you."

Evans nodded as though he'd heard that opinion of his former position before. "As Darlene can tell you, there's a lot more to our part of the government than just making sure food is safe for eating. The work we do touches the lives of virtually every American. It's our responsibility to provide a sufficient, safe, nutritious food supply, produced in a sustainable and environmentally supportive way."

"Doesn't seem like anybody would want you out of office for that," Kim said.

"I suppose the frame-up could have had nothing to

do with my being the secretary, but there are lot of variables that go into what we do. We've got local food producers pushing an agenda counter to what the major growers demand. Environmentalists lobby hard for more sustainability, and we've got technological advancements in fertilizer, seeds, and pesticides to keep track of."

Darlene felt a chill go through her and went rigid in her seat.

Kim noticed and placed a concerned hand on her knee. "You okay?"

To her great dismay, Evans's explanation of the issues surrounding farming reminded her of her father, only in the darkest days, before financial reversals and unremitting melancholy caused him to press a shotgun up beneath his chin and pull the trigger.

Darlene nodded and took a sip from a glass of water. "I'm fine," she said, knowing that her friend could tell she wasn't. "Russ, do you have any idea who might have set you up?"

"Take your pick," Evans said. "Every decision makes someone a winner and someone a loser."

"I wish there were something I could do to help," Darlene said.

"Actually, there is."

"Name it."

The former agriculture secretary's face tightened. "After Martin told me he intended to appoint me head of the USDA, I began developing a legislative agenda for our first term in office. My aides have a series of bills drawn up that I was going to present to the president when . . . when I resigned. They involve everything from school lunch requirements to the handling of foods containing genetically modified organisms. I don't have much I'll be leaving behind, but I would love to see those bills get submitted by the president and passed. I was hoping that because of your and my history and your commitment to kids' nutrition, you might help that happen."

"Does the president know about these bills?"

"No. I tried getting them to him, but it was too late. He doesn't want to hear from me. I'm pretty sure the woman Martin has lined up to replace me has no intention of following through on any of my programs. I've got nothing left, Darlene. My friends are bailing on me as if I were septic. My integrity's been plowed to the roots. These are good, important pieces of legislation. If they go under, my last shred of dignity and purpose goes with them."

Darlene bit at her lip and tried to keep Evans's profound sadness from becoming too much her own. "No promises, but have them sent to me," she said.

The three turned as the door behind them was opened by Victor Ochoa.

"Mrs. Mallory, Ms. Hajjar, I'm sorry for bursting in like this, but there's been a multiple shooting with deaths in Kings Ridge, Virginia. We feel you should return to the White House until we have more information."

"Deaths? Do you know how many?" Kim asked.

"It looks like seven. We should know more by the time we get you home."

Seven people shot to death.

Darlene felt ill. Countless terrible, vivid images began flashing through her mind. She hadn't ever told anyone except her husband, but as a teen, she had been the one to discover her father's body.

"You just have to make every day precious," Kim said as they gathered their things. " 'Cause you never know."

CHAPTER 8

The final battle for Dr. John Meacham's life was over almost before it began. On a vent, with IV blood pressure support and other meds, he was essentially being resuscitated before his heart stopped beating. Dr. Schwartz, the salaried intensive care specialist, who had deferred to Lou for the insertion of the chest tube, administered some cardiac stimulants without any success, and then, after no more than ten minutes, turned to Lou.

"Do you see any reason to continue, Doctor?" he asked.

Lou flashed on the day when he and Meacham had first met at the Physician Wellness Office. Meacham was as tight as a drum skin, and positive that he would never be allowed to practice medicine again. Lou, as a survivor of disaster in his personal and professional lives, knew otherwise. Most of that first session had consisted of him exposing his new client to the life strategies of AA—strategies that he had ridiculed at first as being naïve and simplistic—until he actually began to use them in his life.

Meacham had caught on quickly. With the help of an AA sponsor and people at the rehab, his need to drink ceased almost immediately. Following that, his hair-trigger temper gradually came under control.

Now this.

"I can't think of anything else we should be doing, Dr. Schwartz," Lou heard his voice saying as if from down a long tube.

Schwartz looked up at the clock and nodded toward Sara Turnbull. "Seven forty P.M.," he proclaimed.

And just like that, John Meacham's life was done.

"Has his wife, Carolyn, been around?" Lou asked, realizing that in the craziness of the hours just past, he had lost track of some of his own civility.

"She was in the family room a little while ago," Sara said. "Should I check?"

"No," Lou said. "I know her. I'll go."

"Out the sliding doors and down the hallway to the left."

Head down, consumed by heavy sadness at the senseless deaths of so many, Lou stepped through the unit doors.

The husky detective was still at his post. "So, Doc, how's it going in there?"

"It's not," Lou said.

"Dead?"

"Dead."

The cop nodded. "Whether it's cops' bullets at the scene or a shiv in the back in the slammer from one of the other inmates, these things almost always seem to end this way. Well, there go the answers."

"I suppose," Lou replied, wondering how easy it would be for him to let matters drop.

The cop was right. There was still a boatload of unanswered questions, starting with the meaning of the words *no witnesses*.

Lou opened the lounge door. The modest room, furnished in vinyl, with dog-eared magazines scattered about, was deserted. His eyes went first to a television set mounted catty-corner, high up on the far wall. The volume was turned off, though Lou could easily read the CNN news flash graphic from across the room.

BREAKING NEWS: SUSPECTED MASS MURDERER IN CRITICAL CONDITION.

"Not anymore," Lou murmured, wondering if the grim outcome would have been any different had the local neurosurgeon not gone probing blindly for a bullet in or near the area of the brain dealing with cardiac rhythmicity.

He averted his gaze from the broadcast just as the door to the family room opened and Carolyn Meacham entered. She was slight woman with carefully trimmed gray hair and more makeup than Lou felt she needed. It was surprising that there were no family or friends with her, but perhaps some were on the way. Her makeup did nothing to disguise her pain. Without a word, she raced across to Lou and threw her arms around him, burying her face against his chest.

She was a spirited woman—a New Yorker, Lou thought he remembered, with a hard edge. He had liked her from the very beginning. In all the time he had dealt with her and Meacham, he had never once seen her cry. Now, her tears flowed liberally. It was impossible to imagine what she must have been experiencing since receiving the news. Her three children were all in their teens.

"He's dead, isn't he?" she asked before pulling away.

Lou nodded. "Just a couple of minutes ago. I came out here from D.C. to see if I could help, but there was really nothing I could do."

"He was fine when he left home, Lou. He's been going to meetings and staying sober, and this morning when he left for the office, he was fine."

"Where are your kids?"

"At my sister Rosalee's in Chantilly. When the news broke, I had her pick them up at school and take them to her place to keep them away from reporters."

"Good move. Do you want to go in to see him?"

Carolyn hesitated, and for a moment Lou thought she was going to decline. Then she nodded and took his arm. Her sobbing had already ceased.

The scene in Meacham's cubicle had largely been cleaned up when they arrived. Nurses had respectfully not pulled a sheet up over his face, although they had left a bandage in place over the bullet hole. Death, as Lou had often encountered it, even violent death, frequently had a calming effect on a patient's countenance. To some extent, that was the case here.

Carolyn stood motionless for a time, gazing down at the man she had shared a life with for so many years— the interested, interesting caregiver who would never get the chance to see their daughters into womanhood.

"What happens next?" she asked stonily.

Lou felt himself react to her abrupt change in tone. "Now you have to sign some papers with the nurses and John's body will need to be autopsied," he said simply.

Carolyn glanced over at him. "Is that really even necessary? Isn't it obvious how he died?"

"It's standard practice for all homicides."

Carolyn shook her head. "Let's go," she said, spinning and heading out the door with Lou rushing to keep up.

There were no final caresses, no request for a minute alone, no more tears. It was as if someone had thrown a switch, making Carolyn Meacham aware of the horribleness of her husband's crime.

Lou gave passing thought to asking what her husband might have meant by the cryptic remark, *no witnesses,* but this hardly seemed the time.

"I need to pick up my kids and go home," Carolyn said with no emotion.

"I'll drive you."

"I'm fine to drive."

It was an order, not a statement.

"Well, you may be fine to drive, but you're not okay to be alone. I'll ride with you. We can talk in the car. Then, if need be, I can take a cab back here."

Carolyn made no attempt to talk him out of it.

Outside, the rain had picked up and the fog had thickened. The unseasonable chill persisted. It was Carolyn who first spotted the crowd of reporters lurking about her silver Volvo SUV. Many were using makeshift plastic tarps to shield their equipment from the rain. Lou, headline news himself when the DEA and police descended on his home and arrested him for writing prescriptions for himself, marveled at the resourcefulness of the vultures—how they already knew this particular car belonged to Carolyn Meacham.

As if underscoring his thoughts, their camera lights lit up as soon as he and Carolyn neared. He wondered how long it would take for them to come up with *his* name. Calls to Filstrup would be sure to follow.

Oh, happy day.

Lou pulled Carolyn close to him, shielding her from the onslaught. Reporters shoved their microphones in her face like mothers trying to force-feed their children, and shouted out questions that became garbled as they clashed with one another in midair. Carolyn was silent ice, her head high, her intelligent green eyes fixed straight ahead. Through the swarm, she somehow managed to get her door unlocked, and then reached across the seat to open Lou's side. He tossed his rain-dampened jacket into the backseat and quickly climbed in. Carolyn turned the ignition key. The reporters banged on the windows and doors, and stepped aside only when the car began to move.

"Lou?" she said.

"Yes?"

"Something made him do this. He was not a violent person. Something made him do what he did."

Lou passed on the urge to remind her that a few years ago, her husband had nearly gotten booted out of medicine for losing control.

"I suppose that's an understandable feeling," he said instead.

As she pulled onto the driveway, John Meacham's widow left rubber on the wet tarmac of the doctors-only parking lot.

"Find out what happened, Lou," she said. "Find out why John killed those people."

CHAPTER 9

They drove largely in silence, wipers on intermittent, traveling along a country road that snaked through a hilly landscape. Dusk had passed, and night had settled in quickly, but Carolyn did not appear bothered by the headlights of the vehicles splashing past in the opposite direction. In fact, Lou guessed she might be going as fast as any of them.

"Are you all right to be driving?" he asked.

Carolyn sighed heavily. "I need to be driving," she said. "Even in this crappy weather, I need to be doing something. Just sitting in that lounge . . . waiting for news . . . trying to make sense of it all . . . hoping he would live, praying he would die. It was so horrible, so lonely, Lou. You couldn't possibly imagine."

A beloved husband dead. Hundreds of lives irreparably shattered. Carolyn left to dwell in the aftermath.

Those were Lou's thoughts before he said, "No, Carolyn, you're right. I couldn't imagine."

They fell back into the heavy silence. The Volvo's

wipers now beat a steady rhythm against the driving rain. Fog transformed the approaching headlights into a hazy glow that stretched across the darkening horizon. Even with bad visibility, the rain-slicked road, and Carolyn's above-the-limit speed, there were drivers daring enough to pass them when permissible.

Carolyn made a disgusted sound when one zipped by. "I'm not going to speed in weather like this," she said.

Lou reached for his jacket in the backseat and fished out his cell phone. He assumed that Renee had already seen news reports of Meacham's death, but knew, since she and Emily were there when the call came in from Filstrup, that she'd want to hear directly from him. He began keying in Renee's number, when he felt the SUV shift hard to the left. His seat belt went from loose to taut in a blink, keeping him from being thrown against Carolyn.

Before Lou could regain his bearings, the car swerved again, this time to the right. The tires lost traction on the rain-soaked road; suddenly the Volvo was fishtailing, lurching violently from side to side. Moments later, Carolyn had calmly regained control. Her speed had, if anything, increased.

Lou flashed on the possibility that she had insisted on driving because of some kind of suicidal urge.

She veered right, then left, then right again.

Lou's stomach dropped as though he were front seat in a roller coaster. The left wheels of the SUV crossed the solid center lines twice, one of those times coming close to crossing into the oncoming traffic. But in both instances Carolyn pulled the car back just in time. Her expression had grown tense, her eyes narrowed.

She leaned on her car horn and began flashing her lights at the driver in front of them. "Get out of the way! Move over!" she shouted.

"Carolyn! What's going on?" Lou cried out. "What are you doing?"

Carolyn's eyes remained locked forward, unblinking. She continued to flash her lights and beep her horn. "Move over!" she yelled. "Get over now!"

"Please slow down! Carolyn, slow down and pull over!"

Instead of responding, Carolyn steered the SUV into oncoming traffic, presumably to try to pass the car in front. But here the road turned, and Lou saw the dotted yellow dividing line become a solid one. In the next instant, he was blinded by a set of powerful headlight beams. He heard a deep-timbred horn—not a car's beep, but something much larger. Lou's stomach knotted. The horn had to be an eighteen-wheeler. A second later, he saw the rig emerge from the fog like a huge phantom. Carolyn, acting unfazed, continued on a straight course, unable to pass the car to their right. She sped forward as though playing a game against the forty-ton machine.

"Look, Lou," she called out, still surprisingly calm though her voice had an anxious edge. "The car three ahead of us. Its left taillight is out. Someone's going to get killed unless we warn them. There's been enough death today."

"Carolyn, let it be! Slow down. Please, slow down!"

The car boxing them in accelerated. Lou reached across his seat and took hold of the wheel, pulling it clockwise, aware that the move might well cause Carolyn to lose control.

"Lou, don't do that! I have to warn him!"

The tires slipped several feet, then gained purchase, pulling them into the right-hand lane. Lou released the wheel. The car shuddered and rose on two tires. There was a ferocious crack as the rig sheared off the left-side mirror. The rush of wind as it flew past was probably all that kept them from flipping over.

"Okay, now, Carolyn," Lou said with as much insistence as urgency. "Pull over there and let me drive."

Again she leaned on the accelerator and the horn. "In this fog, somebody is going to ram into the back of them."

"Carolyn, don't!"

She turned the wheel right this time, attempting to pass the intervening car via a narrow, muddy soft shoulder. Lou sat pressed against his seat back, unwilling to grab at the wheel again. The speedometer moved upward.

Forty.

Fifty.

Fifty-five.

Carolyn Meacham looked purposefully ahead, beyond reason.

"Carolyn, stop!" Lou screamed. "You're going to kill us both because a guy's taillight is out!"

They raced even with the car to their left. The driver leaned on his horn and refused to slow down.

Lou could feel the high center of gravity in the SUV threaten to flip them. Every jolt on the uneven ground seemed magnified.

"They're just two cars ahead."

Patches of fog flew past like ghosts. Then, Lou froze. Through one of the patches, directly in front of them, a speed limit sign had appeared.

"Carolyn!" he shouted. "Get back into your lane! Do it now!"

Instinctively, Lou clenched his teeth and readied himself for impact. They were going sixty.

Lou couldn't hold back. He leaned as far to the left as his seat belt would allow, grabbed the wheel, and pushed it counterclockwise. The Volvo skidded into a left turn and fell behind the car Carolyn had been trying to pass. Perhaps instinctively, she slammed on the brakes. The front two tires dragged along the grassy shoulder, kicking up dirt and rocks. The sign slammed into the hood and sheared off, vanishing upward into the mist. Then, in a full spin, the car left the road. Lou saw a tree materialize from the fog. He shut his eyes tightly and raised his arms to his face for protection. The impact wasn't as violent as he had expected.

Lou's head snapped against the window beside him as the Volvo spun viciously. Splintered glass exploded into his face and cut his neck. The rear of the Volvo was still in the center of the road. Then, without warning, the coaster ride was over.

"Carolyn, are you all right?" he said, wiping at his forehead and seeing blood on his hand.

"Did you see that?" she asked him, her breathing not far from normal. "Did you?"

"You mean the taillight?"

"Yes, the taillight. Drivers never fix them until the vehicle-inspection people tell them they have to. That guy could have caused an accident."

CHAPTER 10

Throughout most of the bizarre chase to overtake the driver with one working taillight, Lou remained in what he called "emergency calm"—a state of heightened awareness and preparedness, cloaked in an external composure. It was a reaction to crisis shared by those caregivers whose business often revolved around sudden changes for the worse in their patients—intensivists, anesthesiologists, surgeons, physician assistants, nurses in the ER and various units, EMTs, and paramedics.

Now, with the immediate danger over, it was as if whatever had been blocking the surge of adrenaline through his body had been removed. His pulse had doubled—or tripled, he was breathing heavily, if not hyperventilating, and when he opened the dashboard compartment looking for tissues, his hand was shaking.

The cut to his brow did not look like much, and pressure with a wad of Kleenex quickly stopped the bleeding.

"Carolyn, can you get us out of the road?" he asked, his voice louder than he had intended.

John Meacham's widow nodded weakly and drove the Volvo farther onto the roadside's muddy shoulder. She appeared dazed, though to Lou's relief, uninjured. Still, he checked her head, neck, and extremities and palpated her chest and abdomen for areas of tenderness. His blood pressure cuff and other instruments for emergencies were in a large medical bag, which he kept in the trunk of his car, but he assured himself that her cardiac rhythm was under a hundred and regular, and her radial and carotid pulses were strong.

Finally, using a flashlight from the dash, he did a crude neurologic exam, including eye movements and pupillary response.

"What did I do?" Carolyn muttered. "What the hell did I just do?"

There were several cars stopped behind them. Lou gave the thumbs-up sign through Carolyn's window, and the drivers slowly pulled out and drove away. Two of them paused long enough to say they had called 911.

"Lou . . . that taillight . . . I was so worried the missing light would cause an accident. . . ."

Her voice trailed away. She continued staring blankly out the windshield at the rain. Her hands, right at two o'clock, left at eleven, gripped the wheel tightly as though she were still driving. Lou took an umbrella from the rear floor and climbed out of the car. His left knee was stiff, and had probably taken a hit, but it was not nearly sore enough to keep him from tomorrow's sparring session at the Stick and Move Gym. He took in several sharp breaths of chilly night air and tested the rest of his limbs. Nothing. Next, he made a quick circle around the Volvo. The damage appeared minimal. He waved to a driver who had slowed down, signaling that everything was okay. Then he climbed back into the car.

Whatever had possessed Carolyn seemed to be resolving. Her eyes were no longer glazed. Her hands had relaxed.

"Carolyn, the car should be okay to drive, but this time if it's alright with you, I'll do the driving."

"That would be fine," she said, still somewhat vaguely.

Lou patted her on the shoulder. "Everything is going to be okay."

"Lou, what did I do?"

"Look, you experienced a major trauma back in the hospital. You weren't thinking clearly. That's all. It happens in extreme stress situations. A person just does something . . . something irrational. We see it in the ER all the time."

He felt a flash of embarrassment at what might be construed as a reference to Carolyn's husband.

"I was so worried about those taillights," she said again as Lou gently separated her hands from the steering wheel. "What's going to happen to me now?"

Before he could answer, a siren blared behind them, and then whined down into silence. The flash of blue strobe lights danced erratically inside the Volvo's interior. Lou glanced in the side-view mirror to see a plus-sized police officer exit his vehicle and snap open an umbrella. The policeman sauntered over to the driver's side of the car and shone a powerful flashlight beam through the rain-spattered window onto Carolyn's face.

"Oh, goodness," Carolyn said, gripping the wheel once again.

Lou set a cautioning hand on her arm. "Roll down your window and let me do the talking," he whispered. "You don't have anything to worry about."

Carolyn did as he asked.

The officer, umbrella keeping them both dry, bent at the waist and poked his head inside the car. "Anybody hurt?" he asked. He spoke with a modest Southern drawl. His eyes, which Lou read as showing no threat, scanned the two of them with concern.

Carolyn immediately became more animated. "Oh, Gilbert. Thank goodness it's you," she said, talking without taking a breath. "This was all my fault. I . . . I was chasing down a car in front of us that had one broken taillight. I got so worried they were going to cause an accident, that I ended up having one myself."

Lou gripped Carolyn's arm. She nodded and stopped. He climbed out of the car, opened his umbrella, and still slightly favoring his leg, walked around to the officer. "Officer, my name is Lou Welcome. I'm an ER doc from Eisenhower Memorial, and a friend of Carolyn's and . . . um . . . of John's."

"Gilbert Stone. Chief of police of Kings Ridge." Stone took his hand and, maintaining steady eye contact, squeezed it with near bone-crushing force.

Cap Duncan, Lou's mentor and owner of the Stick and Move, had once told him that any statement of superiority or control a man wanted to make should begin with the handshake. Lou wondered now if the husky lawman was trying to do just that. He gave thought to matching or besting the man's grip, but set the notion aside in his dumb-moves file.

Stone shone his flashlight on Lou's face, momentarily blinding him. "You sure you're all right, son?" he asked.

"We're both fine. Thanks."

"Given what you do and where you do it, I'm inclined to trust you in that regard."

"I appreciate that."

Stone inspected the front end of the Volvo and what remained of the sign, and let out a high-pitched whistle, not so different from the sound his cruiser's siren had made. Beneath the lawman's wool-lined bomber jacket, Lou saw a tan shirt with a silver metal star pinned to the breast pocket, and a perfectly knotted black tie.

"Guess we got real lucky here," Stone said, hoisting up his dark brown pants over an ample belly. "You say you're a friend of Mrs. Meacham?"

"I am—was—friends with her husband as well."

Stone's thin lips folded into a crease that vanished inside his mouth. "Any ideas why he did what he did?"

"Well, no, except to say I can't imagine him doing it."

"But he did."

"Yes, he did," Lou echoed grimly.

He considered sharing details, right then and there, about the bizarre happenings in the ICU at DeLand Regional, and how they dovetailed with Carolyn Meacham's odd behavior, but decided this wasn't the time or place.

"It's been a hell of a day." Stone sighed, his eyes locked on Lou's.

"Tough day, indeed," Lou answered.

"You sure you're in no need of medical attention, son?"

"No, thank you. I'm all right."

Stone just nodded. "Okay. Like I said, I trust you. Now, then, you have something you want to tell me about the accident?" Stone continued his hard stare.

"This accident is all my fault," Lou said. "I never should have let her drive. She's in no condition, given what happened today, but she absolutely insisted. Said it would be best if she had something to focus on. I'd really hate to see her in trouble with the law after what she's just been through."

Stone's grin was impenetrable. "So you're saying it didn't happen quite the way she said it did?"

By then, the two men had connected.

"What if I told you the wheels lost grip? Rain-slicked roads and all," Lou said.

"Well, I'd be inclined to believe you. My doctor was Carl Franklin, one of the best we ever had. At the moment, I am having some mighty harsh feelings toward the man who killed him. But that doesn't translate to the man's wife. I didn't know the Meachams that well, on account they haven't lived in Kings Ridge very long. But what I did know of them, I had nothing against— even John's history of trouble with the medical board a few years back."

Lou tensed. This was no hayseed sheriff. For however many years he had been the man in Kings Ridge, Gilbert Stone was not merely rattling about the town, procuring coffee and doughnuts. He was in charge of it. He also hadn't hesitated to mention Meacham's history to what should have been, until now, a total stranger. Either Stone was indiscreet to a fault, or somewhere in the course of gathering information about his fiefdom, Dr. Lou Welcome's name had bopped across his desk.

Lou warned himself to stay sharp.

"I wish I could explain why John did what he did," he said.

"Me and you both, son," Stone replied. "It sure don't make no sense."

"I'm glad you understand my concern for Carolyn."

"Oh, I do, I surely do."

"So just a ticket, then?"

Stone put his campaign hat back on. "Like I said, I'm sure Carolyn's been through hell today. Let's make sure her car drives fine, and I'll send her off with a warning to be more careful on these slippery roads."

"Wonderful."

Stone hesitated a beat, then locked on to Lou's eyes once again. "And I'm going to send you off with a warning as well," he said.

"Me?"

"If you know something about my town, or the people in it such as Carolyn and John Meacham, or anyone on the staff of our hospital, and you choose to keep that information hidden from me, you won't find me to be so easygoing."

CHAPTER 11

The president and First Family lived on the second and third floors of the White House—fifteen bedrooms and fifteen bathrooms, along with a sitting room, kitchen, dining room, and spectacular solarium. Darlene had done her best to make the master bedroom feel homey and familiar to her, but to no surprise, she had yet to completely succeed. At heart, she would always be a farmers' daughter—a woman of down-to-earth taste in furnishings and art.

She and Martin slept in an 1820s four-poster tiger maple bed that she had chosen from notebooks of photographs that the Office of the Curator had provided to her. The rest of the room's décor was more conventional and modern, although piece-by-piece she was changing it. Perhaps if they made it to a second term . . . at that moment, a big *if*.

Despite her well-intentioned efforts at bedtime meditation and yoga, Darlene still felt restless enough at times to accept some help from the vial of sleeping pills in her bedside table. Tonight, with continuous news coverage of the horrific events in Kings Ridge, Russ Evans's sad visage embedded in her mind, her lingering anger over Martin's decision to leave her solo at the Boys & Girls Club, and a full schedule facing her in the morning, she had little doubt there was an Ambien in her near future.

She was sitting upright in bed, rereading a paragraph from the current issue of *Food Health*. Finally, unable to advance past that page, she set the magazine aside and returned her attention to the eleven o'clock news, which was reporting on the latest developments in the Kings Ridge tragedy. Details of the crime and of Dr. John Meacham's life were continuing to emerge, but there was still no clear explanation for what the man had done. A physician murdering patients and staff in his office. People remained in shock and desperate for answers.

She clicked off the television, picked up her magazine again, and had just finished the page when the bedroom door swung open. The President of the United States slipped inside, threw his jacket and power red tie over a chair, bent down, and kissed her on the forehead.

One look at his tired eyes, gaunt face, and graying temples, and she felt compassion and the stirrings of forgiveness for the man she had vowed to love until death. Martin had been a rodeo jock in college, and it was his piercing blue eyes, powerfully set jaw, and cowboy good looks that had first attracted her to him. Then she came to know his droll wit, tenderness, and the bottomless compassion for the causes he believed in. From that admiration came a profound and deepening love.

If there was any aspect of his personality she had to work to accept, it was the power of his ambition.

"Sorry I'm late getting up here. I had to give a statement about the killings in Kings Ridge."

"How terrible that is. Everyone seems shaken. I saw you commenting on the news a little while ago. You did an excellent job. Very honest and from the heart."

"Thanks, princess. The whole thing is just awful. Right out of the blue, the guy goes postal."

"I don't think that's a phrase you want to use in public."

Martin chuckled. "No, I suppose not. Especially since the union endorsed me. You got anything on under there?"

"Nothing that can't be taken off with the flick of a finger in, say, a nanosecond."

He slowly lowered the sheet. His eyes sparked. "You are just the best thing I've seen all day," he said in a worn voice.

Darlene had promised Russ Evans she would at least speak to Martin on behalf of his legislation. But the way Martin looked to her now—haggard, creases like canyons cutting across his forehead—she felt herself having second thoughts. The old saw about carrying the weight of the world wasn't completely true for many, but it was for him. She lowered him to his belly and kneaded his shoulders.

"You could have seen me earlier," she said in a soft voice.

There was a passing instant when she wished she had kept her feelings about the dedication to herself, but she had strong beliefs that a marriage without communication was doomed to turn toxic.

Martin swung around, pressed a warm hand to the side of her face, and gently caressed her cheek. "I'll make it up to you," he said before giving her a quick kiss on the lips. "I know that I disappointed you today, and I'm sorry. Really and truly sorry."

Darlene smiled down at her husband. Whatever effects of the job she had observed seemed to have diminished. Her heart filled with love and her eyes must have reflected her desire, because Martin rolled over and kissed her hard on the lips, cupping her breast in his hand. Her mouth opened in response and she kissed him back, deeply. Their lovemaking had been occurring less frequently of late, coinciding not so much with pressures of the presidency, but with the time that Martin's outbursts had become more common.

He slipped off the rest of his clothes and moved her down beside him, his hands continuing to explore the spots she liked. His touch brought Darlene a profound feeling of comfort and desire. She felt him becoming aroused, and herself beginning to respond. Perhaps this night, the Ambien would stay in the drawer.

"So, baby," Martin said, beginning the sort of banter he enjoyed during sex. "Tell me something else about your day."

Darlene tensed.

No lies, no evasions. That was the unwritten rule of their marriage.

She once again flashed on Russ Evans's sad, desperate face.

"Actually," she said while Martin worked at her neck with his lips, "there is something I need to discuss with you. But it can wait."

Martin moaned in her ear. "Hmmmm . . . sure . . . get it off your chest if it will help you relax. You seem a little tense."

Darlene gazed up at the ceiling as he continued to explore the soft curves of her chin, neck, and breasts. He was right about her feeling tense, even though he was, as usual, unwilling to take any responsibility.

"Russ Evans came to the dedication today," said quietly. "We didn't see him there, but afterwards, he followed us to the Bar None and asked us to meet with him in private upstairs."

Martin stopped kissing her and remained motionless. The temperature between them dropped several degrees.

"And did you?"

"Did I what?"

Martin sat up. The ice in his eyes was reflected in his voice. "Meet with him."

"I . . . didn't see what harm could come of it. I mean, we have known each other since we were kids. Kim was with me, and . . . and Victor was right outside."

Martin swung onto the edge of the bed, but never took his suddenly hard eyes from her. "I can't believe you met in public with that pervert," he said. "Do you think I don't have enough problems without my wife adding to them with the man who is already the biggest blight of my administration?"

Reflexively, Darlene pulled the sheet up to cover her

breasts. "That's a cruel thing to say, Marty. We three were alone in the upstairs of the restaurant. No one except the agents even saw Kim and me go up there. Russ Evans was our friend. He believed in everything I stand for. Hearing him out seemed the least I could do."

"You had no business talking with that man. He's a disgrace. An utter disgrace. He humiliated the both of us."

"He says someone set him up."

"People like him always say that after they're caught."

"Martin, have you ever considered that what happened to Russ could have been a politically motivated frame-up?"

At this, the president leapt off the bed and stormed across the room, breathing heavily. "What would make you even imply such a thing?"

"Well, when he asked to see me, I thought he was going to try to position himself for a presidential pardon. Use me to get to you."

"Go on."

"But he didn't do anything of the sort. All he cared about was some legislation he's been working on. He wanted me to tell you that the laws are important ones and that people, and especially children, shouldn't suffer because of him. He asked me—no, more like begged me—to convince you to read over his bills and support his programs. That was it. That was the only thing that mattered to him."

Martin's face turned crimson. "You're kidding me, right? Darlene, you really are a gullible hick. Please, tell me this is a joke."

"Martin, I—"

"You what? You what, Darlene? You had drinks with a pervert, and then you chat it up with him about a program that hasn't even been formally presented to me!" His anger had charged the air like lightning, fueling itself before a strike.

"Martin, please, you're sounding unreasonable."

"You have no business talking to Russ Evans!" he shouted, pounding the top of their bureau and sending a velvet-lined box of costume jewelry spilling across the floor. The mouth that had moments before been kissing her was now contorted into a snarl.

Darlene kept her eyes locked on him, watching with concern as he stalked back to her. Her chest tightened, and for a brief moment she felt trapped between her husband and the headboard of the bed. Then the president sat down on the edge of the mattress, just as gently as he'd done earlier. He put his hand on her knee. She could feel her leg shaking.

"Sweetheart," he said, "I am so sorry for going off at you like that. Just the mention of that man's name is enough to make me go crazy. With all the pressures I have, right before my reelection bid is to start in earnest, I've got to live with the fact that I nominated a child predator to join the highest ranks of my administration."

"But maybe, just maybe he's innocent."

"We both know that isn't true," Martin said, "but I also know how important kids are to you, so I'm going to make a deal. I'll read whatever Evans's remaining people submit. Then we'll see."

"Thank you. That's all I'm asking."

"But you have to make a promise to me."

"Anything. Anything at all."

"You are never, and I mean *never,* to speak to Russ Evans or mention him in my presence again. Promise me that, Darlene."

Again, she conjured up an image of Evans sitting across the table from her—a soul adrift and without hope of rescue. Despite her lingering doubts and the horrible accusations against the man, her heart ached for him. But loyalty to her husband was by far the stronger pull.

"Of course," she said. "I promise. Come closer, now. Let's start over again."

Darlene turned off the bedside lamp, but Martin quickly switched it back on.

"I've got work to do," he said, pulling on a T-shirt and a pair of sweats. "You get some sleep. I'll be in later and see you in the morning."

"I . . . I'm glad I told you," she said, more than a little bewildered.

"Me, too," he replied, grinning without warmth, "because I already heard about the meeting from one of the other agents."

CHAPTER 12

Stick and Move was a thousand-square-foot gymnasium located amidst a stretch of warehouses within walking distance of Lou's two-bedroom apartment. Inside were three boxing rings, each the standard twenty-feet-by-twenty. Heavy bags hung from one side of the gym like trophy sharks on a dock, and a row of pear-shaped speed bags were wall-mounted to the other. There were several stationary bikes, a quality set of free weights, wall-length mirrors, plenty of room for jumping rope, and several sets of medicine balls.

And best of all from Lou's point of view, it smelled like a serious gym.

A day had passed since the horror of Kings Ridge. Lou's knee had calmed down from a four out of ten on the stiffness scale to maybe a two. The gym was active and noisy when he arrived to train. Cap Duncan, sparring helmet in place, was already in the ring, pounding his gloves together and dancing—a glistening, graceful block of granite on legs. He noted Lou's arrival with hungry eyes, and motioned him through the ropes. Cap was Bahamian black, shaved bald, and fit—*ripped* was the gym rats' word.

A good guess would have placed him in his twenties, but Lou had organized a surprise fiftieth birthday party for him two years ago. Cap, who along with a bank or two, owned the place, was short for Cap'n Crunch, a moniker he earned during a brief but highly touted professional boxing career, largely because of the distinctive sound that noses made when he hit them.

Crunch.

"Hey, there, Doc, with all that you talked about at the meeting last night, I thought you might not make it in."

"I need this more today than ever, Cap."

Lou threw his ragged sweatshirt aside and worked the kinks from his neck. He was two or three inches taller than his sparring partner, in addition to being a decade younger, and his well-developed shoulders formed a decent *V* with his waist. But it would be difficult for anyone who compared the two men to believe that he was the harder puncher—and they would be right.

The two of them had connected the day that Lou arrived from six months of treatment at a rehab center in Atlanta and moved into an attic room in the halfway house where Cap was a counselor. When the financing came through allowing the purchase of the Stick and Move, Lou went to work there and the fighter became his trainer and his AA sponsor. There was no one on the mean streets or in the recovery community that Cap didn't know, and few on either side who didn't respect him.

With his hands already hot and sweaty inside his

gloves, and his wrists stiff from athletic tape, Lou moved to the center of the ring, still working the tightness from his shoulders and neck, and wondering if he should say something about the bandage on his forehead beneath the front of his helmet.

"So, how's your day been?" he asked, finagling with his mouth guard to sound intelligible.

Cap's first punch, which seemed to have arrived out of nowhere, caught Lou on the side of his headgear.

"If you're in the ring—"

"I know, I know," Lou said, finishing one of Cap's favorite aphorisms, "be ready to get hit."

"So, what do you think this is? Ballet class?"

Cap's words were thick from speaking over and around his mouth protector, but Lou knew his translation of them was close enough. He circled, assessing his options, but not yet ready to commit to any punches. Then he made his second mistake, glancing down, momentarily mesmerized by the older man's footwork. This time, he saw Cap's jab coming from the right, but was no better at defending it. The blow connected against his temple with a solid thump.

"Remember how I said I'd drive you to the meeting on Friday?" Lou said, already beginning to breathe heavily. "Well, another cheap shot like that and you'll be going by cab."

"Oh, yeah, I forgot you were just in a car accident," Cap said. "Tell you what, I'll go easy on you this session."

"By easy, you mean?"

"You'll only need to soak for an hour in the ice tub." He grinned broadly around his green mouth guard.

Lou blocked a left-right combination and returned one of his own, which barely connected. Cap could still fight him almost blindfolded. In order to do much of anything against the man, he was going to have to concentrate.

Childless, but married "a few times here and there" when it suited his purpose, Cap had devoted his youth to boxing, spending every waking hour training in grungy gyms, slowly climbing the amateur ranks. He could dazzle opponents with his footwork, but it was his punching, as powerful with his left as he was with his right, that garnered the most attention. As a kid, he fooled around with alcohol and reefer, but then a trainer set him straight. He gave up smoking and drinking, and began to care for his body through diet, vitamins, and more training.

Eventually, Cap got his big break, scoring a professional fight against a much-hyped contender for the IBA's middleweight belt. The fight that should have made his career was ultimately what landed him in the same halfway house where Lou would one day reside.

Alone in the dressing room, only minutes before the bout, Cap received a bouquet of flowers along with an envelope containing five one-hundred-dollar bills and a note instructing him to lose by a knockout in the seventh round. Cap knew it was a mob thing. In his circles, talk about fixing fights was as common as advice shared on punching technique. But instead of losing the fight,

Cap beat his opponent to a pulp and won a technical knockout in round two.

He never got to box professionally again.

Before his next scheduled bout, the state boxing federation pulled him from the card, citing a positive test for performance-enhancing drugs banned under their governance. Forced out of the sport he loved, he soon began taking narcotics to help ease his emotional pain and humiliation. The back alleys of D.C. became his home, a brown bag his constant companion. People whom he suspected had set him up offered him work as an enforcer, but he never took the jobs. Finally, when he had suffered enough, two more people came—people from AA.

"You're slow tonight, Welcome," Cap said after he threw a series of blazing-fast jabs, purposely pulled to keep from doing any real damage. "You sure you're all right to box?"

Lou got in a quick, effective body blow and danced away, preening. "I'm fine," he said. "I need this to clear my head."

Lou bobbed and weaved while circling his friend. He feigned a couple jabs that Cap shrugged off. Sweat was engulfing both men now. Cap's shaved pate was glistening beneath the incandescent overheads. No matter what was ever troubling Lou, sparring like this was the treatment.

"Did you gash your head?" Cap asked, jabbing at but not hitting Lou's forehead, indicating the bandage was visible from underneath his headgear.

"That accident was the craziest thing," Lou said.

"Yeah, how so?"

Lou bobbed again, and this time got in one good shot to Cap's jaw. Then he danced back and dropped his red mouthpiece into the palm of his glove so he could be heard more clearly.

"Carolyn Meacham, the dead doc's widow, was convinced the busted taillight on the car in front of us was going to cause an accident, so she ends up causing one herself, trying to catch up and warn the driver."

Cap waited until Lou had reinserted his guard, then almost immediately hit him with two quick punches—one to either side of his face. Lou thought he heard a crunch from the vicinity of his nose, and his eyes teared. He wiped at the area with the back of one glove and checked for blood. None.

"Keep your hands up, Doc! Hands up! Now, go on."

Lou increased his movement around the ring. Sweat was pouring off him now, stinging his eyes. He loved the feeling.

"After the crash, she couldn't explain why she'd gotten so reckless," he said. "Lucky for her, she knew the chief of police. He let her off with just a warning, if you can believe it."

"I can't believe you can't keep your hands up," Cap answered, stepping away and removing his mouth guard. "Take a moment without the guard. I think trying to talk is wearing you out."

Lou obliged, and took a few deep breaths to catch up. "Just for a minute or two," he said. "I promise to keep my hands up. Did you get everything I said about Carolyn Meacham?"

"Most of it. Obviously she was distressed about what her husband had done. It could have been that. Any clue what set him off?"

"No idea," Lou said. "He really was a talented doctor and an interesting guy. His AA recovery seemed right on track, and he hadn't had any issues with his temper since he got in trouble four years ago."

Cap continued shifting from foot to foot like a runner at a red light, staying loose. "I heard on the news," Cap said, "that one victim, before she died, had said something about 'no witnesses.' They were speculating that's what Meacham was saying during his rampage. 'No witnesses.' I suppose it had something to do with that lady he was yelling at."

"What lady?"

"On the news. I saw them interviewing her. Apparently she left the office right before your pal went ballistic—so to speak. She said that Meacham had screamed at her about her weight and that she ran off in tears. She got home, turned on the TV, and saw the shooting on the news."

"First I'm hearing of that," Lou said. "I probably should have been watching more TV."

"Nobody should ever be watching more TV, bro. Unless it's the Friday-night fights. So, what was this 'no witnesses' thing all about?"

Lou toweled off and, feeling himself beginning to stiffen, started his own side-to-side shuffle. He needed more sparring time, but Cap was one of the wisest people he knew. If the man was interested enough to ask, his question was worth answering.

"According to the police," Lou went on, "the only victim who lived long enough to say anything quoted Meacham as saying, 'No witnesses.'"

"That's strange."

"I agree, but why?"

"Because if I understand what went down correctly, the potentially strongest witness, the woman I saw interviewed, had left the office before the shooting."

Puzzled, Lou looked across at his sparring partner. "What are you getting at?" he asked.

"The kids from the street—the ones I train—they'd call that *redonkulous*."

"Redonkulous?"

"Yeah, it's a portmanteau."

"Portmanteau? I always thought you spent too much time reading."

"I have a vocabulary notebook. I hardly ever get to use what I write down in it, but here's my chance. *Portmanteau* means a new word formed by joining two others and combining their meanings. Redonkulous is a blending of the words *ridiculous* and *donkey*. It implies something bizarre, or impossible to the extreme."

"Why donkey?"

"Poker donkey," Cap said matter-of-factly.

"What's that?"

Cap shook his head in dismay. "Doc, you need to hang on the streets more often. Get back in touch with the people. Poker donkey is just what it sounds like—a really bad poker player."

"Okay, I got it. So why is what I said redonkulous?"

"Say it's true, and Meacham was shouting 'no witnesses' while he's gunning folks down."

"Okay."

"Why would he be worried about witnesses? What did he think these people had witnessed?"

Lou's chest began to tighten as an anxious feeling took hold. "He'd be worried they had witnessed him yelling at a patient. John was already on probation with the medical board about his drinking and his temper, which is why he was under PWO supervision. An outburst like that might have cost him his license for good."

"No witnesses," Cap said. "But this lady he yelled at, she'd already left the building before he started shooting. Obviously, she was a witness, and someone he couldn't get at now."

"You think John realized his mistake after the shootings?"

"Otherwise, he probably would have gone after the lady and plugged her instead of himself."

"It's possible," Lou said. "It's sort of like Meacham's widow realizing after the fact how she caused an accident because she was trying to prevent one. If that's the case, then Carolyn wasn't just traumatized by her husband's death. She was acting just as crazy as he was."

Cap reinserted his mouth guard, put up his gloved hands, and resumed his fancy footwork. "Not just crazy," he said. "Redonkulously crazy."

CHAPTER 13

Babs Peterbee, the sixty-three-year-old matronly receptionist, greeted Lou's arrival with a look befitting a funeral. Lou was accustomed to seeing the effervescent woman lodged behind her desk in the cramped Physician Wellness Office. But throughout all the tragic clients, disciplinary hearings, and budget crises, he had never seen her looking so deeply concerned.

"He's waiting for you in his office," Peterbee said as he approached her meticulous workstation.

"Mood?" Lou asked.

"Cat 5. I'm so sorry, Dr. Welcome."

It was a poorly guarded secret that the staff at the PWO measured Walter Filstrup's demeanor on the Saffir–Simpson scale, the one used by meteorologists to rate the power of hurricanes. The director seemed to enjoy his reputation and fostered it. Most days, Filstrup was a Category 2: strong winds. A couple of times that Lou remembered, he spiked up to a Category 4. But never in the two and a half years since the shrink was hired to run the PWO had he been labeled a Cat 5 by any of the staff.

"The only thing I have to fear, is fear itself," Lou said, giving Peterbee a Winston Churchill *V* before he remembered that the quote was from FDR.

Okay, he was more nervous than he was willing to admit.

"I wish that were the case, Lou. I really do," she responded. Peterbee puckered her face, possibly holding back tears.

"Hey," Lou said, "we both know I've been through worse."

"Just don't let anyone change you. Since you got here, you've made a huge difference in the lives of a lot of people."

"I can only be me," Lou sang to the tune of the Sinatra song.

The PWO somehow managed to squeeze four cubicles, a reception desk, small conference room, supply closet (where they also kept the printer and fax machine), and Filstrup's office into 850 square feet of space. Teeth on full clench, Lou knocked on the director's closed door, imagining his dentist, Dr. Moskowitz, poised by one of the space-age chairs in his dental office, licking his chops as a couple of crowns drew ever closer.

Ready for battle, he thought.

"Come on in," he heard Filstrup say. The man sounded bright and unburdened.

Another bad sign.

Filstrup's office was, as usual, cluttered and uninviting.

His bookshelves overflowed with medical textbooks, and his desk was lost beneath dictations, articles, and client's charts—an absolute HIPAA nightmare. By contrast, the psychiatrist himself was neatly and nattily dressed in a favored blue suit, crisp white dress shirt, and solid gray tie. He was a trim, modestly built man. His horseshoe head of hair was a chestnut brown, his glasses gold wire-rimmed, and his face without distinctive features.

Filstrup took off his glasses, cleaned them with a tissue, and rubbed at his eyes. "Sit down, Lou," he instructed. His deep baritone was belied by his size.

Lou removed papers from the Aeron chair, set them down on the carpeted floor, and took the seat himself.

"So, how are you holding up?" Filstrup asked.

There was no detectable anger in his voice, which was a source of some surprise. Where was the rage? That crimson forehead?

"I'm doing okay, Walter," Lou said, "given the circumstances. How about you?"

"I'm doing all right—given the circumstances," Filstrup said.

It's over, Lou realized at that moment. *Walter is calm because it's already over.*

"Walter, let's cut to the chase," Lou said. "I'm assuming you asked to meet with me to discuss the situation in Kings Ridge."

Now almost smirking, Filstrup snapped open up a case file that Lou assumed belonged to John Meacham. Lou watched as his boss flipped unhurriedly through the pages.

"We talked about this case when I took over as director for the PWO. Do you remember?"

Lou managed a microscopic nod. *How in the hell could I forget, Walter?*

Walter Filstrup had assumed the helm of the PWO from Dr. Abigail Stevenson with all the grace and patience of a deer trapped in a living room. His first act was to demand that the two assistant directors review, in front of him, all the active cases. The ADs were Lou and a passive little psychiatrist named Ollie Comer, who had been there since the program's inception twelve or thirteen years ago, and was on the tail end of a profound, protracted burnout.

The discussion surrounding John Meacham was not pretty. During the pitched battle over Lou's choice of treatment, Comer, who was not in recovery, and had actually been Lou's monitor following his release from rehab, said not a word.

"John Meacham should have been seeing a psychiatrist," Filstrup said now, echoing his position from that unpleasant day after he had taken over the operation.

"You say it like it's a fact, Walter," Lou countered, as he did then, "as though there isn't another option that would have worked."

"For a case like John Meacham, there isn't," Filstrup shot back.

Now Lou had to once again clench his jaws to keep himself from a useless, inflammatory, snide retort.

When Filstrup took over the PWO, John Meacham was doing just fine. He was attending AA meetings daily, sometimes twice a day, abstaining from any alcohol or other drugs, and not surprisingly, given the work he was doing on himself, keeping his anger issues in check. Twelve steps to remaking a life—and John Meacham had taken them all, and would keep on taking them, Lou firmly believed.

"Alcoholism is a disease, not a moral issue, Walter. We've been through this before."

"No, you've been through this with me. And I haven't agreed."

"You haven't listened. I know what I do here works. I have successful case after successful case to prove it."

"Why? Because you were once a drug addict yourself? That gives you all the authority here? It's been my opinion, Lou, that your past experiences don't help your judgment. They cloud it."

"John didn't need psychotherapy, if that's what you're getting at," Lou said. "He needed to get sober and to keep going to meetings, and that's what he was doing."

"Until he killed seven people. I can't think of one of your cases that shouldn't have involved some degree of psychotherapy," Filstrup said. "I conducted a thorough review of your clients, including ones from before I joined the PWO. You recommend a comprehensive mental health course of treatment less than ten percent of the time in your substance abuse cases."

"Because that's not the way we're going to get their licenses reinstated," Lou said, feeling heat beginning to scorch the back of his neck. "Psychotherapy can drag on and on, when recovery is no farther away than attendance at meetings and adherence to the principles of AA, the first of which is that you can't drink. There may be other approaches and programs that will get drunks sober, but this is one that I know works. That's why I haven't gone out of my way to recommend any others."

"So John Meacham is a success by your standards?" Lou took in a sharp breath.

Here we go.

"No," he managed, no longer able to cull the strain from his voice. "Obviously, something went terribly, terribly wrong with John. But I was monitoring him, Walter. He was doing everything required of him. He was happy and productive. We never got a positive on his urine tests. This wasn't about alcohol."

"My point exactly, Welcome. This is a straightforward mental health issue. It always was."

Redonkulous.

Cap's portmanteau popped into his head. The boxer was right, and so was Filstrup. And so, for that matter, was he. Meacham was crazy at the moment he fired those shots—absolutely insane. But something had created the insanity, and it was nothing that Freud or Jung or any therapist could have couched out of him.

"We have an obligation to protect the public from doctors who pose a danger to their patients," Filstrup was saying.

Lou shook his head in dismay. "No, Walter," he said, "that's what the board of medicine is for. Of course we need to pay attention to that, too, but we also have an obligation to our docs. Sometimes we're all they have— the only ones who are going to give them the benefit of any doubt. The only ones who know and can vouch for the extent to which they are recovering from their illness."

Filstrup had had enough. "John Meacham did not receive proper treatment," he said, "and that's exactly what I told the PWO board."

Ka-boom! Ka-pow! Dr. Louis Francis Welcome, exit stage left.

"I don't believe I've ever seen you move this definitively on a case, Walter," he said.

"Now that's the wise-ass Welcome I know. It's elementary, my dear Watson. You didn't follow my recommendation. You went out on your own, like you always do with anybody who has a drug and alcohol problem. And now you are up to your glutes in casualties and disgruntled board members."

Casualties.

Anger tightened around Lou's chest. He forcefully reminded himself that there was nothing to gain from going off at the man verbally, or throttling him by the throat. Filstrup was like someone who knew nothing about weapons being presented a .45 and a full box of ammo.

"Listen, Walter, I think you should just get to the point."

"The point is," Filstrup said, slowing his speech to intentionally drag the announcement out, "that after considering all the facts in this case, the board has unanimously approved your suspension from the PWO pending any appeals, effective immediately and without pay."

Lou showed no surprise because there was no surprise to show. Surprise would have been crunching Filstrup's peanut nose with a sharp left cross.

"I was right to recommend Meacham for a return to practice," Lou said finally. "I like this job and I'm good at it. Somewhere out there are answers as to why this happened—answers that don't have anything to do with his need for psychotherapy. And when I find out what those answers are, I'll be back to petition the board to reinstate me. The work we do here is too important to be victimized by your narrow views."

"The only answer you're going to come up with, Welcome, is that I was right."

Lou was on the street a block from the PWO headquarters with no recollection of leaving the office or the building. The early afternoon was starting to get seriously warm. His mouth became dry, and he realized he was only a short walk from the dark, cozy, air-conditioned comfort of the Tam o' Shanter, for years his favorite bar.

He walked without thinking of anything but how upset he was with Walter Filstrup. The man was wrong. As usual, he didn't have any understanding of alcoholism or addiction. The science was there—irrefutable identical twin studies and other excellent pieces of research. Alcoholism was a disease.

Lou stepped beneath the rough-hewn carving of the hat and the words THE TAM swinging over the heavy wooden doorway. The Scottish poet Robert Burns had written the epic poem in 1790, and more than once during his years of drug and alcohol excess, Lou had regaled the patrons of the place by reading the tale of a man who drinks too much and must race a hallucinated Devil for his life.

Inspiring bold John Barleycorn!
What dangers thou canst make us scorn!

How in the hell could Filstrup blame him in any way for what happened in Kings Ridge? Suspending him this way was like shooting the bearer of bad news.

The sounds and smells of the Tam started tapes whirring in Lou's head. His mouth became even drier. He licked his lips and began thinking how easy it would be to get even with Filstrup by just getting smashed. Furious now, he took a step toward the already-crowded bar. Then he took another.

At that moment, other tapes began playing—snatches of nine years of meetings and long walks and talks.

. . . No one ever said it was always going to be easy. . . . Pick up the phone before you pick up a drink. . . . It's perfectly okay to want *to. . . .*

Lou wasn't even aware he had taken out his cell phone.

"Cap, it's me," he heard himself saying. "I'm inside the Tam. . . . No, I haven't. . . . Okay, I'll get out now. . . . Ten minutes. I'll be out there."

Sunshine replaced the comforting gloom. The music and the tapes stopped. Robert Burns's poem faded.

Lou walked across the street and leaned against a building to wait for his sponsor. Nine years and he still wasn't safe.

Without constant vigilance, he realized, he never would be.

CHAPTER 14

Unable to clear John Meacham out of his thoughts, Lou headed back to the town of Kings Ridge.

The decision to share some of what he knew with Gilbert Stone had essentially been made for him by Cap Duncan and Walter Filstrup—the one, who was certain that there was a pattern of extremely odd thinking and actions at work in the community, and the other, who had decreed that Lou was to have an unexpected bolus of free, unstructured time on his hands.

Stone strode into the police station waiting area from behind an imposing steel door. He was dressed as on the night he and Lou first met—tan uniform, black tie, metal star. His engaging smile showcased what Lou guessed were top-of-the-line caps.

The night just past had been a frantic one for him, with calls from a dozen or so of his PWO clients, who had been informed by Filstrup of his suspension. The best Lou could offer them was his assurance that he would fight to restore his status and continue to be available to them in an unofficial capacity. In the meantime, he promised each of them that he would do everything within the limits of his new situation to continue to help them.

Lou had come away from his roadside encounter with Stone toting a wariness of the man's oblique manner of asking questions, and an uneasy respect for the degree to which he had his finger on the pulse of his town. Kings Ridge may have looked and felt like Mayberry R.F.D., but this man was no bumpkin.

"Dr. Welcome," Stone said, shaking Lou's hand like a human garlic press, "good to see you again, son. That knot and cut there on your head look to have settled down pretty good."

"It's fine. Please, call me Lou."

"Lou it is," Stone replied, his expression as inscrutable as it had been at the scene of the accident. "I almost said, 'Welcome, Dr. Welcome.' I suppose you get that a lot."

"From time to time," Lou understated.

In fact, except to tell him and his brother that their name came from "someplace in England," their father had no knowledge of or interest in its origin. Over the years, Lou had developed a number of different responses to inquiries about it, ranging from that it was modified from the Finnish word *velkommen,* which was a soft, incredibly cuddly arctic hare, to that his great-great-grandfather had it officially changed to Welcome from the Welsh, Getthehellawayfromhere.

"Thanks for seeing me," he said this time.

"No problem at all. When a person calls with something to talk about pertinent to a multiple-homicide investigation, well, naturally that person becomes an immediate priority. Now, let's go chat in my office."

The sprawling redbrick, one-story station was, according to its cornerstone, just four years old. Stone's office occupied the entire end of one wing. Two long opposing walls of glass were shielded by drawn blinds, the wall facing his massive oak desk was a bookcase filled with law tomes and other professional volumes. In addition, there were a number of contemporary thrillers, including what appeared to be close to the entire Colors collection of John D. MacDonald, one of Lou's favorites. The wall behind the desk featured laminated testimonials and a variety of photos of Stone, posing with a who's who of state and national dignitaries.

Nice digs.

On the trip back to Kings Ridge, Lou had wrestled with a serious moral dilemma: how to discuss his relationship with John and Carolyn Meacham without violating the legally protected confidentiality of the PWO. It certainly seemed from news broadcasts as if Walter Filstrup had already released details of the murderer's relationship with the organization. It was safe to assume that wily Gilbert Stone knew at least some of Meacham's history, information probably unearthed beginning the day the physician first moved to the area.

How much Lou should disclose now was the issue. Since he'd signed on as an assistant director of the program, he had protected its clients the way he protected the anonymity of people in AA.

Still, as things stood, the odds of his winning rein-statement from the PWO board of directors were about as long as those of a mule taking the Kentucky Derby. To win out, Lou would need to prove that Meacham's actions were the result of something that no monitoring program could ever have predicted. And to do that, he was going to need Gilbert Stone's help.

First, he had to convince the chief of police, and himself, that there might be something wrong at the DeLand Regional Hospital and in his town.

Stone took a spiral-bound notebook from his desk drawer and motioned Lou to a Danish modern chair across from him. "So, let's have it," he said.

"Okay," Lou replied, leaning forward. "Beyond the obvious, I'm beginning to wonder if there might be something really strange going on in Kings Ridge."

"Son, I've been chief of police here for over twenty years. Trust me when I tell you, there's a lot of strange things going on in Kings Ridge. Now, if by strange, you mean an explanation besides insanity for John Meacham's rampage, well, I'm all ears."

"What if I told you that the shootings were a case of flawed reasoning on John's part, and that there might be a similar pattern of seriously flawed reasoning at work in other people?"

"I'd want to know about it right here, right now."

It took fifteen minutes to share what Lou had decided he would—his role with the PWO, Meacham's alcohol-ism and anger management issues, the verbal abuse of a patient four years ago that had gotten Meacham into hot water with the D.C. board of medicine, and finally the verbal assault reported to the police by his patient, Roberta Jennings.

"First of all," Lou went on, "there was no alcohol in his system. Tests for other drugs of abuse are pending, but alcohol was always the one for him—the trigger for his outbursts. Second, it seems as if he kept repeating 'no witnesses' during the attack. What did he mean by that?"

Stone's expression was puzzled. "We know all this, son," he said. "Our detectives and the staties are the ones who are conducting the investigation and doing the interviews."

"Except it doesn't make any sense," Lou countered. "Did anyone ask Carolyn Meacham or any of their friends if he had been acting weird lately? Stange thoughts? Unusual mannerisms? Any neurologic signs— a tic, perhaps? How about Roberta Jennings? What did she have to say? What did she see that afternoon in the office?"

"A man killing his neighbors and coworkers makes no sense at all, I agree. But what's your point?"

"Let's say Meacham was worried about there being witnesses because he knew his behavior would cost him his medical license—possibly for good."

"So, you're claiming that's why he shot all those people?"

"Exactly—to keep there from being any witnesses. Except, he never went after the most important witness of all—Roberta Jennings herself."

Stone just frowned. "Crazy is just that," he said. "Un-predictable. Inconsistent. Maybe the bubble just popped and he saw all that blood and all those bodies, and just like that came to his senses—took his own life before he could do any more damage."

"That's exactly my point. He waited until Roberta Jennings had left the building before he acted. If his real motivation was to eliminate all witnesses, he should have started shooting before Roberta got out the front door. Check with any profiler who knows about workplace violence. I'm sure they'll agree. First kill the object of your rage; then go after the others. Something was going on in the chemistry of Meacham's brain. It may not be something physical like a tumor or blood vessel malformation, but something had disrupted the delicate balance of transmitters connecting the neurons of his brain."

"I suppose we could look into that," Stone said. "I appreciate you sharing your theories with me." Stone looked as if he were about to end their session.

"But I told you there's more," Lou said. "I was there at the hospital for a few hours before John officially died. Some of the doctors and nurses treating him were not following standard protocol for a gunshot victim. Some of their actions were poorly thought out to the point of actually being dangerous."

"Now, wait just a minute," Stone said. "You can slander my dog, and even my children, but don't you go disparaging our hospital. We take a lot of pride in that place. As a doctor, I'm sure you know its reputation."

Lou saw that he had hit a nerve and immediately backed off. But he did tell Stone about Prichap's odd fishing expedition into Meacham's brain.

"Dr. Prichap is pretty new here," Stone replied, "but I've never heard anyone say a bad word about him. I have a cousin the man operated on—a disk, I think, or a spur of some sort. She's dancin' around like a chicken now."

"Well, I don't like to speak badly of any doc, and Dr. Prichap may just have been having an off day, but what he did was illogical and didn't demonstrate the best judgment."

Stone sighed. "You're the doctor, but I'm not sure you're giving me much to go on here. "Meacham could have just snapped after Roberta left the office. Prichap might have felt getting that bullet out was the only chance he had. This doesn't scream pattern to me."

"What about Carolyn Meacham?" he asked, trying another tack. "She almost killed us trying to chase down a driver with *one* busted taillight. She was trying to prevent an accident that would never have happened. Afterwards, she couldn't figure out why she had done it. Flawed judgment again."

Stone appeared slightly more interested. "So, what we've got here are three seemingly illogical acts, each resulting in undesirable outcomes—a shooting, a medical procedure, and a car accident. Is that about right?"

"That's right."

"And what is it you suggest we do from here, Doctor?"

"Let's keep looking for patterns. Something strange and out of the ordinary."

"Other than the obvious."

"Other than the obvious. I think we should interview Carolyn Meacham and the people close to her.

Same for Anthar Prichap and the staff who cared for Meacham in the ICU."

"No way we're going to allow you to do anything of the sort," Stone said. "But I will speak to the staties in charge about your theories."

Lou felt his future with the PWO slipping away. "Chief Stone," he said. "I'm in some real hot water at the Physician Wellness Office. In fact, I've been suspended. The only way I'm going to get my job back is to prove I didn't totally misjudge John Meacham's capacity for violent outbursts. And the only way I'm going to do that is to speak with some of the people involved. How about Roberta Jennings? Is there any way I could talk to her—ask her about John's demeanor right before the shootings?

Stone mulled over the request. "Bobbi's pretty shook up about things," he said, "but she did say she'd try to cooperate in any way she could. . . ." Lou held his breath. Without warning, Stone stood up. "Let me talk with her," he said. "See what she has to say."

"Thanks, Chief. I really appreciate that."

"Well, I appreciate you bringing all of this to my attention."

Lou sat alone for several long minutes, thinking about Filstrup, Meacham, the PWO, and all the docs his suspension had left adrift. He was thinking about calling to check in with Emily when the policeman returned.

"Well, I got good news, Lou," he said, slipping on his wool-lined bomber jacket. "It took a little convincing, but Roberta's agreed to meet with you."

Lou brightened. "That is great news," he said. "What did you have to do?"

"Not much," Stone said, grinning. "I just told her that I'd be right there beside her while you did your questioning. Turns out that was all the convincing she required."

CHAPTER 15

Roberta Jennings lived on a quiet dead-end street in a carefully maintained ranch-style home. Though there were pictures of grown children and grandchildren throughout the house, the décor could hardly be considered child friendly. The living room was dominated by an extensive collection of Lladró figurines, proudly displayed inside two ceiling-high glass cases. The plush wall-to-wall carpet was pearl white, and the furniture was small, firm, and uninviting.

The object of John Meacham's outburst was roosted on a hardback chair, looking about as comfortable as her furniture. Lou noticed a tremor of her fleshy hands as she sipped her tea, and suspected it might represent early onset Parkinson's disease, or perhaps a familial tremor. Meanwhile, the springs of her Victorian sofa were digging into his backside. He tried without success to shift into a more comfortable position.

"Are you sure you won't have something to eat or drink?" she asked him, gesturing toward a platter piled high with Oreos and an assortment of butter cookies.

Beside the snacks was a porcelain teapot, steam wafting from its spout.

"No, thank you," Lou said. "We really don't mean to take up too much of your time."

Jennings puckered her lips, gave Lou a disappointed glance, and then swallowed three of the cookies one after another without much chewing. As a doctor, Lou found it difficult not to feel deep concern for the woman's health, much as he knew John Meacham had done. Jennings's ankles were swollen, purplish, and crammed inside shoes that, at that time of the day, at least, were way too small for her. She wore polyester pants that allowed give for an expanding waistline, and her neck and chin were flabby. Her excessive weight had drained most of the luster from her face, and while Roberta was perhaps sixty, Lou guessed her body's age to be fifteen years older.

"I don't get many visitors," Jennings said after a sip of her tea. "Since Terry died, I haven't been very sociable."

"Terry was—?" Lou asked.

"Her husband. And one of the best guys you'd ever have the pleasure of knowing," Stone interjected. "Me and Terry used to go duck hunting together. Best shot in the county. Ask anyone who knows, and they'd tell you the same. The absolute best shot."

"I'm sorry for your loss," Lou said. "When did he pass on?"

"About a year ago," Jennings said. "He had a heart attack. It happened so suddenly. One minute here, the next minute gone."

"If it was that quick, he probably didn't suffer any,"

Lou said, feeling the response, though well intended, was lame.

"Dr. Meacham pleaded with him to lose weight. Same as he did with me."

He knew you were headed for the same fate, Lou thought.

"I'm sorry I have to bring up those memories of Terry, and also of what happened that day in Dr. Meacham's office," he said, "but Chief Stone told me you might be willing to tell me what you remember."

Jennings looked tense. "I . . . have a hard time just thinking about it," she said.

Again, Stone cut in. "Bobbi, Dr. Welcome, here, is looking to ask some real simple questions. He's promised that if anything he says upsets you too much, he'll skip it."

"Dr. Meacham yelled at me," Jennings said, her voice breaking. "It's as simple as that. Right out of the blue, he yelled at me."

"Besides that," Lou asked, "did he say or do anything unusual? It could have been something minor. A tic perhaps, or an odd movement. Some sort of warning that he was going to erupt. Was he at all unsteady on his feet? Did his speech become slurred or thickened?"

Jennings shook her head. "No. Nothing of the sort. He was lucid, calm, and reasonable, and then he just . . . went . . . crazy."

"And nothing specific that you remember set him off—something you said or did?"

"He weighed me, if that's what you mean."

"Can you tell me about that?"

"He had me coming in every month. One visit he would just check my weight and blood pressure with my clothes on and talk to me about the dietician and whatever program I was trying. The next visit one of his nurses, poor women, would be there after I got undressed to weigh me with a johnny on. Then Dr. Meacham would examine me and order blood if he thought that was necessary."

"And how was your weight this time?"

"I don't really remember," Jennings said, probably quicker than she had intended.

Dead end.

Lou's med school had spent hours teaching the students to avoid the pitfalls of asking leading questions—questions with the answers built in. *Does your chest pain ever go down your left arm and up into your jaw?* He knew he was dangerously close to descending into that approach now.

He flashed on what Cap had said: *Not just crazy, Lou . . . Redonkulously crazy.*

John Meacham had taken a situation every doctor regularly encountered—a patient unable or unwilling to take the measures necessary to get healthy or even to stay alive—and had blown his response far beyond what would be expected or acceptable. It was the same sort of reaction his wife had exhibited when confronting the car with one taillight out.

Don't give up! he urged himself.

"Tell me, Mrs. Jennings, did you have any interactions with Dr. Meacham outside of the clinic? Were you involved in any clubs together? Community organizations? Church groups? Anything like that?"

"Not that I can think of," Jennings said, looking disappointed at being disappointing. "Unless you count him giving me dirty looks when he saw what I was eating at Millie's."

"Millie's?"

"World-famous Millie's Diner," Stone answered. "I can't believe you haven't eaten there, or at least heard of it. If comfort food needed comfort, it would eat what Millie was serving up. Best burgers in the state. Mac and cheese that tastes like what your mama used to make. Chicken wings spicier than Cinemax After Dark. If you haven't eaten at Millie's—hell, son—you haven't eaten. It's about four miles outside of the town center on Highway 82."

"I can't believe you're a friend of Dr. Meacham's and he's never taken you there," Jennings added.

"I work a lot," Lou replied.

"Well, since Terry died, I eat there three or four times a week," Jennings said, gazing wistfully out the window. "Guess you could blame Millie's for some of my issues with Dr. Meacham. I never was quite this heavy, but without my Terry around, well, I just lost the will to cook. Plus my friends all eat there, too, so I have their company. I usually order the corn bread chicken pot pie or beef stew, or if I'm in a real adventurous mood, the creamy Cajun chicken pasta."

Uncertain precisely why, Lou sensed his interest perk. "So, Dr. Meacham knew you ate there and tried to lecture you about making healthier choices?" he asked.

Jennings made a face that suggested Lou had missed her point. "Dr. Meacham and his wife probably ate there almost as much as I did," she said. "Only it seemed like he was a stickler for the lighter fare, like the glazed chicken breast with brown rice or else something like turkey stew. I checked to see if I could catch him eating the macaroni and four cheeses, or the lobster Newburg. But I really never did."

"I can't believe Millie's is news to me," Lou said.

"Is that the sort of thing you were looking to know, Dr. Welcome?"

"At this point, anything you can share with me is helpful."

Chief Stone clearly sensed that Lou's fishing expedition had gone as far as it could. He hoisted himself off the couch with a grunt, then stretched a stiff leg. "Bobbi, you've been incredibly generous with your time," he said. "I realize this has been a traumatic experience for you. If you do happen to think of anything along the lines of what Dr. Welcome was asking about, you know how to reach me."

Lou stood as well and handed the woman his business card. "Do you mind if I write my cell phone number down there?" he asked, realizing that the vindictive Filstrup had possibly already had his extension shut off.

"I hope I've been of some help, Dr. Welcome," Jennings said. "If there is some way to explain this unexplainable evil, I'd do anything I could to assist you."

"You've been most gracious, Mrs. Jennings."

Lou had turned to follow Stone out when his cell phone sounded. The caller ID on the display screen read simply DADDY-O, and the ringtone was the Beatles' "Hard Day's Night." Lou clicked the green Talk button.

"Hey, Pops," he said. "I'm just leaving a meeting. Can I call you right back?"

"I'm starving," Dennis said, ignoring Lou's question. "What are you doing?"

His father had the voice of a four-pack-a-day smoker, despite his never having taken a puff of a cigarette. Dennis Welcome lived in Virginia, about a twenty-minute drive from Kings Ridge, and considered Lou's home in D.C. close enough to permit drop-of-the-hat meet-ups. And as he was again between jobs, and handled being alone about as well as a lemming, the spirit lately moved him to try at least a couple times each week.

"You know what, Dad, I'm pretty hungry myself," Lou said as he followed Stone down the walk to the cruiser.

"Great. Meet me at the Wave Rider in thirty."

Lou knew his father was already salivating to be treated to his beloved Wave Rider Bacon Burger, but he had another idea. "Actually, Dad, I'm thinking we should try someplace different this time."

Dennis Welcome snorted into the phone. "Yeah?" he asked. "What are you thinking?"

"Have you ever heard of a place called Millie's?"

CHAPTER 16

EVERYBODY EATS AT MILLIE'S.

The block lettering above the main entrance was set beneath a ten-foot enamel rainbow.

Judging by the number of cars in the parking lot as the noon hour approached, Lou believed the claim had some muscle behind it. Waiting in the busy lobby for his father, he used the time to scan the photographic history of the place, which had gone from a classic railroad car diner through a number of incarnations and reincarnations. According to the text accompanying the photos, Millie's had opened for business thirty-five years before, with a five-thousand-dollar bank loan, ten soon-to-be maxed-out credit cards, and one very determined owner-cum-cook named Millie Neuland.

The original railroad car endured, and now, glorified by an imaginative designer, held sway at the epicenter of a vast dining room, surrounded by a dozen private salons. Given that Lou had lived in the region most of his life, he was impressed that his path and the restaurant's had never crossed. Impressed, but not that surprised. Renee was totally into foods of various ethnicities, and in his life before her, he ate far less than he could have, worked far more hours than he should have, and spent what money he managed to hang on to in dark parts of the city that featured no rainbows.

In the years since its grand opening, Millie Neuland bought up much of the surrounding acreage, paved a parking area the size of a fairground, and at one point, added a quasi motel on the far side of the lot to house the cooks and waitstaff.

EVERYBODY EATS AT MILLIE'S.

Or works there.

After a lifetime of dealing with his father, Lou became aware of his presence almost before he had entered the building. Dennis Welcome was an expansive, barrel-chested charmer, with a salt-and-pepper crew cut and a deeply etched face that seemed perpetually tanned. His wardrobe consisted of one or two pairs of jeans, heavy, virtually indestructible work boots, and perhaps a hundred flannel shirts of various colors and plaids. This day, he had chosen a forest green.

Dennis was devoted to his two sons and granddaughter only slightly more than to his red Chevy pickup, the 200,000 miles on its odometer, and the LOCAL UNION 589 sticker fixed to the center of its rear window.

Barring the year or so following the cancer death of his wife, he was the most inexorably upbeat person Lou had ever known, except when it came to holding on to his money. Whether it was water bottling, real estate, new toys, or a chain of barber shops, he was as capable

of losing investments as he was at making people believe in them.

Mindless of the milling crowd, Dennis embraced his
older son with a frontal Heimlich maneuver that would
have dislodged a T-bone from the throat of a grizzly bear.

"Food here any good?" he asked, ignoring the menu
Lou had handed him.

"They have everything here, Dad."

"Burgers?"

"If you'd look at the menu, you'd see there's a whole
page devoted to burgers."

"It's like the size of the phone book. Besides, why
do I need a menu when I have a doctor here to look at it
for me? What about just a plain old cheeseburger? They
have any of those? You know I don't like any of that
fancy crap on my cheeseburgers."

"They have cheeseburgers, Dad. Bacon cheeseburgers, too."

"Probably comes with an avocado on it."

"Come on," Lou said, taking his father's tattooed,
solidly muscled arm. "Let's go sit down."

The lunch crowd continued filing in around them to
be quickly tended to by a team of pretty, chipper host-
esses. There were plenty of available booth seats around
the wall encompassing the main dining room, and a
number of empty tables as well. But Dennis, as Lou
knew he would, made a beeline for the counter seat-
ing, insisting as always that he liked being up high,
and that the swivel action of the stools benefited his
arthritic hip.

The counter, like the rest of the massive dining area,

was well worn—possibly by design, Lou reflected, or possibly because of the difficulty in catering to "everybody" while keeping the place buff. Varnish was worn away in some spots, and the brass fixtures were short a good polishing. Still, the overall effect was an inviting charm and warmth. As if to underscore the motto of the place, the walls and wooden pilasters featured autographed photos of celebrities and politicians, usually paired with a perpetually beaming Millie—the quintessential grandmother. Lou recognized two former Virginia governors, several players from the Redskins, Nationals, and Wizards, as well as a rapper whom Emily adored but Renee despised.

As they made their way to the counter, Lou caught snippets of conversation from the expanding sea of patrons. Nearly everything he heard dealt with the Meacham murders.

Lou and Dennis grabbed adjacent stools, sandwiching themselves between two much older gentleman, each of whom appeared to be dining alone. The wall facing them opened on the kitchen, where perhaps a dozen white-uniformed cooks and chefs of various kinds were picking up steam for the lunchtime rush ahead. Flames, fueled by dripping grease, danced in the background, creating sizzling steaks that Lou could smell. The culinary ballet was impressive, and for a time, father and son watched, mesmerized. The stainless steel counters just opposite the grill were lined with cutting boards, large mixing bowls, and trays of vegetables. Movement . . . sound . . . aroma . . .

Cue the cash registers.

It was good to see Dennis immersed in something other than the wall-mounted TVs at his beloved Wave Runner.

The narrow passage between the counter and the kitchen was patrolled by a tall, gaunt waitress with crow's-feet eyes and tousled red hair the same height as her head. Her name tag read IRIS. Nothing about her personality explained why she was working with the public. Not surprisingly, Dennis ordered a cheeseburger, fries, and a Coke.

"We don't have Coke," Iris said.

"Okay, Pepsi, then."

"No Pepsi. We only serve Millie Cola."

"Millie Cola? Lou, what is this place?"

"A place that only serves Millie Cola," he said. "Why don't you give it a try?"

"Okay, one Millie Cola and one glass of ice water on the side," Dennis said.

Iris scowled and wrote on her pad. "And how would you like your cheeseburger?"

"With cheese," Dennis said.

Another scowl.

Lou went for the Cobb salad and an iced tea.

"So . . . how you doing?" Dennis asked once their cadaverous server had moved on.

"You mean about John Meacham?" Lou asked, as usual having no problems reading the man.

"Your brother called. He said he suspected you might have had something to do with Meacham through your work. Apparently, the papers said he was an alcoholic and had been involved with a group like yours in D.C."

"Graham could have called and just asked me. I'm in his speed dial."

"Have they mentioned your name?"

"Not yet."

"But you did."

"I did what?"

"Have something to do with the guy, like Graham said."

"I did, yes."

"And are you in trouble?"

"Speak softer, Dad."

"Are you in any trouble? Graham said you might be."

If Graham, a successful money manager, worked as hard at keeping Dennis away from recurrent fiscal ruin as he did pointing out the mistakes Lou was forever making in his life, there might have been significantly less red ink in the family.

"I'll give him a call later on so maybe he'll stop speculating," Lou said.

He wondered if the younger Welcome had reasoned out that Lou's job might be on the line as well . . . or worse.

"Your brother's smart," Dennis understated. "He figures things out."

"Tell me about it."

"So?"

"So, I don't know. I'm still trying to piece it all together."

Lou could sense the old man to his right straining to listen in. He turned his back a few more inches and lowered his voice even further. If he had known Dennis was going to be in a chatty mood, he would have insisted on a booth. He should have been able to predict it. The violence surrounding the Meacham case was the sort of thing that utterly fascinated his father—and most other people, for that matter.

"He fall off the wagon?" Dennis asked.

"Nope. That much I'm sure of."

"Drugs?"

"You know I consider drugs and alcohol flip sides of the same coin."

"In that case, it doesn't make any sense."

"I agree with you there, Pop."

"No warning?"

"Not that I can find."

"It doesn't make any sense," Dennis reiterated. "Usually a guy goes ballistic and kills a bunch of people, then folks start coming out of the woodwork to say how they knew he was unstable, a loner, distant, that sort of thing."

"So far none of that," Lou said.

"Or else, if it's a serial killer, they all say how he was just the nicest guy in the world, and always had a cheerful word for everyone, and that they can't figure out how two dozen bodies got buried in his backyard without anyone suspecting a thing."

Their drinks arrived. Dennis sipped his apprehensively.

"I don't generally like any excuses for Coke," he said, "but this one's pretty good."

"I'm glad they could please you. You should let the waitress know."

"I don't think she likes me."

"Nonsense. Your charm is winning her over. I can tell."

"So, why are you out here?"

"Actually, I drove out to talk with the chief of police. He set me up to meet with one of the witnesses."

"That was nice of him."

"I suppose. Dad, there's something really strange going on around Kings Ridge."

Careful to keep his voice out of range of the old man to his right, Lou told his father what he had shared with Gilbert Stone. When he was finished, Dennis fixed him with the same sort of curious stare he typically reserved for people with excessive body piercing.

"That *is* odd," he said. "One or two weirdos might be a coincidence. Five or six is a trend—unless, of course, you're overreading things."

"Always possible."

Lunch arrived, and after one bite, Dennis Welcome appeared to have become a convert to the church of Millie Neuland.

"Call me delicious," he said to the reedlike waitress, brandishing his cheeseburger with two hands.

She favored him with an enigmatic smile that might have announced she no longer considered him a form of pond scum.

"Fresh food makes all the difference," she said.

"Yeah? Just how fresh are we talking about here?"

"Fresh as in everything we serve is local. Produce. Meat. We even bake our own bread."

"I would call that fresh," Dennis said, wiping away the juice from another bite of cow.

Lou smiled to see his father so upbeat. With on-the-job injuries, recurrent layoffs, the premature death of his beloved wife, and one financial disaster after another, the man had not had it easy. But one could rarely ever tell.

Without warning, Iris planted her palms on the counter and leaned in close to Lou. "I overheard you boys talking about John Meacham," she whispered. "You know, a bunch of the crunchy granolas around here are talking about having some sort of memorial service for the victims."

"That's nice," Lou said, sensing where the woman was heading.

"But they're also talking about including the murderer. I mean, he *is* a murderer. Seven times over. I say burn the box they've got him stashed away in and flush those ashes."

Lou stopped eating and fixed the woman with a baleful stare. "Dr. Meacham was a friend of mine," he said, sensing he was about to boil over. "He had a wife. Children. It's fine for you to have an opinion on matters, but your opinion is getting close to spoiling my meal."

Iris lost color, topped off Lou's iced tea from a pitcher, and then left, muttering.

"I told you that Graham called, didn't I?" Dennis said, changing the subject with the subtlety and grace of a rampaging rhino.

Lou groaned. "Dad, I said I wanted to enjoy my salad. Now, thanks to you and Olive Oyl over there, my chance of doing that is gone."

"I don't know what you're talking about."

"I'm talking about that you tripped yourself up. Graham didn't call you. He never calls anyone he doesn't have to. My guess is you called him."

"Okay, okay. I called him. Then, a while later, he called me back. Besides, what difference does it make who called who. He's still my son, just like you are."

"You called him with a wild new investment idea."

"This country was built on wild investment ideas. But this is a good one, Lou. A can't-miss . . . Sweet Lou . . . Remember when I used to call you that?"

"Dad, when are you going to learn?"

"This time it's different."

"Let me guess. Medical supplies?"

"Nope."

"Pest-removal services?"

"No, but remind me to check into that one. Look, I'll tell you because you'll never guess on your own. It's gold. Not those sissy Franklin Mint commemorative coins kind of gold—a real mining operation in British Columbia. Riches from the earth. The specs have *fortune* written all over them."

"Dad, you've got to stop this."

"I have the brochures in my truck. I'm just asking that you look them over."

"It's not gonna happen."

"That's what Graham said. Look, just give it a read-through is all I'm asking."

"Fine. I'll give it a read."

"Fine. Can you pass me the ketchup?"

From a spot down the counter, the waitress nodded smugly that she hadn't missed a word of the father/son exchange, and approved of how the discussion had gone. The tolerance Lou had developed for people struggling with their lives was nudged a bit by the woman, though not nearly to his limit.

The distraction was quickly interrupted by a vegetable chef who was turning a row of peeled carrots into perfect orange disks. He performed the maneuver with the dexterity of a neurosurgeon. The movement, like working a pump handle, was all wrist, with the point of the huge blade never leaving the cutting board. The sound of the broad end of the knife snapping down was like an AK-47 submachine gun.

But what caught Lou's eye wasn't just watching the pro at work. It was the youthful, freckle-faced cook directly to the chef's right. The young man's dark brown eyes were fixated on the slicing end of the razor-sharp knife. His right hand was just six inches or so from the carrot pieces that were flipping out from the blade like poker chips. Once, then again, it looked to Lou as if the young man—twenty-two if that—was going to make a move to snatch one of the newly minted coins from the cutting board.

Lou tensed.

The chef, lost in concentration, remained fixed on his gleaming blade, which never came up off the cutting board more than a millimeter or so farther than it had to.

Another flinch from the boy—this time involving not only his hand, but his shoulder as well.

The kid was going to go for it.

Lou felt certain of it.

Pushing back from the counter, he rose from his stool.

No one seemed aware of the drama that was playing out—least of all the husky chef himself.

To Lou's left, Dennis was lost in the glory of his perfect burger.

One more slight tic by the boy, and Lou had seen enough.

But it was too late.

The kid seemed to be lost in some sort of hypnotic fugue state, timing his moves like a striking rattlesnake. His latex-gloved hand shot out toward a particular, perfect orange disk.

"Nooooo!" Lou cried out, toppling his tall stool backwards, and diving, arms outstretched, across the counter.

The heavy ten-inch blade snapped down on the boy's extended thumb with unimaginable force.

Bone cracked like a sniper's shot.

The boy's shriek filled the enormous dining room, accompanied moments later by the screams from dozens of others.

Then there were more, unrelenting shrieks.

From the vegetable cutting board in the kitchen came a geyser of blood.

CHAPTER 17

"Oh, Jesus! My thumb! My thumb!"

In an instant, blood was everywhere, spurting into the air from within the tattered rubber glove and cascading across the wooden chopping board onto the floor.

Lou vaulted over the counter and past the waitress, whose expression gave no indication that the startling event had even registered. He slammed into the chaos of the kitchen through a swinging door with an eye-level porthole as a crush of customers and staff closed in behind him.

"It's Joey!" someone cried out. "Joey's cut his finger off!"

Lou's powers of observation were immediately heightened. Seconds passed as minutes. The world around him began moving in slow motion. His tone became firmer, but his speech slowed. What might have been dozens of factors were analyzed and synthesized at once.

Crunch mode.

"I'm a trauma specialist from Eisenhower Memorial," he heard himself announce calmly. "Please give me room. Give me some room. Someone call nine-one-one and tell me when you've done it. One of you bring over some rubber gloves. The rest of you, back away, please."

Incredibly, the boy was still on his feet, staring down at his hand with what appeared to be little comprehension. Blood had sprayed across his white apron like a macabre piece of spin art. The blade had crunched through the bone just above the metacarpo-phalangeal joint—the knuckle separating the digit from the hand. It had been a vicious cut, requiring almost unimaginably intense force.

The bone had been splintered more than sheared in two. Some soft tissue remained intact at the base—a piece of good fortune that would enable optimum anatomical alignment in preparing the boy for transport. Still, as things stood, two bloody tendons and a bridge of skin were all that kept the digit from dropping into the stack of blood-soaked carrots.

If this were a single finger other than the thumb, it seemed quite possible the hand surgeon would opt simply to complete the amputation. But this was the thumb—the digit that, because it could be pressed against the pads of the other four fingers on the hand, created the opposition that, in essence, separated primates from other animals. Writing, grasping, fine motor skills. For life to go on as it was for this youth, meticulous reimplantation was critical.

And preserving anatomical relationships and circulation had to be Lou's mission. But first, there was the matter of the kid himself.

Lou grabbed a towel and laid it over the boy's hand. Instantly, the white cloth became soaked in crimson.

"Joey, is that your name?" Lou asked, supporting him by the shoulders.

"Joey," the kid managed. He began shrieking again and raised his hand to eye level. Heavy drops of blood fell from beneath the towel.

"He just stuck his hand in there!" the chef cried out, the heavy, blood-covered blade still in his hand. "I never saw him. Jesus, Joey, what in the hell were you thinking?"

Joey's fair, freckled complexion was ashen—one of the early changes of shock.

"All right, Joey," Lou said, "I'm going to lower you down."

"Here you go, Doc," someone said.

A box of disposable rubber gloves appeared on the high bench where the accident had occurred. From his earliest days in the hospital, Lou had to battle against the intense urge to dive right in and help whenever there was an open, bleeding wound. Then articles began appearing in the literature reporting the surprisingly large percent of HIV-positive patients found in sequential testing in both inner city and suburban emergency wards. And finally, conversion to positive happened to a fellow moonlighter who didn't follow protocol, in a small, affluent community hospital, fifty miles outside of D.C.

"Please, no one come near the blood without having gloves on," he said, donning a pair and quickly backing it up with another. "One of you roll an apron under his neck and someone else get his legs elevated with something under his knees and ankles. The higher, the better. If there's a blanket around, put it over him. And I need towels. Lots of towels."

He brought his mouth next to Joey's ear.

"Joey, my name is Dr. Louis Welcome. Call me Lou. Hang in there with me and we'll get you fixed up. Okay?" He took a clean towel and slid it in as a replacement for the blood-soaked one. "Do you have any allergies to medications? . . . Any past surgery . . . ?"

He craned his neck back until he made eye contact with his father. Then he pulled his car keys from his pants pocket.

"Ask that guy over there in the green plaid shirt to get my medical bag from the trunk of my car," he ordered the chef nearest to his left. "Then get me a large bowl of ice water and some dishwashing soap. Dove, Palmolive. Anything you have is okay." The circle of people gathered around them began to close in. "You've got to back up!" Lou said firmly, applying gentle pressure. "Give us more room."

Blood flowed from the wound in thick spurts. Hemostasis? Ice? Cleansing?

He evaluated the pluses and minuses of each maneuver.

Stop bleeding. . . . Get alignment. . . . Sterilize. . . . Protect any microscopic arteries that might still be intact. . . .

Lou made decisions while talking to the boy almost continuously. A single rolled apron had been placed under Joey's neck, and stacks of towels were now elevating his legs from the knees down.

Lou rested the damaged hand palm down on a clean towel, gently adjusting the thumb into an anatomically correct position.

"Okay, Joey . . . listen to me now. . . . Everything is going to be just fine. . . . I'm going to help. . . ."

"Help me," Joey answered back meekly. "Please help me."

"Someone give me a scissors, please."

Lou pulled one of the towels from the pile and cut off a long three-inch strip. Next, he wrapped the strip twice around the middle of Joey's forearm and tied it off. The bleeding began to slow. To add torque, Lou slipped a wooden cook spoon under the strip and turned it until the bleeding began to slow even more. He made note of the time, 12:50. There may have been as much as two hours of wiggle room to keep the tourniquet on before there was tissue damage, but he had no desire to cut things that close.

"Here you go, Lou," he heard Dennis say.

Lou's heavy black leather bag materialized on the floor beside his knee. A number of states had enacted Good Samaritan laws to protect doctors who offered help in an emergency from being sued. But many of those laws were vaguely constructed, and some had even been challenged in court. As a result, there were docs who went out of their way to avoid involvement in trauma or medical emergencies—an aspect of his profession Lou had never been proud of. Instead, he had chosen to make himself better prepared. He carried a well-equipped medical bag in his trunk, and at one point, had actually participated on a committee that helped the airlines to design a sensible and useful emergency first-aid kit that could be placed on planes.

"You still with me, Joey?"

"Yes . . . I'm with you, sir."

The physical evidence of shock had already begun to recede, and some strength had returned to the youth's voice. Bleeding had been reduced to an ooze.

"I need that icy dishwashing soap now," Lou called out.

Given that the ambulance would be there soon, there was little in Lou's emergency bag that would be of major help. But there was gauze and a great splint—thumb-sized, three-quarters of an inch wide, pliable aluminum, backed with foam rubber. And just as important, there was a pair of shears that could shape it. Years had passed since he had put the splints and shears into his kit. Who knew?

He irrigated the wound, carefully wrapped the laceration, measured off a piece of splint well more than twice the length of the thumb and twisted it into a *U* that held the fracture in an anatomically perfect position, with three inches of aluminum extending across the wrist and onto the hand, front and back. Then, again from the kit, he snapped open a chemical ice pack and set it on the bandage. By the time the cold was gone, Joey would be undergoing treatment. Lou finished the job with heavy cotton batting up to the tourniquet and two ACE bandages.

"You're doing great, pal," Lou said to him. "You're one tough customer, I'll tell you that. You are really something. . . ."

Lou checked the youth's blood pressure. One hundred.

Reasonable.

He continued the stream of encouraging banter.

"You're doing just great, Joey . . . just great. . . ."

"Out! . . . Out! Okay, back off, everyone. Please." Millie Neuland came rushing through the crowd. If she had aged since any of the dozens of photographs of her were taken, Lou could see no evidence of it. Gray, tousled hair, round wire-rimmed glasses, bright blue eyes, rouged cheeks, finely painted eyebrows, and a nearly perfectly round face. Her gingham dress, frilly half apron, and single strand of pearls completed the picture.

The quintessential grandmother.

Lou had begun wiping off the boy's pallid cheeks.

Millie knelt next to him, mindless of the blood. "The ambulance is on the way," she said to no one but Lou, a genteel Southern lilt in her speech. "If you're not a doctor, son, you dang well should be. I'm Millie Neuland."

"I guessed. Lou Welcome. I'm an ER doc at Eisenhower."

"Lucky us. Oh, Joey! Can you hear me, baby? You got a doctor right here with you."

Joey's eyes fluttered open. "Hi . . . Ma."

"Your son?" Lou asked.

"Might as well be. His name's Joey Alderson. Been here at the restaurant for years. Looks twelve, but he's near twenty-five."

"Ma, I really messed up this time," Joey managed in a hoarse whisper.

"How bad?" Millie asked Lou. There was emotion in her voice, but her tone was that of a woman used to being in charge and dealing with crisis.

"He put his hand under a knife that was chopping carrots. My father, the guy over there in green, and I were sitting just a few feet away."

"How bad?" the restaurateur asked again, encouraging no mincing of words.

Lou glanced down at Joey, who appeared to have drifted off. "Reimplantation," he said, sensing the word was one that the youth was unlikely to completely understand. "We have some wonderful hand surgeons at Eisenhower Memorial. I can make some calls and we can get him over there."

"I don't know you, and I don't know any of the doctors at Eisenhower Memorial," Millie replied, "but since you work at one of the big hospitals in the city, you might know that many folks out here consider a referral to there tantamount to a death sentence. We're very proud of our hospital here. My restaurant is one of its biggest supporters. In fact, the surgical suite is named for me and this place. Joey's a little . . . limited in some ways. He may frighten easily. The doctors at DeLand know him well. They know how to be sensitive to his needs."

"I understand," Lou said, now measuring every single word carefully. "The metropolitan hospitals in cities like D.C. all have the reputation you spoke about—

mostly because people who are referred in are usually quite ill."

From the distance, they could now hear the siren of an approaching ambulance. Lou knew that, assuming his concerns about DeLand Regional were on the mark, time was running out on his chances to get Joey Alderson into the city.

A frontal assault seemed to be his only option.

With the approaching siren getting louder, he met Millie Neuland's gaze with his, and held it. "Millie, I promise to explain my feelings later," he said, "but I have my reasons—very strong reasons—and I am begging you to allow me to bring Joey into Eisenhower Memorial. . . . Begging you."

The woman, clearly nonplussed by the force behind Lou's words, studied his face.

The siren, now in front of the restaurant, cut off. Moments later, they could hear the voices and commotion from the direction of the main entrance.

Lou felt his heart sinking. There was nothing more to say.

"Well," Millie said finally, "if Joey's going to be trucked into the city, then I'm going with him."

CHAPTER 18

There was a time Kim Hajjar and her three closest D.C. friends met for drinks once a week. But more and more, their good intentions were being eroded by their professional lives. Their meeting spots seemed tempered as well. Gone were the margaritas at Chi-Chi's and Scorpion Bowls down at the Hong Kong. The group of women now preferred quieter watering holes where they could commiserate about jobs, kids, husbands, or in Kim's case, the dearth of quality men.

Darlene would have been a welcome addition to the group, but the Secret Service, along with concerns about paparazzi, made it impractical for the First Lady to join their periodic early-evening revels. Having been to Bar None with Darlene just a few days ago, Kim suggested it would make a good kickoff spot to enjoy a cocktail before dinner at the Blue Crab Grill, the much-hyped new restaurant on Connecticut Avenue.

The women were rarely on time for their own gatherings. Two of them were lawyers, and like Kim, worked hours bordering on the cruel and unusual. Candice, an ob-gyn, was often held hostage by the biology of her patients. Usually, though, the group managed to carve out a few good hours, always ending with the pledge that when the time came for their next gathering, their friendship would override all but the most dire considerations.

That night, Kim showed up at Bar None on time, knowing the others probably would not. Having spent an exhausting day making final preparations for the visit of the President of Ireland and his family, she was happy to have a quiet interlude before the gang arrived.

Kim felt lucky to have nabbed a spot at the bar, but after downing a beer in fewer swigs than she would ever admit, she now needed to use the ladies' room. She loved working for Darlene, but always appreciated the ease with which she could move about when unencumbered by her entourage. There were no advance teams to pass judgment on the premises beforehand, no agents chatting inconspicuously in the corner, and best of all, no one following her to the restroom.

When she returned to the crowded bar, Kim was not surprised to find her place occupied by a woman in her twenties, dressed to attract. Several preppy swains had already picked up the scent and were beginning to circle. She moved downwind to the only empty stool. Unfortunately, the occupants next to her were an attractive couple with lovey-dovey eyes and exploratory hands. Kim sensed the all-too-familiar pang. She had had her chances over the years—a couple of engagements, and even a brief marriage to a man who was all shiny on the outside, but on the inside was searching for Mommy. Now, any man who wanted to learn who she was and what mattered to her would have to do some serious digging.

Might need something stronger than an Amstel Light, she thought.

Kim was working to avoid staring at the happy couple and to keep from lamenting her uninspiring love life, when she felt a gentle tap on her shoulder. Turning, Kim came face-to-face with Nicole Keane's stunning beauty. The two women embraced with genuine affection.

"I thought you said you were trapped in some sort of deposition," Kim said.

Nicole, olive complexioned, with dark, seductive eyes, was as statuesque as any runway model. And although none of the friends could be considered at all unattractive, she was the most hit upon. To the dismay of her would-be suitors, she was also the woman with the oldest marriage license and most number of kids—three.

"Deposition over and done," Nicole said. "It is so weird having the absolute goods on someone, and sitting in a deposition listening to them lie."

"A-gree," Kim said. "I'm as big a baseball fan as the next person, but to hell with a grand slam home run or a no-hitter. Lying under oath is the true Great American Pastime."

"And I am now absolutely ready to participate in the other Great American Pastime." She caught the bartender's eye with little trouble. "Wild Turkey, neat."

"Oooh! That kind of day, huh?"

"Loooooong," Nicole said as her drink appeared on the bar.

Kim could not resist another glance at the touchy-feely couple, and Nicole caught her looking. "Do you think they're really happy?" Kim asked.

Both women watched as the couple kissed lightly.

"I wouldn't say they're *unhappy*," Nicole said. "But I remind you of the first rule of Pepsi Generation sanity."

"I know. I know. Never go around comparing your insides to everyone else's outsides. I think we need to start importing more men. Is it just my imagination, or is every guy in D.C. married or gay?"

"There are still some eligibles rooting about. It's not like you weren't a former beauty queen, darling," Nicole replied. "You just don't flaunt it."

"I don't think my eighty-hour workweeks have done much for my overall desirability, that's for sure."

"Trust me, you're still a stunner," Nicole said.

Kim gave her friend a hug. "Flattery, my dear, will get you another drink."

"And a little cleavage on display will get you half a dozen."

As if on cue, the bartender motioned to Kim and guided a bottle of Amstel Light down the crowded bar to her.

"I take it back," Nicole said. "With a face like that, you can keep your cleavage in the henhouse."

"You sure you got the right woman?" Kim asked the man.

"He was very clear it was for you."

"He, who?" Kim asked, looking over at a pod of perhaps a dozen and a half eager twenty- and thirty-somethings beginning the evening's hustle.

"I . . . don't see him."

"Well, what did he look like?"

"I didn't really notice. He looked like . . . all of them. What can I say? I think he wore glasses. Maybe dark hair. I do know when he passed me the drink, he had slid money for the beer and an extra two bucks between the bottle and the coaster."

"Two bucks?" Nicole exclaimed.

The bartender chuckled. "If it had been a five, I might have remembered him better."

Kim turned the screw top of the bottle and wondered if it had been loosened before. Nothing like a couple of years in the White House to fan any spark of mistrust into a conflagration.

"Throw it away," she said after a moment's thought.

The bartender had watched her test the bottle. "Here," he said, exchanging the Amstel for one from the fridge. "You're ready for a fresh one anyhow."

"You really think it's already been opened?" Nicole asked.

"Probably not, but weirder things have happened."

"You're right there, sister."

The kiss-happy couple gulped down their last swallows and headed for the door. Nicole slid onto one of the vacated stools. The other women were later than usual, she observed. Perhaps it was worth calling. . . . The moment she said the word, the bar phone began ringing.

"The all-powerful Nicole," Kim said before she could

begin wondering why whoever it was hadn't called on one of their cell phones. "Wanna guess which one of them it is?"

The bartender listened for a few seconds, then hung up. "It was for you," the bartender said to Kim. "It was the guy who bought you the beer."

"Inventive," Nicole said.

"Creepy," Kim responded.

The jukebox had begun playing a song Kim knew by the band Green Day.

The bartender leaned toward them to be heard over the increasing din. "He told me to tell you to look under the drink coaster."

"Intriguing," Nicole said.

"Double creepy," Kim replied.

Her brow furrowed as she flipped the cardboard coaster over so that only she could see. Nicole and the bartender waited. The note was written in a small, neat hand. Kim read it and felt her stomach knot. Her heart rate accelerated like a drag racer as she scanned the restaurant.

"Do you see him?" she asked the bartender, now with some urgency. "Are you sure he's not here?"

The man glanced about again, but shook his head. "Like I said, I really didn't take a good look at him. In this place, guys are always buying drinks for pretty women they want to connect with. It's like the coin of the realm. I remember what the women look like more than I remember the men."

The noise level in Bar None had elevated as more people filtered in. The bartender waited until it was clear he wasn't going to learn the contents of the message, and then headed off to tend to other customers.

Nicole scanned the room. "Okay," she said finally. "I give up. What's it say?"

"Nicole, I detest pledging people to secrecy," Kim said grimly, "and the last thing I want to do is upset you. But I need to keep this one to myself—at least for the time being."

"You can't be serious. I tell you about my damn sex life. The good stuff, too."

"Believe me, baby, if I had a sex life, I'd tell you all about it, too. But this is business—company business. If Darlene says it's okay for me to talk with you about it, the first thing I'll do is get you on speed dial."

"Good thing I love you," Nicole said.

Kim embraced her. "Good thing you do," Kim said.

The other two women arrived together, just a couple of minutes later. Per her agreement with Kim, Nicole led them to the far end of the bar so that Kim could speak to a man who seemed interested in her. The new arrivals, giddy to be drifting away from the responsibilities of their lives, acted as if they had just been told of their friend's engagement.

As soon as the three women had melted into the evening crush, Kim moved back from the bar, slipped the coaster from her purse, and read it one more time.

> **Sec'y Evans has been framed. I must speak to Darlene Mallory in secret. If you agree to help arrange the meeting, go put a dollar in the jukebox.**

Kim nodded to no one in particular, replaced the coaster in her bag, and moved slowly across the room toward the jukebox. There was no sense in trying to pick out the writer of the note. Kim was convinced now that he was clever enough to keep himself disguised or concealed until he was ready to disclose himself and his purpose.

It felt strange to know that he was out there someplace, watching. Clearly, he had done his homework. Darlene was the one closest to the president who might be willing, at least, to listen to what this man had to say.

Kim made her way to the jukebox, taking several furtive glances over her shoulder. What if the note was true? What if Russ Evans had been railroaded into resigning? She approached a man leaning up against the brick wall, drinking a Heineken—tall, intelligent, with razor-cut chestnut hair. He looked at her unabashedly as she neared. A chill ripped through her. Their eyes met. She was just about say something, when a flashy blonde in a tight white sweater came and wrapped her arms around his neck.

He gave a *What can you do?* shrug, and Kim slunk back into the crowd.

It had been foolish of her to suspect the man. Whoever wrote the note was frightened enough to take these sorts of precautions. He wouldn't be standing around making eye contact with her.

More people had crammed into the darkened lounge area, making it impossible for her to observe them all. She stopped in front of the wall-mounted jukebox, rifled through her purse, and pulled a crisply pressed dollar bill from her wallet.

Russ Evans has been framed, she kept thinking. Assuming it was true, countless other questions were in need of answering. First, though, there was the matter of proof, and clearly that proof had to be evaluated by the First Lady.

Kim's hands trembled as she inserted the bill into the machine's narrow maw. The song playing at the moment was "Voodoo Child" by Jimi Hendrix—appropriate, she thought, given the sense that she was being manipulated. The bill disappeared into the slot like a snake's tongue retreating back into its mouth. As soon as it was gone, Kim felt a vibration from inside her purse.

Glancing about once more, she opened her bag and took out her iPhone. A year ago, she'd taken a picture of the White House during an August sunset, and liking it so much, she made it her iPhone's background image. But superimposed over that image now was a semi-transparent rounded rectangle bordered by a thin white line. In the center of the rectangle was a single-line text message.

I'll be in touch.

CHAPTER 19

Nearly five hours had passed since the hand team had taken Joey Alderson to the OR. Lou and Millie Neuland regularly checked the empty corridor beyond the picture window wall for any sign of his surgeon. Eisenhower Memorial's interior designers had made the family room as homelike as possible, given the restrictions of a hospital. A forty-eight-inch flat-screen TV covered much of one wall, and according to the laminated instructions tacked beside it, could even stream Netflix. The bookshelves offered a collection of paperbacks, children's books, and magazines. There were also two computer workstations with wireless Internet access, and a kitchenette—everything needed to pass the anxious hours.

Whatever doubt Millie harbored regarding bringing Joey to Eisenhower Memorial seemed to have vanished before the sheer magnitude of the place, and the attention to detail and family needs. But it was the quiet confidence of hand surgeon Dr. Rafe Kurdi, speaking to her hours ago in the ER, that sealed the deal—especially when he shared glowingly that he, his wife, and kids had once, a year or so ago, eaten at her restaurant.

"This is going to be a long and complicated operation," Kurdi explained. "But just as preparing wonderful food is what you do, fixing damaged hands is what I do. Saving Joey's thumb, while preserving as much function as possible, is our goal. We have been aided in this effort by the exceptional work that Dr. Welcome, here, performed at the scene. He has a well-deserved reputation in this place for knowing what he is doing. Joey is a very lucky young man that he was there."

"I'm figuring that out," Millie said. "Dr. Welcome insisted that we come here rather than to our local hospital."

Lou could hear the unasked question in her voice, and knew that sooner or later, he might have to explain why he believed there was something terribly wrong in Kings Ridge and also at her beloved DeLand Regional. Lou pictured Joey Alderson twitching with anticipation as he timed his lunge beneath the huge chopping knife, going for a single, bright orange slice of carrot. Was he yet another example?

Lou checked the wall-mounted clock. Nearly eight. The stress was showing on Millie's face. She hadn't appeared at all frail until now. Lou took hold of her hand, which was surprisingly callused.

The woman smiled grimly. "I don't know what I would have done without you," she said, pulling a tissue from her purse to dab at her tears.

"He's going to do fine. After all these years in the ER, I can tell a battler when I see one."

"Do you have any idea what could have happened back there in my kitchen?"

"I saw most of it developing, and right up until the last second, I didn't believe he was going to do it. Has he ever done anything that impetuous or poorly thought out before?"

"Joey's a little what you might call accident prone. That's why they know him so well at DeLand."

"I see."

"But he's not really reckless—certainly not in this way."

"Back at the restaurant, you used the word 'limited' when you spoke of him. What did you mean by that?"

Millie sank down on a sofa, and Lou did the same on the far side.

"Joey came to my office one day when he was just thirteen," she said. "He told me he was looking for a job. I still have no idea how he found me or how he got out to the restaurant. I tracked down his family—what there was of it, anyhow. No father. Alcoholic mother. Joey was the oldest of four. They lived in a dump of a place in Baxter. Family Services was about to move in and dole out the kids to foster homes. I talked them into letting me have Joey. Even though he had some learning issues, and an attention problem, he graduated from high school when he was nineteen. A few years after that, I set him up in a small apartment in the Dorms. That's what I call the place out behind the restaurant where some of the staff stays. He does a good day's work, and the rest of the staff really likes him and sort of protects him, if you know what I mean."

"I do."

Lou was unable to reconcile anything in the boy's history with what he and Dennis had witnessed, and this hardly seemed like the time to start barraging Millie Neuland with probing questions. Still, she continued her narrative with no prompting.

"Now, don't get me wrong," she said. "Joey is hardly a regular guy. He's sort of, I don't know, quirky sometimes."

Lou perked up at the word.

"Quirky?" he asked.

"You know, odd, strange. He's not exactly obsessive, but he gets onto a hobby and goes overboard with it. It's sort of like he gets fixated on things."

Like that piece of carrot?

Lou began ticking off what he knew about conditions that featured fixations without dominating obsessive compulsive behavior. His list, as might be expected from an ER doc, was a short one—variants of autism such as Asperger's syndrome, and . . .

"Can you give me some examples of things that Joey's gotten locked in on?" he asked, wondering about Carolyn Meacham and her nearly deadly fixation on a busted taillight.

"The last thing Joey really got into," Millie said, "was learning how to tie knots. I once bought him a book of over a hundred different knots, thinking he probably wouldn't have enough of an attention span to do much with it. It took him two or three months, but he learned to tie every one of them. Eventually he could even do a bunch of them blindfolded. It was amazing to watch."

"How long ago was that?" asked Lou.

"Maybe two Christmases. And before that, it was puzzles. And before that, radio-controlled cars. Using a kit, the boy built one that went faster than I'm comfortable driving. Then he just lost interest and went on to something else."

"So he's been like that for a long time?"

Lou tried to keep the disappointment from his voice. If Joey's behavior had been a recent development, it might have been an interesting avenue to explore. Instead, it appeared to be just another in a string of dead ends.

"Oh, he's been that way ever since I've known him," Millie said. "Now, I can't be certain I've touched on all his hobbies. Joey's a very private person, and not a boy anymore. I make it my business to keep out of his world. He has a driver's license and an old Ford pickup, and pretty much comes and goes as he pleases. I don't go traipsing about his apartment at the Dorm, and he doesn't invite me over for dinner." Millie said that with a laugh, and then added, " 'Cause everybody eats at Millie's."

"And to your knowledge, he's never behaved irrationally? Done anything dangerous?"

"No. Oh, no. Joey's a stickler for the rules. My only demands of him besides honoring the Ten Commandments are that he's on time for work and polite to everybody. He's never let me down on either regard."

Their conversation drifted off, and for a time, Millie dozed and Lou read some articles in an emergency medicine journal.

They were startled upright when the door to the family room swung open and Dr. Kurdi entered. He appeared as fresh as he had when he left to do the case, and he was smiling pleasantly, almost ecstatically.

"It went as well as we could have hoped," he said. "I'm optimistic that we're going to get a significant amount of function back."

Lou had been imagining what Joey's life of hobbies would have been like missing a functional thumb.

"That's great news, Rafe," he said.

"You get as much credit for the success as we do."

Millie squeezed Lou's arm.

"Can we go see him?" she asked.

"In a little while, one of the recovery room nurses will be in to get you. He's still pretty out of it from the anesthesia. He'll need to stay here for a couple days. We want to keep a close eye on him and give him pain meds and IV antibiotics."

"Well, that's fine," Millie said, a note of disappointment in her voice. "I'm not much for driving any distance, but there are plenty of folks at the restaurant who will come and get him. In fact, someone will come and get me tonight. I'm just glad he's going to be all right."

Lou put his hand on Millie's shoulder.

"It's no problem for me to bring him back to Kings Ridge when it's time," he said. "In fact, it would be my pleasure. I'll drive you home later tonight, too. I have a couple of new CDs I want to listen to on the way back home. Also, I work right down the street at the Annex, so I can pop in as much as I want. And I'll phone you with progress reports. How would that be?"

Most of Millie's wrinkles vanished around a bright smile. "How would that be?" she echoed. "Let me put it this way. Neither you nor Dr. Kurdi will ever have to pay for another meal at Millie's again."

CHAPTER 20

Lou rolled double sixes and moved his pewter Scottie dog ahead twelve spaces. Emily reacted immediately, springing from her beanbag chair, and tapping feverously at the IN JAIL square on their Monopoly board.

"Oh no, you don't," she said. "That's your second double in a row. You've got to go to jail."

"No, no, no," Lou countered. "It's *three* doubles in a row and go to jail. Two in a row and I get to buy North Carolina, which I, in fact, am about to do."

This was a serious development, and the teen's somber expression reflected it. Her father already owned two monopolies to her one. North Carolina would give him a shot at putting her away. Her usual strategy of acquiring railroads at any and all cost along with the orange or red monopoly wasn't working out.

"I'm sure it's two doubles," Emily said, as she plucked up Lou's dog and set it on the jail square. Lou picked up the piece and reestablished it on North Carolina.

"Three," he said.

"Two." Emily moved the terrier back to jail.

Lou sighed deeply and spoke through clenched teeth. "Okay. . . . Let's . . . get . . . the . . . rules."

"We're not getting the rules."

"Because you know that I'm right."

"No. Because I know that *I'm* right. And giving you the rules would be the same as admitting that I could be wrong."

"I could always send you to your room."

Emily's face lit up. "I knew it. I knew you'd resort to that. You should be ashamed of yourself."

"Okay, I'm ashamed of myself. Go to your room!"

Lou could not keep from smiling as well. These were the times he treasured the most—though this one would sadly be ending soon. It seemed that with each passing day, Emily was becoming sharper and more fun. He loved spending time with her at his apartment, even though Renee rarely missed an opportunity to disapprove of his chosen neighborhood. The cozy two-bedroom place above Dimitri's Pizza, across the street from the gym and not far from his old halfway house, had served him and, more important, Emily quite nicely.

"All right, then, the rules," Lou said.

Emily dug out the flimsy, Scotch-taped rule booklet from underneath a pile of tattered Monopoly money.

"Come and get it!" She tossed it between them.

When he reached for it, she dived at him and wrestled him facedown onto the rug, bouncing on him until he cried uncle. When she let up and rolled off, he quickly read, " 'If you throw doubles three times in succession, move your token immediately to the space marked *In Jail*.' "

Emily looked at him, batting her eyes. "I'm sorry, Mr. Butler," she said in a heavy Scarlett O'Hara accent, "did you say something?"

"Not really."

"Good, because when it comes to rules, frankly, my dear, I don't give a damn. They're stupid."

"Oh, they have their place," Lou said.

Emily harrumphed. "Do you know how many rules Steve has?" she asked. "It's insane over there. But he's still like way more strict with me than with his own brood."

"That's a little hard to believe."

In a split second, she went from lying on her stomach to sitting in a lotus position. "Oh, trust me," she said, "it's true."

"Example, please."

"Okay. He and Mom won't let me have my computer in my bedroom, and when his brood is with us, he lets David have his."

"You can't have your computer in your bedroom here, either," Lou said.

"That's not the point. The rules should be the same for everybody."

"How are you and Steve getting along these days?"

Lou knew the answer to that question. Renee had filled him in on Emily's more recent flare-ups with her husband, and had even asked Lou's help with reining in her temper.

"Steve's all right, I guess," Emily said. "When he's not trying to be my father."

"From what I've heard, I don't believe he thinks of

himself that way," Lou replied. "I know he loves you, and wants only what's best for you."

"Well, what's best for me is getting rid of the no-laptop-in-my-room rule."

Lou frowned, but it was hard for him to maintain a stern expression. His daughter's spirit reminded him of her mother.

"You know, sweetie, part of the art of living is knowing when you can break the rules, and when you can't."

Emily made a sourpuss face. "I prefer to follow your example," she said. "You don't take shit from anybody."

"Hey, come on. You have too much class for that kind of language. And for your information, I've managed to get myself into quite a few pickles by not following the rules, so don't make me your shining example there."

"Yeah? Name one?"

"Uh . . . how about, God grant me the serenity to accept the things I cannot change, the courage to change the things I can—"

"—and the wisdom to know the difference," Emily said, finishing the Alcoholics Anonymous Serenity Prayer that Lou had long ago imprinted on her. "Okay, but that's different. You had a problem and you dealt with it. I'm talking about rules like what you fight against at the Physician Wellness Office all the time."

Lou's chest did a double-clutch. How much had Renee told her? Did she know about his suspension—that Filstrup blamed him for what Meacham had done?

God grant me the serenity . . .

"What about the PWO?"

Emily shrugged. "Just that you say you're always fighting with your boss because you know that you're right and he's wrong about something. You don't play along just to play it safe. You fight for what you believe. And I believe if David can have a laptop in his room, I can have one, too."

Lou quickly decompressed. She knew nothing. But, he decided, it was time she did. "That's not always a winning strategy," he said. "There are times you can be wrong, even though you're right. Does that make any sense?"

"No."

"What if I told you that because of my tendency to trust my judgment *more than* the rules, that I'm currently not employed with the PWO."

Emily went pale. "You got fired?"

"Not fired exactly, but I'm not in good standing right now with our board of directors."

"What'd you do wrong?"

"Let's just say that if I listened to my boss and some others who didn't feel as strongly as I did, things might not have gotten so drastic so fast."

"So if you hadn't always been trying to prove that you were right, you might still be working there. Is that what you're saying?"

"Something like that, yeah. Listen, I don't want to see you complicate things with Steve. Give him a chance. Don't fight him at every corner. Show him that you at least respect his judgment. Ask him what you could do to earn the same privilege that David has. Maybe the answer will surprise you. Maybe it will turn out to be something simple."

"Now you sound like Mom."

"Well, your mother is a very intelligent woman."

"And beautiful."

Lou nodded. "Yes, and beautiful."

"Very beautiful," Emily said.

"Very beautiful."

"And incredibly talented."

Lou sensed something was afoot. "Yes, your mother is very talented. She's a great cook and fabulous dresser."

"You forgot to mention a brilliant psychologist."

"One of the best around."

"And that you'll never meet a woman who'll compare to her."

"Quite possibly so. It's true your mother has set a very difficult standard to meet. And I say my nightly prayers of thanks that you inherited so many of her wonderful qualities."

Emily was smiling—beaming was more like it. Then Lou realized that she was looking past him. He twisted around.

Renee was standing in the doorway, her set of his apartment keys in her hand. "Oh please, guys," she said. "Don't stop on my account."

PTER 21

Kim Hajjar beamed at the orderly behavior the children from the inner city Young People's Chorus exhibited as they passed through White House security at the southwest entrance. No pushing. No horseplay. No yelling.

A darn fine start to the day.

Looking like a mother duck with four dozen ducklings in tow, she led the children to the Rose Garden via a series of well-marked paths that took them around the back side of the West Wing. The chaperones flanked the line and brought up the rear of the procession.

Hopefully, over the years, she thought, *some of these kids will visit the White House again. After that, who knows?*

The morning was already quite warm, and the cloudless sky guaranteed it would get even warmer. Forecasts had predicted rain throughout the day, so Kim saw the cooperating weather as a sign that the event would proceed without incident.

The buses had shown up on time. One hundred and

fifty folding chairs were in perfect rows on the Rose Garden lawn, facing the podium and a set of risers. Refreshments were being served. The green, white, and orange Irish flag stood to the left side of the podium and the Stars and Stripes to the right. There was a buzz of conversation from the assembling crowd, many of whom were from a guest list that she had helped to compile.

And the best part was that Martin Mallory would, in all likelihood, not be a no-show today. Kim, working with the president's chief of staff, had assured herself of it. Just the same, she breathed easier when she saw Martin standing beside Darlene, chatting with some dignitaries. Despite his expertly applied makeup, the president looked drawn and haggard. By contrast, Darlene was radiant in a simple white Christian Dior dress and cloche hat adorned with a silk bow and rosettes.

The children filed into the Rose Garden as orderly as they had passed through security. Kim enjoyed seeing the awe in their faces as they took in the grandeur and beauty around them. The crabapple trees were no longer flowering, but the roses, tulips, primroses, and grape hyacinth were in spectacular bloom. The constant chirping of birds added a natural accompaniment to the quartet of professional musicians playing traditional Irish music.

Kim and Darlene's eyes met.

The brief exchange said much. At least for this morning, Martin had come through, and there had been no word from Double M—the name they had chosen for their mystery man. After reading the handwritten note

on the back of the Bar None coaster, Darlene felt in-
trigued and vindicated.

"I knew it. I just knew it," she had said once, then
again during their closed-door meeting in her office.

"But why would somebody go after Evans?" Kim
asked.

"You remember what he said to us at the Bar None?
His office impacts local food producers, major growers, environmentalists, even the manufacturers of fer-
tilizers, pesticides, and seeds. His policies affect millions
of lives and probably trillions of dollars. Any number
of his positions might put him in someone's cross-
hairs."

Kim thought back to their conversation with Evans—
his frustration and almost palpable frailty. She warned
herself not to jump to conclusions about his innocence.
She wasn't connected to him as intensely as the First
Lady was, and needed to remain objective. Double M
claimed to have proof. For Russ Evans's sake, she hoped
the man would not stay hidden for long.

The folding chairs were rapidly filling. Kim sig-
naled to the head of the Young People's Chorus that the
children should take their positions on the riser. The
kids looked super, and no doubt, Darlene was imagining what it would be like going from exam room to
exam room in her office, taking care of every one of
them. *You can take the pediatrician out of the practice,*
Kim was thinking, *but you can never take the pediatrician out of this woman.*

She straightened out a couple of chairs and patted
two of the younger kids on the shoulder.

It was showtime.

From the podium, with the emblem of the presidential seal facing the crowd, she instructed people to take their seats. There was a rustle of movement and the dwindling murmur of voices as the guests settled in. Darlene was seated to the left of the podium. President Callaghan's husband was seated to the right. Both presidents had musical cues that would instruct them when to enter.

"Is POTUS in position?" Kim spoke into her radio.

A crackled reply came back, "Ready to go."

"Good."

Kim nodded to her assistant, and moments later the musicians began to play the Irish march "Wind That Shakes the Barley." President Callaghan emerged through the Oval Office French doors to enthusiastic applause. She stood in front of the podium, waving to the powerful and influential guests, many of whom had Irish heritage, strong ties to her country, or both.

Scanning the crowd, Kim stepped away from the podium and listened from the lawn nearest to the risers. She was startled by a light tap on her leg and looked down to see a mocha-skinned girl with ebony pigtails, wearing the plaid pinafore and black tights of the girls, smiling up at her shyly. Kim knelt down.

"Honey, you're supposed to be on the riser with the others," she whispered. "Your song is right after President Mallory makes his entrance."

"But I need to tell you something," the child said in a honey-sweet voice.

"Me? What is it, sweetie?"

"A man said to tell you that your present is in your purse."

Kim took in a sharp breath.

I'll be in touch.

"What man?"

"The one who came up to me right after I got off the bus."

"Do you remember what he looked like?"

"He had a red and white Washington Nationals hat on. They're my favorite team."

The crowd was settled, and Kim realized that the director of the chorus was looking over at them.

"Everything okay with Simone?" he said in a stage whisper.

"Fine," Kim said. "You did good, Simone. You did perfect. Now, go back with the kids and give us a terrific concert."

A Washington Nationals cap.

Double M seemed to be an expert at disguise by diversion. Give a person like the bartender and this child something easy to focus on, and in all likelihood, that would be all they recalled.

Kim glanced quickly around the Rose Garden, just as she had that night in Bar None. The results were the same.

Nothing.

Yet somehow, Double M had managed to slip something into her purse. The man was sharp, resourceful—and quick.

The Irish march was over, and the musicians had begun "Hail to the Chief." With the first notes of the

James Sanderson march, Martin Mallory emerged from the Oval Office to what Kim considered a polite standing ovation. As he waved to the crowd, she checked her shoulder bag. A small white box, held closed by a red elastic, rested on top of her clutter. It weighed no more than a couple of ounces. Nothing to be wary of.

Stepping backwards out of the line of sight of almost everyone, she pulled the elastic off. The box held six compartmentalized pieces of chocolate. It took Kim a few seconds to realize that only five of the pieces were real candy. The sixth small chamber contained something else.

Something not at all edible.

An earpiece.

"Hail to the Chief" was winding down, to be followed by the national anthems, but Kim could hardly hear the music. Her pulse was a kettledrum in her ears.

Ahead and to her right, the president was waving and smiling for the cameras.

Kim pretended to adjust her earring and fiddled with the small apparatus until it slipped inside her left ear. Immediately, she heard static, then a man's tinny voice, probably electronically altered. Still, his words, even heard through her pulse, were quite audible.

"This is the end of the recording. It will loop for ten minutes more before its contents become permanently erased. Darlene Mallory must listen to this recording and agree to help."

CHAPTER 22

Already on high alert, Darlene tensed even more when she saw Kim approaching. Something had happened between her chief of staff and the young girl from the chorus. And whatever it was, Darlene strongly suspected, had something to do with Double M. Then, when Kim stealthily brought out a small white box from her bag, opened it, extracted something, and quickly closed it again, she was certain.

Martin was at the podium now, waving to the crowd. God, but he loved his job. Each percentage drop in his popularity had been like a dagger in his heart.

Hard as his plummeting numbers were on him, both physically and mentally, he maintained an unyielding belief in his programs and in his vision for the future of America. But lately, reassuring him, deflecting his bullwhip temper, and validating his decisions had become something of a second full-time job for Darlene.

Then there was the matter of her pledge not to contact or mention Russ Evans to him again. It was for this reason Darlene had decided not to tell her husband about Double M—at least not yet. She never had much in the way of craftiness, and Martin generally could see right through her when she tried holding anything back from him. Revealing her connection with D.M., as she and Kim sometimes called the informant, had to be carefully orchestrated, and kept secret until she knew what the man was about.

Kim stood by Darlene's right shoulder, blocking most angles, and bent down far enough to whisper in her ear. "It's him."

"Now?" The First Lady kept her gaze forward and her face expressionless.

"Lower your hand," Kim said.

Darlene did as instructed, keeping her fingers curled to form a makeshift cup. The plastic object Kim placed there was smaller than a marble and surprisingly heavy. At the same moment, Martin began his address. A screech of feedback from the podium's single microphone sent a flock of birds into flight, and the AV tech scurrying for his control knobs. Martin tapped twice on the microphone head.

"There," he said in a voice now rich with electronic reverb, "the First Lady is always telling me to expect the unexpected."

The laughter was prolonged and genuine.

"That feedback was probably caused by this earphone," Kim said. "Very powerful. Double M knows his stuff."

Darlene nodded, smiling for those still looking at her. Kim straightened up and stepped back toward the crowd.

"Thank you all for being here today," Martin continued. "This is a wonderful opportunity to express America's deep gratitude and appreciation to a country that shares so many of our values. Our bond is formed not only in the history we share, but in the perseverance that defines our two nations. And I say this not only as a president who can claim and document a deep Irish heritage, but also as a man who is extremely fond of a perfectly poured Guinness."

The laughter this time was even more enthusiastic.

Darlene knew this speech well, and was prepared for the reaction to Martin's Guinness joke. The timing couldn't have been more perfect. With the attendees distracted, she pretended to adjust her earring. The earpiece slipped into place without any difficulty.

The first thing she heard was a brief, rather unpleasant hissing sound. It was followed quickly by a clearly understandable man's voice that sounded as though she were hearing it through a tin can microphone.

"Darlene Mallory must listen to this recording, and she must agree to help."

Through her left ear, Darlene could hear her husband speaking.

"Before I begin my remarks, and before President Callaghan delivers hers," Martin said, "it is my great pleasure to introduce the Young People's Chorus from Washington, D.C., who are here today to welcome us all with their moving rendition of 'The Face of the Waters.'"

The children began to sing. The harmonies of their angelic voices engulfed the remarkable scene.

"You don't have to be afraid of us," Darlene heard a man's harsh voice say. "You come well recommended for this part, so all you have to do is follow my instructions."

This was a different voice from the one she had attributed to Double M. Her stomach dropped as if she had fallen off a roof. She glanced over at Kim, who looked curious but also apprehensive.

The man continued. "We're not going to take the blindfold off you. If we do that, we'd have to kill you."

Darlene gasped. The voice was calm and as clinical as a science teacher. Educated and probably middle aged, she thought. She wondered briefly about the technology being employed. Was the voice being transmitted, or was it actually held in the device itself?

"You can speak any time something isn't clear to you. Understood?"

A stuttering woman's voice—no, a girl's—said, "Yes. I . . . understand."

Darlene felt bile in her throat. In front of her, macabrely, the children continued their pristine hymn.

"All right, then. Let us review the role you have agreed to play. I need to be certain you understand it perfectly. Where are you going to meet Secretary Evans?"

"At the Motel Six on Georgia Avenue. I'll take a cab and have it drop me off a block away." The girl sounded less fearful now. There actually was some strength in her voice.

"How will you get the key?"

"Room twenty-four is registered to William Betancourt. I'll show the front desk clerk my ID and tell him that I lost my key. The clerk will see that I'm on the room registration, and give me a replacement."

"What time will you do this?"

"Three o'clock in the afternoon."

"Good. What will you do inside the room?"

"I'm going to get undressed. And then I'll wait."

"What are you waiting for?"

"A man—Secretary Evans."

"Can you describe him from the photographs we gave you?"

"He's in his fifties. He's not very fit. He has brown hair, but not a lot of it."

"Good."

"When he knocks on the door, what will you do?"

"I'll drag him into the room. Then I'll push him onto the bed."

"You'll straddle him?"

"Yes."

"Kiss him?"

"Yes."

"Good."

"What else will you say?"

"I'll tell him that he's got me very excited. I'll put his hands on me to show him just how much. I'll tell him that I'm going to do it just the way he likes, really, really slowly. If he lets me, I'll undress him."

"If he fights you?"

"I'll act as if it's all part of the game he likes. I'll keep straddling him. When he tries to get out from under me, I'll make sure it looks like we're playing. Getting physical." Her tone had gotten even stronger.

"Good."

"Once I'm off him, I'll start screaming for him to get out."

"What then?"

"I'll wait twenty minutes. If the police don't show up, I'll call them myself."

"What will you tell the police when they show up?"

"I'll be crying. I'll pretend to be scared. I'll tell them that I'm a self-employed escort and that he was my client. A regular."

"When they ask you if you know who your client is, what will you tell them?"

"I'll say that his name is Russ Evans and he's the Secretary of Agriculture. I'll tell them I had decided to record us fucking. I'm going to use that word, too. I'll tell them that the video camera was recording when he got rough with me after I told him to leave. Then I'll show them where I hid the camera and tripod."

"You're very good at this," the man said.

"When will I get paid?"

"Soon. Very soon. Half now, half when you're done. You did terrific here. It will be a pleasure working with you."

"Thank you."

Darlene stared blankly ahead. Her hands were trembling and her breathing was shallow. A cold sweat had formed on the back of her neck and dripped unpleasantly down the inside of her blouse.

The voice of Double M returned. "If you want to

help Secretary Evans, we must meet. There's an alley behind the movie theater on Columbus Avenue. Eight P.M. tomorrow night. Come alone. Tell no one except Kim Hajjar about this recording. Lives are in danger."

The children finished singing and were rewarded with rapturous applause. Darlene rose to her feet, applauding, though numbly. He legs were Jell-O.

"This is the end of the recording," Double M said. "It will loop for ten minutes more before—"

The recording went silent.

CHAPTER 23

Despite knowing that Joey Alderson was in his mid-twenties, Lou had trouble not thinking of him as a boy—especially following the disaster at Millie's. For much of the early drive from the hospital back to Kings Ridge, Joey stared contentedly out the window, making no attempt to initiate conversation. His thumb and hand, immobilized in plaster, were supported in a sling.

Over the two days before picking Joey up for the ride home, Lou had twice stopped by the hospital to see him. The first time, Joey was heavily medicated and barely able to put two words together. A day later, Lou managed to engage him in a brief conversation. Even though Joey was sweet and eager to respond, there was no question that he was, as Millie had said, limited. He had almost no insight as to why he had put his hand in harm's way for the sake of getting at a piece of carrot.

"How you doing over there, buddy?" Lou asked, wishing he had had the time to clean out his Toyota before putting a post-op patient inside it.

Joey's smile was engaging. "I'm doing fine," he chirped. "How are you?"

"Doin' okay, Joey. Doin' okay. Listen, Joey, I don't want to upset you any, but I wonder if you've had any more thoughts about what happened at the restaurant."

"You mean with my thumb?"

Lou groaned inwardly. "Exactly. I'm still trying to figure out what you were thinking."

Lou caught Joey's shrug out of the corner of his eye. "All I could think about was how badly I wanted that carrot."

The vapid response was no surprise.

"You didn't think you might get hurt?"

This time, Joey turned and gazed across at him. His expression was blank—not deep in thought, not searching for an answer to Lou's question, but seemingly disconnected from his mind. Lou realized he had seen a similar expression before. Carolyn Meacham stared at him without comprehension moments after she had abandoned her reckless pursuit of the sedan with a broken taillight.

A parody of Dylan's classic crossed Lou's mind.

The answer my friend is blowin' in Kings Ridge. . . .
The answer is blowin' in Kings Ridge.

Joey pointed out the window at a roadside exit sign. "Can you get off here?" he asked.

"Sure," Lou replied, grateful to have anything approaching a meaningful exchange. "What for?"

"I've got to get to the pet store before I go home."

"I didn't know you had any pets," Lou said.

Joey placed his left index finger to his lips, letting Lou know it was a secret. "You won't tell Millie, now, will you? She doesn't really allow any animals in the Dorms."

Lou flashed on his discussion with Emily about bending rules. He didn't feel he had been all that convincing, but at least she had left his apartment with a promise to give Steve a sporting chance.

"No problem, pal," he said. "So what do you have? Dog? Cat?"

"You'll see," Joey replied mischievously.

Art's Critters was a small storefront operation sandwiched between an optician and a cut-rate jeweler in a modest strip mall. Lou offered to get whatever was needed, but Joey refused. He fished a thin, tattered wallet from his jeans and strode excitedly into the store. A few minutes later, he emerged carrying a medium-sized brown paper bag.

"Can't wait to get home," he said.

When they arrived at Millie's, the lunch rush was over, leaving plenty of available parking spaces. The restaurateur was waiting for them just inside the entrance, and burst out the front door before Lou shut off his engine. She was carrying a cardboard box of food. Lou helped undo Joey's seat belt, then reached across his lap to open the passenger door. Joey set his bag on the floor before getting out.

"Hi, there, buddy," Millie said.

"Hi, Ma."

Millie set the box on the ground and gave Joey a

quick peck on the cheek. Lou popped the trunk and set the food inside.

"I just put some snack stuff together for you. You can come over to the restaurant for your meals if you're up to it."

"Oh, I'm up to it."

"The report is good. His surgeon thinks we're looking at maybe seventy-five percent functional recovery. Maybe more."

"Joey, you sure you don't want to stay with me?"

"No, Ma. You know how happy I am to be in my own place. All I thought about in the hospital was how much I just wanted to get home. I have some pain medicine that I don't even think I'll need, but if I do, I can take one or two every four hours, and some infection medicine I need to take twice a day."

"He needs to go back in three days," Lou said. "I think I can adjust my schedule to come out and—"

"Nonsense. I have people who will drive us. You've been just wonderful, Lou."

"He's going to help me get settled in at my place," Joey said, perhaps a bit too quickly. "I'll be at the restaurant for dinner."

"Very well, dear," Millie said. "You know how I respect your privacy. That's your home not mine."

Millie thanked Lou again, wrapped him in her arms, and stood on her tiptoes to kiss his cheek.

The Dorms, ten or twelve units, white vinyl siding, black shutters, was nothing special. In fact, despite well-trimmed hedges and several small flower gardens, it reminded Lou of the sort of motel that might have rates by the day, half day, or hour. Unfortunately, it also reminded him of places he once took refuge in when he was in no shape to go home.

Never again, he thought, violating AA's most essential day-at-a-time maxim. *Never ever again.*

The print curtains looked fairly new, and there were brass numbers nailed to the front of each red painted door. Joey lived in unit number six.

Carrying his package inside his sling, Joey fished his key ring out of his pocket and unlocked his door. Lou followed with the cook's small duffel bag and then the carton of food.

Cozy, he thought. *Cozy and surprisingly neat, but small.*

There was a kitchenette and an adjacent dining area with a table for two that Lou guessed most often sat one. The sitting area featured a brown tweed sofa, modest flat-screen television mounted to the wall, and a couple of area rugs that covered part of a parquet floor.

"Where do you sleep?" Lou asked, noting that what was probably the door to a bedroom was closed.

Joey pointed to the couch. "It folds out into a bed," he said. "It's more comfortable than you'd think."

"Oh, trust me," Lou said. "I know all about foldout couches. What about your pet? Where do you keep it?"

"Them, not it. They're in the bedroom," he said. He nodded toward the closed door. Again, there was playfulness in his expression.

"So what's in the bag?" Lou asked.

Joey pulled out what looked like a Chinese food leftover container and clumsily opened the top a bit.

Scampering about on the bottom were two small brown mice.

Ah, pet mice, Lou thought. *Harmless enough.*

Still, he understood why the young cook was reluctant to have Millie know about his hobby.

"Ready to see something cool?" Joey asked conspiratorially.

"Ready," Lou said.

"You got to promise not to tell," Joey said.

"Scout's honor."

Joey turned the knob and nudged the door open with his foot. A strange, musty odor immediately wafted out. The first thing Lou saw were two workbenches, with tools spread across the top. There was a small, empty wire cage at one end with a mouse wheel in it. But the main attraction was in the center of the room—a huge Lucite cube, six feet on each side, raised off the floor a foot or so on a heavy wooden platform. Fixed to the top of the cube and plugged into a wall socket by a long cord was what appeared to be a ventilation apparatus. There was also an inch-in-diameter Lucite tube, bent upward at a ninety-degree angle and sealed at the outer end with a rubber stopper and inside by what appeared to be a levered trapdoor.

Warming lights were clipped to two of the four sides, illuminating a tall, irregular mound arising from the floor at the center of the cube, and looking somewhat like the spired castle of a Disney princess. In one corner of the floor was a dish of water. In another was a mound of what looked like a mix of wood pieces and sawdust.

A complex mouse habitat, Lou thought. *Just the sort*

of thing the eccentric kid of a hundred knots would build.

Then he stopped and caught his breath. The surface of the castle was moving.

"Get it?" Joey asked proudly. "The mice aren't my pets. They're the *food* for my pets."

"Pet what?" Lou asked, his voice breaking between the words.

He remained fixed to where he was standing, unable to advance as he struggled to sort out what he was seeing.

"Termites," Joey said simply. "Beautiful, aren't they?"

"Termites?"

Lou could see them now—a sheet of constant motion coating virtually the entire castle. He managed a couple of baby steps toward them.

Termites—huge termites, some of them half an inch long or more.

"Joey, I'm not any kind of a bug expert, but I do know that termites eat wood, not mice."

Lou tried with minimal success to tie the bizarre scene to the events surrounding Joey's nearly amputated thumb, and the other strange behaviors he'd observed since coming to Kings Ridge.

"You watch and then tell me what these guys can and cannot eat," Joey said.

He removed his arm from the sling and used it to hold the animal container while he removed one of the mice by its tail and set it in a mason jar with a cotton ball on the bottom. The other mouse he placed in the wire cage.

"I have to knock this fellow out first," Joey said. "The termites won't eat them if they're dead, and I don't want them to feel any pain."

Lou watched, transfixed, as Joey poured a bit of liquid onto the cotton ball.

Chloroform.

In seconds, the mouse was on its side.

Joey used a long forceps to pick up the limp animal. Then he removed the rubber stopper from the Lucite access tube, set the mouse inside, and nudged it onto the small trapdoor with a thin stick, all the while, softly whistling the theme from *The Andy Griffith Show.*

Then, after giving Lou a final look at the ingenious setup, the cook pushed down the lever opening the trapdoor.

Instantly, the lower third of the princess's castle flowed like lava onto the inert mouse, covering every millimeter of it. There was a loud clicking noise that reminded Lou of rain pelting against a tin roof.

More insects—huge heads with black pinchers and yellow bodies—poured or flew around it. The clicking sounds intensified as the swarm became more frenzied. The animal corpse, for surely it was already that, was now encased in a ball of clamoring insects at least three inches around, each trying to burrow down onto the meal. Then, just as quickly as the termites advanced, they began to retreat back to and into the mound. The clicking decreased in volume until it could no longer be heard.

Lou circled the table, never once averting his gaze

from the frightening diorama. He expected he'd see the remains of the meal, mauled and bloody.

But there was not any blood to be seen.

What Lou witnessed instead, was nothing.

There was no mouse left at all.

CHAPTER 24

Lou felt leagues better the moment he set foot inside Cap's Stick and Move. One good whiff of stale gym air with its distinctive blend of sweat, cheap aftershave, and bleach, and he felt he was home. But he still could not forget Joey Alderson's astonishing termites. Before heading over to the gym, he had made a quick search of the Internet, but could find no entomological evidence that such creatures existed.

Only they did.

The image and hideous clicking of that amber-colored swarm totally consuming a mouse in a matter of seconds would stay with him indefinitely. Lou wrote down the name and number of Oliver Humphries at Temple University in Philadelphia, listed as one of the experts in the field of termite entomology. If time allowed, he might give the man a call.

Joey was extremely excited at Lou's stunned reaction to his pets, and offered to drop another mouse into the Lucite habitat. Lou politely begged off an encore, but did ask where he had come up with the bugs.

"I can't show you today," Joey had said, a broad smile creasing his boyish face. "But come back on the weekend, and I'll take you there. I think you'll be pretty amazed."

"I'm pretty amazed right now," Lou had said, "and a bit horrified, too."

Lou concentrated on the young fighters chasing their dreams, and Joey's nightmare bugs gradually receded toward the back of his consciousness. As always, the gym was a sanctuary for his brain. The grunts, soft thud of boxing gloves, and rhythmic skip of jump ropes across the cement floor were symphonic.

After changing quickly in the locker room, Lou slipped on his bag gloves and got to work on the heavy bag. Cap was in the ring nearby, training a young fighter who had pretty decent moves. Lou started off with a set of straight jabs, remembering what his mentor had told him about not telegraphing the punch by leaning forward. Then he switched over to a rapid-fire combination set that included a mix of jab-cross, jab-hook, and jab-hook-hook punches. By minute five of his ten-minute set, he was sweating profusely and feeling almost airborne. He tried to focus on his punching technique, but then a surprising thing happened.

He found himself thinking about Renee.

Thud. Thud. Renee. *Thud.* Steve. *Thud.* Emily. *Thud.*

Steve was a decent-enough guy, Lou convinced himself as he walloped the bag with his hardest punch yet. Maybe he was a little dull and set in his ways, but at least he had a big heart and good intentions. Besides, Lou knew sparks were not a guarantee of a successful marriage. Heck, he'd given Renee enough of them to start a matrimonial forest fire, and look where that got him.

Lou had come to believe that Renee loved a solid 95 percent of him during their eight years of marriage. It was that remaining 5 percent, the addict who lied about his drug and alcohol use, that Renee could not endure. As in many failed marriages, she discovered Lou's unacceptable 5 percent only after she had said, "I do." As a recommended part of his recovery, he had done his best to make amends to her. Now, all he could do was to support her in her marriage and continue to push that 5 percent further and further from his life. When the time was right, someone would show up who could help him get over her.

Thud. Thud. Renee. *Thud.*

Lou slammed the bag a few more times, then stepped aside when Cap came over and hit the bag with a beautiful sequence of jabs. He seemed to be exerting little effort, but his punches sounded like gunshots. Throughout the remarkable barrage, he continued smiling.

It's good to be the king.

"Where you been?" Cap asked as he unleashed an uppercut that would have put a full-grown gorilla on its back.

"Long story," Lou said.

"Well, you might want to make it a short one," Cap said without sounding the least bit winded. "I just got a call from the street that there are two guys lurking outside the gym, snapping pictures of this place, your building, and what I think is your car. What have you been up to?"

Lou felt as if he'd just been on the receiving end of one of Cap's punches.

"I guess stirring somebody's pot," Lou said, wrapping his arm around the swinging bag like they were dancing partners. "What kind of guys are we talking about?"

"They look like muscle," Cap said. "Thick, beefy guys. The kid who called seemed sure they were packing heat, and I don't think he's ever wrong about such things."

"So do we invite them up for a workout?"

"That's up to you and how interested you are in them."

"I'm plenty interested."

"Then we turn the tables and follow them," Cap said after delivering a right cross that sent Lou staggering backwards off the bag. Sooner or later they'll get tired of hanging around, and probably nervous, too. I'm betting sooner. This is hardly their kind of neighborhood."

"How am I gonna tail *them* in the car that they've been tailing?"

"Leave that to me," Cap said. He smacked the heavy bag one last time, hard enough rattle the chains.

Following Cap's instructions, Lou grabbed a couple of slices of pizza from Dimitri's, making a conscious effort not to look around while making the purchase. Outside, the two men in a black Cadillac sedan rolled past, then past again in the other direction.

"Be careful to act nonchalant," Cap had insisted. "You don't want these guys getting suspicious."

Lou carried the pizza box upstairs to his apartment. Once inside, he turned on the TV and took out a slice. He felt like a duck in a carnival shooting gallery walking back and forth in front of his apartment windows while eating a slice of four-cheese with mushrooms, but he wanted to be certain he was seen from the street below.

Again, Cap's idea, not his.

Lou's cell phone rang. He stepped away from the windows to answer it.

"They're on the move," Cap said. "They think you're in for the night. Let's go."

Lou raced down the back stairwell, threw open the unalarmed fire exit door, and stepped into a narrow alleyway. A beat-up Chevy Prizm, sans hubcaps and the passenger-side mirror, sped down the alley toward him and flashed its lights once. The rear door opened and Lou scrambled into the backseat as the car kept rolling. Then, as soon as he slammed the door, it accelerated.

Cap was driving, but Lou did not recognize the two twenty-something black men in the car with him. The one sitting beside Lou was clean-shaven with short, tightly curled hair. He was big, as in "needs to buy an extra plane ticket to fly" big.

"Ah man, I smell pizza. You bring us any pie?" he asked.

"After we get back to the gym, it's my treat."

"Terrific. I do a large with everything. Hold the anchovies."

"Lou, meet Notso," Cap said from the driver's seat.

Notso's beefy hand enfolded Lou's like the wrapping on a burrito.

"Notso?" Lou asked.

"His real name is Anthony," the man riding shotgun said, "but his last name is Brite."

"Got it," Lou said, suppressing a smile. "You okay with that, Mr. Brite?"

"My mother's the one who first called me it, so I guess the answer's yes."

"And you would be?" Lou asked the second man.

The man maneuvered around to get a better look at Lou. He was slightly built, a while from his last shave, and was wearing a gray T-shirt, tattered at the neck. His left ear was studded with a lone diamond, while his tortoiseshell glasses gave him an air of intelligence. He reminded Lou of Spike Lee—minus the New York Knicks gear.

"Name's George," he said. "George Kozak."

His hand was to Lou's as Lou's was to Notso Brite's.

"Okay. Notso and George," Lou said. "Pleased to make your acquaintances. I'm Lou Welcome."

"That's *Dr.* Lou Welcome," Cap corrected. "So behave or he'll take out your liver."

"Fat chance," George mumbled, turning to face front again. "Yo! Yo!" he cried out. "You're losing 'em, Cap. Hell, man, you need me to drive?"

"I didn't even want you to *come*."

"Yeah, sure. You know you can't separate me from my car."

"That's right," Notso chimed in, "or me from my Glock."

He pulled his handgun from a shoulder holster beneath his black Windbreaker and set it on his lap.

Lou's heart stopped. Then, with utterly unpleasant slowness, it began pumping again. Two decades in the ER had featured far too many gunshot wounds, and far too many deaths of all ages. He could count the number of times he had held a gun on the fingers of one hand, and could not even stand being this close to one.

Handguns and beets, he had said on more than one occasion, enumerating the two things in the universe he hated most.

"Jesus, Notso, put that thing away!" he snapped.

"Easy, Lou," Cap said. "The muscle we're tailing are almost certainly packing. Notso just wants to be prepared. Stow it, big fella."

Notso looked at Lou queerly and slipped the Glock back into its holster.

"Who the hell are these guys, anyway?" George asked.

"I have no idea. Did you get a look at them?"

"A couple of white guys with thick necks and bulges in their jackets. One of them has a cheesy mustache."

"Meet any thick-necked white guys lately who'd want to tail you?" Cap asked, making another turn.

"What are they driving?"

"See that Caddy a few cars up ahead?" Cap said.

"Yeah."

"Well, that's them."

Lou leaned forward to get a better look. "Don't know the car," he said. "Thanks for putting your piece away, Notso. I work in an ER and I've seen too many holes in too many people."

"Don't worry about my cousin," George said. "My aunt got it right about him. The only thing we're going to be shooting with on this trip is my digital camera."

"What's the camera for?" Lou asked.

"Information, my friend," George answered as he snapped a couple of pics of Lou without triggering the flash. "We don't know what we're going to find, so this way we can capture the memories."

"Where'd you get that camera from anyway?" Notso asked. "Yo mama's so poor, she can't even pay attention."

"Funny," George said, feigning a laugh. "I got it from school, blubber belly. It's for a project I'm doing."

"You're in school?" Lou asked with more incredulity than he had intended.

"Yeah, college," George said.

"*Community* college," Notso corrected.

"Oh, shut the fuck up, you bucket of lard. Last time you picked up a book you freaked out because it had already been colored in." He turned back to Lou. "I'm a sophomore—well, a junior with four more credits."

"That's terrific," Lou said. "What are you majoring in?"

"Biology."

"He's learning how to grow weed," Notso said.

"You wish. Believe me, if I ever start growing weed, you'll be the last to know."

Cap groaned his displeasure. "George, will you shut your mouth and keep your eyes locked on that car ahead. This ain't a joke."

"Why do you think I called you about them? I know bad when I see it."

For a short while, the four fell silent. Cap managed to stay four or five cars behind the Caddy without losing sight of it. After a mile or so, it turned onto the highway headed west. Another mile, and Lou had it figured out.

"Cap," he said. "I believe I know exactly where these guys are headed."

"Yeah? And where's that?"

"Kings Ridge, Virginia," Lou said.

Notso smiled. In the flash of approaching headlights, his teeth shone. "That's way cool," he said. "I ain't never been to Virginia before."

CHAPTER 25

Darlene knew what she was about to do might end her marriage—if not in fact, then at least to all intents. Martin had learned about her meeting with Russ Evans almost as soon as it happened. Should he learn of this one, he would never understand—especially if she turned out to be wrong about Evans.

But she wasn't wrong.

An anxious young woman's voice on a high-tech recording told her so. And hopefully, very soon, she would have proof. Of course, it was always possible that the tape was a fabrication, but to what end? Even if someone put together a fake, even if the young woman was an actress, Russ Evans was finished politically.

The three cars escorting Darlene and Kim to the movies—a town car and two nondescript sedans—pulled to a stop a block past the iconic Regent Street Theater. Dusk was settling over the district. During the intentionally circuitous ride from 1600 Pennsylvania Avenue, Darlene gazed out at the streets teeming with people, moving through their lives, making connections only when they wanted to. She had willingly given up that privilege when she and Martin entered the campaign. Now she felt wistful that Russ Evans could no longer walk comfortably among people without attracting unwanted attention.

With half an hour to go before the movie, the advance team of agents completed its assignment with trademark efficiency and radioed to Victor Ochoa that it was safe for Buttercup and Wildcat to enter the theater. Darlene had forgotten the name of the film they were going to see until she read it posted out front on the illuminated marquee. Double M had chosen a PG-13 chick flick.

Darlene's mouth was dry with tension. She was defying the man she had married, and about to deceive the people who had been sworn to protect her at any and all cost. But her friend since childhood and more recently her professional soul mate had been destroyed—framed. And now, the man she and Kim called Double M wanted her help at least to clear Russ Evans's name.

Why? With nothing tangible, what does he expect I can do?

Darlene pushed the questions to the back of her mind. It was imperative that she remain sharp—aware of everything and everyone around her. Slipping free of Ochoa and his crew was not going to be easy, even though only he and a female agent named Bonnie would actually be in the theater, seated in the back.

Darlene wore a pair of tinted glasses with thick white frames, and an auburn, shoulder-length wig beneath a gold print satin scarf. The outfit was one of several—

the most effective, in fact—that she used when she wanted to keep gawkers and disrupters to a minimum. In addition, she had on a pair of faded blue jeans and a brown leather jacket with the Hard Rock Cafe emblem sewn onto the back.

Ochoa handed Kim and Darlene their tickets. "Bonnie and I will be in the back," he said. "Just make sure you take the seats we've designated for you."

"Sorry it's not your type of movie, Victor," Kim said. "My girlfriend told me that there are no car chases, and no one gets shot."

"Hey, I like sweet, endearing romantic comedies as much as the next guy who gets paid to carry a gun."

Darlene hooked her chief of staff's arm and, eyes down, escorted her into the theater and down to two seats on the side aisle. There were fifteen or so other patrons scattered throughout the remaining seats, but none anywhere near the two of them. The film, nearing the end of its run before DVD, seemed to have been carefully chosen by Double M, and to this point, at least, no one appeared to be paying any attention to them.

"How are you holding up?" Kim whispered without turning.

"I don't have butterflies flying around in my stomach," Darlene said, "if that's what you mean."

"Well, that's good."

"I have buzzards."

"Oh."

"What if this is a bad idea? A trap of some sort. Terrorists."

"Double M is incredibly resourceful and inventive. I

think if he wanted to get to you, he could have done it already. No, he wants your help, and if you want to help Russ, you're going to have to trust him—at least this once."

The on-screen ads had given way to the previews. Subtly, Darlene glanced down at her wristwatch. "One hour to go," she whispered.

"Keep your eyes on the screen," Kim said, giving Darlene's hand a squeeze.

The sixty minutes seemed interminable. Finally, Darlene tapped a fist on Kim's knee, rose from her seat, and headed to the back of the theater.

"I'm going to use the bathroom," she whispered to Bonnie.

"Stay here for half a minute."

"You can check out the room, but please be sort of quick about it."

"Are you okay?"

"I will be once I get in there."

By agreement, she stood resting her elbows on the back wall and waited.

Darlene knew Bonnie was startled by her uncharacteristic abruptness, but it served its purpose. The woman checked the bathroom in thirty seconds or so and pronounced it empty. Moments later, Darlene was inside.

Grateful for the many hours she had spent with her yoga instructor, personal trainer, and in the White House gym, she crossed over to the pair of sinks and nimbly pushed herself up onto the one farthest from the door. It was no problem to slide the curtain aside on a small transom window that was now level with her waist, and to undo the latch.

As soon as she pushed open the window, a well-manicured hand featuring a shade of nail polish identical to her own gripped the sill from the other side. Then a woman's head popped into view. Wearing the same wig, glasses, and satin scarf as Darlene, she climbed through the window, then stepped on the edge of the sink and dropped to the floor with a cat's grace. The jeans and Hard Rock jacket completed a striking match.

"Madam First Lady," the woman said as Darlene helped her down, "I'm Nicole Keane, Kim's friend. It's a pleasure to meet you. The stepladder is right outside. You won't have any trouble."

It was difficult for Darlene to keep from staring at the lawyer, whom Kim had described as the perfect body double.

"A ten-finger boost and you're out of here," Nicole said.

"Kim's by herself ten rows down the second aisle. Just keep your head down and avoid any eye contact with the two agents in the last row. They think I'm in a hurry to get back to the movie, and won't expect any chitchat. In fifteen minutes, Kim is going to tell them I have an upset stomach, and ask them to check the bathroom again. Then she's going to come get you at your seat, and we'll switch back."

"I've got the plan memorized like it was one of my court briefs."

"Perfect."

"Ten-finger boost," Nicole said, interlocking her fingers. "The ladder's right under the window."

"Is he there?" Darlene asked.

"I didn't see him. Just the ladder."

Darlene set her foot onto Nicole's makeshift hoist, slipped easily through the window, located the ladder with her foot, and climbed down into the dimly lit alley behind the theater.

CHAPTER 26

The alley appeared deserted. There was a Dumpster nearby that reeked of popcorn oil, and several cars parked against old brick buildings beneath a lattice-work of fire escapes. Darlene stepped out into the glow of a single hooded bulb at the end of a metal pole pro-truding from the theater. There were several similar lights spaced along the alley.

"Hello?" she called out in a strained whisper. "Are you here?"

Silence, and then, "I'm here."

It took several unsettling seconds to locate the source of the voice. A tall man, six-foot-one or so, with broad, powerful shoulders, approached her from behind a parked car. He wore a baseball cap and glasses with a thick black frame, and had a neatly trimmed full beard. He was probably good-looking, but in the gloom, with the glasses and the beard, it was hard to tell. Darlene guessed him to be about forty. He was wearing a pat-terned blazer, blue oxford shirt, and crisply pressed pants.

A man of the outdoors, she decided.

He remained a couple of yards away, his eyes never leaving hers.

"Kim and I call you Double M for 'Mystery Man,'" she said.

He held an electrolarynx against his throat, making his speech eerily robotic—and not identifiable. "Good nickname," he said.

"You can come closer. I'm not afraid of you."

Double M closed the gap between them by half, but declined taking Darlene's extended hand.

"My name is Alex," he said.

"That's not your real name, is it?" Darlene said.

"No, but that doesn't matter."

His electronic voice was creepy, especially given the setting, but Darlene was determined not to react. "Okay, then, Double M Alex," she said, "you want this to be our level of trust, that's up to you."

"I would be in great danger if my identity became known."

"Well, we don't have much time. What are we doing here?"

"Trying to save lives." He studied Darlene as though she were an equation to be solved.

A professor or a scientist, she guessed. "Go on," she said.

"First of all, you need to know that the recording you heard was real."

"I believed it was. Otherwise I would not have risked so much for this meeting."

"You may have to risk even more."

"Who was on that recording?" asked Darlene. "Who was the girl? The other man speaking? What happened to her?"

Behind his lenses, Double M's eyes narrowed. "At this point, I can't reveal who is involved in that tape."

Darlene was beginning to feel exasperated with the man's paranoia. "What is it you want from me . . . Alex?"

Double M sucked in a nervous breath. "You must use your influence to get your husband to reinstate Secretary Evans."

Darlene tensed. "Is Evans behind this?" she asked.

"I don't even know the man."

"Well, I'm sorry, but that can't be done," Darlene said. "Politics simply doesn't work that way. Russ Evans has resigned, and he's embarrassed the president."

"There's nothing in the Constitution to prevent reinstating him," Double M countered.

Darlene stifled a laugh. "One thing I've learned from my years as a politician's wife is that the Constitution may be a marvelous framework, but it isn't politics."

Double M appeared agitated. "We can't let the president's nominee get appointed. Russell Evans must be returned as Secretary of Agriculture, and soon."

"And lives depend on it."

"They might."

"*Might?* Well, from what I can tell, Gretchen Rose has impeccable credentials and widespread support. Her approval by Congress is all but assured. Are you suggesting that she is somehow involved with what I heard on that recording?"

"Indirectly," he said.

Darlene felt herself emotionally pulling away from the man. Assuming Russ had been framed, she wanted to do anything she could to help him, but it didn't feel as if this skittish man was the answer.

"By indirectly, you mean—?"

"It's about her policies," Double M said.

"So did Secretary Evans's policies get him framed?"

"Yes."

"You need to tell me more. Our time together is running out. You need to come clean with me, and you need to do it right now."

"I'm sorry. I can't do that."

"Can't, or won't?" Darlene replied, folding her arms tightly across her chest.

"I have my reasons for being oblique."

"I sincerely want to help my friend Russ," Darlene said.

"Then you're going to have to trust me without getting all the facts. That's the deal."

"At least tell me what's at stake here. Tell me why it's so imperative that Gretchen Rose not be appointed."

"It's impossible to say precisely what's at stake. But it could be a great deal."

Darlene frowned. "Okay, we're done. I've put a lot on the line to meet with you this way, and I'm very disappointed that I took the risk. I don't appreciate circuitous conversation. You won't get my help this way. There's just too much at stake for me."

Shoulders sagging, Double M turned and appeared ready to depart. After one unsteady step, he whirled back around. "Her name is Margo."

"The girl on the recording?"

"Yes."

"So, in order to get my husband to reinstate Russell Evans, you want me to find this girl named Margo."

Double M reached into his jacket pocket, and Darlene had a flash of panic that he was going for a weapon. Before she could react or even process the thought, his hand came out holding a handkerchief.

"I have something for you," he said, reaching into his jacket with the handkerchief to withdraw a letter-sized white envelope. "As you heard on the recording, she's a prostitute. I'm sure of that. Besides her name, that's all I know. Inside this envelope are several photographs of her that I took. Her face is partially obscured, and I never got a clean a shot, because I was trying to be discreet. But I've also included a flash drive with an MP3 voice sample that could be used for matching purposes, as well as the girl's fingerprint, which I lifted using a piece of Scotch tape off the chair she was sitting on. Do you know people who could help?'"

"I might."

"I heard her mention she was living in D.C."

"Well, that might be useful."

Double M handed over the envelope. Darlene's heart sank as she flipped through four grainy color photographs of a titian-haired, blindfolded girl with a willowy frame, both seated upon and standing beside a wooden chair. Not much. Not much at all.

"I'm not making any promises," Darlene said. "I assume from the precautions not to leave your fingerprints that I can keep these."

Double M adjusted the electrolarynx against the side of his trachea. "I was hoping you would. If I learn any more, I'll get the information to you."

"Come on, Alex. You can at least be honest enough to tell me you're holding stuff back."

"Okay, let's just say I've told you everything I can."

"May I ask why you approached me and not my husband?"

"Your husband won't believe the tape recording is real. In addition, he has too much to lose by reneging on his stance. He respected Russell Evans when he nominated him, but he's not nearly as intensely connected to the man and his policies as you are."

"And how are you so sure about my feelings toward Evans?"

"Because I read your interview in *Time* magazine where you talked about knowing him since you were children, and you likened him to your own father. I did extensive research about you. From what I've learned, I know that the comparison to your father isn't something you would have made lightly."

Darlene was impressed. "Just so I'm clear—you want my help to find this girl, and then I'm to arrange a meeting between her and my husband. I would be doing this to convince my husband that Russ Evans was framed and must be reinstated."

"That's correct. I also suspect he would have to arrange some sort of a presidential pardon for Margo."

At that moment, a small pink rubber ball arced out from the bathroom window and bounced several times across the alley before disappearing under a car.

"That's the signal from Kim," Darlene said. "She and Nicole are in the bathroom. I have to get back inside. She set her foot on the bottom step, then paused. "How should I contact you?"

Double M reached into his jacket again and took out a cell phone. "This is a disposable cell phone. Nobody will be able to trace your call to me, and you won't be able to trace me from it, either. There's one recent call on it. Ring that number only when you have something to report. Afterwards, please completely destroy the phone."

"Whatever it is you're going through seems agonizing," Darlene said. "I'm truly sorry."

"I knew you'd understand," the man said. "I'll take care of the ladder."

Darlene ascended the remaining steps, gripped the window's edge, and silently hoisted herself back into the bathroom.

Victor Ochoa approached Darlene as she and Kim were exiting the theater. "May I speak with you a moment in private?" he asked.

Kim had been talking nonstop about the movie, in effect allowing her to transmit a plot summary to Darlene, just in case.

"Of course, Victor," Darlene said.

Ochoa escorted her to a secluded corner of the theater.

"What's up?" Darlene asked. Her heart was a jack-hammer in her chest. She knew Victor well enough to sense that something was very wrong. His expression did nothing to dispel that notion.

"Listen, I'm on your side," the swarthy agent said evenly. "I have one job to do and that's to keep you safe."

"And you do it well," Darlene said, trying not to stammer.

"Not when you sneak through a bathroom window to rendezvous with a tall muscleman in the alley behind the theater."

"Victor, I—"

"It's not my business to know all the details of your life," he said. "But it *is* my business to know where you are and who you're with. Look, I'm not your husband and I'm not here to judge you. I've worked for three First Ladies before you. I trusted them and they all trusted me. But if I find you're not trusting in me anymore, if I find you're playing games that are keeping me from doing my job, then my allegiance will have to go someplace else. Is that understood, Madam First Lady?"

Darlene felt her throat tighten. "You won't tell my husband?"

"Not if you stop trying to sneak away."

Darlene squeezed Ochoa's arm. "I'll explain to you soon," she vowed.

"Not necessary, but I'd appreciate that."

"I'm lucky to have you."

"No, that guy you met back there is lucky," the graying agent replied. "If I hadn't seen that envelope come out of his pocket, he would have developed a new orifice or two in his body."

CHAPTER 27

Just past the sign for Kings Ridge, the Caddy made a sudden left turn onto a poorly lit road—two narrow lanes, no dividing line, few cars. Cap was forced to drop back until their quarry's taillights were red peas in the mounting darkness. They continued west into the day's final blush of sunlight.

"Getting tougher," Lou said to Cap.

"The only thing we have going for us is that there's no reason for them to suspect anyone's tailing them."

"If this is what Virginia's like," Notso chimed in, "I choose our hood any day."

"I hear there's a collection bein' taken to send you out here permanently," George said.

A mile . . . then another. Now there were no cars coming the other way, and only darkness between them and the glowing red peas. They bounced across a railroad track and rolled past several white-painted corrugated hangars with NO TRESPASSING signs mounted to the outside walls.

Cap cut the Chevy's headlights, plunging the car

into darkness. The blackening sky made it difficult to follow the winding stretch of road that snaked around low hills and paralleled a small rill on the left. Soon, though, the curves straightened out and the landscape turned flat again. On both sides now, there was nothing but corn.

"So, Welcome, where do you think they're headed?" Cap asked.

"No idea," Lou replied.

"Is this the way to John Meacham's house?"

"No. We'd be headed in the opposite direction if that's where they were going. It looks like all there is out here is farmland."

Notso pointed out the window. "Zat wheat?" he asked.

"Is wheat green, Notso?" George answered. "Do you even know what wheat looks like?"

"I know what wheat looks like," Notso said, folding his arms across his chest in a pout. "Look, man, it's dark outside. Quit ridin' me."

"Well, it's *corn*, you big goof. Acres and acres of fuckin' corn."

Lou glanced out at the stalks on both sides of the road, rippling in the light night breeze like a vast emerald ocean.

Cap decelerated. "I think they've turned left," he said.

He waited a few seconds before catching a flicker of the sedan's taillights through a path cleared in the corn. A minute later, he made the same turn. Tailing the Caddy was becoming more challenging.

"All this corn is making me hungry," Notso said, rubbing his ample belly.

George turned around. "Seriously, Brite," he said. "Could you please talk about somethin' other than food."

"Jes sayin' I'm hungry is all," Notso answered. "Why y'all buggin' me so bad? Can't a man want to eat?"

"No!" Cap and George said in unison.

For a few minutes, they rode in silence.

"Anyone ever hear the expression 'knee high by the Fourth of July'?" Lou asked.

"I have," Cap said. "It has to do with corn. My gramps used to grow it in a corner of the backyard of his place in North Carolina. It means something like if the stalks weren't knee high by July fourth, the crop would be bad."

"Exactly," Lou said. "That's what I remember, although I have no idea who I heard it from. Well, it isn't July yet, but that corn is certainly way higher than my knees."

Cap turned left again, this time onto a gravelly dirt road. The stalks on each side towered upward like a ghostly army. Rocks, coupled with potholes and the gathering darkness made driving without headlights tricky. Lou felt every jolt of the low-riding Prizm as it struggled to negotiate the uneven terrain.

George pointed up ahead. "They're turning again," he said.

"I got 'em," Cap replied, swinging the car onto an even narrower dirt road that was carved into a seemingly endless expanse of corn.

"You sure you can find your way out of here?" Notso asked, looking around anxiously.

"There's always a way out," Lou said, patting the hefty man's shoulder.

Notso was rubbing the gold handcuffs pendant he wore as if the miniature manacles were rosary beads.

Again, the car jostled from side to side as the wheels found more ruts.

"Shit," Notso said.

"What is it?" Lou felt a tingle of alarm.

"I dropped my gun."

Before anyone could comment, he reached above his head and flicked on the car's interior light.

"Notso!" Lou yelled, covering the light cap with his hand and quickly flicking the switch off. "What are you doing?"

"Sorry, man," he said, "but I got to find my gun."

"We told you to leave it in your holster."

"I got nervous, so I wanted to be sure I could get at it."

Lou glanced up just in time to see the sedan's taillights, perhaps a quarter mile ahead, go dark. Cap pulled over to the edge of the narrow road, car wheels crunching corn stalks underneath, and shut off the engine. Save for the white noise of insects and the swishing of the corn, the silence was heavy. After a minute, his window open, Cap restarted the engine and inched forward. Ahead, the blackness intensified.

"Stop, Cap," Notso said with authority.

"Why?"

"'Cause I'm gettin' out to walk on ahead of you.

They might call me Notso Brite, but that don't mean I make the same mistake twice. I got hearing like a shark."

"What in the hell are you talkin' about?" George said. "Sharks live in the fuckin'—"

Notso was already out on the road, gun in hand, lumbering ahead through the night.

Cap followed for a few minutes, then pulled to the side and cut the engine. He, Lou, and George joined Notso in front of the Prizm and moved cautiously ahead.

"Will you put that gun away?" George snapped at his cousin. "Who do you think you are, Arnold Schwarzenegger?"

Cap shushed them harshly. "Stop talking and listen."

Insects and corn. Nothing else. Insects and corn.

Notso did not stay silent for long. "It sure is quiet out here," he said in a reasonably hushed tone. "Spooky quiet. Man, I couldn't sleep a wink if I didn't hear sirens and car horns all night."

Lou grinned. Over the years, the urban theater had taken up residency in his soul, and he often said as much to Renee when she suggested that he move to a neighborhood more conducive to raising Emily.

Cap had wandered over to the corn. He snapped off an ear and inspected it. Then he pulled back the leaves and held it up to capture what little bit of light existed where they were. "Weird," he mused.

"What?" Lou asked.

"I remember my grandpa telling me that each corn stalk makes one ear, but this one has four and—"

There was no chance for him to say more.

Two gunshots pierced the blackness.

Lou looked ahead at Notso, thinking the big man had mistakenly fired his weapon, but Notso was looking around, confused.

Three more gunshots rang out.

"Run! Scatter!" Cap cried.

Another shot.

Notso groaned loudly, doubled over and clutching his stomach, and stumbled into the corn, Cap following. Lou and George thrashed into the jungle on the opposite side of the road. Stalks lashed at Lou's face and arms as he plunged into the blackness.

There were more shots, coming from not far away.

Then, from somewhere across the road, Lou heard Notso Bright's voice. A single, grunting, agonized word. "Shit!"

CHAPTER 28

Lou stumbled into the dense corn, quickly losing his footing and falling hard. Air exploded from his lungs. Thick stalks snapped in half with a sound like breaking bones as jagged edges sliced his face and arms. Dust coated his mouth and throat.

Gunfire seemed to be erupting from all directions, piercing the darkness with flashes of light. Crawling deeper into the corn, Lou had become separated from George. Movement of the stalks tipped the gunmen as to where he was, and instantly, bullets snapped through the leaves overhead and slammed into the ground close enough to spray clumps of dirt into his face.

Pivoting his body, Lou flattened himself in a deep furrow between two rows. Then, lying motionless in the dark, he listened.

"One's down," a gravelly voice called out from somewhere behind him.

"Stay cool!" The angry warning emanated from just a few feet to Lou's right.

"We're closing in on two of them!" the first man yelled back.

Lou kept still and forced his breathing to slow. He sensed movement. The man was on the move.

Moments later, Lou heard Notso Bright groaning in pain and crying out.

"I'm shot . . . Cap, help me . . . Ca—!"

Two quick shots cut him off, and then there was silence.

"Got him for real, this time," the gravelly voice cried out.

Lou's heart sank.

"Let's get some light on this situation."

Floodlights affixed to widely spaced poles flashed on, creating a shadowy, artificial day. Lou could see almost everything around him. He was readying himself for a dash deeper into the corn, when he heard three quick pops of gunfire from his right, accompanied by the sound of shattering glass. The two spots nearest him went out instantly.

"One of 'em has a gun! He just shot out two floods."

Lou managed a cold smile. George must have brought more than a camera with him.

"Hey, Welcome, that you?" the man closest to him called out. "Your fat black friend is dead. Toast. You should have stayed at home, because you're next!"

It was strange for Lou to hear his name called, but not surprising. Clearly, his mounting suspicions about Kings Ridge had gotten someone's attention.

There was a sudden, intense rustling of corn from

some distance away to his right, and moments later the gunman shouted, "Drop it, asshole! . . . I said drop it!"

He had George.

"Welcome," he called out a minute later, "I'll give you until five to show yourself! Then I'm gonna blow this little sucker's head off. . . . One . . ."

Lou judged the killer to be some twenty feet directly in front of him. After rising slowly, he remained hunched over as he moved ahead.

"Two . . ."

"Lou, the motherfuckers shot Notso!"

"Three . . ."

"Fuck you! Go ahead and shoot me, you prick!"

In the eerie glow from one of the remaining spotlights, Lou could see the gunman's broad back, one shoulder, and the gun he held pointed at George's head.

"Four . . ."

"I'm not afraid of you, you fat—"

Blood running down from gouges in his forehead and neck, Lou had moved as close to the man as he could chance.

One . . . more . . . step . . . and . . .

"Five!"

Ten feet away, George was on his knees. His glasses had been knocked off, and Lou sensed the frustration and anger in his eyes.

But no fear.

"That's it, Welcome. His blood is on your—"

Bellowing, Lou exploded from his crouch like a football lineman.

The gunman whirled awkwardly and George rolled at his legs, connecting just below his knees. The man managed two quick shots, but he was off balance, and the slugs slapped harmlessly into the soil.

Driven by a burst of adrenaline and countless hours of sparring, Lou's fists came up. He landed a powerful left-right-left combination to the larger man's jaw, snapping his head from side to side like a puppet's. His knees already wobbly, he dropped his gun and staggered backwards. Lou launched himself again, pummeling his face and the center of his chest.

Both men went down, Lou on top, still hammering downward with as much power as he had in him. It was as if he were punching stone. The man, with at least a four-inch and fifty-pound advantage, reached up and grasped Lou by the throat. He was a beast, and his hamhock hands were pure power. Lou tucked in his chin to protect himself, but too late. His trachea and larynx were seconds from collapsing.

Still on top, he slammed his forehead down onto the man's nose. Blood burst from both nostrils, but incredibly, the killer's grip hardly lessened. His teeth were bared in a snarling rictus, and Lou's vision began to dim. Grinning obscenely, he rolled Lou onto his back. Thick dollops of blood splashed down into Lou's eyes.

He landed two more wild blows, but the behemoth simply squeezed harder. Lou's flailing weakened. It was over. Images of Emily and Renee, his father and brother took over his thoughts. At the instant his vision went completely dark, he heard a loud gunshot followed by a muffled cry of pain from on top of him. The flow of blood from the man exploded into a fountain, and he toppled limply to the ground.

Gasping, Lou could only lie where he was.

Finally, he managed to turn.

The huge killer lay motionless beside him, blood soaking through the groin of his trousers. Then Lou realized that the top of his head had burst open as well.

George knelt nearby, smiling proudly. "I couldn't find my thirty-eight," George said, "but this damn water buffalo had a cannon. Just look at this thing. This is some serious firepower."

Groaning, Lou forced himself to his knees. George's bullet had gone straight up between the man's legs and had blown off the top of his head.

Serious firepower, indeed.

"Nice shot," Lou understated.

"You all right, Welcome?" George asked. "You look like something Jason got ahold of in *Friday the Thirteenth*."

Lou pawed at the gore on his face with the sleeve of his jacket. It took some work, but gradually his vision cleared. "I'm okay, thanks to you," he whispered. "I'm sorry about your cousin."

"I can't believe this has happened. We gotta find him. He's not dead. I know my cousin, Welcome. He's not dead!"

"We'll look for him as soon as we can," Lou said, knowing in his heart what they would find. "We've got to get back to the car. We can call for help, provided there's any reception."

"How many you estimate are out there, not countin' him?"

"I'm guessing four. Could be five. Stay low, George, and try not to fire that thing anymore unless someone's about to kill me again."

Crouching low, Lou moved ahead, pushing the densely packed rows of corn aside. George followed closely. They found the road again, and after a careful walk along the edge, saw George's car. The overhead spotlights had been shut off. There was no sign of Cap or Notso.

"Cap!" George cried out anxiously. "Where you at, man? Notso! Cap!"

"George, keep it quiet!" Lou whispered harshly, but his warning came too late.

Gunfire erupted from across the road, forcing them back into the corn. Bullets streaked past them from several directions, but their cover held. Sticking close together, they pressed deeper into the corn. At that instant, the silence was pierced by a low rumbling, coming from the direction in which they were headed. Shoulder to shoulder, they ducked down in a furrow. The noise built steadily until it seemed like a jet engine had fired up and was heading toward them.

"What the hell is that?" George asked.

Lou stood up on his tiptoes and peered over the corn.

Instantly, his blood turned cold.

CHAPTER 29

Advancing rapidly toward them through the darkness, looking like an attacking spaceship, its bank of headlights blazing, engine roaring, was a massive combine harvester. Attached to the front end of the harvester, whirling at a blurring speed, was a cylindrical threshing reel, at least twenty feet wide. The machine, with tires taller than Lou, was shearing stalks off at ground level.

Wind generated by the rotating blades sprayed dirt toward Lou and rushed ahead with enough force to throw him off balance. In the brightly lit cab, he could see the silhouette of the driver and wondered what George and he must have looked like to the man.

Helpless was the only word that came to mind.

Most frightening to him about the thresher was its speed. For several precious seconds, he was frozen—almost literally, a deer in the headlights of the powerful beast. The gap between him and the machine seemed to be closing rapidly. Finally, with no specific plan in mind, he whirled to his right. Nimbly, the combine responded. Moments later, Lou tripped and fell, pitching facefirst onto the rugged ground.

"George! Run! Get out of here!" he shouted, stumbling to his feet.

He could barely hear himself over the roaring engine, and knew there was no way George could hear him.

The screech of the razorlike blades was deafening, and the skill of the driver had him persistently locked between the headlights. Slivered stalks flew out from the base of the apparatus like daggers. A shot rang out from the right, then another. Bullets sparked off the metal framework of the cab. A third shot seemed to spiderweb the windshield.

Lou saw the muzzle flashes and located George, thrashing ahead through the corn, firing over his shoulder like a sharpshooter in a Wild West show. For the moment, at least, he seemed to be well beyond the far end of the screeching rotors.

Lou was dead center.

George got off three more rapid shots. Then, it seemed, he was out of ammunition. It didn't matter. The bullets had done nothing to stop, or even slow the combine. Still, Lou was concerned that there was space for the thresher to swing from him to George.

Still fixed between the headlights, he began jumping up and down, hollering and frantically waving his arms above his head. The move sealed his fate. The thresher made an adjustment, and he quickly became the chosen one.

Fifteen feet.

Ten.

The noise was deafening now.

In seconds, it would be over.

Five.

Lou spun to his left and tripped on a root, rolling his left ankle. He pitched forward like a baseball player diving headfirst into a base. Unlike the rest of the cornfield, the soil he landed on was muddy and dense. He flattened himself out, hands stretched over his head, jaws clenched, waiting for the blades to tear him apart.

But there was no impact.

He had fallen into a trough, he realized—not a furrow between rows, but something deeper, an irrigation ditch. The roar and wind as the harvester passed over him were like a tornado. The ground shook violently, and the blades actually swept across his back. A millimeter or two more, and he would have been shredded.

As soon as the harvester had passed over him, Lou scrambled from the ditch and hobbled toward where he reckoned the road was, feeling every step in his ankle. Just as he was losing confidence in his sense of direction, the densely packed stalks fell away. He stumbled out into the roadway, torn and completely covered in blood and dirt. Some distance away, he could hear the combine, swinging about for another run at him. Headlights appeared up ahead, flashed twice and went out. A car came skidding toward him through the darkness. Lou tensed, ready to dive back into the corn. The headlights urgently flashed again and the approaching car slowed.

Cap leaned out the driver's-side window. "Quick, get in the car, Lou!" he cried.

Lou clambered into the backseat, relieved to see George sitting up front, and immediately grasping the significance that there were only three of them. Cap spun the car 180 degrees, sending a pillar of dust swirling into the night sky. The car fishtailed several times on the dirt road before finally catching traction. Lou looked behind him and saw the bank of lights from the harvester fading in the distance.

Unable to stop shaking now, he kept on looking until the machine had vanished from view.

CHAPTER 30

At one o'clock in the morning, beneath a densely over-cast sky, the vast cornfields all looked the same.

Each turn Lou directed Chief Gilbert Stone to take led them to another narrow dirt road that cut through another field. With a gentle breeze fanning the tall stalks, it all seemed so peaceful—so far removed from the guns . . . and the combine harvester . . . and the blood . . . and the death. But the nightmare had been real, and Notso Brite had apparently paid for some-one's paranoia with his life.

It had taken most of an hour before the 911 call from Cap's cell phone had directed a cruiser from the Kings Ridge police station to where the three of them were waiting in George's car. The officer, on orders from Stone, had led Lou and the others to the station, and after photographing Lou, fixed him up with a shower and a set of clothes. Even after washing off the blood and caked soil, he looked beaten and totally spent. His face had half a dozen gouges, and his knuckles throbbed. Nasty crimson bruises encircled his neck like a cleric's collar. Worst of all, his ankle was quite swollen and was monitoring every heartbeat.

The small motorcade consisted of two cruisers. Stone drove lead with Lou riding shotgun and Cap and George seated quietly in back behind a wire mesh screen. Two officers occupied the second car. Even staying under fifteen, nothing Lou or the others described was of any help in leading Stone to the spot where they were ambushed. Thirty minutes passed. Then another thirty. Several times, Lou thought they were on the right track. His pulse spiked, only to quickly settle down at the sight of a road sign or a house or outbuilding that told him they were still in the wrong place.

Stone was patient and understanding, but several times suggested that they might do better to suspend their search until daylight. Lou was adamant they continue.

"Look at my neck!" he insisted. "I didn't do this to myself. There are at least two bodies out there—one of the men who was trying to kill us, and our friend Anthony Brite. Cap saw him get shot."

He glanced back at his stoical friend and wondered what Gilbert Stone was thinking about him and George.

"Turn here," Cap said suddenly.

"Turn here?"

Lou nodded and Stone made the right. The other police car followed them onto yet another narrow dirt road. Both drivers cut to their fog lights and slowed to five. There were no distinctive tire tracks on the dirt road, but there was something about the interface between the road and the stalks that seemed familiar.

"Cap, you sensing something?" Lou asked.

"Maybe."

"Duncan, do you really think you killed somebody, too?" Stone asked.

"Well, first of all, while one of them was shootin' at me like Wild Bill Hickok, another one charged me. I hit him with a right cross to the throat that would have stopped an elephant. I didn't have time to stick around and check the guy's pulse, but he didn't seem to be doin' much moving."

"Three dead and no bodies," Stone murmured thoughtfully. "Not your everyday case."

"They're out there," Lou said, gazing out the window and trying not to feel hopeless.

"We should have left a bread crumb trail," George added.

"We'll find him, George," Lou said, somewhat buoyed that they hadn't seen anything that meant this could not be the road. "We'll find him. . . . Wait! Stone, up there! Up ahead!"

Stone slammed on the brakes. Twenty feet ahead on the right was a gnarl of tread marks.

Lou clambered out of the cruiser, cringing when his ankle bore weight.

"What do you have?" Stone asked as he and the others approached.

Lou pointed at the disrupted ground ahead. "This is it. We were here."

"You sure? Could just be farm machinery," Stone said, climbing out with the others and panning the area with his flashlight.

"Mighty small machine," George said. "I wish we had brought my car out here with us so we could compare, but these tracks are bald in the same places my tires are bald." He got low to the ground and felt around the depressions in the road, then nodded authoritatively, as if he actually could tell.

With renewed tension, the group climbed back into the cruisers. The fog lights were turned off, and they slowly rolled ahead. They had gone a quarter mile or so when Lou exclaimed, "Look! Look at the corn over there."

The fields on both sides of the road, for as far ahead as they could see, were mown flat. The six of them stepped out into the cool early morning and listened. Nothing but the heavy white noise of humming insects and swishing stalks of corn, where such stalks remained.

"This has been threshed," Lou said.

"What does that mean?" Stone asked.

"It means someone flattened these fields."

Stone scanned the area with his flashlight. It looked like the model of a nuclear winter.

"This is where these gunmen attacked you?" he said.

"I'd bet on it," Lou said, excited at last. "We didn't pass any other fields that had been cut down like this. It's a huge cover-up."

"I agree," Cap said.

Lou limped into the field.

Was it possible this wasn't the place?

He inhaled deeply, tasting the air, and then inspected a handful of chopped-up stalks and leaves. "This field looks like it was very recently cut," he said. "These plants haven't decayed any, and you can still smell diesel in the air."

Stone shook his head. "I want to believe you, Welcome," he said. "I really do. But I still have trouble wrapping my brain around the extent these killers went to in order cover up what you say happened here."

He took his powerful flashlight out again and shone it at one of the overhead spotlights—then at another. None of them was lit, but all the bulbs appeared intact.

"I thought you said you shot out the lights," Stone said. For the first time, there was a note of cynicism in his voice.

"They could have been replaced," George said.

"And we could be in the wrong place. You guys haven't spent much time out here in corn country, if you've spent any at all. It's sort of like another planet to you. You could be feeding off one another. We see that sort of group dynamic from time to time. It's like a form of hysteria or mass hypnosis. You start following some suspicious thugs out of the city, and get yourselves double-crossed and ambushed. No one's attention to details is all that sharp. The stories get twisted on one another."

Cap strode up to the police chief and, hands on hips, glared down at him. It was as if Michelangelo's *David* had decided to confront the tourists who were gawking at him. "Do I look hysterical?" he asked.

Lou, who was kneeling nearby, inspecting the soil, glanced back at his chisled friend and grinned.

"Duncan, don't get me wrong," Stone was saying. "I

just think we should go at this in the morning with a lot more men and some dogs."

Cap took a step back.

"What about Notso?" George insisted.

"Notso's dead," Cap said. "I saw him get shot."

"I don't give a damn what you saw. I'm not leaving my cousin out here in this stinkin' field to get eaten by animals."

"We don't even know if this is the right field," Stone said.

Lou felt the situation getting tense. He did not know George well enough to predict his actions or whether Cap would be able to control him. He imagined him facedown in the dirt with his hands cuffed behind him and Gilbert Stone's knee in the small of his back.

At that moment, Lou's hand brushed over another clump of dirt. This one had something hard embedded in it—something hard and sharp. So sharp that it took a few seconds for him to realize that he had been cut. He inspected the side of his palm. Blood was oozing out of a half-inch-long slice. Carefully, Lou worked his fingers around the edges of the object that had cut him. He scraped the dirt away and was left with a large shard of glass—thick, textured glass.

"What's that?" Stone asked, inspecting the object with his flashlight.

"Broken spotlight glass, if I'm not mistaken," Lou said. "I'd guarantee it."

"Told you!" George chirped.

Stone fingered the glass.

"Well?" Lou asked.

Stone shrugged. "Well, I think it's time we go pay a visit to William Chester."

"Who's that?" asked Lou.

"The guy who owns these fields, that's who."

CHAPTER 31

A twelve-foot-high vine-covered stone wall enclosed Cross Winds, the Chester estate. Stone left his two officers to continue patrolling the fields, and then drove Lou, Cap, and George to the far western part of Kings Ridge and up a broad circular drive lined with trees. A security guard posted at the gated entrance checked everyone's ID before calling inside and granting the group passage. Mounted security cameras monitored their arrival.

Ah, the joys of big bucks, Lou thought sardonically.

Cross Winds was a resplendent two-story neoclassical mansion featuring large, gently arched windows, and stone chimneys. The windows were dark from within, save for one on the first floor.

Even in the darkness, it was obvious the grounds were a source of pride to the owner. The grass, cut to the height of a putting green and tastefully illuminated by a series of in-ground lights, glowed the color of a polished emerald, while the hedges were pruned with a carpenter's precision. Sprawling rock gardens and flower beds completed the remarkable landscape. Protruding past the corner of the main house was a portion of a large, dimly lit greenhouse.

The odd quartet proceeded up a short flight of stairs and onto a wide veranda that featured a dozen classic rocking chairs. Lou's ankle challenged him with every step. Stone used a huge bronze wolf's-head knocker to confirm their arrival, and in seconds, a cast iron lantern dangling overhead bathed them in a diffuse incandescent glow.

The massive front door opened, revealing a round-faced man in his mid-sixties—swarthy and fit in a weight lifter's sort of way. He had narrow Eastern European eyes and thick silver hair combed in a sideways part as straight as the hedge trim outside. Despite the early hour, it seemed as if he had not been sleeping.

"William Chester," he said, shaking each man's hand as he directed the group into the elegant foyer inside.

His hands were thick and powerful, and Lou wondered if he might be putting something extra into each squeeze—an immediate message as to who was in charge and not to be trifled with. The gesture was understandable. On their drive over, Lou had used his smartphone to research the man. Chester's rise to industry dominance would have sent Horatio Alger scurrying for his typewriter.

Chester, age five, along with his father, mother, and a sister, immigrated illegally to the United States from Poland as stowaways onboard a cargo ship. Having spent their life savings to secure safe passage, the family changed their name from Chudnofsky to Chester, and settled down in a single room in the heart of Manhattan's Hell's Kitchen. Chester would later say the run-down building where his family lived would have been condemned had it not been needed by the city to house the rats.

Eventually, Bernard Chester found employment in the garment district. However, the family's good fortune proved short-lived. Carlo Gambino, of the Gambino crime family, assumed control over the district, and Bernard became a leader among those opposed to him. William had just turned eleven when his father, along with several others, was gunned down.

Penniless, Chester supported his family by sweeping floors in a plant wholesaler. Within a year, he had shown an unusual aptitude for stimulating plant health and growth, and was hired away by the Barlow Seed Company—first as a salesman, then as an assistant manager to Donald Barlow, who subsequently became his mentor. By the time William was thirty, he was managing the Barlow Company, which was by then among the twenty top-grossing operations of its kind.

When Barlow died suddenly and without family, his company passed to Chester. The subsequent growth of Chester Seed and Fertilizer, soon to be Chester Enterprises, put the company among the top ten in the industry worldwide.

Barlow died suddenly.

The phrase, from the Wikipedia article on William Chester, resonated in Lou's mind. Over the final mile to the Chester mansion, he searched Donald Barlow on Google, then Yahoo, and finally Bing.

The third try was the charm.

A small article in a thirty-three-year-old issue of the *Miami Herald* reported the accidental death of seed giant Donald Barlow, who was washed overboard during a surprise squall while sailing aboard his fifty-two-foot yacht, *Green Thumb*.

The only other one on board at the time was Barlow Company executive William Chester, who immediately radioed the Coast Guard and followed their instructions. Despite Chester's efforts, and an extensive sea and air search, Barlow's body was not recovered. Police say that a cause of death hearing, routine in such deaths at sea, will be held in the near future.

William Chester, impeccably dressed in deck shoes, chinos, and a turquoise knit shirt, led the quartet to a conference room just off his study, offered them soft drinks and water, and motioned them to take any seats they wished around what looked to Lou like a mahogany table that might have cost the total of all the furniture he had ever owned.

"Well, gentlemen," Chester said in a calm, authoritative voice, "I confess that I am rather shocked at the story as Chief Stone has related it to me. Suppose each of you give me your version. And please, take your time."

"How far back would you like us to go?" Lou asked.

"Why, back to the beginning, of course, Dr. Welcome. Why don't we begin with you, and then Mr. Duncan, and finally, Mr. Kozak here?"

Lou noted how smoothly Chester demonstrated that he knew their names after just a single introduction. Another well-mastered display of control.

Lou began with the retelling of Joey Alderson's injury and the subsequent drive home with him from Eisenhower Memorial.

"I don't know when these two thugs started following me," he said. "It could have been several days before that. But this past afternoon, George and his cousin Anthony Brite noticed them checking out my building, and we followed them back out here."

"Anthony Brite is the man whom you say was gunned down?" Chester asked.

"That's right, man!" George exclaimed. "He was my cousin, and those dudes of yours burned him! Bastards!"

For several moments, there was absolute silence.

Then Chester nodded minutely at George. His expression was placid, but his narrow eyes were ice, and fixed on George like an infrared sight. "Young man," he said finally, "you are a guest in my house. And as long as I treat you with civility and respect, you will honor me with the same courtesy. Is that clear? . . . I said, *is that clear*?"

Lou felt the man's power. He also sensed strongly that the word *boy* had barely gone unsaid.

George seemed unable to respond. "Got it," he finally managed, eyes to the floor, his usual bravado gone.

"Chief Stone," Chester said, "my orchids are a source of calm and balance for me. I think I would prefer to continue this discussion in my greenhouse, or if you prefer, sometime tomorrow—perhaps out where these gentlemen say they were attacked. I can ask my field manager to meet us there, and perhaps one or two of my attorneys as well."

Stone silently polled the others. "It's your house, Bill," he said. "Let's take this meeting outside."

The group stood and parted like the Red Sea as Chester strode past them, through a set of French doors, then down a long corridor to a rear door that opened on one end of a magnificent, fragrant greenhouse, perhaps the size of a hockey rink. With the touch of a button, the subdued lighting brightened, and soft classical music—Beethoven, Lou guessed—flowed through speakers that seemed to be everywhere.

The entourage followed Chester into densely humid air that was rich with the aromas of flowers and ripe fruit. Lou picked up the scent of chocolate, raspberry, and citrus the most strongly. The flowering plants, he realized, might all be orchids.

Chester paused, perhaps to appreciate his visitors' collective awe. He then lifted a specialized gauge and began testing a nearby flower bed, which seemed to consist of an earthy mix of moss and bark.

"It is a common misconception that orchids are difficult to grow," Chester said while sprinkling water here and there. "But the truth is, you just have to be aware of their needs. I think of orchids not as plants, but as a civilization—a culture whose customs I have come to know intimately. Do you enjoy gardening, Dr. Welcome?"

"Mr. Chester, forgive my impatience, but we have a very serious situation here," Lou said. "Men have been killed in a field that you own, our friend among them."

Chester stopped taking measurements, settled himself with a breath, and gave Lou a curious stare. "Dr. Welcome, I did not become a person of influence, possession, and power by not knowing precisely what was going on around me. As I told Chief Stone when he called, I have received no reports of any disturbances in any of my fields."

Lou began to bristle. "I don't care what reports you received or did not receive, Mr. Chester," he said. "Our injuries can tell you what happened out there. Our stories coincide. We were ambushed and attacked with fists, with guns, and with a combine harvester. The area where it took place has been mown clear, and the bodies, including Anthony Brite's, have been removed."

Stone positioned himself between Lou and Chester, perhaps sensing the simmering exchange might boil over. "Bill," Stone said, clearly wishing he were anyplace but there, "Dr. Welcome believes he has evidence that the spotlights they claim to have shot out were replaced."

"I can't believe it," Chester snapped. "If such a thing transpired, I can assure you, none of my employees was involved."

"Funny that these nonemployees knew how to drive your combine harvester," Cap said.

Chester's eyes flashed.

Lou almost cracked a smile, imagining what the man was thinking, being spoken to in such a way by someone he probably considered so far beneath his status.

Chester brushed the comment aside with a wave of

his hand. "Believe me," he said, "operating farming machinery is not nearly as difficult as growing these orchids, especially when the keys are left in the ignition slot, as is often the case here. I've warned my people against such practices, but alas, they don't always listen."

"Show him the glass," Cap said to Lou.

Lou handed the jagged piece of broken glass to Chester, who inspected the heavy shard like a gemologist.

"And what do we think this is?" Chester asked.

"Floodlight glass," Lou said. "As you know, the lights are on poles twenty feet above the ground. I found this at the base of one of the poles. Who besides one of your employees would and could repair the floodlight that George shot out?"

George broke in, "And why would your field be threshed after we left it? I'll tell you why—" he pointed his finger at Chester— "a cover-up, that's why."

Stone gripped George by the wrist and forcefully lowered his arm. "Son," he said, "you'd best watch how you speak to Mr. Chester—especially in his home. He's agreed to help us, and your accusations aren't helping anybody. Got it?"

George nodded glumly.

"It's all right, Gilbert," Chester said. "Obviously these men have experienced some sort of trauma, and quite possibly on my land."

"Any idea who might have been involved?" Stone asked.

"No, but I can assure you it was no one in my employ. I'll be happy to make my employee records available to you."

"I appreciate that."

Chester turned his attention back to Lou. "Is it possible that in all the confusion you've described, Dr. Welcome, you merely thought a floodlight that had shattered some time ago had been shot out? Floodlights do break from time to time, kids and rocks and thermal changes, you know. Perhaps the piece you've found is an old one."

"That's not possible," Lou said coolly. "I know what I saw. A man died next to me. I saw him get shot."

"Then are you sure you were in the right spot? The fields can become quite disorienting, especially at night."

"We strongly believe that was the spot," Lou said.

"My, my," Chester said. "This is certainly quite distressing. Gilbert, I'll phone Stewart right away."

"Who is Stewart?" Lou asked, his patience walking the edge.

"He manages all my fields," Chester said. "I'm not denying some version of what you have said actually occurred, but I will strongly contest that any of my people were involved. I assure you, Gilbert, you'll have my full cooperation."

"Thank you," Stone said, looking satisfied. "We're going to bring a K-9 unit out to the fields later this morning and start searching for their friend."

"That sounds like a fine idea," Chester replied. "Is there anything else you think we should be doing?"

"Well," Lou said, "I do have a question about your corn."

"Go on."

"Your plants seem quite high for this time of year."

"And one other thing," Cap said.

"Go ahead, Mr. Duncan."

"I thought each stalk produced one ear. One of the stalks I checked had four. The other had five."

Chester chuckled. "I'm pleased to meet an amateur agrarian," he said. "Some kinds of corn still make one ear per stalk, but many others are hybridized and produce two and even three. Still, our corn is special. I'll show you why." Chester led them over to a row of baskets filled with flowers of a stunningly iridescent blue. "We've been experimenting with a new type of fertilizer in our fields. It's the same formula that I've used to help grow these magnificent blue *Phalaenopses*. This type of orchid is often extremely difficult to grow, especially with color this brilliant. But thanks to our breakthrough fertilizer, the task has been made remarkably easy. I'd tell you more about it sometime after our patent issues are dealt with, but for now, I must pay homage to a busy day ahead by getting some sleep."

At that moment, the greenhouse door flew open, and in stepped a well-groomed, nattily dressed man of slight stature, perhaps five-foot-seven. In his early forties, he was quite handsome, with chiseled features, raven hair gelled straight back, and dark, piercing eyes.

"What's going on here?" the new arrival asked sharply, moving so that he stood shoulder to shoulder next to Chester, and eyeing Lou, Cap, and George as if they had dropped in from Mars.

"Ah, Edwin," Chester said. "It appears we have had a disturbance in one of our fields."

"Then what are you doing even talking to these people without our attorney?"

Chester actually seemed somewhat cowed next to the man. "I just didn't feel it was necessary," he said.

"Sometimes I wonder how you've made it this far, Father."

"Gentlemen," William Chester said, "I'd like you to meet Edwin Chester, my son."

CHAPTER 32

Edwin Chester stood motionless beside his father, at the center of the magnificent greenhouse. Lou introduced himself by name, but the scion made no attempt to shake his hand. Cap and George received the same chilly greeting.

Edwin's gaze turned first to Stone, then back to Chester. "What sort of disturbance?" he asked, gesturing toward Lou and the other two. "What happened to these men?"

"We were attacked," Cap said. "Ambushed. That's what happened. And in your father's cornfield."

"What's my father's is mine," Edwin said. "Ambushed by whom? What are you talking about?"

Lou paid close attention to Edwin's reaction. His surprise appeared to be genuine, as did his indignation about having to deal with this situation at all.

"These three are from D.C.," Chester said. "They say they followed two men out here whom they believed were following them. They claim there was an ambush and gunfire, and that at least two men were killed. One of them was their friend."

"My cousin," George corrected.

"Chief Stone is here to investigate, and I've offered our complete cooperation."

"That makes no sense," Edwin said. "Why would somebody attack these men in our cornfield? Have you contacted someone from Hensley's? They're on call to us twenty-four/seven. That's why you pay them that ridiculous retainer."

Lou took a step forward. "I believe I know *exactly* why we were attacked," he said, addressing both Chester men.

"And who the hell are you?"

"Edwin, Dr. Welcome, here, is an emergency physician at Eisenhower Memorial," Stone said.

Lou was unable to ignore the fact that William was concerned as to why the ambush could have happened, while his son seemed interested only in absolving them of any responsibility.

"Go on," Edwin said, as if he expected Lou wouldn't speak without his permission.

"I've noticed an unusual pattern of behavior among people in Kings Ridge," Lou began. "It seems that my observations may have attracted the attention of the people who ambushed us—or else of the people who hired them."

"What sort of behavior?" Edwin asked.

"For me, it all started with the John Meacham shootings," Lou said.

"Meacham!" William exclaimed. "What in the hell could that crazy murderer have to do with your being ambushed in our field?"

It was the first crack in the man's composure. Continuing to select each word with care, Lou reviewed his job with the PWO, his relationship with Meacham, and the reason for his trip to the hospital in Kings Ridge.

"I don't think John knew what he was doing when he shot those people," Lou summarized. "His judgment was impaired and—"

"Of course his judgment was impaired!" Edwin cut in. "He was deranged. He had proven that before, but apparently you weren't paying attention then. Now you're consumed with guilt and willing to pin the blame on anyone and anything except your bad evaluation of the man."

"Up until the day he killed those people, Meacham had been doing fine?" Stone asked, as if he expected Edwin to jump down his throat.

"Perfect, from all I can tell," Lou replied.

"Then what happened?"

"That's what I'd like to find out," Lou said. "You see, I think Meacham is the tip of an iceberg."

"Explain," Edwin said curtly.

"From what I can tell, he wasn't deranged in the sense that he had gone crazy," Lou replied. "It seems more as if he was profoundly confused—as if his logic and reasoning deserted him."

Lou went on to review the police report of the woman who survived long enough to describe Meacham's repeated muttering of the phrase *no witnesses* during his rampage, even though the most important witness of all, Roberta Jennings, had long since departed the office.

"That does sound strange," Edwin said.

Lou sensed that he had now lost the older Chester completely, and knew that he had never made a dent in Gilbert Stone. But there seemed to be at least a glimmer of interest from Edwin. Lou decided it was worth pushing his theories.

"And there's more," he said.

He recounted the baffling and at times risky medicine being practiced by several of the staff at DeLand Regional, Carolyn Meacham's dangerous car chase, and finally, his observations surrounding Joey Alderson's near amputation, and the young chef's admission that he had no idea why he chose to reach beneath the deadly blade when he did.

"In each instance," he concluded, "it appeared that there was a temporary loss of judgment—a gap in thinking or, if you will, a lapse of reason."

"Oh, Jesus," Edwin muttered when Lou had finished. "This is absolute rubbish. It is preposterous to think that you'd be the target of a deadly ambush, like you claim happened, just because of your theories, which are utterly baseless."

Lou's patience with the man was wearing thin. "Baseless? Chief Stone, how many residents are there in Kings Ridge? Seven thousand?

"Ten," Stone grumbled, clearly wishing they could all call it quits.

"Ten," Lou echoed. "Even allowing for the fact that

not everyone working at the hospital is from Kings Ridge, I've just identified roughly ten people who have exhibited these symptoms, and that was without even searching for them. Now, I was never a biostatistics whiz in med school, but I did pass. I imagine that someone who knew what they were doing and crunched the numbers would tell us there is no coincidence at work here."

"Ridiculous," Edwin said. "Please, Gilbert, tell me you're not buying in to this nonsense?"

"We're investigating all possibilities, Edwin," Stone said.

"We'll cooperate in the morning when our attorneys are present. But for now, I ask that you all leave these premises immediately so that my father and I might attempt to get some sleep."

"Of course," Stone said.

Without reaction, William stalked from the greenhouse, and Gilbert Stone led the others through a door leading to the front lawn.

Lou was the last of the group to leave.

Edwin was standing by the door, and as Lou passed, Edwin seized him tightly by the arm. "What in the hell is really going on, Welcome?" the man whispered harshly. Despite the difference in their height, he fixed Lou with an icy glare.

"I thought I just told you," Lou said, pulling his arm free and not backing off a step. "There is something deadly wrong going on in Kings Ridge."

CHAPTER 33

Darlene wore a brunet wig in addition to the same white-framed tinted glasses she had on the evening she met with Double M. The disguise worked well. In her tight-fitting jeans and studded leather jacket, Darlene blended in perfectly with the other nighthawks enjoying an early-morning meal at Chef Chen's. No one in the eatery seemed to recognize the First Lady of the United States, seated alone in a back booth, not far from the kitchen.

Victor Ochoa, on high alert, was at a lacquered table directly across from her. He sipped absently at his tea while constantly scanning the room—especially the main entrance.

The girls weren't going to show.

Darlene made the briefest eye contact with the man committed to protecting her at all costs, and shrugged. Her pulse had been racing since she met him by the exit in the basement below the White House pantry. Ochoa was driving his private car, and his composure kept her reasonably grounded.

"I need your help finding this girl," she had said to him on the ride from the movie theater back to the White House. She handed him the stack of photographs that Double M had given to her.

Ochoa studied the images and set them facedown on his lap. "Is she a prostitute?" he asked.

Darlene was stunned. "How did you—?"

"Just a lucky guess. Secret Service agents like to think we're a special breed of law enforcement, but underneath the dark suits and shades, we're really all just cops at heart. This her fingerprint?"

"Yes. And that's a sample of her voice. Her name may be Margo. That's all I have."

"That's a lot. I've got a few friends working with D.C. vice. If it's all right with you, I'll let them look these over, and see what they come up with."

What they came up with was the name Margo Spencer, a doe-eyed sixteen-year-old, seasoned call girl, who disappeared shortly after Russ Evans resigned, but before his case was prosecuted. In fact, without access to their star witness, the U.S. Attorney's Office in D.C. opted not to bring the case to trial at all. Evans's disgrace, the head of the office begrudgingly decided, would have to be punishment enough. The police and FBI could not explain why Margo had disappeared. Because of her age, she'd been spared the limelight that had shone on other women who played a part in the downfall of other well-known public figures.

"I would imagine she's laying low until the noise surrounding Evans dies down," Ochoa said.

"I don't think so, Victor," Darlene replied. "I think she's afraid of the people who hired her."

Ochoa's contacts gave him the names and photographs of three women whom they believed might have been friends with Margo. The three, known to vice as Jewel, MonicaBelle, and Debbi, were still holding on to their looks, and worked for various high-end escort services. They also periodically fed information to vice in exchange for being left alone. Ochoa had been tipped that they often met at Chef Chen's after finishing an evening of work. The best he could do was to get a message to the one named Jewel that there would be easy money to be made should the three of them stop by Chen's at two.

Darlene did not sip her wonton soup, so much as she kept stirring it with her plastic ladle. The meetings, first with Evans at the Bar None, then with Double M in the alley, had her on edge, and she had been eating very little.

Victor might be able to sneak her out of the White House once, he told her, perhaps twice more, should the girls be no-shows this morning, but each such departure carried with it increasing risks, most notably with Martin. His tension, as he stepped more and more out onto a rocky campaign trail, was becoming almost palpable, and Darlene felt increasingly uneasy around him. Kim had actually and earnestly suggested they find a way to get some counseling, but Darlene laughed off the notion, replying that trying to do so would be like asking her husband to deal with his fear of heights through a set of skydiving lessons.

She was settling herself down by playing through a number of the more wonderful memories of the early years of their marriage when, at 2:15, the front door swung open and three striking women strode into the restaurant. Darlene looked over at Ochoa, and he confirmed her suspicions with a nod.

The women did not look exactly as they did in their photographs. MonicaBelle, a redhead, was now a platinum blonde with her hair tied back. Jewel wore glasses, and Debbi had morphed from a pixie-cut brunette to shoulder length. They wore elegant stiletto-heeled boots and skintight designer jeans that Darlene put at three hundred a pair, minimum. Their gold jewelry jangled like wind chimes, and she caught the aroma of perfume mixed with the odor of cigarettes as they passed. A closer look, and she upped her initial estimate of their ages to thirty or even somewhere north of that. MonicaBelle and Debbi slid in across from Jewel two booths away. Before too much longer, Darlene found herself thinking, life was going to start getting harder for the trio.

Ochoa waited for the women to place their orders before he approached.

"Oh, handsome," Debbi said, curling her lower lip in a pout, "I'm afraid our meters stopped running a while ago."

The three burst out laughing. Ochoa joined in at a reduced level.

"This is easy money," he said. "You don't even have to get up."

"Oooh, kinky," Jewel said, and the trio exploded again.

Ochoa waited until their mirth had drifted off. Then he swung a chair over from the table behind him, made sure no one was watching, and slid three hundreds in front of each of them. "I'm not here for that," he said. "I just want to talk."

Jewel flipped the bills with the edge of her thumb. "This won't even get us through five minutes at Nordstrom's makeup counter," she said.

"Sorry, I'm low budget."

"Fed?"

"Sort of . . . Yes or no?"

The women took a silent poll, and nodded. Quickly, the nine hundred vanished.

"I'm not alone," he said, motioning for Darlene to join them.

"Oh, you *are* a kinky one," Debbi murmured, her accent Hispanic.

Darlene took the space next to Jewel.

"So who's your cute friend?" MonicaBelle asked Ochoa.

"My name's Brenda," Darlene said.

Jewel's pale blue eyes fixed on her, and for a moment Darlene thought her disguise had failed. Then the call girl simply smiled, nodded, and said, "How're you doin', Brenda?"

Ochoa was on his feet, hands on Darlene's shoulders, ready to move out the door if necessary, but the scattered patrons in Chef Chen's seem to be paying little, if any, attention to them.

Darlene motioned him back into his seat. "Ladies, this handsome guy is Victor. His job is to keep me safe, and thankfully, he's very good at it."

"He's the one who sent that note to me at the agency, right?" Jewel asked.

"You got it," Ochoa said.

"My kind of man," MonicaBelle said. "Great hands. That's how I judge a guy—by his hands."

Darlene moved the group closer. "Listen, we need your help locating a girl whom we think you know. Can Victor show you some pictures?"

MonicaBelle appeared suspicious. "You gonna try and take back the cash if we don't know her? Because—"

"No," Darlene said. "The money is yours regardless."

The girls took another quick poll, then shrugged their agreement.

"Okay," Jewel said. "Show us what you got."

Ochoa brought out a stack of police photographs. He and Darlene chose to avoid any of the ones Double M had taken with his cell phone. He spread the pictures across the table, arranging them so that each woman had some images to examine. Debbi and Jewel looked them over, but their expressions revealed nothing. MonicaBelle, on the other hand, connected with the girl right away.

"This is Angela," she said.

Darlene tried to conceal her disappointment. "I'm sorry, I should have told you," she said. "The girl's name is Margo."

"Yeah and my name's Queen Latifah if the price is right," MonicaBelle answered.

"What are you saying?" Ochoa leaned across the table to ask.

"I mean she might have said her name is Margo or Fargo or whatever," the woman said. "But I know this girl well. We used to work for the same service. She was younger than me, so I kind of looked out for her. A real looker, in my opinion—natural, if you know what I mean. Didn't need no makeup—at least not yet. Girl's name was Sylvia . . . Sylvia Winger. But she went by Angela."

Was.

Darlene and Ochoa exchanged tight-lipped glances.

"Well, Angela, or Margo, was coerced by somebody into framing a good friend of mine," Darlene said. "We promise that we mean her no harm. We just want to talk to her."

"That's impossible," MonicaBelle replied.

"Almost anything is possible. I'm pretty well connected."

"You could be the pope, for all it matters, but nobody can keep Angela safe now. She's dead."

The words, though no longer totally unexpected, fell like hammer strikes.

"Oh, that's terrible," Darlene said, her voice breaking. "Do you know what happened to her?"

"She moved to Tampa to be with her mom a few months ago. I got a postcard from her."

"Do you know how she . . . died?"

Without Margo, Martin would never believe Double M's recording was real.

"She drowned," MonicaBelle said simply. "Washed

up on a beach after she'd gone missing from a party. Her mother found my number in her things and called to tell me. You can imagine how she was feeling. Angela was a baby."

"I'm so sad. Would it upset you if Victor tried to learn the details of her death?"

"We don't mind," the woman said. "You really seem like a nice person."

"So are you—all of you." Darlene didn't have to force the sincerity in her voice. She extended her hands, and the three escorts covered them with theirs.

Darlene nodded to Ochoa, who pulled a BlackBerry from his jacket pocket as she looked over his shoulder, watching him key the name *Sylvia Winger* and the word *Tampa* into the Google search box. Margo's photo—possibly from high school, appeared in a search result set that included the girl's obituary. They read through the short paragraph, and then an earlier account in the *Tampa Tribune* of her death.

"It says here that the toxicology was positive for alcohol. Three times the legal limit. No one seemed to know or care where she was partying."

"Accidental drowning," Darlene said to the women. "It makes sense the police here didn't know about her death. It wasn't suspicious, so the Tampa cops had no reason to publish her picture on any of the law enforcement databases."

"I never knew her to be that heavy of a drinker," MonicaBelle said, "but then again, I didn't know her all that well."

"Victor," Darlene said, her voice strained, "I need to

make a call. I'll be in my booth. I'll be right back, la-dies. This would be a good time to have the waiter bring your food."

Back at her booth, she retrieved the cell phone Dou-ble M had given her, accessed the preentered contact number, and then pressed Send.

Double M answered on the second ring. "You found her?" he asked excitedly.

"She's dead," Darlene said softly, close to tears over the hardness of the world for so many like Sylvia Winger. "We may be at a dead end, ourselves. My hus-band has forbidden me to discuss the Russ Evans case with him or even to mention his name. I believe you when you say the risk involved if we can't get Russ Evans back to work is substantial, but without the girl's testimony, there's nothing I can do to help."

"That's not entirely true," Double M said. "I think I have another idea."

CHAPTER 34

Cap pulled off the road and onto the gravel shoulder about a mile from the Kings Ridge police station. The heavy sense of loss among them had taken over. George, who had done a remarkable job of maintaining his composure, stumbled out of the car, dropped to his knees, and pounded the ground, sobbing. Then he vomited. Afterwards, he washed out his mouth from a bottle of water that Lou had accepted from William Chester, and cried some more.

"They shot him," he sobbed. "They fuckin' shot him, and now Notso's gone forever."

Lou crouched down and set a comforting hand on the young man's shoulder. Then he helped him back to the Prizm.

"We don't know for sure that he's gone," Lou said. "Maybe they took him somewhere. He could be a prisoner—a hostage."

"Who's they?" George shouted.

"Well, if you believe Chester, it's somebody who doesn't work for him."

"Yeah, well, I don't believe Chester at all," George said. "That guy's a liar. He wouldn't last five minutes on the street without all that money to protect him. People would see through him in a second."

Daybreak was approaching. Scudding clouds concealed the bright moonlight. Only the drone of night-time insects broke the otherwise heavy silence.

Lou thought about his own family. He and Graham were not that close—certainly not the kind of friends George and his cousin Notso were. He wondered how he would react if Graham had violently died. He would certainly demand answers and would likely stop at nothing to get them. Lou and George might have come from different worlds, but for them at least, the language of family was a constant.

Headlights from an approaching car illuminated the roadway behind them. Reflexively, the three of them dropped down beside the Prizm. Lou tensed while Cap reached for a rock to use as weapon. The car rumbled past them without slowing. Lou felt his tension ease. He took out his smartphone and went straight to Google.

"Wish you didn't turn that gun over to Chief Stone," Cap said to George, dropping the rock.

"He asked for it and he's a friggin' cop. What in the hell was I supposed to do?"

"You did right. Sorry, pal. I'm a little short on sleep."

"When did Stone want us back here?" Cap asked Lou.

"He said eight. Do you guys want to go home and shower, then come back?"

"That's only a few hours from now," Cap said,

checking his watch. "I can call someone to open Stick and Move. What do you say we go back to those fields and do some more searching on our own."

"I'm in," Lou said, stifling a yawn. "I don't have to be at the ER until tomorrow.

"What are you looking up?"

"Corn."

"Learning anything?"

"Maybe. Back at the house you asked Chester about the number of ears on a stalk. It says here one or two—three at the very most. But I can't find anyplace that says four or five, and look, there's a five right there."

"They look like torpedoes," Cap said.

Lou broke off an ear from the top of a stalk, stripped it, and snapped it in two at the center. Then he started counting kernels.

"This is incredible," he said. "It says in this article here that because of the way an ear develops, there are always an even number of rows of kernels—usually fourteen or sixteen. This one has twenty-four. Multiply the number of rows by the number of kernels per row, and you get how much corn there is per ear. This article says between four hundred and six hundred, depending on whether the ear has fourteen or sixteen rows. Well, this monster has about fourteen hundred."

"Plus all those extra ears per stalk," Cap said.

"Exactly. That's a powerful lot of corn."

"It's more than that," George said. "It's Frankencorn."

"What?"

"Frankencorn. I did a paper on the genetic modifications in the fishing industry, and they used the term

Frankenfish to describe these genetically engineered humongous salmon."

"So that's what you think these ears are?"

George snapped off an ear, peeled the leaves, and held it up, turning it from one side to another. "That's it, exactly," he said. "I'm sayin' it's Frankencorn. Freaky corn. I'm sayin' it ain't natural. GMO, baby. Genetically modified organism." George flipped the ear aside disdainfully.

Lou went back to his smartphone. "It says GMO is pretty common now in the corn business. In fact, it's the rule more than the exception, but mostly because the ears have engineered resistance to the pesticides that are sprayed on them. Same for most agricultural plants. Whatever it is, it certainly seems as if this Frankencorn isn't the result of some superfertilizer like Chester claims."

"But if GMO is so common," George asked, "why would Chester lie about it?"

"That's what I'm asking myself," Lou said. "Why would he lie?"

CHAPTER 35

Sebastian Bachmeier donned a pair of safety glasses, then released the top button of his meticulously pressed lab coat. His unshaven face was sunken from lack of sleep, but his ice blue eyes sparked with excitement. Though he was a strapping German, standing six-foot-three or -four, Sebastian looked pocket sized when compared to the massive array of scientific equipment crammed inside his laboratory.

He was standing in front of a long conveyor belt that at first glance appeared to be painted gold. But a closer inspection would show it to be covered with kernels of corn. The belt zigzagged like an amusement park ride throughout the enclosure. When Sebastian spoke, his deep, accented voice reverberated off the steel walls of the underground facility like the cries of a lost spelunker.

"This is experiment number seven-thirty-eight in our efforts to create an effective biolistic delivery mechanism to transfect gold particles coated with the DNA

plasmid we have code-named MB45R directly into the
corn seed. This represents the final set of experiments
before certifying the process we have dubbed RAP-
TURE for commercial readiness. Though the outcome
of RAPTURE will obviate the time-consuming and
resource-intensive sexual process for creating hybrid
corn seed, rest assured, this transformative technology
cannot be extended to human reproduction."

Sebastian chuckled at his own humor. His giddy
mood resulted from years of seventy-hour workweeks
that were about to pay off to the tune of a multibillion-
dollar technologic breakthrough. Sebastian paused here,
mesmerized by the significance of the moment.

"Soon, farmers the world over will be able to custom-
order corn seed with the unmatched yield potential
of our TruGrow genetics. I am now going to demonstrate the process used to make the TruGrow corn
seed. This technique not only delivers the holy grail
mark of three hundred bushels per acre, but also dramatically speeds up the time to market by using actual
kernels instead of the widely accepted tissue-culture
process."

Sebastian approached a gleaming stainless steel apparatus suspended directly above a section of the conveyor belt. A long bazooka-like tube extended downward
from the apparatus, its muzzle about an inch above the
corn kernels.

"I have increased the PSI of the helium powering
our gene gun, ensuring low transfection efficiency to
obtain the optimum number of transfected neurons in

the kernel's targeted cells. To save time, I have preloaded the gun with pellets coated with a mix of positively charged gold particles and the MB45R DNA plasmid. In ten minutes' time, the gun's self-loading mechanism will transfect enough corn seed to plant a thousand acres. It would take six months to replicate this process using hybrid corn and tissue cultures, with substantially lower yield."

Sebastian reached for a tablet PC that was secured to a concrete support post with several strips of Velcro. As he was tapping on the computer's display, a series of machines instantly thrummed to life. The conveyor belt groaned and shook as the roller mechanisms became engaged. The corn needed to travel fifteen feet before the first batch could be blasted by the gene gun's massive barrel.

Sebastian put on his protective earphones, anticipating the loud boom to come. The conveyor belt stopped in the expected location.

However, the gun failed to fire.

Seated feet up on his desk, across from his built-in forty-eight-inch television, Edwin Chester watched the informational video, made three months before, for perhaps the twentieth time. Each time, his research assistant behaved as stupidly as the last. Edwin held his thumb on the button of the DVD remote and considered shutting off what he knew was to follow.

Sebastian removed his earphones and rubbed his chin, perplexed. "Hmmmm," he said as he ruminated on the problem. He sauntered over to the gene gun, where he inspected the barrel in search of the malfunction.

Stop! Edwin urged silently. *For God's sake, you stupid bastard, stop.*

The scene moved on with the inexorableness of a glacier.

Sebastian could not discern the nature of the problem from an upright position, so he knelt on the concrete floor. Using a penlight, he peered into the dark aperture.

Power down. Jesus, Sebastian, cut off the fucking helium, and power down.

Sebastian turned toward the camera and smiled. "The contact points in the firing mechanism are off by a millimeter or so," he said. "I should have it fixed in no time."

Sebastian pulled down on a lever, which raised the barrel of the gun two feet. The repositioning allowed him access to the gun barrel's internal mechanics.

Corn seed scattered onto the floor as Sebastian wriggled himself into a supine position on the conveyor belt. Then he reached one hand into the gun barrel and began to fiddle with the connection until there was a satisfying click.

"You stupid bastard," Edwin said out loud. "You know better than to do this."

As always, there was nothing he could do.

Sebastian again used his penlight to peer into the muzzle. A thin smile creased the corners of his mouth.

Success.

A second passed.

Edwin cringed and sank farther down in his chair.

His eyes refused to close.

The deafening pop from the huge gene gun seemed louder every time—like the backfiring of an eighteen-wheeler. The sound was followed immediately by a faint discharge of smoke from the barrel.

Sebastian cried out and rolled off the conveyor belt in obvious agony, clutching his face. Blood instantly seeped out from between his fingers and spewed through multiple punctures in his neck. He lay on his back on the corn kernels, his body jerking spasmodically as jets of scarlet sprayed the equipment and soaked the floor beneath him. Then he lowered his hands and pressed futilely against the skin over his carotid arteries as if knowing that was where the wounds were mortal. The thousands of gold pellets embedded in his face were like an obscene Seurat painting.

Shrieking in pain, Sebastian began picking at the pieces of searingly hot gold microshot. The pellets, used for inserting the DNA plasmid into the kernels, were cooking him alive. Blood continued spurting from his neck while his gold-pockmarked face smoked from the embedded metal.

He writhed on the floor, screaming and pleading for help, gurgling on blood that had seeped inside his mouth and down his throat.

The handsome German, an obsessive weight lifter, was already a corpse whose head and neck were virtually the same golden color as the corn surrounding him.

Edwin snapped off the video playback. Sebastian's gruesome remains, for a moment frozen on the screen, faded into black.

He had seen enough of the scientist's bizarre death—especially now that he had the first inklings of an explanation for the man's behavior—an explanation provided unknowingly by Dr. Lou Welcome.

CHAPTER 36

Lou and the others spent an endless day searching for Notso in the cornfields. The dogs Stone had brought in barked excitedly a couple of times, but then quickly fell silent.

"Rabbits," their handler said.

After three hours, George's spirit was broken. His plea for a chopper was brushed off as being fruitless with the corn being as dense as it was. He continued going through the motions of a search, scuffing through the tall stalks and grumbling about Frankencorn. But it was clear he was spent, and in great despair about having to report his cousin's probable death to his aunt.

Not unexpectedly, Cap was a giant, forging ahead tirelessly over ground they knew they had covered before. Lou found himself wondering how different the man's life would have been had he simply been allowed to live it. Still, over the years, the two of them had been to countless AA and NA meetings together, and not once had he heard Cap complain about his lot.

A power of example he was called by most of those who knew him.

"We're not done looking," Stone said to the trio when they got back to the dirt road where their vehicles were parked. "But the dogs are beat. We'll call in the staties and resume searching in the morning."

"What the fuck for?" George muttered. "Notso's dead, and you know it."

"We're still viewing this as a search-and-rescue mission, son," Stone said in his soothing drawl. "If your friend is wounded and somewhere out in this cornfield, we'll find him. I promise you, we'll find him."

Cap could no longer hold back his irritation. "And what about the guys who tried to kill us?" he snapped. "You still viewing this as a crime scene for that as well?"

Stone showed no outward signs of losing his cool. "This whole investigation is going to take some time," he said. "You've got to give us a chance to do our jobs."

None of the three from D.C. bothered to respond. Instead, they climbed into the Prizm and headed east, back to the District.

Cap dropped Lou off at home only after getting assurances that he would call at the first hint of a return engagement from the muscle who had started it all.

Lou trudged up the staircase to his apartment, then fumbled to unlock his door. Between extended shifts on his feet in the ER, and sessions at the gym, he was in better than decent shape. This fatigue, he knew, was something else—a combination of frustration, bewilderment, and anger, mixed with a good-sized dose of fear—fear not so much for himself as for Emily, Renee, and Steve, as well as his father and Graham.

It was hard to believe the thugs who had followed him home and later ambushed the four of them were through with him. It was also hard to believe they would stop at anything to achieve whatever it was they were being paid to do.

One of the most interesting things to come of all that had happened were Lou's thoughts of his brother. For reasons that were never completely clear, probably Graham's shame over Lou's addiction and months in rehab, the two of them had drifted apart over the years since Graham entered college, and Lou's life began its gradual deterioration. What Graham would never know, Lou hoped, was that the two occurrences were connected.

Soon before Graham was to enter Georgetown, their father buried himself beneath yet another financial avalanche—this one an absolute crusher that left the man virtually penniless and without hope of recovery. Unwilling to deprive his second son of a college education, Dennis had turned to Lou, who was already generating a salary as a resident. Dennis assumed, without blinking, that Lou could and would help him out. After all, he contended, he had been there as much as he could when it was Lou's college and med school tuition at stake. Surely Graham, the stronger student of the two, deserved nothing less.

In the beginning, Lou managed, and Graham excelled. Then marriage and Emily forced Lou to add more moonlighting shifts until sleep became a major problem. Enter the friendly, neighborhood amphetamine dealer, and still more hours of work. It was something like the so-called death spiral that figure skating pairs performed—the woman stretched out almost completely supine, being spun faster and faster by her partner, and closer and closer to the unyielding surface of the ice.

By the time the world and the DEA came crashing in around Lou, Graham had his MBA and was excelling as a businessman, and the distance between the two brothers could be measured in light-years.

The first thing Lou did after a walk-through of his apartment, and a glance into his closets, was to check his e-mail, thinking that he might have received something from Filstrup at the PWO. Nothing. Lou leaned back and stared at the ceiling, consumed by a heavy melancholy. He was disconnected from the thing in life outside of his family that meant the most to him—being able to help sick docs who, more often than not, had very few people, if anyone, on their side. Now, for the second time in his life, he was one of them.

Working through the stack of spam and e-mail from clients who had chosen to ignore his status at the PWO further darkened Lou's mood. In fact, the only thought that appealed in the least was flopping facedown on his pillow and lying there until sleep brought him some relief. It was then he realized that there was another unread e-mail lost in the remaining spam—this one marked URGENT. The subject line read: *Regarding Events in Kings Ridge*.

Lou's mouth went dry.

Dr. Lou Welcome:

For reasons that cannot be revealed, I have become aware of your investigation into the peculiar behaviors exhibited by some residents of Kings Ridge, Virginia. Like yourself, I believe these odd incidents may be connected. Your help is required to prevent what may be a looming disaster.

At precisely ten o'clock on the date of this message, your apartment door buzzer will ring. When it does, you are to go downstairs, where you will find a waiting car and driver. You must then do as he asks. Guaranteed, you will not be harmed. But if you want answers to your questions, then you will comply with this request.

Do not try to determine the source of this message. I have taken the necessary precautions to safeguard my anonymity.

If you are willing to do as I request, please respond to this e-mail with the word WILCO in the message body.

Please, you must help.

The message was unsigned. Lou knew that *WILCO* was a military term meaning, "will comply," but that did not mean the message sender was government. He looked up the Web site, anonymousspeech.com, from which the e-mail had been sent. According to the site, which Emily would probably understand better than he did, the service provided the message sender with guaranteed anonymity by constantly moving its Web servers, which were located outside the United States, to different countries, while ignoring all government requests for subscriber information.

Lou felt more curious than apprehensive. A trap of some sort seemed possible, but if so, it was a clumsy one.

You will not be harmed.

At least whoever had written him admitted knowing that there had been trouble.

The people who had followed him before the nightmare in Kings Ridge knew his name and where he lived. They were resourceful and violent. If they were set on harming him, warning him to the contrary made little sense.

No, Lou concluded as he sent the WILCO message and then headed off to shower, this was not a trap.

At 9:15 he toweled off and changed into comfortable jeans and a tan canvas L.L. Bean polo shirt. Then he folded some turkey, sliced tomato, and horseradish mustard in a wrap and finished it with a handful of chips, a can of Diet Coke, and a Kosher dill. At 9:40 he called Emily.

He wanted her to hear his voice as much as he needed to hear hers.

Their conversation was nothing out of the ordinary for them—school, weekend plans, and life at home. It pleased him to learn that the tension with Steve had lessened, and that a conversation with him, one on one, had resulted in his agreeing to allow her to use her computer in her room.

"I'm really proud of the way you're handling this, honey," he said.

"Thanks. I was a little surprised when he caved in. It turns out he was just trying to help Mom, who was worried about a report from Ms. Sternweiss that I wasn't checking over my math homework."

"But you're doing better at it?"

"Starting to."

"That's great, Em. Just great."

"Dad?"

"Yeah?"

"Are you okay?"

Lou nearly stumbled on his reply. "Of course I am. Why would you ask?"

"Nothing. Just a weird little chill I had."

"Well, I'm fine. Everything's fine. I love you, honey."

"I know. I love you, too, Daddy."

"You be good to your mom. Okay?"

"I will. . . . You sure you're all right?"

"Tired, but otherwise fine and ready for a Monopoly rematch. I'll see you Saturday, okay?"

There was another missed beat from Emily's end, then, "Okay, Daddy. Bye."

Lou set the phone back in its cradle and braced his arms against the end table. His knees were putty, and the fullness in his chest felt like a balloon.

What in hell have I gotten myself into? he asked once, then again.

He was still leaning against the end table when his apartment buzzer startled him. He glanced at his Timex, a Father's Day gift from Emily.

Ten o'clock on the nose.

Lou considered grabbing a kitchen knife, but decided against it.

The e-mail made him believe that whoever was waiting for him downstairs wanted his help—for what, exactly, he'd find out soon. Still not completely trusting his knees, Lou held on to the railing on the way downstairs. *Breakthrough or danger?* Despite having showered, he was starting to sweat. His body was pulsating with a nervous energy.

You're going to see your daughter on Saturday, he said to himself. *You're going to be fine.*

At the foot of the stairs, Lou peered out through the front door's sidelight window at a large sedan—possibly a town car. A man, graying hair, sharp looking in a dark blazer, tie, and khaki pants, waited beneath the porch bulb. Lou opened the door to accompany him to the car, but the visitor stepped inside the tiny foyer. Lou judged him to be a light-heavyweight, and in shape. Still, his eyes were kind, and Lou felt no threat.

"Dr. Welcome?"

"That's right."

"Turn around, please, and put your hands on the wall. I've got to frisk you."

No introduction, and Lou didn't ask for one. This was a driver—professional muscle. And judging by his not-overwhelming size, a tough one at that.

William Chester, Lou thought. The bodyguard had to be working for the seed magnate.

Lou spread his legs and set his palms on the wall, grateful that he had left the knife in the kitchen. When the driver finished, he escorted Lou down the outside stairs to the town car, idling by the curb. The car's tinted rear window slid down as they approached. Lou was surprised to see a striking, well-groomed woman sitting alone in the backseat. She looked out at him, smiled thinly, and nodded.

Lou caught his breath as recognition took hold.

He had seen Darlene Mallory on television, in the papers, and in magazines, but this was the first time he had seen her in person. His initial impression was that none of the photos or video footage had done her even remote justice.

CHAPTER 37

Darlene opened the car door and slid over halfway to make room.

Lou stayed where he was, scanning the street.

"Is there a problem?" she asked.

"That depends."

"On?"

"On whether there are any thick-waisted, bad-tempered, neckless men watching us, and whether your driver can handle himself the way I think he can."

"Victor is Secret Service and very protective. He shoots anyone who even looks at me cross-eyed, then he asks questions later."

"Good thing I can't cross my eyes," Lou said through the window. "Nice to meet you, Victor."

"And you, Doctor. Not to worry about the other thing. I have an agent at the end of the street covering our back. Besides, I hear you're a decent boxer."

"Only when the other guy isn't hitting back."

Lou climbed in next to the First Lady.

"I've been looking forward to meeting you, Dr. Welcome," Darlene said.

Lou's throat went dry as he struggled to find his voice. In the ER, he knew he was sometimes known as Dr. Cool, for the way he kept it together even in the worst emergencies. In fact, over the years, he had treated a number of prominent politicians and even a couple of well-known celebrities without losing his objectivity, except once when he asked for a photo signed to Emily from the previous year's winner of *American Idol*. But in the presence of this woman, he felt extremely unsettled.

"Please call me Lou," he managed. "I've found that being called doctor often carries with it heightened expectations."

"I've noticed the same thing," she said, her grip on his hand warm and confident. "Darlene works fine for me."

"That's right, you're a doc. Do you miss it?"

"Only every day."

"I'm not surprised. Even after all these years and a gazillion patients, I still love it each time I step into the hospital. It's the one place in the universe where I actually feel like I know what I'm doing."

Her smile canceled out his self-consciousness. "Same here," she said. "My office was my sanctuary. I still think I could tell you something special about every single one of my patients. Pardon me for asking, but are you okay? You look a little pale. Sorry if I'm out of place, but once a doctor, always a doctor."

"And a perceptive one, at that. You're the second

woman who asked me that question in the last hour.
My thirteen-year-old daughter, Emily the Sorceress, di-
agnosed me over the phone as not being my usual bub-
bly, positive self. Forgive me . . . Darlene. I didn't tell
Em, but just a day ago, I was being chased through a
cornfield by some professional killers who, when they
weren't shooting at me, were trying to run me down
with a combine harvester."

"Ouch! As the daughter of a wheat farmer, I know
those harvesters. Thank goodness they're not too ma-
neuverable."

"Actually, I was six-foot-nine before this one got
me."

"Well, no wonder you look a little peaked."

Lou loved her laugh.

"Under normal circumstances, I'm a certified, dues-
paying nonsleeper," he said, "but there's *no sleep* and
there's running for your life from people who want to
shoot you or chop you up *no sleep.* I'll look less chalky
soon."

"I'm working on a pretty endless day, myself. I
promise we won't be long, but I want to hear about
everything."

No, no, take as long as you like, Lou found his inner
voice saying. *Take all night.*

"Don't worry about that," he said. "I'm tough."

"My daughter, Lisa, is locked into me like a Patriot
missile, just like Emily is to you. She has a tougher
time getting a read on her father, but as you might have
discerned if you're at all political, not many people do,
if any."

Darlene's expression was enigmatic, and Lou wondered if the statement was calculated or had just slipped out. He suspected it was spontaneous. This was not a woman who measured her words.

"I vote," he said. "Does that count as being political?"

"It counts more than everything else put together. Good answer. Hey, Victor, this guy comes as advertised. I like him. Let's go to Plan B."

"You got it."

Keyed by Victor, the window between the front and backseats glided shut. As the Lincoln eased away from the curb, Lou turned to look behind them, but never made it past Darlene. He was stunned to realize that the First Lady was staring at him as well.

She made no attempt to look away.

He could not remember ever being so immediately attracted to a woman who was not Renee, and warned himself to remember he was compromised by stress and exhaustion, and she was more than compromised by the obvious.

He felt a slight burning in his cheeks and suspected he no longer looked pale.

Darlene spoke first. "Do you need anything to drink?" she asked. "Water? Soda?"

"I'm fine, thanks."

He wondered if she knew that he didn't drink alcohol. He could see the car had a small well-stocked bar. She could have offered him a cocktail. Victor knew about his boxing. Had she been studying up on other aspects of his life? She said he came as advertised. They had to have done some homework on him.

"Before we begin," she said, her directness not at all surprising, "you should know, if you don't already, that my chief of staff and I did a little research on you when I knew we two might meet. Nothing too elaborate—mostly a little background checking, some phone calls, and Google and Yahoo, plus a dab of LexisNexis."

"You wouldn't be the first. What did you learn?"

"Let's see. From several sources, we learned that you don't get along all that well with the head of the Physician Wellness Office. We also learned that the poor doctor who went crazy in Virginia was back at work because you felt he was ready."

"That about summarizes it. Anything else?"

"From Google, I learned that you dug yourself out of a hell of a hole about nine years ago, and have helped a lot of other troubled doctors over the years since then. From Google Images, I learned that you don't photograph well and that your eyes are your best feature."

"My dentist, Dr. Moskowitz, would say it was my teeth, except he worries that I grind when smart, terrific-looking women say nice things to me."

"Thanks. Are you grinding now?"

"Down to the nubs."

That smile.

"I won't say stuff like that again, Lou," she said. "Sorry. I can be a little flip and flirty at times, and I have a tendency I'm not proud of to fish for compliments."

"Not to worry, I have dental insurance. So . . . you checked me out, you e-mailed me, I'm here. What can I do for you?"

"Well, first of all, I wasn't the one who e-mailed you."

"No?"

"It was a man my chief of staff, Kim Hajjar, and I call Double M. It's short for *mystery man*."

"And who is your mysterious Double M?" Lou asked. "And more important, what's his connection to Kings Ridge, Virginia?"

"Believe it or not, I don't know. Our guy is either extremely cautious or absolutely paranoid. He has made it clear to me that his life may be in danger if his identity becomes known. He contacted me because of my friendship with Russell Evans—"

"The secretary of agriculture?"

"Former. He and I played in the Kansas dirt together when we were children. It was through me that he became friends with Martin. I'm sure you heard about the scandal involving him and a young woman, and his subsequent resignation."

"Of course. I'm glad to hear that he's not guilty, but I tend not to judge people, so I hadn't formed any opinion."

"That doesn't surprise me. Double M wants me to convince my husband to reinstate Russ and get him back to work. He said the secretary was framed because of certain of his policies, but he didn't say which ones."

"Do you have any thoughts about that? I had heard that the FDA and the Department of Agriculture were at war over lots of things."

"Because the food manufacturers don't have to tell people precisely what goes into the food they're eating. For example, the way the current legislation is set up, most products that are GMOs are exempt from the label saying they're a genetically modified product. Their argument is that foods developed using new genetic methods don't differ from the real-deal foods in any meaningful way. For instance, cows that are fed on GMO grain—are they GMO cows or not? The problem is that the government hasn't made it clear who is in charge of what."

"Go on."

"I've recently been given new information from Double M. It's that information I've come here to discuss with you."

"Do you trust him?"

Darlene sighed. "Alas, my best quality and worst shortcoming are the same. I trust everyone—at least until they've given me serious reason not to."

"In that case, I can't think of a worse game for you to be in than politics," Lou said.

"Amen to that. But don't forget, I didn't choose politics. I chose Martin."

Lucky Martin. The thought popped uninvited into Lou's head, and began to nest.

"I voted for your husband," Lou said, "partly because I have the same problem you do with trust, and I read more about you as a doc than I did about him as a politician."

"Well, then, you'll want to listen to this."

Victor continued driving as Darlene handed Lou an

envelope containing the materials Double M had compiled regarding the call girl he knew only as Margo. Using a set of headphones Darlene provided, Lou listened to the audio of the girl prepping to entrap Russell Evans and being obliquely threatened should she fail to perform up to expectations.

"The man's voice, whoever it is, is digitally altered," Lou said, pulling the headphones away as if they were burning his ears. "Whoever your Double M is, he is an expert in electronics or has one on his payroll."

For a time, they rode on in silence.

"Tough stuff," Darlene said finally.

"She sounds awfully young. I can't help thinking about Emily."

"Same with me and Lisa when I first heard it."

"Do you know what's become of this girl?"

Darlene's expression grew strained. "Supposedly accidental drowning while staying with her mother in Florida. Lots of alcohol in her system."

"Damn."

Victor cruised past American University, then down Arizona Avenue, and finally to a parking spot just off the Palisades Playground.

"You okay?" she asked.

"A little shaken, but I'm anxious to hear how this all connects with Kings Ridge."

"In that case, let's walk a bit."

They stepped out of the car into heavy, damp air and headed down a narrow, paved bike trail, deserted this time of night. Lights from the city reflected off the rippling water of the Potomac. Victor followed a good distance behind.

"I took Emily here when she was younger," Lou said.

"I like to ride here when I have time."

"With the president?"

"That would happen only if it would help him in the polls. Plan B was for Victor to come here unless I gave him a signal that I wasn't interested in talking to you."

"Let's hear it for Plan B," Lou said.

CHAPTER 38

"Martin absolutely deplores Russell Evans for humiliating him at a time when the polls have him at an all-time low. Russ's father was a farmer like my dad, but Russ got a master's degree and ended up going into academics. I always felt close to him. He and I are mutually interested in kids' nutrition. Martin has forbidden me even to mention his name."

"That's got to be hard," Lou said.

Walking slowly through the dense night, the two physicians shared information along with bits about each other's lives. Their conversation was easy and animated except for Lou's account of the almost-certain death of Anthony Brite, which was obviously painful for her to hear. After a while, it was as if he and Darlene Mallory had been longtime friends. Still, the tension that had brought them together was never far from the surface.

Lou sensed another feeling building inside him as well—the excitement of merely being close to her.

"Assuming those killers are connected with Russ

Evans and Double M," she said, "Anthony's death only underscores the importance of our figuring out what's going on."

According to Double M, she went on, Gretchen Rose, whose name the president had submitted to Congress as Evans's successor, had strong views on states' rights and limitation of federal involvement in setting agriculture policy. Evans was close to her polar opposite.

"And that horrible tape?" Lou asked.

"Martin is quite the skeptic, and is already extremely prejudiced against Russ. I needed to find the girl on that recording to convince him that someone was manipulating his administration. Sadly, that's not going to happen now. But Double M has another plan—something that he's asked me to make happen. That's where you come in."

"Tell me."

Darlene tucked her hands into the pockets of her Windbreaker. "It's all about corn," she said.

"That's about as far as I had gotten in Kings Ridge," Lou replied, "before the well ran dry. I feel like the six blind men each trying to describe an elephant."

He described the findings that led him, Cap, and George to refer to William Chester's crop as Frankencorn.

"Double M has never mentioned anything about this to me until today," Darlene said, "but he called and said that rather than try to get Russ Evans reinstated when the president won't even allow his name to be spoken, I should concentrate on stopping a shipment of corn that's loaded on a cargo train scheduled to head west. I don't know who supplied this corn, or precisely where it's going or when, but I've been told that this shipment must be stopped."

"Darlene," Lou said, "is there any way, any way at all, that you can tell me something about this man that would help to figure out who he is? It may be very important."

Darlene sighed deeply. "I've met him, but it was pretty dark, and he had on glasses with heavy black frames and a baseball cap—a Nationals cap, I think. He spoke to me using an electrolarynx, even though there was nothing that I could see wrong with his neck."

"Probably just distorting his voice," Lou said. "Go on, please."

"Well, he's a big man—probably taller than you."

"I'm almost six-one when I don't slouch."

"Okay, six-one and a little on the husky side. He had a full beard, but I thought it might be fake. I promised I wouldn't push him to tell me who he was. He said he would be in great danger if his identity became known."

"I won't ask again. He wants the corn shipment stopped by the president? What could be wrong with it?"

"I don't know," Darlene said. "According to Double M, you might have the answer to that."

"Me? I don't know anything about any shipments."

"No, but Double M says you know a lot about the residents of Kings Ridge exhibiting very strange behavior. Apparently he believes there's a connection."

Lou flipped through the people he had spoken to since Meacham's killing spree, focusing on those who were above average height and husky—Gilbert Stone, employees at DeLand Regional, members of the police department, farmers he had met at the Grange Hall— where he also posted a notice asking for any information surrounding shootings in the Chester Enterprises fields, or any stories of severe lapses in reason or judgment. Then there were the politicians he had yet to meet, and others who might have feelings pro or con regarding Russell Evans. The list was already daunting. In fact, Lou realized, Double M could easily be an actor hired by Russ Evans, and the tape could be bogus.

Lou stopped as though he had just walked into a wall. "Hey, what if it's the corn itself?" he asked.

"The corn?"

"The Frankencorn. What if it's somehow toxic for people?"

"Meaning that this shipment of corn and John Meacham are connected?"

"Well, I didn't think the killings had anything to do with corn until just now," Lou said. "But I can see the possibility." Then he related what he had observed about the corn—the unusual size and growth. "When we spoke with William Chester, he tried to convince us that the corn was just the by-product of a new type of fertilizer Chester Enterprises is patenting."

"Genetically modified organism," Darlene whispered. "So, do you think that Double M works for William Chester?"

"I don't know," Lou said. "There could be hundreds of corn shipments headed west."

"Even if we narrow it down to a specific company, Double M is concerned about only one specific cargo train filled with corn."

"So where does that leave us?" Lou asked. He realized he was intentionally avoiding too much eye contact with the woman, fearing she would feel, correctly, that he was staring.

"My instructions were to get you and Martin together. I guess Double M wants you to tell Martin what you've just told me."

"Why? If Double M's not going to tell us which train we've got to stop, what good will that do?"

"Maybe he'll give us that information after you talk to Martin," Darlene offered.

"Maybe. From what you've told me about your husband, I don't think he's going to do anything without demanding to know who Double M is."

"If that's the case, I will tell Martin what I know. I certainly understand there may be lives at stake, but I can't begin to tell you the measures this man has taken to keep his identity a secret. Martin's out of town right now. There's no way I can get you a meeting with him until he gets back. Lou, if it is the corn, how do you think it's affecting people?"

Lou shook his head. "I just don't feel like I know enough, unless . . ."

"Go on, please."

"From what we could tell, there are hundreds, probably thousands of acres of that GMO corn growing in Kings Ridge."

"And?"

"And what if the problem is something airborne," he said.

"Pollen?"

"Sure," Lou said, "pollen! The tassels on the ears produce pollen that gets dispersed by the wind."

"Airborne! That's how people could be getting exposed. They could be inhaling the pollen and be allergic to it."

"That would certainly explain some things I haven't been able to understand."

"Explain what things?" Darlene asked.

"The termites."

Lou glanced back to ensure that his sudden enthusiasm hadn't brought Victor any closer.

"Termites?" Darlene echoed. "What on earth do—?"

Lou put one foot up on a bench, leaned on his knee, and recounted the astounding setup at Joey Alderson's small apartment, and the piranha-like efficiency with which his termites had totally dispatched a mouse.

Darlene listened wide-eyed, occasionally brushing her hands down the length of her arms, as though the termites Lou was describing were crawling there.

As he expected, Darlene gleaned the significance of the tale immediately. "You think this airborne toxin causes mutation in the insects?" Darlene asked.

"I think along with a number of other questions, it's one worth answering."

"And how do you propose to go about doing that?"

"Dr. Oliver Humphries," Lou said.

"Who?"

"One of the world's leading experts on termites. My

smartphone and I are sort of joined at the hip. I found him while I was Googling 'flesh-eating termites' after my visit to Joey's. I certainly hadn't connected the little beasties to corn, but I was running out of paths to follow in investigating John Meacham's rampage."

"So you had already planned to speak with this bug man about these termites?"

"Yes. I have an appointment with him the day after tomorrow. Now I have more questions to ask him, such as whether some sort of airborne mutagen might be at work."

"And if perhaps the effect on people is different from that on the termites, but caused by the pollen nonetheless," she said with new excitement. "Where is he based?"

"He teaches entomology at Temple University in Philly."

Darlene turned and beckoned Victor over. An exchange Lou could not hear followed, with Victor doing a lot of head nodding and Darlene a lot of talking. Victor ended the conversation with another quick nod, then retreated back to where he was. Darlene returned to Lou's side.

"So," Lou said, "did you tell him I was delusional and needed to be closely watched?"

Darlene smiled. "No, I don't think you're delusional at all. What I told Victor was to make arrangements."

"Arrangements for what?"

"I've decided that we're going to speak with your Dr. Humphries together."

CHAPTER 39

Roberta Jennings was through being fat.

For the third time this week, she had overeaten at Millie's and vomited up much of her meal. It was her ninth or tenth unintentional purge for the month. Even that would not have been so bad if she had just dropped a pound. One lousy pound. Instead, though, she had gained three.

It's time for a change.

Roberta had survived a lifetime of obesity by internalizing her struggles. She endured endless taunts during her school years and later had learned to ignore the snickering at the office and whispers at restaurants. Her self-esteem was all but gone by the time she finished middle school. She chose the persona of a giggly, cheery friend to all. But in truth, the horrible ache inside her never abated. If not for meeting and marrying Terry, there was no telling what she might have done.

Now, with him gone, even the simple joys of life were lost to her. Magazines she'd once loved depressed her. She detested those emaciated waifs called models, so thin, they'd blow off the page in a strong wind. Still, though it sickened her even to inhale the aroma of fast food, or to gorge herself at Millie's, she could not stop.

This is it.

If Terry were alive, perhaps he'd have been an inspiration to cut back. Even though it never seemed to be a big deal to him, he always told her to mind her weight, which she had failed to do to the tune of thirty new pounds since his passing. Several reassuring friends convinced her that she suffered from an addiction, like an alcohol or drug problem. She appreciated their opinions because addiction meant disease, and disease meant her weight problem was not entirely her fault. But her plunges into Weight Watchers and Overeaters Anonymous were utter failures, as was the drawer of half-empty pill bottles from various TV infomercials.

And blaming her condition on bad genetics was like blaming her parents, whom she loved, and who weren't even alive to defend themselves. Making matters even worse, John Meacham, that sorry excuse for a doctor, had blown his top over *her* failure to lose weight. People who once were supportive and sympathetic to her now eyed her with contempt. She had actually gotten several notes—anonymous, of course, and simply left in her mailbox—blaming her for his death.

If you could have kept to your diet, those people would still have their lives, one had actually written.

She simply could not stand being overweight another day.

Liposuction was clearly the answer. Roberta had arrived at this decision after extensive research and before the insurance company arrived at theirs. By the time her request was denied by them, she wanted liposuction more than she wanted air. But fighting Terry's illness had taken all their savings, and the price tag of twelve to twenty thousand dollars was more than she could handle. She could sell all her figurines and still cover only a fraction of the cost. Then what? Sell all her furniture, too? Take out a third mortgage on the house?

Fortunately, there was another way.

She could quite literally cut out the fat without incurring any of the expense. She had found the answer on the Internet during her hours of research. Terry would have been so proud of her resourcefulness. He would never have approved of such an expenditure.

Never.

But free was a different story.

Roberta returned to the kitchen and the checklist she had meticulously put together. She then covered a portion of the linoleum floor with a faded bedsheet. She was not feeling the least bit nervous. The commitment to alter her life in dramatic fashion had replaced any fear and trepidation with euphoric waves of adrenaline.

After meticulously centering the sheet, she crossed over to the granite-topped island—the home improvement she and Terry had scrimped and saved for over five years ago. There, carefully laid out on a freshly laundered white towel, were long and short carving blades from her butcher block holder, and a gleaming X-Acto knife she had bought expressly for this procedure. Beside them were three of Terry's Percocets and a glass with three fingers of brandy. There was also a bottle of rubbing alcohol, a cigarette lighter, several ice packs, and a pile of gauze pads.

Smiling excitedly, she set the pills on her tongue and washed them down with the brandy.

This is it.

The knife she selected for starters had a thick and meaty blade. It was deeply curved. Her excited expression reflected off its shiny surface. She grabbed the sterilization kit, a lighter, and some rubbing alcohol.

"I'm going to be thin!" she sang, testing the sharpness of the huge knife against the pad of her thumb. The tremor usually present in her hands actually seemed less than usual. Still, she applied only the slightest pressure and opened a thin sliver that promptly began oozing blood.

"I'm gonna be the biggest loser. The biggest loser is what I'm gonna be. . . ."

Roberta sucked the blood from her thumb.

Li-po-suc-tion.

She sang the word in her mind as she admired herself again in the knife's gleaming blade.

The brandy and Percocets were kicking in faster than she had anticipated, and she realized she was having trouble controlling her tongue. Best to hurry.

She placed a kitchen chair on the bedsheet, grabbed a blue Rubbermaid bucket, and set it at the foot of the chair. "Be prepared for something of a mess," one set of Internet instructions had warned. A few towels and some gauze, and she was all set. On the towel beside the X-Acto knife were several threaded needles.

Ready.

Oh, I wish Terry could see me, Roberta lamented as she set a bath towel across her lap, unbuttoned her blouse, and pressed an ice pack against her belly to numb up the skin and constrict the blood vessels.

"Getting ready," Roberta announced, though her speech now was quite thick and slurred.

She sat down on the chair and picked up the knife.

"I can do this," she said, pressing the knife against her massive belly. "I can make it all go away."

The huge blade easily sliced through skin. It hurt—more than she expected it to, and she cried out at the pain. But then, just as quickly, it went away. Roberta pressed on.

Her eyes rolled back. She cried out again as she forced the blade through half a foot of saffron-colored fat. Blood began to spray out onto the towel, the floor, and into the blue bucket.

I'm getting thinner already, she thought.

She dug the knife in deeper, and began slicing away huge chunks of fatty tissue and dropping them to the floor and into the bucket. Her hands and arms were slimy with a shimmering mix of blood and grease. The terrible hurt accompanying each jab gave way to a dreamy light-headedness.

Barely looking down at what she was doing, Roberta widened the incision and continued carving away fist-fuls of fat. Her dizziness intensified. The floor around her chair was awash in the slick mix of blood and adipose tissue.

Terry Jennings, wait until you see me. I'm going to be so beautiful . . . so thin and so beautiful.

Her vision began to blur. Still, she could make out the massive incision, and the intestines that had now slid out onto the blood-soaked towel. She felt confused—lost and uncertain what she had done or why. The large knife clattered to the floor. That was the problem, she realized. She had forgotten to sterilize the knife.

Oh, Terry, what have I done? Roberta thought as the darkness enveloped her. *What have I done to my-self?*

Moaning, she lost her strength and tipped over with her chair.

Then, abruptly, her moaning stopped.

CHAPTER 40

Darlene instructed Victor to pull into a largely deserted area of Fairmount Park's verdant Belmont Plateau and asked that he keep as far away from the other parked cars as possible. Another Secret Service transport vehicle, part of her usual escort group, parked on the opposite side of the lot to avoid attracting unwanted attention.

Victor shut off the engine and opened the moonroof. "I'll wait outside," he said. "Keep an eye on things, check for photographers."

"Thank you, my friend," Darlene replied. "We won't be long."

It was the second time Victor had driven her and Lou Welcome to a park after peak hours. She knew it was the agent's job to protect her with his life, but she also knew that ultimately his responsibility—everyone's responsibility, for that matter, was to her husband. If he reported to the president on her growing friendship with Lou, and on their trip together outside of Washington, the tension that had been developing between her and Martin might well explode.

But she felt a connection with Lou, and wanted to get to know him better, and that was that. It said a lot for the status of her marriage that she had given precious little thought to asking Martin's permission for the trip. After all, he had made the decision to start his reelection campaign without discussing it with her.

With Victor gone, she and Lou spent a quiet couple of minutes gazing out the town car's bulletproof front windshield at the twinkling skyline of downtown Philadelphia, in the distance. She sighed deeply.

"Are you all right?" Lou asked.

Darlene nodded emphatically, but sensed she wasn't convincing. Good doctors, and Lou certainly seemed to be one of those, often possessed the ability to get more out of a facial expression than they could out of lab tests. Martin, though a lawyer, had a knack for reading faces as well. Lately, though, his concerns seemed more global than with any individual, including her and Lisa. Darlene knew she was enjoying Lou too much to try to be an enigma.

"I used to come here with Martin whenever we had a campaign stop in Philadelphia," she said. "I fell in love with the view. I think the Philadelphia skyline is one of the most beautiful anywhere."

"I'm glad you brought me to see it," Lou said. "You're right. It's spectacular."

"I probably shouldn't have done this," she said.

"Nonsense. We've got an hour to kill before our meeting with Humphries."

That's not what I meant, and you know it, she thought.

"It's silly, really," she said, "but I've never come to Philadelphia without stopping here. Martin and I would look out at the skyline and each make a wish."

"So it's a tradition."

"It started off as that, but it's morphed into more of a superstition—like a chain letter that warns you of a curse unless you continue it. If you don't wish upon the Philadelphia skyline, something bad is going to happen. Pass it on."

Lou laughed. What surprised her was not the warmth of his laugh so much as how much she enjoyed hearing it. She could barely believe it, but Dr. Darlene Mallory, caretaker of thousands of children over the years, First Lady of the United States, woman of the year in countless magazines around the globe, was feeling giddy—schoolgirl giddy.

"Well," he said, "I see this as a hell of a lot healthier superstition than coming up here to eat a Philly cheesesteak sandwich."

"Mmmmm, now me want cheesesteak sandwich," she said in the imitation of Grover from *Sesame Street* that her patients loved to hear her use.

She added Lou's grin to the things she liked about him, and tried to remember the last time she and Martin had sat alone together laughing at anything.

"So what did you wish for?" Lou asked.

"I can't tell you that," she said with indignation. "Have you not ever studied anything about the art of wishing?"

"The farthest I've gone was when I was in my second month of rehab, writing four pages of *Wishing for*

Dummies. I must have learned something from it, because after the third month, I got out."

"From what I have learned, a lot of people have benefited because you did."

She wondered what Lou would say if he knew she had wished that Martin could have his warmth and connection to people. There was something about him, a serenity and sense of place, that put her instantly at ease. If she were injured or ill in an ER, she decided, the best thing that could happen would be lying on a gurney and having him show up at her bedside. Maybe it was just the way a good doc made people feel. Whatever the explanation, spending time with Lou Welcome was reminding her of things that she and Martin had lost on their nonstop path to the White House.

"I keep promising Emily that I'll take her to see the Liberty Bell one of these days," Lou said.

Darlene smiled, grateful to be distracted from her thoughts. "Your daughter's never been?"

"No," he admitted, folding his lower lip down. "She's also got her heart set on running up the steps of the Philadelphia Museum of Art and doing the *Rocky* dance."

"Thirteen is such a great age," Darlene said wistfully.

She had been warned by friends early on that after Lisa hit first grade, the years would fly by instead of crawl. Now her baby was a busy college sophomore, moving ahead with her own life, and all Darlene had of those early years were photographs and memories.

"The divorce has made me miss time with Em," Lou said. "That's the hardest thing in my life."

"You said the divorce wasn't your idea. I would imagine there's some guilt roiling around that."

"Her mother's a really good egg, who just ran out of gas after a couple of self-destructive years on my part. She's married to a decent-enough guy now, and is as happy for my recovery as I am. Whatever guilt I still feel toward Em I make up for by allowing her to drink Diet Coke when we're together."

"The beverage industry loves my husband, but they sure don't like what I have to say about their products."

"Is it hard for you?" Lou asked, "the spotlight? . . . The constant scrutiny?"

Darlene tried to shrug off the question. "It's gets tiring," she confessed.

"I'll bet."

"We can't be normal. For starters, most couples can have a slight argument without making the front page of the tabloids. We can't risk a cross word or look outside of our bedroom. When we began this journey, Martin made me a promise. He said the responsibilities of the country wouldn't eclipse his responsibilities as a father and husband. I never questioned his resolve. But now, I've realized my own naivety."

"In what way?"

Darlene found herself liking the way Lou was looking at her—steady but relaxed eye contact, with no hidden agenda or preoccupying thoughts. She tried reminding herself that he had the advantage of not having to compartmentalize his life the way Martin did. But in the end, she felt unwilling to fight her attraction to the man.

"Before Martin took the oath of office," she said, "I read everything I could about being a First Lady. There's no provision in the Constitution for the president's wife. No formal job description, either."

"You were a doctor. It must have been hard for you to go from having a very clear set of guidelines to none at all. Maybe you could start doing some version of medical practice."

"Believe it or not, I never even considered that."

"Well, like you said, there's no job description for what you do."

A pleasant silence followed, which became prolonged enough to begin to feel edgy.

"Well, it's time," she said, clearing her throat and checking her Movado—a wedding present from Martin. "How about we go visit Dr. Humphries and see what he has to offer to untangle this conundrum."

"Great idea." Lou paused a beat. "Can you make another wish on the Philadelphia skyline?" he asked, eyes fixed ahead.

"Sure," Darlene said. "Nothing in the rules of wishing says I can't."

"Then how about just wishing that everything becomes clear . . . on every level."

CHAPTER 41

Lou had imagined Dr. Oliver Humphries would be a small-framed, skittish fellow with oversized glasses—something akin to some of the arthropod phylum he studied. To his great surprise, Humphries looked nothing like a bug, but rather, possessed an uncanny resemblance to the rock star Sting. The entomologist's two-toned hairdo was cut short on top, with dyed-blond spikes held straight by a vigorous application of gel. One of Humphries's ears was pierced, a silver dragonfly dangling from a small chain, and a silver stud could be seen depressed into the side of his left nostril. Even more distinctive were his muscular arms, which featured an array of brilliantly drawn tattoos incorporating insects of all types—flying, crawling, stinging, and praying.

They were in Humphries's modest office on the second floor of the Bio-Life Building. Photographs of the scientist on expedition to every conceivable climate adorned the walls, along with half a dozen framed degrees and testimonials, including a doctorate from UC Davis.

"Well," Humphries said, "I guess your friends from the Secret Service found me no threat."

"Actually, they were quite interested in you and wanted to stay and hear what you had to say," Darlene replied.

Humphries pushed aside a stack of papers and several magnifying lenses, and slid a spiral-bound notebook in front of him. Lou's immediate sense of the man was completely positive.

"So, then, let's talk termites," Humphries said as he studied what Lou assumed to be notes taken from their phone conversation.

"Were you able to find any documented examples of flesh-eating termites since we spoke last?" Lou began.

Humphries drummed his fingers on the desk and pursed his lips. Despite the gold band on the professor's wedding finger, Lou imagined his offbeat good looks acting like pheromones on the coeds in his classes.

"To be honest, Dr. Welcome—"

"Lou, please."

"And Darlene. I'm a pediatrician, so I should be able to understand anything the ER doc over here understands."

"To be honest, Dr. Lou . . . and Dr. Darlene," Humphries said. "I didn't look very hard."

"Because you found one?" she asked.

"Because they don't exist. At least not naturally."

"Could they have been another sort of flesh-eating insect?" Lou asked. "An unusual species of the Dermestid beetle perhaps?"

Humphries's eyes brightened. "I admire anyone who comes to my office prepared. The skin beetle is a good guess, but unfortunately, all known species are scavengers."

"By that you mean they don't live off live flesh?" Darlene interjected.

"That's correct. The Dermestid beetle is often used in taxidermy and some natural history museums to clean animal skeletons. There's also a medicolegal aspect to the beasties' handiwork, helping forensic investigators determine time of death. But I've never come across any accounts of this particular beetle consuming live flesh. Besides, they don't fit the description of the insects you saw, Lou. The adult beetles have oval-shaped bodies, concealed beneath hard scales."

"What about mutation?" Lou asked.

Humphries pondered the question. Darlene caught Lou's sidelong glance and nodded her excitement.

"A mutation that transforms a detritivore into an omnivore . . ." His voice trailed away in thought.

"Detritivore?" asked Darlene. "Like *detritus*?"

"Precisely. Your Latin hasn't deserted you, Doctor. Organisms that obtain nutrients from decomposing organic matter. Garbage eaters. It appears that everything I read about your intelligence is accurate."

"Why, thanks, Oliver," she replied with her ice cream–melting smile. "I'm afraid I'm much more used to reading about my waistline or makeup or wardrobe than my intellect."

Humphries took a moment to compose himself and continued. "In any event, I can't fathom an environmental factor that would cause such a mutation. I've studied entomology for most of my life and have been to every continent except Antarctica studying bugs—termites especially. I've discovered at least two new species, but never encountered anything close to what you've described. It's one of the reasons I was so eager to meet with you. If such an insect were naturally occurring, well . . . it would certainly generate a lot of buzz in the industry." The entomologist chuckled.

"Nicely done," Darlene said, picking up on the play on words before Lou. "But you just said 'naturally occurring.' What about a nonnatural environmental shift of some sort?"

"Something man-made?"

"Yes," Lou said, perking up at the thought. "A man-made airborne contagion of sorts."

Humphries slipped back into his contemplative mode. "There's certainly evidence of insect behavioral shifts as a result of, let's say, light pollution, or thermal factors, or air pollution, or various forms of radiation. Have you followed what's been happening to the honeybee population?"

"I have," Darlene said while Lou was shaking his head. "Colony collapse disorder."

"Right on, ma'am. The explanation for CCD is still widely disputed. The number of Western honeybee colonies have been declining quite impressively for a couple of decades, but more rapidly over recent years. Some of my colleagues are blaming biotic factors such as viruses or mites, but others purport that environmental shifts—cell phone radiation, pesticides, even genetically modified crops are to blame."

Lou's face lit up. "So, it's possible that GMO crops caused the bees' colony collapse?"

"Evidence for that is slim and certainly not proven as far as I know. It's still a controversial subject at best."

"Could the pollen from GMO crops be a contributing factor?" Darlene asked.

Humphries shook his head—a firm warning not to jump to any conclusions. "It's almost impossible to say. If that were the case with your termites, I'd expect there would have been a corresponding mass kill event, or perhaps a dramatic reduction in the termite population. A full-on mutation would be something quite startling."

"But assuming what I observed is fact, how would you explain it?" Lou asked. He felt like he was feeling his way down an endless pitch-black corridor.

"I couldn't," Humphries replied. "That's my point. Not by nature, anyway."

"Or by mutation," Darlene added.

"Or by mutation."

"So, what now?" she asked, unable to mask her disappointment.

"I'd say the best thing for us to do now is have a look at those bugs," Humphries was saying, apparently unaware of the subtext going on between his visitors. "Dr. Lou, you promised to bring me some samples?"

Lou nodded, and he hoisted his briefcase from the carpeted floor.

Darlene's eyes widened. "You had those flesh-eating bugs with you this entire time?"

Lou grinned sheepishly. "I didn't want you to get creeped out before the expert was around to assure you that these guys can't eat through glass."

Lou handed Humphries two large covered baby food jars. In one of them, the bottom was nearly coated with termites. The other contained a single gigantic bug, pumpkin in color, with a segmented body, long scimitar-shaped pincers, and pure white disks where its eyes might have been.

"Joey, the collector I spoke to you about, assured me that the huge, puffed-up one is a queen."

Darlene shivered and hunched her shoulders, per-haps again imagining the bugs were crawling up her arms. She glared at Lou but could not hold the reprov-ing look very long. "No secrets next time," she said, her eyes glinting.

"No secrets, pal," Lou replied. "Next time I'm carry-ing carnivorous termites, you'll be the first to know."

"Oh, she's the queen, all right," Humphries was say-ing. "The queen of queens. My lab is next door. Let's go there and have ourselves a closer inspection."

Humphries took great care to maximize the limited space in his windowless lab. A Corian-covered counter extending out from the far wall provided enough sur-face area for three distinct workstations. There were microscopes, centrifuges, and other lab equipment rest-ing on a table.

Glass-fronted cabinets contained shelving stocked with glass beakers, jars, flasks, and coils of plastic tubing. Dozens of scientific tomes were neatly arranged in a bookcase on one wall. At least three of them, Lou noted, were written or co-authored by Humphries himself. On the opposite wall stood several specimen cabinets, holding containers with various insects inside them, some living and some not.

Again, Darlene caught Lou's eye and shivered.

Humphries crossed to the cabinets, where he retrieved a jar containing a small battalion of fairly large live ants. After slipping on a pair of latex gloves, he transferred the termites Lou had brought to a large flask and closed the opening with a rubber stopper. Next, he skillfully used a large dropper to remove half a dozen ants and deposited them into the flask. There was an instant rush of activity as the termites' amber bodies swarmed the ants, which were nearly the size they were.

The attack was as ferocious as the one on the mouse in Joey's bizarre terrarium.

Within seconds, there were no remnants of the ants whatsoever.

It took Lou most of a minute to realize he'd been holding his breath. He let the air out slowly. A glance at Darlene told him she had been doing the same thing.

Using a large magnifying glass, Humphries silently studied the termites with a child's wide-eyed enthusiasm. "Just what I thought from the pictures you texted to me," Humphries said. *"Macrotermes bellicosus."*

"That's their name?" Darlene asked. "It's almost as scary as they are."

"Macro means 'large' and *bellicosus* means—"

"Warlike," Lou and Darlene said in unison.

"You got it. *M. bellicosus* is an African breed. But these were found in Virginia?"

"That's right," Lou said. "In a town named Kings Ridge."

"Well, obviously somebody imported them . . . illegally, I suspect. Or, I guess, accidentally. *Macrotermes* are builders—architectural masters." Humphries put a stopper on the flask and set it back down on the table. "The African sun is a brutal force, which the *bellicosus* termite has managed to tame. Their mounds are the largest non-man-made structures in the world. They build thermoregulated chambers inside them that maintain a temperature of precisely eighty-eight to eighty-nine degrees, with ventilation ducts that continuously refresh their air supply. The temperature is critical because their primary food source, a fungus, won't grow in any other temperature. I spent six months in Africa studying these critters. Marvels, really. Absolute marvels."

"Ever see them eat a lion?" Lou asked. "Because the swarm I witnessed could probably do just that."

"No," Humphries said dismissively. "Their primary food source is that fungus, or else they chew up wood and digest whatever nutrients they can."

"So how do you explain what you just saw?"

"That's just it!" Humphries exclaimed with youthful exuberance. "I can't!"

Lou and Darlene exchanged excited looks.

"So what's next?" Lou asked.

"I'm going to dissect Her Majesty, if you don't mind. I need to look at the queen."

Within minutes, Humphries had the queen termite

under a microscope. His fingers moved with remarkable delicacy and economy of motion. On occasion, he would pause to wipe sweat from his brow, a move that made the tattooed insects on his arm appear to come alive.

Lou and Darlene huddled close by and watched in silence.

"This is odd," Humphries said, mostly to himself.

"What? What's odd?" Lou asked.

He and Darlene had moved in closer. Their arms were touching, but neither attempted to pull away.

Humphries looked up from his microscope, his expression bewildered.

"This queen is about twice as large as the average *M. bellicosus* queen. This one here is more than ten centimeters. Her egg-laying capacity seems to have been doubled as well. Maybe tripled."

"What does that mean?" Darlene asked.

"It means that if these insects exist in the natural world, they would probably have more egg-laying capacity than any creature on the planet. The fecundity of these termites suggests they could cause a very serious environmental imbalance."

"So, do you think it's a mutation?" Lou asked.

"No . . . I don't," Humphries stated. "If this were a naturally occurring mutation, at some point I, or one of my colleagues, would have seen these insects in the wild. Their breeding would be massive and impossible to contain. We're talking a major shift to Mother Nature's already tenuous balance. I think these insects were engineered in a controlled environment."

"Engineered? How?" Darlene asked.

"My guess is radiation," Humphries said. "I'd have to run some tests on the samples you brought, but my bet is I'll find high levels of ionizing radiation that produced an abundance of free radicals within the termite's cell structures."

"You think somebody mutated these termites to increase their size and egg-laying capacity?"

Humphries nodded. "I do. And I further suspect that the radiation and hybridized breeding resulted in the mutation that altered the termites' natural diet. I think that's how these herbivores became flesh-eaters."

"Why would anybody want to breed a termite that produces more eggs?" Lou wondered aloud. He looked over at Darlene and saw that she had turned pale.

"Lou," she said, "the corn. You told me it was bigger than a normal ear and had a lot more kernels on it, too." She pointed to the jar of termites. "What if that's how they're growing corn like that?"

Lou understood immediately. "Oliver," he said. "Could the DNA from this termite be inserted into the nucleus of a corn seed?"

"Of course," Humphries said. "The DNA transfection process would allow cross-breeding with any number of species."

"What would you call corn that was cross-bred to include the DNA of a mutated termite?"

The entomologist laughed at the notion. "I don't know what I'd call it," he answered. "But I know what it isn't."

"What's that?" Darlene asked.

"It isn't corn," he said.

CHAPTER 42

While waiting for Joey to emerge from the staff entrance to Millie's, Lou checked over the large piece of equipment Oliver Humphries had lent him. The ground-penetrating radar system looked like a jogger's stroller, minus the canvas seat where the infant would go. It had a twenty-inch front wheel and two twenty-four-inch rear wheels, making the contraption reasonably easy to transport. The 270 megahertz antenna was encased inside a bread box–sized container and secured to the underside of the carriage. The antenna was capable of broadcasting subsurface images to an eight-inch display screen mounted between the handlebars.

Perfect for locating termite tunnels.

Humphries felt confident that a single termite tower did not preclude the possibility of there being others nearby. In fact, the tattooed entomologist thought it strange that only a single tower existed in a given area. If these termites had escaped from a lab where they'd been radiated, as Humphries believed to be the case, then there should be a ventilation shaft connecting the isolated mound to the rest of the colony.

The *Macrotermes bellicosus* species were strange, almost mystical creatures. Their huge towers, Humphries had explained, did not provide habitation for the colony. Instead, scientists believed the elaborate Tolkien-esque structures were built for the thermoregulation vital for growing the fungus essential to their diet. The ground-penetrating radar might not provide answers to any perplexing questions, but it would help to find other mounds by detecting the subsurface ventilation shafts joining one colony to another.

Lou was leaning against the machine, rereading the manual, when Joey slammed open the screen door and, blinking against the glare, bounded into the bright early afternoon sun. He looked dressed for a safari—tan khaki shorts, knee-high socks, and a wide-brimmed sun hat. Lou was pleased to see that he had been taking good care of his surgically repaired hand.

"Hey, big guy," Lou said, "that wound dressing looks great."

Joey's freckled face crinkled in a broad grin. "Millie and Tommy, the head chef, drove me back yesterday to have the thumb checked again. It looks really scary, all black and blue and greenish, but Dr. Kurdi says it's doing terrific and that it's going to work as good as my other one. So, what's that thing?"

"It's a device to help me locate other termite mounds," Lou said, pausing before adding, "if there are any others."

"Well, I hope you pumped up the tires real good, because it's a few miles' walk from here to the mound—maybe four."

Lou sighed, pulled off his Nationals cap to wipe sweat from his brow, and looked out at the shimmering heat rising up off the road.

"Four miles, eh? Can't we just drive there?"

"I only know how to get there by walking," Joey said.

"Do we need a map?"

"Wouldn't know where to look on it. The directions are all up here." He tapped his forehead with his good hand. "One of the things I really enjoy doing is exploring the cornfields."

"And you think you can find the mound by walking?" Lou grunted as he pushed the cart hard enough to build up some momentum.

Joey marched ahead as they passed the Dorm and then left the vinyl-sided apartments behind.

"I spent two years walking every bit of the cornfields," Joey said, loud enough not to have to turn his head. "Acres and acres and acres. That's how I found my special termites. I know these fields like the back of my hand." He held up his heavily bandaged arm and laughed.

Lou imagined how difficult it was going to be pushing the contraption through the deeply furrowed fields.

So much for AA's golden admonition not to project.

He recalled Joey's obsession with knot tying and Millie's acknowledgment that he got fixated on certain things. As Lou trudged along, grateful for all the hours he spent training in the ring and on the bags, he hoped Joey's navigation obsession also included the shortest and easiest route to get to where they wanted to be.

Forty-five minutes later, Lou's sweat-drenched T-shirt was plastered to his chest like a second skin. Of all the cornfields Joey took him through, this one was proving especially difficult to negotiate. Loose soil and tall stocks from Chester Enterprises' genetically modified corn crop made for extremely slow going. Joey offered to help push, but there was no way Lou would risk anything happening to the thumb he had helped to save.

If there was a positive aspect to the difficult and dusty passage, it was that his attention was largely fixated on moving ahead. Still, thoughts of Darlene were never far from the surface. Between reestablishing himself in the ER, demonstrating his work ethic at Physician Wellness, spending time with Emily, getting to meetings, and working out with Cap, he had precious little opportunity to meet women. AA was famous among its members for having a saying to fit every situation or occasion. The one he liked to fall back on when it came to having a social life, was *Time is nature's way of keeping everything from happening at once.*

Unfortunately, there was no saying that applied to what was happening between him and the president's wife.

As much as Darlene dared, she had decided to confront her husband when he returned from his campaign trip later in the day regarding Double M, Russell Evans, William Chester, the *bellicosus* termites, and the elusive trainload of corn. Her goal was to set up a meeting between the president and Lou to review the bizarre and sometimes deadly pattern of behavior that Lou had observed among the citizens of Kings Ridge.

Lou felt embarrassed about his near obsession with the woman, but decided that so long as he could keep his fantasies and projections from getting the best of him, he could only do what he could do.

Another useful saying.

Eventually, he and Joey emerged onto a narrow dirt road. Lou paused and scanned the track and the surrounding fields. "I know this place," he said.

"Well, the mound I found is in the woods off the end of this road. Not far now."

"This is near where I was attacked."

"Attacked?"

"Never mind," Lou said quickly.

He remained on high alert the rest of the way. If Chester's corn was the source of all the troubles in Kings Ridge, it was likely that the mogul's henchmen would be stationed someplace close by. The afternoon was virtually windless, and he kept a cautious lookout for any movement of the stalks, while at the same time scanning the dense rows in a futile attempt to spot Anthony Brite's body.

At the end of the dirt road, Joey veered into the woods to their left, and Lou followed several paces behind. The cart's bicycle-like tires were designed to traverse difficult terrain, making it fairly easy for him to maneuver over the ground's exposed roots and rocks. The two of them bushwhacked their way another quarter mile or so. Although Joey seemed confident, Lou, now grimy and soaked in sweat, was beginning to have doubts. Gratefully, his ankle was not aching badly.

"Bingo!" the young chef cried out from some distance ahead.

Lou took a moment to settle down the burning in his chest, then headed toward Joey's voice. The packed-mud *bellicosus* castle rose from the forest floor like a rocket on its launching pad. There were hundreds of large termites scattered along its length, and dozens more of them flying around like an air force fighter squadron.

"Whoa!" he whispered, marveling at the staggering height and geometry of the thing. "It's awesome."

"Don't I know it!" Joey said. "*Awesome* is the word."

The jagged, conical tower, two or three feet taller than Lou, was peppered with impressively large termites. It looked like a decaying tree trunk, sculpted with spires and crevices.

From about two feet away, Lou cautiously circumvented the spectacular construction. "Amazing," was all he could say. "Absolutely amazing."

"Well, I've got to go," Joey said with singsong nonchalance.

"Go? What are you talking about? Where are you going?" Concern crept into Lou's voice.

"Why, back to work, of course," Joey said. "I did tell you I had to work a double, didn't I?"

"Actually, no, you didn't," Lou replied, laughing nervously. "Joey, what if I can't find my way out of here?"

"Oh, the trail behind us is pretty well marked now.

You can follow the dirt road back there, and skip the cornfields entirely. It'll only add two or three miles to your return trip."

"Two or three miles? Joey, I don't even know where this gizmo is going to take me, let alone how to get back from there." The notion of being back in these fields in the dark of night was not the least bit appealing.

One look at Joey, and Lou's distress quickly began to ebb. The kid had done his best.

Lou had read two historical accounts of the Louis and Clark expedition. If they could accomplish their remarkable, uncharted journey, he could find his way back to the restaurant. Still somewhat apprehensive, he thanked his young guide.

"If you find a queen, let me know," Joey said. "Even though they can make a new one, the colony is struggling without a leader. They need a purpose."

"Will do," Lou said, holding up one of the specimen jars he had brought. "And thanks for sacrificing your lady to the greater good."

"I was just kidding, Doc. Don't try to find one. She'd be deep within the colony. Before you got to her, you'd be hamburger."

Joey tipped his hat, waved good-bye with his heavily bandaged hand, and was gone. Lou listened until Joey's footfalls had disappeared into the dense woods. Finally, when the only sound in the still afternoon was the continuous scraping and scratching from the *bellicosus* termites, he powered up the radar machine.

Despite the bug repellent he had swathed on himself, he wondered at what distance the insects would sense the presence of live flesh, and organize themselves for an attack.

The ground radar system whirred softly as it came to life. The cart's handlebars vibrated, causing Lou's forearms to tingle. The display screen went from deep gray to varying lighter shades. The background colors were of no interest to him. They represented natural soils, not the organized, hyperbolic reflections of air tunnels within the ground, which were black.

Lou maneuvered the radar closer to the tower, fearing that the ground beneath him might cave in. The first subsurface ventilation shaft came into clear focus a foot from the conical structure. The markings on the radar's display screen looked like flickering, serpentine shapes—black, projected onto a gray background. As Lou moved the antenna away from the ventilation shaft, the change in reception altered the subsurface reflection, causing the curved shape to disappear from the screen. By trial and error, he learned that so long as he had the black patterns on his radar display, he was standing over one of the ventilation shafts.

Using a pad and pencil, Lou mapped a number of the largest shafts, keeping a careful log of the orientation and length of each on graph paper Humphries had provided. Each of the tunnels led to a small hole in the surface topography along with a baseball-sized depression in the soil that contributed ventilation to the remarkably constructed tower.

Sweaty and aching, Lou mapped the entire area until one quadrant, which he had labeled *SE*—southeast—caught his attention. It contained a thicker, curved black shadow than the others—a dark snake that went to the edge of the screen and did not seem to have an end. Lou wheeled his apparatus ahead and followed the winding shape on his display as it led him away from the huge structure and deeper into the forest.

One hundred yards . . . two hundred . . . three . . .

The shaft was still beneath his feet, running parallel to the surface, about two feet deep.

Eventually, Lou emerged into a broad clearing about the size of a football field, with a single-story, windowless brick structure at the far west end. There was a narrow unpaved access road just opposite from where he stood, which opened into a small dirt parking area. There was a single empty car standing in the lot—a large black Mercedes four-door with Virginia plates.

The ventilation shaft remained at the center of the screen, although the depth seemed to have increased—perhaps three feet now, maybe even a bit more. Lou followed the shadow until it came to an abrupt end at the south-facing side of the building. At that point, the depth of the serpentine ventilation tunnel increased sharply, and moments later, the radar display screen turned totally gray.

Lou checked his machine, which seemed to be functioning all right. The shaft appeared to have disappeared into something much larger—a subterranean chamber of some sort.

Lou sensed there might be something underneath him. He flipped through the instruction manual, but it was quite technical, and there was no explanation for something like the phenomenon he was observing. The one thing he felt fairly certain of was that the fearsome *bellicosus* termites in the forest and subsequently in Joey's Lucite terrarium were originating here.

Scanning the surroundings for cameras, he walked the radar around the building. There was a slight crack in the foundation, and he wondered if farther down, the bugs had escaped that way. There was a green metal door by the east corner. Lou carefully tried to open it, but it was locked. He backed away and wheeled the radar machine into the woods.

Given his experience with the gunmen, the deserted Mercedes was unnerving.

Still, Lou felt desperate to get inside the blockhouse-like building. A possible solution, he decided, was among the contacts in his cell phone—Chief Gilbert Stone.

Three rings and Stone answered. "Stone here."

"Chief Stone, it's Lou Welcome."

"Welcome. Everything okay? What can I do for you?"

"Do you know anything about a windowless brick building in a clearing not too far from where we got attacked?"

"*Allegedly* got attacked," Stone corrected. "Sounds like the old power and water transfer station. Why? What's up?"

"I'm in the woods outside of it right now. Do you think you could get over here? I may have found the source of the Kings Ridge problem."

"You stay put, Welcome, and keep out of sight," Stone said. "I'll be right there."

"The door's locked."

"No problem," Stone replied. "I have a key."

Soon, Lou thought excitedly. *Soon it's going to be over.*

Starting to chill from the evaporation of his own sweat, he slid down to the base of a white ash, clasped his arms around his knees, and waited.

Soon . . .

CHAPTER 43

The crunch of Gilbert Stone's cruiser on gravel startled Lou from an exhausted, dreamless sleep. He wiped salt and perspiration from his eyes, rose blearily to his feet, and reentered the clearing, wheeling the ground radar system ahead of him. Stone parked near the Mercedes, emerged from the cruiser, hoisted his heavy utility belt above his ample belly, and then settled a campaign hat over his mop of graying hair. Lou met him at the blockhouse, outside the green door.

"Anybody else coming?" Lou asked, glancing down the road.

"I've got two teams on standby," Stone answered. "Tell me everything. What's that contraption you've got there?"

"It's portable radar. I think the corn Chester is growing is poisonous."

"Poisonous?"

"I know it may be hard for you to believe, but I think William Chester is producing vast amounts of corn, genetically modified to grow larger and faster by combining it with the genes of a large African termite called *Macrotermes bellicosus*—perhaps the most reproductively proficient animal on the planet."

"And you think this corn is somehow poisoning the citizens of my town."

"I do."

Stone made the same high-pitch whistle that Lou remembered from the first night they met. "So what on earth brought you way out here?" Stone asked, gesturing to the woods surrounding them.

"You remember Joey, the cook at Millie's who nearly got his thumb sliced off?"

"Of course."

"Well, a couple of years ago, Joey found these huge mutated termites in the woods and made them his pets."

"Mutated?"

"Termites," Lou repeated.

"How are they mutated?"

"Well, first of all, they're bigger than other termites of the species, and second, they eat flesh in addition to their usual diet."

"Holy gravy," Stone said, making that whistle again. "So what do these bugs have to do with corn?"

"Well, initially I thought it was airborne contagion—inhaling pollen from Chester's modified corn—that caused the odd behaviors taking place around town. I went to see a bug expert in Philadelphia to see if that was even possible. Turns out that the termites Joey found are an African species, clearly imported here by someone. This piece of equipment"—Lou tapped the

cart's handlebars—"can be used to track their underground ventilation shafts."

"And you tracked one of these shafts all the way to
this building?"

"That's right," Lou said proudly. "The bugs must
have flown out and started another colony, or else they
escaped through a crack in the foundation. The expert
and I aren't sure, but we don't think it's an airborne
contagion anymore. We think the termites are being
intentionally mutated—radiated, most likely—and
then their DNA is being combined with the corn to get
this huge, rapidly growing, genetically modified, monster vegetable. Frankencorn, I've been calling it."

Stone looked at Lou queerly. "But if it's not airborne, how's it making the people sick?" he asked.

"I don't know."

"Well, we've got to find out. I got some more trou-
blin' news to share with you. More proof, I guess, that
something really wrong is happening here in Kings
Ridge." Stone pulled a kerchief from his pocket and
used it to mop his brow. "Roberta Jennings accidentally killed herself yesterday."

"What?"

"Poor dear took some painkillers and alcohol, then
sliced open her belly with a kitchen knife. Apparently,
she was trying to lose some weight the quick way. The
ME says she cut a couple of arteries and bled to death."

"Oh, God," Lou muttered.

He swallowed hard. Roberta Jennings had completed the pathetic circle John Meacham had begun.
Another terrible decision. Another violent death. Lou

considered disclosing then and there what he knew of Darlene Mallory, Double M, and a huge shipment of corn, maybe Chester's corn, headed someplace by train, but he needed to clear things with her first.

"Can we get inside?" he asked, pointing to the green door. "Do we need a warrant or anything? I'm fairly certain that the source of whatever is going on here is behind that door."

Stone's eyes flashed. "Of course we can get in. I'm the damn chief of police."

"Do you know what this building is used for?"

Stone nodded dully, then said, "Sure I do. Heck, I authorized it."

Lou looked up at the man, bewildered. "Well, what is it?" he asked. "It doesn't look like much."

Stone snorted a mirthless laugh and pointed down. "That's because it's all belowground," he said.

"What is?"

"William Chester's research laboratory," Stone said, a note of impatience creeping into his voice. "We excavated it years ago. He already owned the land and wanted a place where he could conduct research without attracting much attention. Hardly anybody even knows about this access road." Stone pointed to the dirt road behind them. "The seed business is very competitive, you see. Chester was worried about trade secrets being stolen—industrial espionage and such. We gave him the permits to build an underground lab because, well, Chester Seed Company is what makes Kings Ridge a viable community."

"So do you know what they do down there?"

"Not really. The security system feeds to a room in the basement of the Chester mansion—the place you and your friends visited. As far as I know, these people have been complying with all our permits and regulations. We never gave them permission to radiate bugs, though, and turn 'em into mutants, if that's what you're wondering."

"Do you know whose car that is?"

"Actually, I think it's one of Bill Chester's."

"He's here," Lou said. "Maybe he can finally provide some answers. How do we get in?"

"Well, we can pound all night on this door, or we can use this." Looking somewhat puffed, Stone held up a key. "Like I said, I'm the chief of police."

With a turn of Stone's key, the green metal door swung open on well-oiled hinges. Brushed steel wall scones illuminated the cinder-block entrance and a staircase with a metal handrail. Stone removed his gun from its holster and started down, with Lou following.

"Should we send for backup?" Lou asked.

Stone turned. For the first time, his expression had darkened. "I saw what Roberta did to herself," he said. "If the cause of what happened to her is down these stairs, I intend to uncover it here and now."

Lou nodded as Stone cautiously resumed his descent. They came to another locked steel door at the bottom of the stairwell. A keypad secured access to whatever was behind it. Without hesitating, Stone punched in a short series of numbers. Then after a soft click, the red LED light on the pad turned green and the lock responded.

"What now?" Lou asked, somewhat surprised by Stone's familiarity with the place.

"Now we go in," the cop said simply.

Remembering Chester's thugs, Lou glanced up the stairwell behind them, wishing at least that reinforcements were on the way. At the same time, he wondered again about precisely how tight Stone was with the mogul at the center of Kings Ridge's prosperity.

The cop pulled open the door without first peering inside. Either he had no reason to believe any threat existed, or in his zeal to get to the bottom of Roberta's death and the rest of the troubles in his town, he had become reckless.

Or maybe, Lou found himself wondering, *it's the corn at work. . . .*

He fell into step behind Stone and followed him down a short corridor that dead-ended at another windowless metal door with another keypad.

"Better stay back," Stone said. "Not sure what we're going to find behind this door."

At least he's finally being cautious, Lou thought.

Again Stone keyed a number sequence, and again the access panel's red light gave way to green.

"I hope you're right about forging ahead like this, Gilbert," Lou said.

"I've had just about enough strange things happening in my town."

Pistol at the ready, Stone went in with Lou following. The space ahead of them was brightly lit.

Just inside the threshold, Lou stopped abruptly, his mouth agape at what he was seeing. A series of conveyor belts snaked throughout a large area. Corn seed, lit by banks of powerful overhead lights, covered every inch of the conveyor belts in a golden river that seemed to have no beginning or end.

Suspended above the conveyor belt was a thick metal tube, four feet long, with gauges, control knobs along the side, and smaller tubes running down its length. It appeared to be a ray gun of sorts with a short, six-inch muzzle, half the diameter of the main tube. The rest of the space reminded Lou of Oliver Humphries's lab on steroids—stainless steel tables, centrifuges, multiple microscopes, glass cabinets stocked with flasks, beakers, plastic tubing, pipettes, and other scientific materials.

Lou composed himself and quickly covered the gap between him and Stone. "My radar machine picked up some sort of expanse down here," he said. "I suppose this is it. Do you have any idea what's going on?"

Instead of responding, Stone surveyed the crowded underground laboratory, training his gun wherever he looked. With a nod, he motioned Lou down a central corridor toward another door. It was stainless steel, like the others, but this one had no keypad. Lou moved up beside the cop.

"I think you'll want to see what's behind this," Stone said.

"Aren't we being a bit cavalier, not sending for backup?" Lou asked.

Stone did not reply. Still training his gun ahead of him, he opened the door. It seemed to Lou as if the man knew precisely what he would find, and was not at all concerned. From where Lou stood, the space ahead was dark.

Stone disappeared through the doorway, reached to his left, and flipped on high-powered fluorescent lights. Moments later he motioned with his gun for Lou to follow.

Lou hesitated, feeling increasingly uneasy. *Oh, well,* he thought, *in for a penny—*

One step through the door, and he froze.

The space, warm and humid, was at least the same size as the laboratory. Echoing off the stainless steel walls was the machinery-like humming of insects— many, many insects. He stepped forward onto a grated steel walkway with heavy metal pipe railings and three- or four-foot chain-link sidewalls that crossed a pit at least twenty feet deep. The whole space just below the walkway was covered with a dense metal screen. With the overheads reflecting off the fine mesh, it was difficult to see what was in the pit.

But Lou had no doubt.

Stone reached over to the wall next to him and depressed a large red plastic button. Smoothly, gears engaged and the vast screen slid back on tracks and rolled up on a reel at the far end. Revealed below was a terrible, surreal landscape. The sides of the massive pit were lined with brushed stainless steel, gleaming beneath the overheads. The surface of the space looked like an alien moonscape, formed by at least a hundred termite mounds of various heights and sizes, some of which reached upward to within ten or fifteen feet of the walkway. The chilling diorama was swarming with *Macrotermes bellicosi*. Like the mound in the forest, more insects were humming about through the air— some actually flying above the steel catwalk.

For a time, Lou remained transfixed on the bugs below as they moved with blind purpose in and out of the mounds. This was their city—their home. The clicking of thousands of feet and jaws made his fillings ache.

The walkways were three feet wide, crossing at right angles to one another over the precise center of the pit. Thick metal rods, descending from the ceiling, held the walks firmly suspended in place. There was a door ending the walk to their left, and a third door, painted red, directly across from them. That door featured a large decal with the yellow symbol for a biohazard. Even from where he stood, he could read the words below the symbol: CAUTION RADIATION AREA.

Lou batted at a huge termite that buzzed past his face. "Behind that door is where they must be mutating the termites," Lou said as much to himself as to Stone. "And the conveyor belt in the lab we just passed through is where they fire the termite reproductive genes into the corn seeds."

He had been so astonished by what he was seeing that it took some time for him to register that the police chief was not.

Stone nudged the toe of his boot against a sturdy metal pole resting by his foot. The pole had what looked like several extension segments, and the head of it had a rotating claw for grabbing and gripping. Lou wondered if it was used for feeding.

"I'm guessing these are your bugs," Stone said, too nonchalantly.

Lou looked over at the heavy service revolver and felt himself shudder. "No ladders. There's a reason people don't want to go down into that pit. The termites must not be able to scale that surface."

Stone appeared somewhat troubled. "And you think the bugs little Joey adopted slipped out of a crack somewhere in the foundation here?"

"I do. Or else enough of them flew out and escaped this place to start a colony."

"Let's see if we can find where that leak might have happened. That infernal clicking and grinding can really get to you. Can't hardly hear your own footsteps sometimes. It's like they're constantly eating."

But eating what?

Stone stepped out onto the catwalk until he was standing above one of the larger mounds.

Now with his senses electrified, Lou followed. Stone's haphazard approach to investigating the lab and observing the termite metropolis continued to gnaw at him. Even without firsthand knowledge of police departmental procedure, Lou assumed that Stone had violated many safety measures in this investigation.

If he's so familiar with this place, Lou wondered, *why did he even let me come down here? If anything happens to me, it would be Stone's responsibility.*

Lou glanced down into the pit again. Something between two mounds directly beneath him caught his eye—a glint of gold. He strained to get a better look. Then his body tensed and he broke into a chilling sweat. The golden object was a necklace with a handcuff pendant attached—Notso Brite's necklace.

It was at that moment Lou knew exactly why the chief had let him tag along.

CHAPTER 44

Lou had no doubt that any moment he was going to die, and most likely die horribly. Another thing he had no doubt about was that he was not going to go down without a hell of a fight.

He took a single step back to size up his situation and the potbellied lawman whom he was certain was about to kill him. The first thing he warned himself of was that under no circumstance was he going to underestimate the man. Despite his bulk, Stone carried himself with the balance, grace, and confidence of a fighter—probably a brawler. At the moment, though, he appeared totally at ease, almost blissful. Holding his pistol loosely in front of him, he looked like anything other than a man who was preparing to kill.

Lou wondered if Stone was aware that his target had figured out what was coming. More than likely, he decided.

Desperately, Lou searched for a move, any move, that would shorten the odds against him. His advantage was his quickness, his skill as a boxer, and the surprise if he managed to make his play before Stone made his.

Trying to run would result only in a bullet between the shoulder blades. Lou did not know when Stone intended to strike, only that it would happen and happen soon. The pit made for the perfect human disposal receptacle. If the man was trained in martial arts, he might try to gain leverage to flip Lou over the rail. The bugs would devour his clothes while they were mulching his flesh. His bones would be last.

More likely, Stone would neutralize him first with a single shot, possibly to a nonvital spot. From where the policeman was cradling his gun, Lou would have a second or so before he could raise it and fire. Cap would have shown him the move he should go to—possibly a jab-uppercut combination. He would have more confidence if he could connect with a weapon of some sort. Then he realized that he had one in his pants pocket— the pencil he had been using to graph the termites' ventilation shafts.

Stone was gesturing below them and commenting on the setup.

Easy, Lou warned himself as he turned away an inch or so and slid his hand into his pocket. The pencil was there, complete with point.

Perfect.

Lou gestured into the pit. "Look," he said. "Look there."

Stone kept a wary distance and peered below. "I don't see anything."

The termites' clicking seemed to have gotten louder, as if they sensed a meal was on the way.

With thoughts of Emily and their last, too brief, conversation, Lou slipped the pencil out of his pocket, then held it under his wrist and concealed it against the top of the catwalk railing. Leaning forward, hoping Stone would react to his vulnerability, he gestured down at the golden necklace.

Lou's grip on the handrail was tight. His feet were well spaced and his knees wedged up against the sidewall.

Make your move, Stone . . . make your move . . . make your move. . . .

Sweat slickened Lou's grip. He wanted to wipe his hands dry to strengthen his hold, but feared letting go of the handrail for even a moment. Below him, he watched the bugs scamper about. He imagined their jaws sinking into his flesh—digesting him one small piece at a time.

Come on. . . .

One second . . . two . . . three . . .

Maybe I'm wrong about the man, Lou found himself thinking.

The loss of concentration was only momentary, but it was enough.

Stone grabbed Lou by the back of the shirt and slammed the muzzle across the back of his head. Lou was still prepared enough to twist away, reducing the force of the blow. Still, his vision blurred and his knees buckled. He would have gone down had he not been wedged against the sidewall.

"You should have stayed out of Kings Ridge," Stone said, raising his gun for another blow.

Lou released his grip on the railing, ducked as if he were avoiding a vicious right hook, and brought the pencil up behind his shoulder. Still bleary, he approximated where Stone's neck would be and stabbed at it with a broad, sweeping motion. The pencil sank into the muscle beside the man's throat. Lou hoped to tear into the jugular vein, but sensed right away that hadn't happened. Stone cried out and stumbled backwards, raising his gun.

Lou parried the pistol with his left forearm and rammed his fist into Stone's abdomen with as much force as he had ever hit a man. Stone splayed backwards, crashing into the railing and teetering perilously over the edge for a moment before righting himself. The pencil stuck out from his neck like a bloodied yellow dart.

Bellowing like an enraged bull, Stone hunched over and drove his head into the center of Lou's chest. Intense pain exploded from the spot, and Lou's initial fear was that the bone had shattered. His vision dimmed, then went dark. Moments later, when he regained his senses, he was kneeling on the catwalk. Stone was looming above him, clawing at the pencil.

As the pencil came free, followed by a jet of blood, Lou dived for the man's ankles, got ahold of the right one, and twisted it sharply. Stone fell backwards, landing with a force that shook the entire catwalk. Lou straddled him, grabbed his head on each side, and slammed it onto the catwalk—once, then again, and again. Stone grunted with each blow, and finally went limp. Lou, gasping for breath and feeling as if his sternum might have been broken, slumped over onto the catwalk, then painfully pulled himself to his feet.

At that moment, from beyond Stone's prostrate, motionless body, Lou saw the radiation room door swing open. A man dressed in a bright yellow biocontainment suit emerged from the shadows of the room beyond. Groaning with each breath, Lou steeled himself to turn and run, but the suited man held up a hand in a nonthreatening gesture. Then he lifted the hood away from his face.

"Jesus," Lou whispered.

He stepped over the fallen police chief and met Edwin Chester halfway past the convergence of the catwalks. Below them the clicking had grown more intense.

"I was involved in an experiment and didn't hear anything that was going on," Edwin said. "For as long as I can remember, Gilbert Stone has been owned by my father. He can be one of the most heartless, frightening men I have ever met."

"He brought me down here to kill me," Lou said.

"I don't think you'd be the first. He does a lot of my father's dirty work."

"Edwin, this whole business has gotten out of hand."

"I didn't want any of this to happen. I told my father the corn wasn't ready, but he just wouldn't listen."

"I thought you were his protector."

"I am, but that doesn't keep me from trying to cancel out some of the things he does. That's why I contacted Darlene Mallory in the first place."

"You? You're Double M?"

Edwin grinned. "You expected someone a little taller and heavier? I have boots with six- and seven-inch lifts, and specially padded jackets. In my world, trust can be a very expensive commodity. I tend to stand out because of my lack of height, so when I need to, I just do something about it."

"But why the charade? Why didn't you just come forward and tell what you knew had happened?"

"You don't know my father," Edwin said. "He's really a very wonderful man—by far the most important person in my—" His eyes widened. "Lou! Behind you!"

Lou whirled. Stone had unsteadily pushed himself to his knees and, eyes glazed, was fumbling for his gun, which had been on the catwalk underneath him. There were no choices available this time—no strategies. The distance between him and Stone was ten yards. Ignoring the pain in his chest, and keeping as low as he could manage, Lou charged. Stone rattled off two wild shots that clanged off the steel walls. The third one, fired from no more than six feet away, tore through the outside edge of Lou's left thigh.

Lou cried out as he dropped to one knee, but his momentum carried him flailing into Stone, who was bowled over backwards. The pistol went clattering across the catwalk and slid under the railing. Lou pounded the cop in the face again and again. Blood gushing from Stone's nostrils flowed into blood streaming from the hole in his neck. Still, the man was able to shove Lou off and make it to his feet, pulling Lou up

by the shirt and squeezing the air and life out of him
with the strength of a python.

Quickly, Lou's strength began to fail. Stone swung
his hips to the right, lifting Lou's feet off the catwalk
and slamming him against the railing. Lou, now nearly
helpless, tried and failed to drop down to avoid being
thrown over the edge. The pressure of Stone's thick arms
was unbearable. His face, teeth gritted, was a bloody
mask.

Lou pushed against Stone's chest with all his strength,
but failed to put any distance between them. He was
now aware of a burning pain from the muscle where
the bullet had torn through. At that instant, Lou's knees
went slack and he experienced the horrific sensation of
his feet leaving the catwalk. Before he could make another move, he was over the top of the railing. Frantically, he forced his fingers through the steel chain link
of the catwalk wall and gripped it as tightly as he could.

Every breath was an agonizing effort. His feet dangled down, precariously close to the hordes of termites
milling below him. His palms stretched until they
burned. His arms quivered from exertion and utter fatigue. Grateful for the hours of training under Cap's
tutelage, Lou managed to stretch up with his right foot
and slip it over a support beam beneath the walk. At
that instant, Stone appeared above him, his face a hideous mask of gore. Blood, dripping down into the pit
below Lou, sent the colony clicking and scurrying
about. Grinning ferociously, Stone tapped the toe of his
heavy boot against Lou's fingers, sending electric pain
shooting down his arm.

"Fast or slow?" Stone asked. "Your choice."

He emphasized his question with another light tap. Though he tried, Lou failed to keep himself from crying out. His left hand fumbled to improve his grip on the metal. The tightness in his palm intensified.

Emmy, I'm so sorry, baby. So sorry.

Lou tried to will himself to hold on, but felt his grip starting to release. Perspiration was stinging his eyes. His left hand was about to let go when he heard a scream from above, followed by the sound of running footsteps that shook the catwalk.

"No!" Edwin shouted as he charged the police chief.

Buoyed by the attack, Lou managed to tighten his grip. He craned his neck and looked upward just in time to see Edwin swing the metal extension pipe, connecting heavily with Stone's temple. A second blow landed on the side of the man's neck.

Stone staggered back from the sidewall. Swinging his weapon wildly, Edwin charged after him, stumbling against his broad chest. The two men grappled on the catwalk, spinning in circles, with Stone screaming in both rage and pain. Lou tried to pull himself up, but his arms were shaking from fatigue.

Emily. . . . Come on, you idiot, do it for your kid. . . .

He gained a little more purchase with his foot and then finally was able to adjust the position of his hands. Overhead he could see Stone beginning to maul the much slighter Edwin.

He had to get up to help.

At that moment, Edwin made a move, almost certainly unexpected, that spun Stone around and rammed his back into the upper railing of the catwalk. In an instant, locked in each other's arms, the two of them went over, brushing past Lou as they fell.

The heavy thud beneath him was dreadful, and was quickly followed by the unremitting shrieks of Gilbert Stone. But Lou was too weak to turn and look. He hoped that the lack of sound from Edwin meant that the man had been knocked unconscious.

The clicking and cracking from the termite jaws, reverberating off the steel walls, became deafening.

Inch by painful inch, Lou advanced upward along the outside of the catwalk wall, using his foot to push and his fingers to pull. Finally, he was upright, hanging on to the wall. Fearing what he was going to see, he finally had the strength to look down. The two adversaries lay supine, a foot from each other, their hands nearly touching. Edwin was motionless, a pool of insect-covered crimson expanding from beneath his head.

Stone was moaning and squirming with pain. His eye sockets were already filled with termites, and dozens, if not hundreds of them seemed to be forcing their way into his mouth. His lips were moving as if he were trying to speak, but no recognizable words were emerging.

Lou hung on until his wind had somewhat returned. Then he swung his legs over the top railing of the cat-walk wall and dropped to his side on the metal grate, his chest heaving with exhaustion. The bullet wound to his thigh burned, but he knew that with time, the scar would be a memento of what had been the worst day of a life that had experienced more than its share of them.

Below him, the clicking and grinding of thousands of *Macrotermes bellicosi* had built into a turbinelike crescendo. Still laboring for each breath, Lou stumbled to his feet and grabbed the extension pole Edwin had used to save his life. By the time he returned to the spot where he might have had a chance to reach the man, it was way too late.

The bugs were busily eating.

And the scion of Chester Enterprises was already dead.

CHAPTER 45

It took eight minutes for the *Macrotermes bellicosi* to finish most of their meal.

Exhausted and battling pain in his sternum, thigh, and a dozen other areas, Lou sat on the catwalk and averted his eyes. From his days on the streets and in the ER of a tough city, he had seen more than his share of death in its various forms. The images never sat well with him and never would.

When he did manage a glance down, what might have been hundreds of thousands of insects were done. The sounds of the carnage, of human bones being pulverized by insect jaws, would never leave him. Aside from a few shreds, all that remained of the two men below were metal—belt buckles, Edwin's brace, Stone's badge and gun, and two sets of car keys.

Lou was thinking about retrieving the keys when another sound set his heartbeat racing.

An alarm buzzer began throbbing from somewhere beyond the laboratory. Somehow, Stone had managed to avoid the alarm, but whoever had just entered did not know how, or hadn't bothered.

A light fixture encased in a metal cage and mounted just above the entrance to the catwalk began to flash.

Not good.

Lou ran through his various escape options, quickly ruling out going back the way he'd come in. There was a door at the end of the other arm of the catwalk, but if it was locked, he would essentially be trapped. The only other door in the termite lair would bring him into the radiation area. He'd have no time to don a protective suit, but the risk was unavoidable. There had to be an emergency exit someplace, and the radiation lab seemed a good bet.

First, though, he had to get through the door, and then get away from whoever had just entered the lab. Running was not an option. He needed wheels.

Using the extension pole, Lou considered going for Stone's gun, but went fishing for Edwin's car keys instead. If it seemed there was time after snagging the keys, he might take a crack at the pistol. The choice proved to be a good one. The heavy pole was cumbersome to use and was probably intended to grasp much larger objects. Prodding the bloodstained ground near to where Edwin's body once had been, Lou struggled to grasp his keys. The drone of the alarm seemed to be getting more urgent.

Come on, Welcome. . . . Focus, dammit, Focus.

After two futile attempts, Lou hooked the keys, but deflated an instant later when the grip he had secured failed to hold.

Lou inhaled deeply. He needed to slow his heart in order to steady his hands.

Just imagine you're sewing up a squirming little kid . . . don't get flustered . . . just another routine procedure.

One more try, and he was going to give up and bolt. Whether he loathed them or not, he wished he had gone for the gun.

The pulsating alarm was unnerving. There was no way to tell precisely where the intruder was or how many of them were out there. He began considering going for an ambush—hiding behind the door onto the catwalk and using the extension pole as Edwin had used it. The necessity to make that decision never came. One more deep breath, and he hooked the keys. He hoisted them up, thought a second about going for Stone's gun, but decided against it.

Looking over his shoulder, he limped across the catwalk, then disappeared into the radiation room. Whoever was about to enter the termite lair was in for a hell of a surprise.

As the steel door closed behind him, Lou thought he heard the door open at the far end of the catwalk. He slid a dead bolt into place and finally allowed himself to exhale. He had to get out and get out soon, but there had to be confusion on the other side of the door, so he probably had a bit of time to compose himself.

The radiation room was bathed in red light. Lou's eyes were immediately drawn to what looked like a holding tank. It was a massive glass-fronted structure, five feet high and four or five feet deep, occupying most of one wall. Inside the tank were thousands upon thousands of termites, almost certainly, Lou guessed, *Macrotermes*. A long plastic tube rose up five feet from the center of the tank, made a ninety-degree right angle bend, paralleled the floor for fifteen feet or so, and then dropped down into a plastic box the size of a small refrigerator. The box rested on top of a conveyor belt, which would, Lou observed, carry the contents inside a piece of machinery that looked like the X-ray machines found at airport security points.

The purpose of the setup was apparent. A vacuum would suck the termites into the tube, then deposit them inside the box. Afterwards, the box would be conveyed into the apparatus where the insects would be radiated. On the far side of the machine was a door marked simply: EXTRACTION.

Extraction. Probably the removal of the DNA from the termites, Lou decided. Incredible how far the technology had come—absolutely incredible and absolutely terrifying.

He was overtaken by an image of him and people in his life—Cap, Emily, Renee, Darlene, Steve, Filstrup, Brian, Graham, bunched together at some sort of cookout, grinning broadly as they each held out a huge ear of steaming sweet corn swathed in butter and salt.

Here, have a bite. Bon appétit!

Mutation, he knew, was the alteration of the pattern of nucleotide bases in a plant or animal, by natural accident, radiation, chemicals, or other stressors, resulting in changes—often massive ones—in the properties of the organism. Edwin was radiating the *Macrotermes bellicosi,* as Humphries had suspected, causing them to mutate into insects with greatly enhanced fecundity and the secondary ability to consume flesh.

Here, have a bite. Bon appétit!

Now, with the finding of the huge tube in the lab on the other side of the termites' habitat, the cycle from two organisms to one was complete.

The mutated bugs were placed inside the steel holding pen where Edwin, Stone, and Anthony Brite had all perished. When their DNA was needed, somebody would gather up the carnivorous insects and bring them to the extraction room. There, they would be pulverized, and their DNA extracted using large centrifuges. Lou now felt certain the long tube he saw in the other lab was a mammoth gene gun, literally capable of blasting the mutated termite DNA into large numbers of corn kernels.

At that moment, Lou's exhausted reverie was cut short by pounding on the door. The nightmare was hardly over.

On the far side of the lab was another door, this one with a glowing EXIT sign above it. The door at first seemed stuck, but Lou yanked harder, figuring the room was being kept under negative pressure as a precaution against radiation leaks. With a loud rush of air, the door swung open into a cinder-block anteroom, with another door, again marked EXIT, just opposite him. From behind, he could hear the pounding intensify, now with some sort of metal implement. He went through the exit, then up a short flight of metal stairs. The gunshot wound to his thigh, probably responding to a constant surge of adrenaline, was quite bearable. At the top of the stairs was a steel storm door that opened into the floor of a utility shed. After he closed that door behind him, Lou dragged as much weight as he could onto it and exited the shed, squinting against the late afternoon light.

He was at the edge of the woods, bordering the clearing. Through the tree line, he could see Edwin's Mercedes-Benz, Stone's cruiser, and another car, a black Cadillac—almost certainly the car that had followed him into the city, what seemed like eons ago. It appeared empty. Humphries's radar cart was where Lou had left it, but there it would have to stay. His priority at the moment was survival.

Keeping his eyes fixed on the blockhouse, Lou took a couple of tentative steps into the clearing and then ran as best he could to the Mercedes, fired up the engine, and skidded from the parking lot. He had never been much of a car aficionado, figuring that the lust to drive high-end vehicles should be commensurate with one's ability to afford them. But the Benz—the first he had driven in many years—was a car to dream about. With only the slightest punch to the accelerator, it sped ahead, sending a rooster tail of sand and gravel swirling into the still air.

Any confidence he felt about his improving situation was short lived. A hundred or so yards down the road he risked a glance into the rearview mirror.

Trouble.

The Cadillac, emerging like an enraged phoenix from a dense, swirling cloud of dust, was on the move.

It looked as if there were two men in the front, but it was impossible to see behind them into the rear seat. The power of the Mercedes was more than he could easily handle, and he skidded several times from one side of the narrow road to another.

When he finally got the hang of the car, Lou jammed down the accelerator again, and the Mercedes shot ahead with a force that felt like several g's. The Caddy kept pace, and actually seemed to be inching closer. Lou's palms were soaked with tension-driven sweat. He was trying to remain composed, but he knew he was hyperventilating.

It seemed like only a second or two since he had checked behind him, but when he looked again, the Caddy seemed to fill the rearview mirror. Moments later, it slammed into his rear end, snapping Lou's head forward like a whip. The Mercedes fishtailed several times before Lou was able to regain control.

Jarred and disoriented, he failed to notice the men—two of them, he could see now—had drifted to his left and were attempting to pull alongside him. He skidded in and out of a shallow drainage ditch and when he looked back, they had taken over the road. The bull-necked man in the passenger seat was grinning as he opened his window and raised his gun.

Instead of ramming into the side of the Caddy, which was Lou's first instinct, he slammed on the brakes. The other car surged past him, and the bullets from several shots vanished harmlessly into the corn.

Clenching his jaws tighter than seemed possible, Lou spun the wheel to the right. Instantly, he was flying through a dense forest of tall stalks. He punched the accelerator and jounced violently ahead. Tall green Frankenstalks lashed at the windshield like the brushes in a car wash. The soft dirt stole much of the car's traction, but miraculously the tires navigated the uneven, loose terrain. Somewhere out there had to be another road.

Behind him, the stalks were flattened like the wake of an ocean liner—no problem for the Caddy to follow. Lou couldn't see it at the moment, but he had no doubt it was coming. The man at the wheel seemed to be a much better driver than he was, and the car, surprisingly, was at least as fast as the Benz.

The slashing stalks were blinding. From behind, he thought he could see the Caddy again, bouncing through heavy dust. There was a loud crack and his rear window shattered.

Faster, dammit! Faster!

Instinctively, Lou ducked to avoid the spray of dirt and debris now being sucked into the Mercedes.

More gunshots.

The Caddy again closed through the sandstorm behind him.

Then, over the roar of the Benz, he heard another sound—the howl of a powerful engine.

Something big.

A combine harvester, he realized.

Through the stalks he could see the top of the glass cab moving toward him and closing fast.

He was in the ER, now, and things were unraveling rapidly for the patient on the gurney. Blood pressure was plummeting. Heart rhythm was wild and irregular. No time to reason or plan. Only time to react.

Slamming down on his horn, Lou hoped to drown out the engine's sound. Anything to keep the driver behind him from realizing the harvester was there. He intentionally let up on the accelerator, beckoning the Caddy to close in. Dust was filling the Benz and choking him. Corn continued to lash against the windshield. Lou could see just enough to gauge the distance between him and the harvester. Maybe twenty seconds to impact.

Ten tons barreling at him. Probably more.

The Caddy was on his tail now, exploding through his wake like number two in a cigarette speedboat race.

The driver had to be flying blind.

The Mercedes was going fifty.

The Caddy was close on his tail.

At last an advantage.

Blood pressure zero, pulse zero.

No more time.

Go for it!

It was *Rebel Without a Cause,* and he was James Dean, playing chicken with a ten-ton harvester.

Through the windshield Lou saw only green. The Caddy hit him—once, then again.

Fifteen seconds . . .

The harvester was green, he could tell now—green with half a dozen bright orange torpedo-like protrusions shearing off the ears at ground level and sucking them up. The driver was a dark shadow in the glass tower of the machine. Any moment he would realize what was happening, but by then, hopefully, it would be too late for the Cadillac and the men inside.

Number twenty blade, please . . . Chest cutters . . . Rib spreaders . . . Come on, everyone, no time . . . No time!

The gunman in the Caddy fired again. The bullet passed through the opening where Lou's rear window had been, and spiderwebbed the front one. Another shot, more spiderwebbing.

Ten seconds.

Lou ducked low in his seat.

The orange torpedo scoops began turning toward Lou's right.

Time!

Still crouched as low as he could manage, Lou swung the wheel of the Benz sharply to his left, scraping the outermost tube.

The driver behind him had no time to react. Lou sat up just as the men slammed with ferocious force into the front of the oncoming harvester. The Caddy rose up onto its nose and flipped over onto its roof.

Lou accelerated, now following the trail of harvested Frankencorn that hopefully would bring him to a road. When he finally broke free onto yet another narrow dirt and gravel track, he pulled over, coughing, gasping for breath, and then, laughing out loud. Throughout the chase, he had forced himself to think by reenacting the cracking of a patient's chest in the ER, even though he had never actually done the procedure on anyone. It was a game he had played off and on over his career to sharpen his thinking—the emergency specialist's version of a kid counting down the last seconds on his driveway court before taking the final shot in the championship game.

Lou exited the Benz long enough to brush himself off, spit out a mouthful of dust, and stretch. He was safe for the moment, but he knew William Chester was vindictive and deadly. It was only a matter of time—possibly very little time—before the man who had risen to wealth and power on the suspicious death of his mentor went after Renee and Emily.

CHAPTER 46

Darlene waited in the sitting room outside the Oval Office for the chance to speak with her husband. She had hoped to pop in on him unannounced, but understood that at times, even the president's wife was not extended that liberty. Today, it was a call Oval Office Operations Director Cynthia Cuthbert described as "very important."

Cuthbert, fiftyish, single, and as devoted to Martin as anyone on his staff, oversaw who was granted access to the president. She prided herself on being meticulous, serious, and efficient. Although she preferred to work in the shadows, no one in Washington who mattered, or wanted to matter, misjudged her power.

Darlene and she shared a mutual respect though nothing approaching a friendship, and a very important phone call was a very important phone call. Darlene hadn't gotten near the Oval Office yet, but already she felt off balance and uncomfortable.

How will Martin react? How much should I tell him?

Everything, she had decided. He must know everything that she had learned from Double M. The situation was far too grave for her to hold anything back. Unfortunately, even without mentioning her connection with Lou, there was a strong chance her overstressed husband would erupt. Gratefully, the Oval Office walls were soundproof.

"May I get you something to drink while you're waiting for the president?" Cuthbert asked.

The president. Darlene thought, sighing inwardly, *How about "Martin"? Or better still, "your husband"?*

Protocol was invaluable for maintaining order, but Darlene never grew accustomed to how it dehumanized her twenty-five-year marriage. Here, in Cuthbert's realm, Darlene was no longer the man's wife. She was merely another guest, someone with approved access to the president through the same rigors applied to any prospective visitor. More and more she found herself longing to return to their former life together, with the privacy, true intimacy, and, yes, the fun so increasingly lacking in their marriage.

Granted, Lou wasn't the President of the United States. But he did have intense stresses in his life, and he had managed to overcome them and continue active devotion to his daughter, and even to his ex-wife. Darlene felt some guilt at harboring the feelings that she did. But she was nothing if not a woman, and a deeply emotional woman at that. Whether it was guilt or longing, joy or shame, her feelings were her feelings, and she would always own them.

Cuthbert's phone rang and a brief exchange followed.

"The president will see you now," she said.

Rising from her chair, Darlene smoothed out her skirt. "Thank you, Cynthia. I shouldn't be too long."

Had she just said that cynically?

Martin smiled warmly as soon as Darlene entered his office. He came out from behind his expansive desk, took hold of her hands, and gave her a brief, perhaps obligatory, kiss on the lips. "You look nice," he said, though his eyes barely stayed on her.

Darlene sucked in a deep and nervous breath. This wasn't going to be pleasant. "Marty . . . there's something I need to discuss with you."

Martin's gaze became more probing, as if he had begun sizing up a diplomatic adversary. "How about we go to the sitting area? Coffee? Tea?"

"The effervescent Miss Cuthbert already offered."

"Ah, Cynthia—always and ever the right thing," Martin said, favoring her with the boyish grin she liked most.

Darlene sat at the center of one of a pair of peppermint-striped sofas, and was not totally surprised when he took the seat across from her.

"Thanks for making time to see me," she said.

"Nonsense. Honey, what's wrong? You look upset."

She inhaled deeply and let her breath out slowly.

"It's about Russ Evans," she said.

She could see Martin tense. His back became rigid, and the beginnings of a glare materialized in his killer blue eyes.

"I thought we had decided that subject would be taboo," he said, still maintaining control.

Darlene had hoped to keep Victor Ochoa out of this discussion, but now she could see that unless Martin simply threw her out of his office, it wasn't going to be possible. She pressed on, ignoring his tight-lipped reminder of "their" agreement, and extracted an unmarked envelope from her purse.

"The girl who framed Russ is dead," Darlene said, handing Martin Angela's photos.

Martin began flipping through the articles, notes, and snapshots. Darlene watched him for any reaction. She had expected more.

"Okay, what's this all about?"

Darlene told him about Double M, from his first contact with Kim to the horrible recording of threats made to a young prostitute to their meeting at the movie theater and, finally, to the arrangement for Darlene to meet with Dr. Lou Welcome. She also recounted Double M's warnings about a dangerous shipment of corn, Lou's concerns over William Chester's fields, experimental work with DNA taken from mutated termites, and finally, Lou's suspicion that the John Meacham mass slayings and other tragedies and near tragedies were somehow connected to Chester Enterprises' GMO corn.

What she left out was her trip to Philadelphia with Lou. At the moment, there was no predicting how Martin would react. Now, he craned his neck back and stared up at the ceiling, processing what was clearly a lot of information. The creases across his forehead deepened. His lower lip bulged as he ran his tongue across his bottom teeth—a nervous tic predating the days when the two of them first started going out together.

Does he believe me?

Abruptly, Martin rose from the couch and walked to a window overlooking the Rose Garden. Several tense minutes passed. When he turned back to her, his expression appeared to have softened.

He's seeing me, she thought. *I feel him finally seeing me.*

He returned to the sitting area, but this time took a seat next to her. After twenty-five years, there wasn't a posture or body position she couldn't read. This one, his face tight and his weight pulled back from her, she did not like at all.

"Okay . . . okay . . . let's talk," he said.

He leaned back more, his leg crossed, his elbow on his knee, one hand nearly concealing his mouth. For the briefest moment, Darlene felt guilt for having burdened her already overtaxed husband. But like Martin, she, too, possessed a love of country and a responsibility to protect Americans from harm.

"Go on, Martin," she said.

"I want to help you out, here, honey. I really do. But I'm flat out of ideas. So why don't you tell me exactly what I can do?"

She hated his tone and blank look. It was as if she had become an intrusion on his day. "Ignore me if you wish, Martin, but please don't patronize me. You know exactly what I'm talking about and what I want you to do about it."

Martin then nodded. "It seems you're asking me to issue some sort of presidential edict I really have no authority to do, and stop a shipment of corn."

"Precisely."

"And even if I could, even if I had that sort of legal clout, why should I?"

"Because there is strong evidence to suggest the corn on that train isn't safe," Darlene answered.

"Strong evidence? Oh, please, give me a break, Dar. You're being naïve. This is all about someone's petty attempt at inconveniencing a competitor. I happen to know about this corn—a good deal about it, for that matter. I know that it has been thoroughly tested, and found to be perfectly safe. For crying out loud, Dar, your friend Russell Evans is the one who signed off on it!"

Darlene felt as if she had been punched in the gut. It was half a minute before she could speak. Why hadn't Double M told her?

"What is it you know about this corn, Martin," she managed, forcing a modicum of calm back into her voice, "that makes it so easy for you to discount what I'm saying?"

Martin stood and turned his back to her, hands resting on his hips. For those few prolonged seconds, it felt like he was her president, and not her husband. Eventually, he turned back with new resolve on his face—the look of a man about to compromise. "What I'm about to tell you, Darlene," Martin said in a stern voice, "cannot ever be repeated. It cannot leave this room. Is that agreed?"

Darlene felt her chest tighten as her pulse began

hammering. "I'm your wife, Martin. You can tell me anything you wish in confidence."

"That corn is going to save my presidency, and I'd feed it to our family for Thanksgiving dinner. It's that safe."

Darlene sat silent and breathless.

"The economy is killing us," Martin continued. "Americans need jobs, and as things stand, I have no way to come up with them. It's as simple as that. Forget about Democrats or Republicans. When it comes to employment, we're all independents. If I can't get Americans back to work, my presidency—and everything I stand for and was elected for—is over. One term and I'm through. If I'm lucky, history will paint me as a failure. More likely, I won't be painted at all. And I am no failure, Darlene! I'm not about to let the American people down."

Darlene felt herself beginning to shake. "Martin, what have you done?" she asked.

His gaze at her was level. His jaw set. "I cut a deal with the Chinese," he said matter-of-factly. "They're on the precipice of a major food crisis, and they know it. The wealthier Chinese are demanding more meat in their diets, which requires more corn to feed the livestock. The new Chinese wealth is spiking food demands all over the country. Corn has become the key commodity feeding the world. It's in all our processed foods. Feeding corn to livestock that was built by evolution to eat grass is what allows us to eat meat any moment of the day that we want it. Forget the foreign oil debate. We're more dependent on corn for our survival than on any single commodity. The Chinese government realized they simply cannot meet the growing demand using traditional agriculture practices."

"But why this corn? Why not just increase exports?"

"Because we can't grow enough of the stuff," Martin replied, as though the answer were obvious. "Genetic engineering is the only way to make truly high-yield corn. To meet future global food demand, farmers need to grow corn at a rate of three hundred bushels an acre. That's almost a two hundred percent increase from current yields. The Chinese see the long-term value in what we're proposing to trade. This revolutionary corn—the corn on your train—will virtually guarantee China's food security through the next millennium. Ours, too. The Chinese government understands that the fastest way to lose control over their citizens is to allow them to starve. And it will happen, unless the food demand is curbed . . . or met."

Darlene felt ill. Her husband was not only in bed with the Chinese government, but he was in bed with Chester Enterprises as well. She opened a bottle of water and drank without using a glass. "What are you trading?" she asked, her voice breaking nevertheless.

"The technology to make this corn," answered Martin. "The corn shipment you're so concerned about is the first of many planned exchanges with the Chinese. We're giving them enough corn to meet the food demands of a city the size of Beijing, along with the technology to produce high-yield corn on their own."

"You mean the tools to mutate termites and create potentially dangerous food," Darlene snapped.

Martin began pacing. The tic below his lip grew more intense. "What is with you, Darlene?" Martin fired back. "There is nothing wrong with this corn. Why do you think I have the USDA! They have tested it. It was approved by my personally chosen Secretary of Agriculture for human consumption."

"Don't be so quick to discount me, Martin," Darlene said, anger making her voice shake.

"I'm not discounting you. I'm trying to make you understand. There's a difference."

"And how are the Chinese going to save your presidency?"

"Exports support U.S. jobs, and imports displace them," Martin said. "The Chinese control what and how much they import. If they ease up on the throttle just a few clicks, our economists have predicted two hundred thousand new U.S. jobs in half a year. That number is more than enough to change the public's perception of our economy. It will bolster confidence, increase consumer spending, and create even more U.S. jobs. Ultimately, with the tentative agreements we have in place, this corn is going to create two million new jobs. That's how it's going to win me the election. Or maybe you don't understand how politics really works."

Darlene averted her eyes. She hated being belittled, and was incensed at how easy it was for her husband to make her feel that way. "You're the president," she said, her voice hoarse with emotion. "I trust you to do what's best for the American people and the citizens of the world."

"I'm glad you have confidence in me."

"But what if Lou Welcome is right about John Meacham and the other messed-up people in Kings Ridge?"

Martin sighed. "Are we back to that?"

"Do you know how many Chinese there are?"

"Of course I do! Don't insult me."

"Then don't play politics with this. Make sure it's safe. Stop that train."

Martin went red. "I already told you that the corn is safe!"

"This isn't just about an election," Darlene retorted. "Believe it or not, there are more important things in life than winning elections or your precious legacy!"

"Like what?"

"Like me!"

Martin seemed not to have heard her, but he did uncross his arms and softened his expression once more. "Honey, let's not do this," he pleaded. "I'm sorry for what I said about you not understanding politics. I just hate seeing people take advantage of you."

Darlene pulled away. "What is that supposed to mean?"

Martin sighed again. "It means this Double M, whoever he is, clearly knows your weakness and your commitment to good nutrition for all. Bottom line is this guy is a radical. He's a crackpot, using you to get to me. And you just bought into it."

Darlene's bubble of self-control burst. "I saw those mutated bugs, Martin!" she shouted, no longer caring whether the Oval Office was soundproof or not. "They're monsters. They can't be considered food."

Finally, Martin looked as if he were listening. "Where did you see them?"

Darlene sucked in a breath and regretted making the disclosure. "Victor drove Dr. Welcome and me to Philadelphia. We met with an entomologist there. That's how I knew the insects had to have been mutated."

"Victor drove you and some strange man to Philadelphia?" Martin's rage could be felt. "I swear I'm going to have that fucker run out of the service."

"Don't you dare!"

"Then don't you dare go behind my back again, Darlene. You don't know what you're screwing around with. You are way, and I mean way, out of your league here."

"I want you to talk with Lou Welcome," Darlene said.

Martin reddened even more. "I'll do no such thing! You just told me he was a drug addict and an emergency doctor, not a nutritionist! The only arrangements I'm going to make are for you to leave town to have a visit with Lisa until this whole train thing is over and the corn is where it should be—in the ground and on the dishes in China. You need to get some perspective on things, Darlene. Leave the politics to me. I want you out of this. No more investigating. No more talk about Russell Evans, Lou Welcome, or your jaunts to Philadelphia. Is that understood?"

Darlene moved as far away from her husband as she could without actually leaving. "Or what?" she demanded.

"Or I promise you that Victor Ochoa will need to find a new career, and it'll be your fault when it happens.

And if your doctor friend gets in my way, I'll have him hounded until he melts like hot butter."

"You wouldn't dare," Darlene said in a near growl.

"Don't test me."

Darlene and Martin locked eyes, with neither yielding. In many ways, Darlene knew Martin better than he knew himself. Although they often disagreed, Darlene had never known the president to lie to her. His threat to fire Victor, she believed, was not veiled or lacking teeth. He meant what he had said, and would do as he had promised. Darlene felt certain that was true.

But at some point during their argument, his eyes had betrayed him. At some point he hadn't told the truth.

If only she knew what lie he had told.

"Just do yourself a favor, President Mallory," she said.

"What's that?"

"When they ask for someone to write your legacy, don't recommend me."

CHAPTER 47

"Who is this?"

Kim could barely hear the caller above the din of rush hour noise.

She blocked her ear with one hand and moved away from the traffic and closer to the buildings. It had been a brutal day at work, and she had chosen take-home salad from Panera Bread over dinner with a potentially interesting congressman from California.

"Kim, it's Doug, from Bar None," the caller said.

"The bartender?"

"Yeah, Doug the bartender."

Kim became hyperfocused. Why would he be calling? How did he even know her phone number?

"What's up?" she asked.

"Some guy in the bar wants to buy you a drink. He gave me your number and paid me a hundred bucks to call you. Sorry to bug you, but the truth is I can always use that kind of cash."

Kim tensed. "Is it . . . the same guy from before?" she asked.

"Look, you've come in here lots of times with a bunch of great-looking women, and I'm not sure I could pick any of you out of a crowd. People buy people drinks all the time here. I'm just a messenger."

"Could you tell me what the guy looks like?"

There was a pause. "Well, actually, I can. He's old."

"Old? Can you see him?"

"Not at the moment. It's pretty busy right now. He said he'll be sticking around for another fifteen minutes. Longer if you promise to show up. Okay? I got to go."

"Okay," Kim replied to a dead line. "I'll be there."

Not *Double M,* she thought.

No longer feeling exhausted, Kim called Darlene.

"Hey, there," Darlene said, answering her phone on the first ring with an unusually somber voice.

Something was wrong.

"You okay?" Kim asked, already headed toward the Bar None.

"Actually, no, I'm not. Want to talk?"

"Actually, we've *got* to talk."

She told Darlene about the bartender's call.

"If it's not Double M," Darlene said, "it's probably someone with a message from him. You've got to go there right now."

"I'm already on my way. What about you?"

"I'll call or else meet you there as soon as I can. And Kim," she added, catching her chief of staff just before she ended the call.

"Yes?"

"You be careful."

* * *

When Kim arrived, Bar None was enjoying another packed night of deep-pocketed patrons. Spotting an opening at the bar near where Doug was serving at Mach 2 speed, she wormed her way onto the stool and waved for the bartender's attention. When he finally came over, he seemed unaware that he had just minutes ago called her cell phone. He just stood there, waiting impatiently to take her order. The jukebox was blasting a song from the country trio Lady Antebellum, and a dozen young and beautifuls were vying for his attention.

"What can I get you?" he called out.

"I'm the woman you just phoned."

Recognition dawned. "Oh yeah," he said, nodding vigorously. "Here you go." He handed Kim an open Amstel Light, along with a cardboard coaster.

She left the beer on the bar and flipped over the coaster. To her surprise, there was no writing on the bottom. Her heartbeat began to accelerate.

"Edwin told me you'd do that," said a gravelly voice at her elbow.

Kim snapped her head right and saw a cadaverous-looking man in a nicely tailored suit and striped bow tie. Tall and stoop shouldered, the man, well into his seventies, she guessed, extended a bony hand. He had a road map of narrow veins covering his sunken cheeks, and bushy white eyebrows hovering above a set of intelligent chestnut eyes.

"Who are you?" Kim asked.

"My name is Shank, Norman Shank," he said. "I am a friend of Mr. Edwin Chester, and also his attorney."

No business card. Kim doubted she would find a Norman Shank in any listing of area lawyers.

"Go on," she said.

"My instructions were to contact you precisely in the manner I am doing. Regrettably, I am afraid that something terrible has befallen Edwin."

"Edwin?"

"Edwin Chester, the son of William Chester of Chester Enterprises."

"The seed giant?"

"Yes," Shank said. "He is also the man you know as Double M."

"Can we go somewhere and talk?" Kim asked, glancing around for anyone who seemed interested in them.

"According to my understanding, everything that Edwin has to say is contained in here." Shank handed over a large sealed manila envelope. "You see, for some time now, Edwin has instructed me to phone him every day at three o'clock in the afternoon, sharp. If he failed to answer my phone call, I was to send him a text message. Difficult thing, teaching an old man like me how to text. In any event, if Edwin failed to respond to my text within an hour, I was to assume that he was either dead or incapacitated. In that event, I was to contact you via Doug, here at Bar None, and hand-deliver this envelope."

"Double M is dead?" Kim asked, struggling to remain composed.

The lawyer smiled sadly. "The likelihood is that the most dire misfortune has, in fact, befallen him. Once I have done as he requested here, I will set about to learn what has happened, but we must think the worst."

Kim clutched the envelope. "Thank you."

Her thoughts swirled through the implications of Double M's death—either murder or suicide, it seemed.

Shank bowed his head slightly. "I must be going now. Please do not try to contact me. Those are Edwin's wishes. If I learn anything you need to know, I will get back to you." He turned and shambled from the restaurant.

Kim, never losing contact with the envelope, drank half her Amstel in two gulps and again scanned the patrons for anyone paying too much attention to her. The game had changed to serious hardball. Fifteen minutes later, she was considering another beer when her cell phone rang.

"I'm parked right outside," Darlene said.

CHAPTER 48

Kim paid her tab, left a twenty under the coaster, and hurried to Darlene's limo. She was surprised when another agent, not Victor, opened the door for her. Darlene instructed the man and the agent with him to get onto the Capital Beltway and drive until she asked them to return to the White House. As they pulled away, she requested that the privacy window behind the front seat be closed. Then she settled back next to her friend.

"Where's Victor?" Kim asked as soon as they were moving.

"I told him to take a few days off for his own good. Martin wants to fire him for taking us to Philadelphia." Her hands were tightly clenched.

"Talk to me," Kim said, gently loosening Darlene's fists.

Darlene described her fight with Martin, the threats he made against Victor, and what he revealed about trading GMO corn seed and technology to the Chinese for American jobs.

Kim listened in stunned silence, the envelope from Double M resting on her lap. "Have you told Lou about all this?" she asked.

"No. I gave Martin my word that I wouldn't tell anyone, but I'm really PO'ed at him. The choice was between sharing with you what happened and broadcasting his pigheadedness on CNN. I guess I really shouldn't have put you in the line of Martin's fire by telling you."

"Nonsense. I can handle it. I'm just sorry I can't do anything about his deplorable behavior. So, what now?"

Darlene sighed. "I don't know," she said. "I need Martin to meet with Lou. That's the only way he can possibly be convinced the corn isn't safe. But that just isn't going to happen. Lou has joined the ranks of Russ Evans—people I am forbidden to mention in Martin's presence. I swear, Kim, I have never seen such change in a man."

"You don't have to explain, babe. I remember how he was the night we won. Floating right up there overhead with the red, white, and blue balloons. Alas, becoming the most powerful person on earth can cause some pretty heavy changes—like the bite of that radioactive spider did to Peter Parker. Darlene, you don't have to answer this, but is there something going on between you and Lou?"

"Why would you even wonder about such a thing?" she replied, not trying too hard to suppress the glint in her eyes.

"I knew it. I swear, Dar, you have all the guile of a newborn."

"I don't even know what's happening. Lou is the only man I've had these sort of feelings for since I met Martin."

Kim squeezed her hand. "Have you kissed him?"

"No. No," Darlene replied emphatically. "But that doesn't mean I haven't thought about it, especially after that circus today with Martin."

"Careful about doing anything when you're angry. It's someone's rule."

"I understand."

"Whatever you do, I'm behind you all the way."

The women hugged.

"So, tell me," Darlene asked, "what's going on with Double M?"

Kim handed over the envelope, having nearly forgotten it was there. "It's bad," she said. "Real bad." She recounted the upsetting exchange with the man calling himself Norman Shank. "You should open it," Kim said softly. "Read it to yourself, or if you want, feel free to read it out loud."

The pages, several of them, were neatly single-spaced with a double space between paragraphs. As Darlene scanned the first few words, she covered her mouth in horror, then read aloud.

Dear Madam First Lady:

If you are reading this letter, then I am dead. My name is Edwin Chester, and I am the son of William Chester, Chairman and CEO of the Chester Seed Company. This letter is a confession of sorts. It does, in my death, what I could not bring myself to do while I was alive—finally to tell the truth about my father's lies and misdeeds.

Darlene gasped. "Lou was right," she whispered before continuing.

I apologize for all the subterfuge. My reasons for not being more forthcoming were the direct result of my steadfast, unyielding love for William Chester. You can research his most remarkable life, but accounts will paint a very incomplete picture of the caring, loving man whom I have been blessed to call my father. I write this even though I believe he will be found at least partially responsible for my death.

I was born with severe club-foot deformities and was the source of much ridicule even as a young child. My father refused to accept my condition. He took me to the best surgeons in the world and sat beside me for many hours and many procedures as they reshaped my bones. He also pushed me to rise to my potential.

Darlene stopped reading. "I can't believe he's dead," she said, shaking. "And I'm terrified that Martin is somehow involved."

"Please keep reading," Kim urged.

Darlene continued.

My father was nurturing. He was also quite forceful in his beliefs and ways. Most important, he was a constant presence in my very chaotic and inconsistent world. When my mother and sister passed away, it was my father who stepped in, fulfilling the role of parent to such a degree as to earn my unyielding devotion.

He was the first to see my potential as a scientist, and encouraged me to study plant genetics, and to continue through to my Ph.D. William Chester is a true visionary. He foresaw the looming food crisis long before it was even a whisper in the halls of the Department of Agriculture. He saw that the corn yield was the lock keeping us from achieving global food security, and he knew that rDNA would be the key.

"What's rDNA?" Kim asked.
"It says right here," Darlene said.

Recombinant DNA opens the door for the creating of limitless new species, each designed for a specific function, and all created from transplanting the genes from one organism into the genetic makeup of another. Corn is the single most important crop in the global food economy. It is fed to cattle, which in turn provides us with beef. Corn is a key ingredient in almost all processed foods, and a mainstay in most diets. Without a sufficient supply of corn, it can be argued, a country would fail to provide its citizens with the resources necessary for them to live without hunger or fear of starvation. In the global agricultural economy, corn is the king, queen, and most of the court.

To meet the growing demand, our competitors have tried various hybridization techniques, averaging a yield increase of roughly 2 percent per year. But genetic engineering has changed the game dramatically. Yields have been increasing, up to an average of 150 bushels per acre.

However, that is not nearly enough. As a result of the looming corn shortage, in the coming years, Americans will need to decrease their consumption of meat to under 12 pounds per year from an average of 250 pounds per person. Population growth; more industrialized countries; more meat-eating populations; higher demand for convenient processed foods; ethanol-based fuel; these are all factors contributing to a dramatic increase in corn demand. Meanwhile the supply side is under increasing pressure.

Single-handedly, I have developed a solution to this pending crisis. Three hundred bushels per acre of corn is now possible with the technology I have created. However, this technology requires significant genetic manipulation, firstly with a radiation-induced mutation of the African termite species *Macrotermes bellicosus*, and secondly, using rDNA techniques to embed the mutated termite DNA into common corn. I stumbled onto this discovery when I became curious to see how one of the insect world's most fecund creatures could be used to engineer corn genetically to have more kernels per ear and more ears per acre. This represents a dramatic shift from the current yield projection reported by our competitors, which requires engineering corn with built-in pest and pesticide resistance.

The technology I have created, in my opinion, calls for years of testing before it can be safely sanctioned for human consumption. Secretary of Agriculture Russell Evans shared my concerns about this new product. He believed that transgenic corn, that is to say corn created using the DNA of a non-corn species, technically is not corn. In a report filed by the DOA, and now apparently lost, Secretary Evans insisted on the formation of a study commission that would have kept our new corn product out of the food supply for a minimum of five years.

I am afraid that delay translated into too much lost profit and lost acclaim for my father to bear. For this reason, he had Secretary Evans removed from office. As you know, I tried to warn the president about my father's wrongdoings without having to betray the man I love. Secretary Evans was right—the corn needs to be tested further, even though my father insists that intensive human use of our corn, and products derived from our corn, has already disclosed no adverse health effects. But my father is wrong, and Dr. Lou Welcome is right. This corn is not safe.

There is a train being loaded with our GMO corn for shipment by air and sea to cargo planes and tankers bound for China. I believe there are other trains being readied as well. I am sorry now that I did not do more to stop these shipments.

Please understand, that I did what I thought was best. But now it is up to you and President Mallory to do what is right. I am sorry I will not be there to help you.

Sincerely, Edwin Chester.

"My God," Darlene whispered, dabbing at her tears. "The poor man." She then extracted another piece of paper from inside the envelope.

"What's that?" Kim asked.

"It's the copy of the train manifest," Darlene said. "The train carrying the corn shipment." She folded the letter and manifest, then slipped them back inside the envelope.

"What now?" Kim asked.

"Now I call Victor."

"Victor? Why not Martin?"

"If I'm going to speak to Martin again, I want Lou beside me, and Victor is going to help me with that. I told you that during our fight, I knew Martin was lying to me about something. Now, thanks to this letter, I know exactly what lie he was telling."

CHAPTER 49

"You're not making any sense," Renee said, handing Lou a cup of the Darjeeling tea that was his favorite. "You've got to slow down and catch your breath. Can you get into the shower?"

She had cleaned off some of the filth and the worst of his scrapes and cuts, but a glance at himself in the mirror was still frightening. The gunshot wound to his leg burned, but he could tell no serious damage had been done. He took a long sip of tea. Gradually, his hands stopped shaking.

He was in the living room of Renee and Steve's comfortable four-bedroom colonial in Arlington. Emily was in her upstairs room, ushered there by Renee, but only after Lou assured the girl he was okay and got her filthy with a prolonged bear hug. Lou suspected she was near the stairway, eavesdropping on their conversation, but neither parent had the time nor inclination to prevent it.

Renee . . . Emily . . . Steve . . . all of them had to leave town—and tonight.

"William Chester is a powerful, resourceful, vindictive man," Lou said. "Now his son is dead and his whole operation is about to be exposed. He's going to do anything he can to get back at me. Anything. Until we get the police involved and he gets put away, we're all in danger. Believe it or not, today is the *second* time his people have tried to kill me. I need you to get away and find someplace safe until I can straighten all this out."

Renee took a seat next to him on the sofa that was the only piece of furniture he recognized from their years together.

"This isn't the first time they've tried to kill you?" she asked. "Why haven't you told me?"

Lou filled her in on the events following John Meacham's murderous spree.

Her eyes widened at his description of the *bellicosus* termites. "You actually saw a man get eaten alive?"

"Two of them, as a matter of fact. After that, two more guys tried to kill me. If you want proof, the Mercedes I was driving is parked outside absolutely riddled, with the front and rear windshields both blown out."

Lou lifted the bath towel Renee had laid across his lap, exposing the gash on his thigh from Stone's bullet. She rose from the sofa, went to the bottom of the stairs, and called up to Emily.

"What is it?" Emily yelled back without materializing.

"Pack a suitcase, sweetie. We're going to spend a few days with Nana."

"What?" The teen bounded down the stairs as if

teleported. "What are you talking about going to Nana's? For how long? I have plans this weekend."

"Cancel them and pack," Renee said more sternly. "No arguments."

Emily's expression immediately became one of deep concern. "We're gonna be okay, right?" she asked.

Lou hugged her again. "Thanks for not putting up a fuss, kiddo. We're going to be fine. I just need time to straighten some things out."

After exchanging anxious looks with each parent, Emily whirled and raced back up the stairs.

As soon as they heard her bedroom door slam, Renee asked softly, "Why do you think *we're* in danger?"

"Gilbert Stone," Lou said, clenching his battered hands. "He did a lot of research on me. My arrest, our divorce, my reinstatement by the medical board. I have no reason to believe all that information hasn't found its way to Chester."

"It's not your fault," Renee said. "This is the information age, and Stone is—was—the police, and Chester has boatloads of money. If they want us, they'll find us eventually."

"Eventually isn't now. You can't go to Nana's, though."

"Why not?"

"For all the reasons you just said. If they can get to you, they can get to your mother. What about Steve?"

"What about him?"

"Does his company have a retreat—someplace you've never been?"

Renee thought a moment. "No, but a partner at his law firm has a place in the Adirondacks that he keeps offering to Steve. A fishing cabin, I think."

"Perfect. Call Steve, now. Tell him you all need to go there right away. Make him believe you."

Lou watched the color drain from Renee's face. "I'm sorry, Lou. I really am."

No casting blame. No poor us.

This was a hell of a woman.

Those thoughts segued into images of Darlene.

Was it possible? he found himself wondering. Was there any way it could happen between them? Given their situation, given his predicament at the moment, all he could do was smile inwardly. The answers to any questions about him and Darlene Mallory were more than clear: not in this lifetime.

First things first, Cap would remind him. First things first. And the first thing here was to survive William Chester and find a way to bring him down.

"Lou, don't let anything happen to Em," Renee said, sobbing now.

He held her tightly while he tried to quell his own fears. Then he rocked her in his arms, stroking her hair in the way that was still familiar after so many years.

"Nothing's going to happen to her," he said once, then again. "Nothing's going to happen to her, or you . . . or Steve." Lou closed his eyes and whispered the word *hush,* over and over again until her sobbing subsided.

When Renee pulled away, the anxiety in her eyes

had been replaced by resolve. "Go shower off," she said. "I'll call Steve and then I'll get you some clothes."

She took a few steps toward the kitchen phone, then stopped.

"Lou, how are these people in Kings Ridge being infected by the corn? If it's not an airborne contagion, like you originally thought, then how?"

Lou bit at his lip. "I can't figure it out," he said. "I've about torn my brain in half, and I just can't figure it out."

Renee returned to the living room after calling her husband. "He's on his way," she said. "He didn't doubt the urgency for a second. He trusts you, Lou. That says a lot."

"I'll help you pack, as soon as I wash off," he said.

Renee paused. "Who are the people you know of who have been affected?" she asked.

Lou listed off the names.

"Now, what do they have in common?"

"Nothing except the obvious, as far as I can tell," he said.

"No . . . if the symptoms aren't the result of something airborne, then there's got be a physical factor linking them," she said. "You're just too close to it, that's all."

"Maybe. Maybe so. Listen, Renee, you need to pack. Chester has enough money to get at you unless we make it nearly impossible."

"Okay, okay. Just think about it, though." Her voice trailed off.

Lou followed her upstairs and showered in the

guest bathroom. Renee was right. There had to be a connection.

Lou couldn't dwell long on the possibilities. Steve worked in D.C. and would be home soon. Renee had her suitcase at the top of the stairs. The sooner they were on their way, the better, and even then he wouldn't feel safe until he heard they had arrived at the cabin without incident.

He went to Emily's room and helped her gather her things.

"What's really going on, Dad?" she asked, her eyes moist.

Lou patted the edge of her twin bed, and she sat down beside him. The nearness of her comforted him and calmed him more than any medication ever could have. "Like I said, there is a very bad man who wants to hurt me and anyone close to me. He's angry because I can prove the corn he's selling is responsible for that doctor who shot all those people."

"Dr. Meacham, your client from the Wellness Office," she said.

Lou reminded himself never to underestimate or talk down to his daughter. Thirteen going on thirty. "Exactly," he said. "I'm going to go speak to the police, and we're going to do what we can to put a stop to this and put him in jail where he belongs. You can help by doing what Mom tells you. Okay?"

"Dad, I'm scared."

"I understand," he said. "I'm a little scared myself. But once you're away and safe, no one can hurt you and

I'll have time to go and talk to the police. It won't be long. I promise."

Emily wrapped her arms around him and he allowed her to cry until she was able to stop. He was still holding her when an incongruous image popped into his head. It was the image of pathetic Roberta Jennings, seated in her living room, swollen ankles folded over the tops of her shoes.

Tell, me, Mrs. Jennings, did you have any interactions with Dr. Meacham outside of the clinic? Were you involved in any clubs together? Community organizations? Church groups? Anything like that?

And at that instant, the missing piece fell into place and he knew.

Together, he and Emily moved the suitcases downstairs.

Lou was getting a glass of water in the kitchen when he felt his cell phone vibrating in the pocket of the sweatpants Renee had given him. It was a text message from an unfamiliar number.

Darlene?

Lou clicked the message icon, and a photo appeared. His breathing stopped. The picture was of Cap and George. Both men were blindfolded, with their hands bound and suspended above their heads by chains. They were imprisoned inside what appeared to be the boxcar of a train. He could make out the train's open side door, as well as some spray-painted writing on the interior wall. A message accompanied the photograph.

Come to the Chester Enterprises grain silo in Monroe, West Virginia, by eight o'clock sharp, or the next picture I send will have your friends' throats slit open. Tip off the police or anyone else and I'll kill both of them as slowly and painfully as possible, and then, your wife, Renee, and your daughter, 13-y.o. Emily. We need to talk.

"Damn."

"What's going on?" Renee asked from the living room. "What was that?"

"Cap," he said. "It was Cap." He averted his eyes, but not too much. Like their daughter, Renee was a smart bomb for the truth.

"Anything important?"

"Not really," Lou said, unable to keep himself from shaking. "He just wants to get together is all. Listen, can you all take Steve's car and let me have yours? The Mercedes is virtually undrivable."

"No problem. Just put your shot-up one in the driveway. The neighbors don't take kindly to folks who let such things happen to a Mercedes. Here are the keys to my BMW. You bring it back with the windshields all busted out, and you're going to have to open up a lemonade stand to pay for it."

"You have maps in your car?"

"A terrific GPS and a whole road atlas, why?"

"Just some thoughts I want to check on," he said, his eyes averted again.

From what Lou remembered, Monroe was about

twenty minutes south of Wardensville and a good two hours' drive from Renee's house in Arlington. He checked the time. He could make it at the designated hour, but only if he left soon.

At that moment, the house phone rang.

"That was Steve," Renee said after a moment's conversation. "He's about ten minutes away."

"I'm going to head off because Cap doesn't have much time," Lou said, before realizing that he had spoken the grisly, terrifying truth. "Keep your doors locked and the phone handy until Steve's here. Call me when he arrives, and then as soon as you're settled in."

"You be careful," Renee insisted.

"I love you, Daddy," Emily said, throwing her arms around him.

"I love you, too, kiddo. This will all be over soon."

I'm coming, Cap, he was thinking. *You stay strong. I'm coming.*

CHAPTER 50

Lou was a few miles from the grain silo before allowing himself to feel nervous. Throughout the ride, he tried to formulate a plan—any sort of plan as to what he might do once he arrived at William Chester's rural lair. The highest card he had to play appeared at the end of Chester's text message:

We need to talk.

Talking meant there might be some wiggle room. Chester's son and only child was dead. It was a given that the man wasn't going to allow Lou to live. But there was information he wanted that Lou might be able to use to barter for Cap's and George's lives—most likely the identity of those whom he had spoken to about what he knew.

In earlier, simpler days, he had hiked the Appalachian Trail through West Virginia a number of times. The lush forests and churning rivers were just what John Denver had written in the song: "almost heaven." He had actually driven through the hamlets of Wardensville and Monroe once, although he could not remember the circumstances. The towns were somewhere around the junction of state routes 50 and 220. The GPS showed only one major east–west rail line in the area, and his smartphone one corn silo near the intersection of the two roads. It was owned by Chester Enterprises. Obstacle one, albeit a small one compared to those ahead, had been negotiated.

Jaw clenched, he located the track—a pair of parallel tracks, actually—as well as the two-lane roadway that ran alongside them. Unless he came up with something soon, he was going to show up at the rendezvous with Chester less prepared than Emily had probably been for her most recent math test, although if he recalled correctly, she had reported getting an A on it nevertheless.

Lou had considered and rejected bringing a weapon of some sort to this showdown, perhaps a kitchen knife. Given the manpower Chester was sure to have, a slingshot like the one David had used against Goliath would have done him more good. He had decided that going to the authorities was a no-go as well. Cap and George had essentially no time left. Even so, twice, on the drive to Monroe, he grabbed his cell phone to call 911, but could not get past Chester's blood-chilling warning.

I'll kill both of them as slowly and painfully as possible, and then, your wife, Renee, and your daughter . . .

Lou needed only to glance at the horrifying picture of the two men, hands secured by chains, faces beaten to pulps, to convince himself that bringing help would be a death sentence.

Lou took in a deep breath and vowed he would not

let them die. It was his fault that their lives were on the line. Cap had been there for him since the day the two of them had met. George had already pulled himself out of a situation that had buried many others. He was a role model—an important role model to kids from the inner city. His future was full of productivity and service—if he lived. At this point, it seemed like the best Lou could hope for was to find a weakness in William Chester—some miracle negotiation that would save their lives.

No matter what, he wasn't going to go down easily.

The two-hour drive to Monroe felt interminable. His mind wandered through the Frankencorn transmission conundrum and the solution that had to be right. The quiet, tree-lined streets of the village, with its clapboard houses, white picket fences, and old town general store, glided past and vanished in his rearview.

William Chester was nearby now, waiting.

Lou followed the twin rail beds out of town. The trees thinned out and then disappeared altogether. Dusk settled into twilight as the GPS in Renee's car instructed him to turn onto a rutted single-lane road. Lou kept the BMW's speed down, just in case a police cruiser lurked behind a billboard.

It was nineteen minutes until eight o'clock.

Still no plan.

Outside of Monroe, the terrain became flat. The two sets of tracks were on his left, perhaps thirty yards away. In the distance, through the deepening gloom, he could see the silos, brightly illuminated by spots, rising like a mystical metropolis from the tableland. On the far track, the one that he guessed handled westbound traffic, was a train—almost certainly, *the train*. It was a colossus stretching toward the horizon as far as he could see, perhaps a mile or more long with what seemed an infinite number of cars.

As Lou rolled past the caboose, he could see two men inside. They were at a table, drinking or playing cards, or perhaps both. He chose not to cut his lights. There was no need to call any unwanted attention to himself, and he was far enough away from the train, on the opposite side of the other track, that he could have been any traveler heading west.

Lou drove until he was five or six cars past the caboose, then slowed almost to a stop. The behemoth shook as its rusted wheels struggled to inch forward. Then it stopped for a time before inching forward again.

Is it loading?

Lou's heart sank. He had no idea how enormous Chester's train was going to be. Even if he were able to sneak aboard, it would be nearly impossible to locate the car where Cap and George were being held. Then he remembered the number, clearly visible in the photograph.

Fifty-eight.

He checked the picture to be sure. The number was stenciled on the wall behind his two battered friends. Lou looked carefully at the cars as he drove past. Each one was numbered, although in no particular sequence that he could discern. Some of them were standard boxcars and some were grain cars. They represented several different rail lines, and were probably rentals.

But a majority of them, particularly the boxcars, belonged to CHESTER RAIL SYSTEMS and had stenciled black numbers at the center of their side, similar to the numbers inside the car holding Cap and George.

Lou had planned simply to walk up to Chester's storage facility, turn himself over to William, and negotiate—essentially winging it from moment one. Now he increased his speed, searching for car number fifty-eight, and just as important, a way to get onto it. To his left, the train lurched forward again. Another load.

Lou drove a quarter mile. No fifty-eight.

Chester's silos were approaching in the distance. The massive structure was composed of four cylinders, maybe twenty stories high, rising up like medieval turrets. Toward the base of each silo, he could now see long metal chutes—half pipes extending out for loading the corn through hatches in the roofs of the cars. At that moment, the train stopped again and in the distance he could actually see and hear the death kernels, rumbling like golden hail down a chute into an empty car.

Where was this corn headed? Lou asked himself. Who would be eating it? How many more lives would be ruined or lost because of it?

He accelerated slightly. Seven fifty. Time was running out. The towering grain silos drew closer. It was then Lou saw something ahead in the distance—the starlike headlight of an oncoming eastbound train. From what he could tell, it appeared to be moving slowly. The way to get onto Chester's train may have just arrived.

But only if he could find car fifty-eight.

Without hesitating, he floored the accelerator, still searching to his left as the headlights of Renee's BMW played across the sides of the corn cars. The approaching train, a totally black phantom from what Lou could tell, seemed to be crawling ahead, perhaps trying not to disrupt the loading process by sending kernels flying everywhere.

He sped past Chester's silos without slowing. The corn train seemed unending. Still no fifty-eight. Perhaps he had missed it. No matter. If his plan worked, and if fifty-eight was part of the train, he would find it. Finally, he passed the engines—three in all. The head of the dragon. He kept on driving. The black phantom was now a slow-moving eastbound snake with a yellow CSX insignia painted on its two ebony engines.

Ahead, the horizon glowed like the remnants of a settling fire, its red orange hues being nudged into oblivion by the descending night sky.

Seven fifty-five.

Here, the road curved, bringing Lou even closer to the train tracks, now some ten feet to his left. He cut his speed, then confident he had driven far enough, braked to a stop and exited the Beemer. He took the car keys with him, hoping against hope that once Cap and George were freed, all three would be able to make their way back to this spot undetected. Lou took one other item from the car as well, a tire iron. It would probably be that against guns and killers who knew how to use them, but better a tire iron than just his wits.

The huge eastbound freight train lumbered along at

about the pace of a brisk walker. Lou jogged up to it, ignoring painful messages from both his wounded thigh and stiff ankle. Down the track to his left, the lone headlight on the lead engine of Chester's train glowed like a cyclops in the deepening night. Following alongside the CSX cars, Lou checked out the steel ladders on two of them.

From a distance, jumping hobo-style onto such a slow-moving train did not strike him as too perilous. However, from up close, and somewhat hobbled, he wasn't so confident.

Seven fifty-eight.

He had to move. Cradling the tire iron in his hand, Lou caught his breath and jumped at a chest-high rung on the next passing ladder.

The tire iron clanged as he got a hold of the painted metal. An instant later, the hand with his weapon lost its grip on the rung. Lou swung away from the side of the car like an opening door. The tire iron fell to the gravel beside the squealing wheels. Gripping tightly with the other hand, he shifted his weight to counter the momentum, then swung back, hitting his nose hard against the ladder. Instantly, his eyes teared up and his vision blurred. With his hand now freed, he managed to regain his hold. With tears still cascading, and now nearly breathless, he climbed. At the top, he flattened out on the roof and peered across at the trio of engines on Chester's train as the phantom rolled slowly past them.

Next came the unending line of corn cars and box-cars. One by one, he scanned the numbers painted on each. The massive CSX train groaned and shuddered as it passed no more than two feet from the other.

"One-thirty-one.

"Twenty-seven.

"Sixty."

Lou said each number aloud. His heart was racing as the cars glided past. The car he had chosen to jump on was past the silo now. The sound of corn kernels rumbling down the loading tubes was lost in the grinding of the wheels.

"One-oh-seven.

"Sixty-two."

It was just after eight.

Be strong, Cap. . . . You be strong.

"Thirty-six.

"Eighteen."

He looked ahead at the number of the next car he would pass.

There it was! Fifty-eight, right after eighteen.

Lou shifted into a crouch and inched across toward the other train. He would go for the roof of car number eighteen, to avoid alerting any guards who might be in fifty-eight. Time had run out for Cap and George. The fear that was choking his confidence gave way as he readied himself to make the leap. Even though the black phantom was moving slowly, the ground between the two trains was a blur.

One . . . two . . . three!

With all the force he had, Lou launched himself across the gap between trains. He traveled much less distance than he had expected or intended, and landed hard on the roof of number eighteen. However, he hadn't appreciated a slight slope to both sides from the center of the car, and without traction he immediately began to slip backwards.

Unable to arrest his slide, Lou went over the roof feetfirst. At the last possible instant, he caught hold of a rib running along the roof edge, and his arms held. Uttering a soft thanks to Cap for the upper body training, he hoisted himself back onto the car in an awkward chin-up—the second time in eight hours or so his arms had been tested like that.

Eight-oh-seven.

Please, don't let me be too late.

With his body as flat as he could manage, Lou crawled marine-style along the length of car eighteen. Up in a crouch again, he was about to dive above the platform joining it to car fifty-eight, when the train lurched forward to receive another load of Frankencorn. Lou was thrown hard onto his back. Air burst from his lungs, and his head snapped backwards against the unyielding metal.

No time.

Dazed, he again scrambled into a crouch and leapt headfirst from eighteen to fifty-eight. His belly-flop landing was surprisingly easy and silent.

Maybe another prayer is in order, he thought.

If he was right—and he simply had to be—Cap and George were just below him.

The train stopped moving. Glancing ahead, Lou

heard the rumble and saw a rush of yellow corn seed as one of the silos emptied some of its load about four cars ahead.

At the center of the roof of car fifty-eight was a closed hatch. The door's rusted hinges creaked slightly as Lou lifted it open, but the sound of the corn rushing down the loading chute appeared to mask it. Flattened against the metal, he peered into the gloom below. The sliding door on the left side was open, bathing the inside in a dim light from the spots on the silo. He could make out a lone guard—jacket off, gun in his shoulder holster, unaware of the changes above him.

There might be other guards down there, out of Lou's line of sight, but no matter. The flames of his determination were fanned by what he saw just in front of the man below him. Cap and George, neither of them moving, were dangling from a ceiling support on thick chains, their feet barely touching the floor. Even in the dim light, it was easy to see that they had been viciously beaten. Their heads hung down lifelessly.

At that moment, the gunman, tall and blond, with a square-set jaw, glanced up. He moved directly beneath the opening of the hatch, blinking to clear his vision.

Lou clenched his teeth.

He said a silent prayer for God to watch over Emily.

Then he jumped.

CHAPTER 51

Falling prey to his own disbelief, the guard was late in reacting to the movement above him. Silently, arms flailing, Lou plunged fifteen feet chest first, like a sky-jumper in free fall. Below him, he could see the confusion and hesitation in the young man's face. Just before they collided, he thought he recognized him from Chester's cornfield.

"What the—?"

The guard's words were cut short when Lou, head turned to one side, hit him like a cannonball. Lou's knees slammed into his midchest. An older man might have had his sternum or collarbones snap, but the blond was solid and fit. He went crashing over backwards with Lou on top. His hefty pistol clattered away.

Lou's breath exploded out of him, and his right elbow hit with numbing force. His body momentarily went limp from the pain, and he rolled to his side. He was relieved to see there were no other guards. From where he lay, it seemed as if his sudden appearance hadn't registered with either Cap or George. In fact, he wasn't even certain George was breathing.

"Cap, can you hear me?" he said in a harsh whisper. "It's Lou."

A moan and movement of the fighter's head were the response.

The men were suspended from a beam by a single heavy chain, secured by a padlock.

To Lou's right, the stunned guard was groaning and struggling to roll over. He kept pressing against his ears with his huge hands, perhaps trying to muffle the continued explosions in his head. With any luck, the man was out of commission.

Lou crawled to his friends and cringed. Cap's eyes were nearly lost within mounds of swollen bruises. There were cuts on his cheeks and arms, and his lips were split and caked with dried blood. Chester's thugs had accomplished what no opponent in the ring had ever been able to do.

"What took you so long?" Cap rasped, his words thick and barely discernible.

"I'm going to get you guys out of here," Lou said. "Just hang in there."

"Very funny," Cap managed.

Lou was on his feet now, checking George. Gratefully, he was breathing, albeit shallowly and slowly. Lou lifted his head and checked his pupils as best he could. Wide but equal in size. Better than they might have been. George's hands were pitifully swollen, and folded over like rags. Lou wondered if there was any function left in them.

"Lou!"

He was scanning the dark corners of the car for the guard's gun, when Cap grunted a frantic warning and kicked his feet to get Lou's attention.

The guard was on his knees, propping himself up with a hand on each side. He was a beast, Lou realized—huge hands, broad shoulders, and the neck of a linebacker. His platinum blond hair was smeared with blood, probably from a gash at the back of his head. Still, he looked far more lucid now.

Lou scanned the boxcar once more, searching for the gun or some other sort of weapon. The walls and grimy floor beneath him seemed bare.

Where in the hell was the gun?

The guard was quickly regaining his senses and had to be dealt with. If he woke up much more, it would be like being trapped inside a metal box with an angry tiger. Lou had never kicked anyone in the face, but this seemed like the time. He took two steps and swung his right leg up toward the man's chin, as viciously as he could. The guard reacted much quicker than Lou had anticipated, batting Lou's foot aside with the swipe of a meaty arm, and the kick barely connected enough to throw the man off balance.

Trouble.

Lou knew he had only seconds to act. Another kick was probably not the answer. His eyes were drawn to a large amount of excess chain, dangling from George and looped loosely on the floor.

The guard was wobbly, but readying himself to stand. Lou's only hope was that the man's concussion was still slowing him down.

Diving headfirst, Lou grabbed the chain about four feet from the end, and swung it with all his might at the guard's face, connecting with much more force than he had with the kick. The blond reeled as Lou was wrapping the end of the chain around his own fist, creating in effect a set of brass knuckles. A right hook connected solidly enough to send the man spinning onto his face.

Lou leapt on his back and in an instant had the chain wrapped around his throat. Kicking frantically, the guard rolled over, forcing Lou onto his back. But Lou, now beneath him, was still able to keep maximum tension on the chain.

The man, on top, facing upward, was thrashing wildly, trying to break free of Lou's hold. Lou responded by pulling even tighter on the chain.

"Stop fighting," he said through tightly clenched teeth. "You're only going to make it worse."

For emphasis, he used up what felt like his remaining strength to increase the tension.

The guard continued to thrash. Lou kept the chain taut, but the task was getting harder. His own muscles were battered and burning, and he doubted he could hold on much longer. The beast had to black out. Turning his head for better leverage, Lou held on.

At that moment, where the floor met the wall, in the darkest corner of the car, he spotted the gun. There was no way the guard could have seen it there yet.

Was the man losing consciousness? Getting foggy? It certainly didn't feel like it. Could Lou beat him to the gun and get set to shoot it? Close call.

Lou's arms were on fire now. If anything, the guard's struggles seemed to be intensifying. His weight, pressing down, was making it hard for Lou to take in a full breath. He felt his strength beginning to go.

This was it.

Somehow, he had to get the beast off him and go for the gun.

At that moment desperation took over, and with absolutely no idea what he was about to do, Lou tilted his chin down, released the chain, and with all his might, bit the man at the base of his neck. At the same moment, he shoved upward as forcefully as he could. The guard, wrestling with the chain, and now in intense pain where his shoulder joined his neck, offered no resistance.

Lou shoved him aside and scrambled for the gun. The guard actually managed to grab him by the ankle, but it was too late. Lou spun around and leveled the pistol at the man's chest.

"One more move and you're dead!" Lou snapped.

The guard, the chain loose around his neck and blood flowing freely from the deep bite Lou had inflicted, sank back exhausted and beaten.

Painfully, gasping for air, Lou struggled to his feet. "The key . . . now!"

The guard unwound the chain and let it fall. "I don't have the key," he said, barely able to be heard over his hoarseness. "Mr. Chester has the key. He's the only one."

"Stand up and pull your pockets out."

The man did as he was ordered. Nothing but a wallet.

Next Lou warily retrieved his jacket from where it had been laid over a folding chair. Nothing in the pockets but what seemed like a full magazine of ammunition.

Lou flipped open the wallet. "Dolph, that your name?"

"You fucking bit me, you bastard."

"I'll look for some soap to wash out my mouth. Okay, Dolph, where's Chester? . . . I said, where in the fuck is Chester? Tell me now or I swear I'm going to shoot you in the knees."

"He should be at the silo, waiting for you."

Lou turned the man around and jammed the muzzle hard up against his spine, noting with some satisfaction the continued bleeding from the deep gouge he had created.

"Nice going, Doc," Cap managed. "I'm proud of you."

"Just be strong. . . . George? . . ."

No response.

An idea had begun to take shape.

"Where to?" the guard asked.

"On your face, Dolph. Right here. Dammit, I'm in a very bad mood, and I won't hesitate to shoot. Now on your face!"

The guard complied.

Lou wrapped the jacket around the pistol and, closing his eyes tightly, shot the padlock twice—once on the bottom and once on the side. The jacket did a lousy job of muffling the sound, and the lock fell in two beside the prostrate gunman. Lou undid the chain and kicked it aside as both George and Cap crumpled to the floor, groaning.

"Cap, can you stand?"

"If my arms don't fall off. You are a piece of work, Doc. An absolute piece of work. I think now you just been carrying me in the gym."

"Aw, shucks," Lou said, helping his friend up while keeping the gun leveled at Dolph. "Okay, Cap. Can you get down from here? Good. Just stand close to the car and keep your eyes out for trouble. Now, Dolph, this guy's name is George. If he doesn't make it, you don't make it. Got that? I said *got that*?"

"You bit—"

Lou swiped the muzzle hard across the back of the man's neck. "Up, let's go."

Glaring at Lou, Dolph pulled George to the doorway, jumped down, and hoisted the young botanist onto his shoulders as if he were a doll.

Then Lou followed, knelt down, and peered beneath the train. The last of the cars of the black CSX train had picked up speed, and were just rolling off toward the east.

"Almost home, Cap," he said. "Kneel down and tell me if you think you can make it across."

"Piece of cake," Cap said.

"Okay, then, we're going to slide underneath this car and across the tracks. Dolph, you do exactly as I say, and none of those pretty women out there will have to go looking for another guy. My friend, here, looks like he can handle George, and that makes you expendable."

"No, you're the one who's expendable."

Lou whirled to the voice.

William Chester was standing beside an empty grain

car, shielded by a wall of half a dozen beefy men, each with a gun trained on Lou.

"Drop it, Welcome," Chester continued, "and get inside this car. We need to have a chat."

"Let these men go, and I'll chat all you want," Lou said.

"You had your chance," Chester said. "I only give one. Company policy."

Before Lou could respond, pain exploded from the back of his skull, and his world went dark.

CHAPTER 52

Lou could hear himself groaning, but did not have the strength to open his eyes. There was an intense throbbing from the back of his skull. Gradually, he was able to blink. His surroundings were blurred. The smell, a dusty, heavy farm odor, was much stronger than the one inside the boxcar where Cap and George were being held. Maybe some sort of grain car, he thought.

He brushed his hand over a huge knot on his scalp. *Stupid!* He had let one of Chester's goons get behind him. Things came into focus and he rolled onto his side. The car's interior was alarmingly dim.

Directly overhead, twenty feet or so, a round hatchway in the roof, not totally sealed, let in the only light. Lou pushed himself upright and walked his hands around the metal walls. No steps, no ladder. No way out. The rectangular space was not the full size of one of the cars. It was half as large, maybe a third—a full-sized car partitioned off, he guessed.

From nearby he heard moaning and crawled toward

the noise, trying to ignore the shell bursts from the back of his head. As a doctor, he would often ask his patients to measure their discomfort on a scale of zero to ten, with zero being none and ten being the worst pain imaginable. Taken as individual injuries, his head and the bullet wound in his thigh hovered around a seven each. Bearable. When he finally located the source of the moaning, his own discomfort all but vanished.

Cap and George lay huddled together on the floor of the grain car, hidden by shadows and propped up against one of the walls.

"Hey, pal," Cap said weakly. "You okay?"

Typical of the man.

Lou's vision adjusted even more. Neither of the two was restrained—a bad sign.

He stood, shakily crossed to Cap, and gave him a hand up. Cap's grip was all but gone. He had absorbed more beating. Aside from swollen eyes and a freshly split lip, Lou saw that he was also missing two front teeth.

"Oh, Cap . . ." Lou's anguished whisper echoed in the empty chamber.

"Two on one, I'd bet on me any day. Four on one, it's still gonna to be close. But five or six? Bad odds, brother."

"You're a lion, buddy," Lou said. "They really did a number on you."

Cap shrugged. "Hey, like they say after those horror stories at meetings, at least I'm sober."

George had absorbed another pounding as well, but

he actually seemed more conscious. He cried out when they tried to move him.

"I think they busted him up inside," Cap said. "Maybe some ribs."

Instinctively, Lou checked George over. He was battered, but his pulse was holding.

"We've got to find a way out of here," Lou said. "There's nothing resembling a ladder."

"What about this hatch?" Cap asked, tapping his foot on a spot on the floor.

Lou felt around the edges of a square hatch in the floor, three by three, that lay directly beneath the round portal above them. He was looking for a handle or lever of some sort, but it appeared the hatch opened only from the outside.

"Fill from the top, empty from right here," he said.

"A giant steel coffin," Cap replied. "I think Chester's not taking any chances."

Lou sighed heavily. "I'm sorry about this, Cap. It's my fault you're here."

"Nonsense, I don't remember you forcing me into tailing those guys to Kings Ridge."

"Thanks for saying that."

"And don't you start thinking you're not going to see Emily again. Because that's not going to happen. Not on my watch, it ain't. We'll think of something."

Before Lou could respond, the portal above fully opened, and artificial light from the mammoth granary brightened the space.

"Well, hello, down there," Chester called out.

Lou could see the man, backlit from above. "Let us go, Chester!" he yelled up to him. "It's over." Echoing in the chamber, Lou's punchless order made him feel infinitesimally small.

"First things first, Doctor," Chester replied. "Who knows?"

"Who knows what?"

"Don't play me for the fool," Chester said. "Who knows there might be trouble with our corn? Who have you told?"

"I haven't told anyone," Lou called out.

"That's bullshit!"

Lou knew their situation was hopeless. Desperately, he searched his thoughts for something—anything— he could say to change matters.

"Okay," he tried, "every major newspaper and network is going to run stories about you and Chester Enterprises mutating termites and engineering poisonous corn, and then shipping it off for sale before testing it properly. If I don't get out of here to recant my story and explain that you aren't responsible, you and your company are finished."

"You did no such thing!" Chester yelled down. "I know precisely when you killed my son and when I text messaged you that photo of your friends, there. You didn't have the time to do anything. Nice try, though."

"I didn't kill your son, Chester. Your flunky Gilbert Stone did. Edwin saved my life when Stone was trying to kill me. Now, what do you want?"

"I told you," Chester said. "I want to know who you've told."

"Nobody, that's the truth."

"You're lying."

Lou hesitated. "You're right," he said. "I did tell somebody. Somebody very important, who will destroy you. Agree to let us go, and I'll tell you everything."

"No," Chester said. "Let me show you what I'm going to do if you continue to mess with me."

He reached beside him. A mechanical whirring heralded a grain chute being lowered into the mouth of the porthole.

"Chester, don't do this!" Lou screamed.

"Tell me who you told."

Chester pulled on a lever next to his shoulder. There was a thunderous *whoosh* accompanying a storm of corn kernels. Instantly, dust filled the compartment, blocking out much of the light and sucking up nearly all the air. Lou managed a small breath and then held it. The dust thickened as corn continued pouring down. Lou had rafted the powerful New and Gauley rivers in southern West Virginia. The roar of the corn was like riding down a Class V rapid. The kernels struck like BBs.

All at once the rush of corn seed stopped. Lou and the others were gagging and coughing. For a few moments, it seemed as if George had stopped breathing altogether. Lou's eyes were afire. Dust continued billowing, filling the steel coffin, which now seemed oppressively small. Some of the dust, but not nearly enough, swirled upward and flowed through the open portal. Like an emphysemic, Lou put his hands on his knees to assist his breathing. Dust covered his face and hair. The back of his throat felt raw and dry. In what seemed no time, the level of corn had already reached his ankles.

"Cap," he wheezed, "we've got to get George."

The two men stumbled and slipped as they worked over to where George lay in half a foot of kernels. On three, they hoisted him to his feet. George cried out in pain.

"Who did you tell?" Chester called down again.

The three prisoners were standing on the hatch—George, unable to lift his head; Lou and Cap, peering up at Chester's silhouette. The swirling dust made the man appear to be hovering within a cloud.

"The president," Lou said. "President Mallory knows, but I don't think he believes me. You have my word. Let us go and I'll tell him I was wrong."

Chester jeered. "Of course the president knows," he said. "This is his corn as much as it is mine."

Lou and Cap exchanged bewildered looks.

"Chester," Lou called up, trying another tack. "You don't want to do this. This isn't what Edwin would have wanted."

"You have no right even speaking my son's name," Chester said, spitting in disgust.

"I told you, I didn't kill him. Stone did."

"Bullshit! You know what? I really don't care who you told. You killed my son. That's enough."

"Your son was trying to stop you from sending this shipment. He was trying to get Russell Evans reinstated

and have him make you test this poison more carefully."

The seed baron's silence brought Lou a jet of hope.

Then, without warning, Chester pulled the lever again.

More deafening noise, more spattering corn, more
dust, more choking, more stinging. Breathing again
became virtually impossible. Lou's chest constricted.
His throat closed altogether. They were suffocating—
drowning in dust. Together, he and Cap were forced to
their knees. They sucked air through their dust-coated
shirts, but the maneuver was of little help.

Then, again, as quickly as it began, the rush of corn
ceased.

The two of them coughed and gagged. Probably
mercifully, George had again drifted into unconscious-
ness. Somehow, Lou and Cap had managed to hold on
to him. Now, they hoisted him upright between them.

The corn was above their knees.

"Had enough?" Chester yelled down. "I'll give you
one last chance to tell me the truth and make me believe you. Who else did you tell about my corn?"

"Nobody knows about it," Lou replied with no force
behind the words.

Chester waved down to them. "This is it," he said.

"It's the truth," Lou managed. "You've got to believe me."

He could see Chester reaching again for the lever.
But there was no noise, no waterfall of corn and dust.
No suffocating air.

Instead, there was what sounded like the crackling
of gunfire.

Lots of gunfire.

Lou closed his eyes, flinching with each crack, in anticipation of being shot. The gunfire continued in rapid spurts, but to Lou's growing surprise, no bullets struck the inside of the grain car.

"What's happening?" Cap shouted to Lou.

"I don't know. Someone's shooting. I thought they were shooting at us—some sort of a revenge game."

More gunfire erupted, followed by explosions that shook the train.

Then there were helicopters swooping overhead. One of them hovered above the portal. Men, caught in the spotlights from the silos, seemed to be fast-roping down toward them.

More gunfire. More explosions.

Through the din, Lou heard Chester cry out. The silhouette above Lou clutched his shoulder and pitched forward, still holding the lever on the chute. Again, the corn kernels and dust poured down, but this time, William Chester became part of the deadly cataract, twisting in the air as he fell. He landed heavily on his back, not five feet away from where Lou and the others were struggling to stay upright and breathe.

Corn pelted Chester's body and face. He struggled to sit up, but his efforts only drove him deeper into the feather bed of kernels.

The man's mouth contorted in a silent scream.

Within seconds, corn had completely buried him. Briefly, Chester worked his head free and craned his nose and mouth toward the portal, but the level continued to rise.

With the corn already at Lou's chest, there was no way he could even move.

"Help me!" he thought he heard over the rush of seeds. "Help me!"

Corn had covered Chester's nose and eyes. His mouth seemed to suck in one final breath. A moment later, he vanished.

The flow of corn was nearing Lou's shoulders. The pressure against his body was enormous, and he reflexively began reviewing the physiology of crush injuries. Muscle death, swelling, loss of function, renal shutdown, and all sorts of cardiac and pulmonary problems.

How would dying that way compare to suffocating in corn?

The horrible din was diminishing as well. Lou no longer heard what he thought was gunfire. Maybe the noise had been something mechanical? He looked over at Cap. The rising corn was at the level of the man's upper chest. George, wedged between them, mumbled incoherently. He was buried to his throat. Lou tried to reach over for Cap's hand, but was immobilized within a cocoon of kernels. Still, through the intense dust, they could see each other well enough to exchange looks of helplessness.

"Got any ideas?" Lou asked, surprised at how calm he was feeling next to the man who had been such a perfect friend.

"Yeah," Cap said, "the Serenity Prayer."

"This is going to be tough on Emily."

"She's a strong girl, Lou. She'll be all right."

Lou lifted his chin. No use. The corn was already nearing his mouth. His ears and nose were filled with dust. Kernels continued to sting them like angry hornets.

"I wish you had my two inches," Cap said, noting Lou's struggles to keep his head up.

Lou, spitting corn seed out of his mouth, glanced glassy-eyed over at his friend.

He could read Cap's lips: . . . *The courage to change the things I can, and the wisdom to know the difference.*

Lou said the last words out loud, clenched his jaws, closed his eyes tightly, and inhaled one deep, final time.

Corn slid up and over his mouth. There was no way he could hold his breath any longer.

I love you, Em. I love you.

Her beautiful face was there with him, smiling.

All became silent.

Then, with another rush of sound and a sense of movement, the darkness turned to a dim light.

"I'm looking for Dr. Lou Welcome. Is Dr. Lou Welcome here?"

Disoriented and confused, Lou opened his eyes. He was on his back alongside the track. Spotlights were shining down on him from the Chester Enterprises silos. He had an oxygen mask on. Everyplace around him was corn—piles and piles of golden kernels. *Frankencorn.* Sitting beside him, brushing dirt and corn from his face, was Cap.

"Hey, there, boss," Cap said. "Welcome to the land of the living. There's a guy calling out your name. I think he wants to talk with you."

Lou pulled the oxygen off. He had to clear his throat and spit out a gob of thick mud in order to speak. "George?"

"Medics took him away," Cap said. "One of them gave me a thumbs-up, so I think he's not in any big trouble."

"Medics?"

Lou's head cleared rapidly. He rolled over onto his side, gagging and coughing. Then, with Cap's help, he sat up and looked around. In every direction were crumpled-up parachutes. There were dead bodies, too—a row of them, being dragged away from the train and lined up by soldiers in black greasepaint. Lou recognized Chester's man, Dolph, as two soldiers set his body down next to the others. He was bloodied, and it appeared he had been shot many times. The landscape was complete and total carnage.

To Lou's left was the grain car. Its hatch was open, and the contents of the bin had been emptied out onto the ground.

"Chester?"

"The medics took him, too. I'm no expert on dead, but he sure looked it to me.

A soldier approached, his face also blackened. "Lieutenant Brad Taylor, United States Army, Second Ranger Battalion. Are either of you Dr. Lou Welcome?"

"I am," Lou responded weakly.

"Do you need your oxygen mask, sir?"

"If I have trouble breathing, I'll put it back on."

"Very well. I'm glad you're okay, sir. I have been instructed to tell you that President and Mrs. Mallory send their regards."

CHAPTER 53

Millie Neuland unlocked the front door of her restaurant and motioned for Lou to come inside. She had on what he had come to believe was her standard uniform—a light blue gingham dress and frilly half apron. Her broad smile upon seeing him rivaled the brightness of the midmorning sun.

"Dr. Lou!" she said, wrapping him in her arms. "What a pleasant surprise. I'm so glad to see you. Are you all right? Your face looks a little bruised."

"I'm fine, Millie. Fine."

"Wonderful."

Behind Millie, across the vast restaurant, Lou could see half a dozen cooks and an equal number of waitstaff, all getting ready for what was sure to be another busy day.

Everybody eats at Millie's, he was thinking.

"Business as usual," he said.

"Business as usual," Millie echoed. "Come in, come in."

Millie seized Lou tightly by the arm and guided him into the expansive foyer.

"So, what brings you out here so early?" she said. "You know you don't have to beat the crowd to get served first."

Lou grinned. "If the truth be known," he said, "I came here to talk to you. Is there a private place we can sit down?"

"Why, of course, dear. My office is on the second floor." She gestured to a staircase off the right side of the foyer and undid a velvet rope so they could ascend.

Shuttered office doors lined one side of a long carpeted corridor that was interspersed with foldout tables, on which there were several fax machines, a printer, and reams of copy paper. There was also a water bubbler and mailbox cubby system, in addition to numerous employee notices on bulletin boards—OSHA-type stuff. Taped to the wall was a poster announcing an upcoming softball game against a rival restaurant.

"Lots of excitement in the news today," Lou said as Millie unlocked a door at the end of the hall.

"I should say. Soldiers dropping out of the sky in the middle of nowhere to subdue a drug king—that certainly *is* exciting. Can I get you some tea? Coffee? Eggs? We're going to begin our breakfast experiment in another month."

"Thanks but no thanks," Lou said.

Millie's office, a modest, windowless space with a ceiling that was peaked like the roof above it, was sur-

prisingly uninviting. There were no framed pictures
about. No motivational posters adorning the walls.
Not a single cookbook, either. There was just a simple
desk, two chairs, several filing cabinets, and a lot of
papers.

All business.

Lou closed the door behind him as he entered.

"This used to be a supply closet," Millie said, gesturing him to the classic hard-backed maple kitchen
chair on the guest side of her desk and taking what
looked like a high-end orthopedic desk chair on the
other.

"So why'd you make it your office?" he asked.

"Oh, I didn't want to be tempted to spend too much
time in here. You can't understand your customer if
you're not *with* your customer. Know what I mean?"

"I don't think there's a restaurateur who knows their
customers like you do," Lou said.

"Everybody eats at Millie's," she replied cheerfully,
picking up a menu off her fairly cluttered desk to show
Lou the saying printed below her rainbow.

"That commando raid in West Virginia," Lou said.
"Actually that's what I came out here to talk with you
about."

"Now, what a strange thing for you to do," she said,
her blue eyes narrowing slightly and surrendering some
of their sparkle.

"Not so strange," he said. "I'm not sure what your
news source was, but the raid had nothing to do with
drugs."

"Now, how would you know that?"

"Because I was there," Lou said.

Millie tried for a quizzical look, but her eyes had grown hard. "And if the raid had nothing to do with drugs," she asked, "exactly what did it have to do with?"

"Corn. It had to do with corn."

"Oh?" Millie crinkled her nose and smiled at him benignly. "I'm afraid I'm not following."

"Renee," Lou said.

"Who?"

"My ex-wife, Renee. She's the one who really figured it out for me."

"Figured what out, dear? You're not really making any sense."

"You see, once I realized that William Chester's corn was the cause of all these people periodically losing their judgment and doing crazy, sometimes dangerous things, I was looking for a common thread— something that would tie John and Carolyn Meacham, Roberta Jennings, Joey Alderson, and the staff at De-Land Hospital together. I kept thinking it had to be airborne, or how else could those people have become affected as they did."

Millie Neufeld was granite now. "I'm afraid I still don't get you, Doctor. Perhaps you'd better come back another time."

"But then it hit me. On the helicopter ride back from West Virginia, we actually flew somewhere near your place. By then I already knew. Just as you said, everybody eats at Millie's."

Millie, her smallish hands gripping the edge of her

desk, glared across at him. "Why don't you stand up, Lou?"

He did as she asked.

"Will you take your shirt off, dear?"

"Wire?"

"I just want to make sure our conversation stays private, if you know what I mean."

Lou took off his shirt, and Millie gasped at the extent of his cuts and scrapes. He pulled up his pant legs, too, then put his shirt back on.

"I don't have a wire," he said.

"And you don't have any proof, either, my friend. Merely allegations."

"The FBI could seize your invoices. I bet they'll find you have a very limited number of food suppliers. I bet they'll also find that each of your suppliers can be traced to a food processing plant owned by Chester Enterprises and its subsidiaries. Like I said, it's all about corn—specifically, Chester corn."

"Interesting concept. The trouble is, I wouldn't be so foolish as to keep any invoices around."

"What percentage of the food you serve is processed from that stuff?"

"I couldn't say."

"Yes, you could. How about Millie's Cola? Who makes that?"

"You mean the fructose in it? I think you already know the answer to that question."

"And your beef?"

"All of it corn fed," Millie said.

"Chicken the same?"

"Chicken. Turkey. Taco shells. Cola. All my pasta. Customers almost never complain, either. My cereal. My frying oil. My biscuits and grits. Cookies. Chocolate. Potato chips. Yogurt. Mayonnaise. Margarine. Ketchup. Salad dressings. Syrup. Even our wheat bread has some corn baked in it. Forget amazing grace, we're talking amazing grain! You asked what percentage? The answer is almost everything on my menu."

"Millie, why did you do it?"

"Do what?"

"Feed your customers Chester's corn."

A wistful look overcame her. "Do you have any idea how hard it is to survive in the restaurant business these days?" she asked. "The economy was tanking and it was taking my customers down with it. Food prices were going up high and fast, but the bigger chains could keep their prices low because of volume. I didn't have that luxury. The only way I could have stayed profitable was to raise my prices and lose my customers. Then Mr. Chester came along."

"Mr. Chester is the one those commandos were after. He's dead."

Millie stiffened momentarily, then quickly regained her composure. "I'm sorry," she said.

"What kind of deal did he offer you?"

"He needed a place to test his products for allergenicity and other health effects, and he needed it fast. All I had to do was buy my food from his processors. I tasted everything first, of course. It was good, high-quality stuff. No problem there. Plus, he funded my retirement by just a little bit."

"What's a little, Millie? What was selling out like this worth to you?"

"Enough to let an old lady leave it all someday."

"And Stone?"

"He was paid to keep an eye on things. He did whatever William asked him to. If there was trouble with any of the deliverers, he would take care of that. Little things that I guess added up to a lot. You sure William's dead?"

"Sure as sugar," Lou said. He shook his head in dismay. "Did you know what Chester was doing? Why he needed to get that corn of his into the marketplace so rapidly?"

"A retirement fund buys a lot of silence. I didn't really ask."

"So you had no way of knowing that his experimental corn could dangerously diminish the decision-making capacity of your consumers?"

Millie shrugged. "I just knew that they were loyal and regular customers. But Chief Stone did ask me to keep a close lookout for anything unusual in any of them—allergic reactions, skin problems, and such. And as I said, there were none."

"What you were looking for was only the tip of the iceberg—the things you can see."

"If you say so. Why hasn't everyone who ate here over the last eighteen months suffered these lapses?"

"Maybe they have, to a greater or lesser degree. We may never know if the problems were related to how much people ate here or just an allergic, idiosyncratic reaction, but I am positive that your food is the cause.

And regardless, Millie, what you did was illegal, wrong. You knowingly fed your customers food products that were not FDA approved or even tested."

"You have no proof of that. I'm just a business-woman running a business. I bought my food from the supplier that gave me the best deal. Proof, Doctor. You have no proof that I did anything wrong."

Lou sighed aloud. "Why don't you come with me, Millie."

She followed Lou out into the corridor.

"Do any of these offices have windows overlooking the loading zone out back by the kitchen?"

Millie nodded. "All of them, except of course for mine."

Lou opened the door to the next office he came to, letting Millie enter first. He watched her walk over to the large picture window, then saw her shoulders sag when she looked outside. Lou came over to stand beside her. The loading zone was a beehive of activity. Outside were police cars and several official vehicles from the FDA, DEA, and EPA. They were taking food out of the kitchen and loading it into FBI vans.

"The agents closed this place until they can get statements from your employees. They're downstairs doing that now. They have a court order, but I told them they could wait to give it to you."

"Why, aren't you the foxy little fellow, Lou Welcome. Too bad I'm not a big fan of chicanery."

"The FBI doesn't need invoices when your food can be tested for the DNA of mutated termites."

"Is that what Chester used to make his food? Bugs?"

Millie's insouciance made Lou boil. "There's a lot at stake here, Millie. Lives have been lost and destroyed because you closed your eyes to what was going on. You're going to be found guilty—either by the law or the IRS."

"Well, you should know something yourself, Doctor."

"What's that?"

"I may not be getting everything William was going to pay me, but there are plenty of top-of-the-line defense attorneys who love to eat at Millie's."

CHAPTER 54

"I can't make myself be happy," Lou often liked to say to anyone who would listen, "but I can always make myself not be miserable."

He sat alone in his modest living room, imagining what a shot of Jack Daniel's would taste like right about then. Not that he was about to dash off to the bar, but he knew he was making the conscious decision to spend some time wallowing in his own melancholy.

On the surface, it didn't make much sense.

He had friends, family, a job that mattered (hopefully, as soon as he sat down with the PWO board and Walter Filstrup, *two* jobs). He had helped save the health and lives of countless people, and had at least brought some closure and understanding to those poor folks killed in John Meacham's office, as well as to Carolyn Meacham and her children. Cap and their young friend George were going to be okay, and in another day, Emily, Renee, and Steve would be headed home.

In addition, last night, Lou had driven to the White House to participate in one of the most momentous decisions in the history of American politics—the decision of a sitting president whether or not to resign.

Therein, he knew, lay the source of the gloom engulfing him at the moment.

He didn't know for certain, but he strongly suspected that Martin Mallory was going to leave office and return home to Kansas as penance for dealing untested, genetically modified Chester Enterprises corn to the Chinese in exchange for jobs. Lou also felt fairly certain that First Lady Darlene Mallory would be going with him.

It was nearly nine at night, just over two days since Lou had hugged Emily and Renee, and set off for what he honestly believed were going to be his last hours on earth. Now messages had maxed out his answering machine, and calls were flooding his cell phone as well. The newspapers were gradually piecing together the story, and his name was beginning to pop up. It would, he knew, get worse—undoubtedly much worse.

Already, several reporters had found their way to his front door, to the Physician Wellness Office, and even to Cap's Stick and Move Gym across the street. Lou saw none of them. Nor had he turned on his TV.

Falling for Darlene as he had was stupid, he knew—childishly dumb, especially after knowing her for such a short time. It was easily the most un-Lou thing he had done in longer than he could remember.

And, oh yes, she was married.

Although she had never said anything outright, he sensed her feelings for him were growing as well. But that only made things harder.

At least, he decided now, he was being forced to come to grips with something that had gotten lost amidst all the gratitude he felt for having gotten straight and sober, having a great relationship with his ex and his daughter, and having his medical license restored, now without restrictions.

He was lonely.

Fantasizing that Darlene might fill that void had been where he went off the track, so to speak.

Smiling at the irony of the image, Lou padded to the kitchen for some cold cranberry juice and a four-pack of SnackWell's vanilla cookies. There was nothing that could happen in his life that the combination of the two wouldn't help. He had just returned the Ocean Spray to the fridge when his doorbell buzzer went off. Nine thirty. A little brazen of this reporter—no, a lot brazen. Ready to dismiss whoever it was with a lesson in civility, he stalked to the intercom.

"You're way out of line coming here at this hour," he snapped. "Now, go home and write a story about consideration for others."

"Lou, it's Darlene," her voice said softly. "Can I come up?"

"Of course you can come up," Lou said well after he had buzzed her in.

Moments later, she was there beside him, and all the work he had done reeling in his feelings crumbled. She was wearing jeans and a Windbreaker as she had when they first met, and just as then, she was one of the most beautiful women he had ever seen.

"I figured you came to my house last night," she said. "The least I could do was come to yours."

The summons to attend a critical meeting at the White House had come from Martin Mallory's chief of staff, Leonard Santoro. Lou was ushered into the Cabinet room, where most of the Cabinet, as well as the vice president and Speaker of the House questioned him politely about what they called the Chester Affair. The president showed up toward the end of Lou's testimony, and the First Lady arrived just as Lou was about to leave. Aside from shaking his hand, and a moment of eye contact, there was no obvious connection between them. When the session was over for him, Lou was escorted without comment to his car. He drove home with the strong sense that Mallory's presidency was about to come to an end.

"I like your place," Darlene said, taking a spot on the couch without waiting for Lou to offer her one.

He took the other end, knee on a cushion, hands folded in his lap. "Thanks," he said. "Next to some other places I've lived, it's the Taj Mahal. Emily likes it here, and that's what really counts, and I love being right across the street from the gym. Do you want something? Milk? Juice? Cookies?"

Darlene shook her head. "I won't stay long. Is Emily okay?"

"Doing fine. Hopefully, she'll never know how close she came to being fatherless."

"I know. Martin and I listened to your testimony last night from his office. What you and your friends went through was so damn horrible. You were terrific, by the way."

"Thanks. I probably wouldn't have been able to speak if I had known you were listening."

"You do know that sending in the Rangers was Martin's idea, yes?"

Lou nodded. "His man Santoro told me. Santoro didn't say so, and maybe he didn't know, but I was pretty sure you had something to do with it."

"When I found out about the deal with China, I pushed and shouted for that train to be stopped. I spoke about what you and I had learned about Kings Ridge. I even pleaded with Marty that there were more important things in life than being president if it came to that. For the first time, he didn't simply dismiss me out of hand. He just got real quiet and still, and then asked to be alone. When he called me back into his office, he told me he had spoken with William Chester and told him he was going to cancel the deal with the Chinese. He demanded the train be stopped immediately."

"But Chester refused."

"Exactly. There was a lot of money at stake, not just for the corn, but for the technology. Billions, I think."

"I wouldn't be surprised," Lou said.

"Chester said the cargo ships and planes were waiting, and the shipments were going to happen no matter what. He also said that you were totally wrong and the corn had been proved safe through thousands of trials in humans. Martin mentioned the communication you and I had with Edwin, and Chester went ballistic. If he had to, he said, he would divert one of the trains to one of his distribution centers here in the States and give the corn away. Then he would just make a deal with the Chinese himself. Martin decided that Chester had gone over the edge. He sent in a reconnaissance flight and got the report that there were armed guards and that men were being held at gunpoint beside the train."

"Guess who," Lou said.

"I know. Well, Martin tried one last time to reason with Chester, but apparently the guy actually hung up on him. That's when Martin sent in the Rangers. Their instructions were to avoid bloodshed at all costs and take Chester and his men prisoner. But before they could do that, some of Chester's goons started shooting. You know the rest."

"I'd like to say I'm sorry, but you, your husband, and the Rangers saved our lives." Lou chewed on his lip for a time, then reluctantly asked, "So what happens next?"

He could see the answer in her eyes.

"Martin met with his people and discussed if there was a spin they could put on things that would at least get him through to the election. If he just stayed in the race, there was no predicting what might happen. They considered telling the world that a large shipment of drugs was involved, but in the end they decided that there were too many ways things could break down, and they would end up with another Watergate on their hands."

"So he's just going to go with the truth."

"It came down to being guilty of a colossal lapse of judgment, or trying to get away with an equally grand lie."

"You and Lisa should be proud of him."

Darlene's eyes had begun to well. "Lou, before he went out to tell his advisers his decision, he asked me if I would stay with him if he resigned. I wasn't surprised that I told him I would. What I was surprised about was that I found myself thinking about you when I did. Weird, because we've known each other such a short time."

"Believe me, I've been thinking the same sort of thing."

"I felt pretty sure that was the case." Darlene shrugged *what can you do?* but her expression said much more. "I think the announcement is going to come tomorrow. It's a shame. Martin's not a bad man. He just made a bad mistake."

"Is Victor outside?" Lou asked.

"Nope. He gave me his car when I asked. I came alone. Wasn't sure I'd remember how to drive. I didn't even know if you'd be home. It's silly, I know, given our situations, but I . . . I just wanted to be sure you knew that when Martin leaves, I'll be going with him."

"Why wouldn't you?" Lou asked, swallowing against the sudden appearance of a softball in his throat.

"As I told you, he and I were on shaky ground before all this happened. I was seriously starting to think about a separation, even before I met you."

"That would have been hard."

"I don't care. After you and I met, those thoughts intensified. I don't believe I've ever met a man as genuine and caring as you are. If Martin hadn't made the call to Chester, I really think I would have left him."

Lou flashed on the corn rising past his mouth and nose, and actually managed a grim smile. "I don't think we would have benefited much as a couple if that's the way it had come down," he said.

"I suppose not," she said, her expression bittersweet. "Lou, I know it's not fair, but please, come and sit by me here."

Lou hesitated and then did as she asked.

She set her hand on his and made no attempt to stem a gentle flow of tears. "I can't leave Martin," she said. "Not now. Not after the choice he made. Not after he . . . saved you."

"I understand."

"It won't be right for me to contact you once we're gone, but if there's ever anything you need, anything I can do for you, please get ahold of me."

"I understand," Lou said again. "Do you think you would ever go back into medicine?"

"I don't know. I hope so."

"So do I."

"Lou?"

"Yes."

"I'll never forget you."

He started to speak, but she silenced him with a finger to his lips. Their kiss began as a gentle touch. When it ended, she stood, but motioned him to stay where he was.

Then she smiled, wiped her tears with the back of her hand, and headed downstairs, softly closing the door behind her.

Read on for an excerpt from
Michael Palmer's next book

POLITICAL SUICIDE

Available in hardcover
from St. Martin's Press

PROLOGUE

May 3, 2003

The three men, members of Mantis Company, slipped
out the open hatch of the C130 transport as it flew sixty-
five thousand feet above the world. They had trained for
this jump countless times. Their gear, ballistic helmets,
oxygen masks, Airox O2 regulators, bailout bottles, all
fastidiously maintained, assured them a successful landing. Altimeters marked their belly-to-earth rate of descent at one hundred fifteen miles per hour. Minutes of
free fall were spent in an effortless dive, with the men
dropping in formation, still and straight. Automatic acti-
vation devices engaged the parachutes eight hundred

feet before impact, the lowest altitude allowed for combat high-altitude/low-opening jumps.

They descended through the low cloud covering like missiles, emerging out of nothingness beneath a starless predawn sky. Their landings, each completed with a puma's grace, would have made their instructors back at Quantico proud. Perfection. Mantis demanded nothing less. In silence, the three exchanged their polypropylene undergarments, vital to protect against frostbite at high altitudes, for white cotton robes and the traditional head coverings of Taliban fighters. Then they zippered shut their fifty-pound combat packs.

Wearing their dusty garments, the men anticipated they would not immediately rouse any suspicion. Each of the three had a tanning-booth tan supplemented by professionally applied makeup, as well as a closely trimmed moustache and a fully grown beard. Moving stealthily, the trio blended in with their surroundings—a mountainous, rocky region in southern Afghanistan, barren as a moonscape.

"Any injuries?"

"No, Sergeant," the two men replied in unison.

"Miller, how many klicks to the target?"

Miller checked his handheld GPS.

"Five kilometers south, southwest of the target, Sergeant."

"Gibson, ditch the gear."

Gibson knew not to look long for a suitable location in which to hide their parachutes and other equipment. By the time any Afghani stumbled upon the array of high-tech military paraphernalia hidden behind a jagged boulder, it hopefully would be too late.

They walked in single file, moving silently across the rock-strewn terrain, with Miller and his GPS taking the lead. Behind them, dawn rose in streaks of brilliant pinks, yellows, and blues—giant fingers extending skyward, beckoning the new day. If anyone had checked the men's pulses at that moment, none would be above fifty.

Miller found the road, a rutted stretch of dirt that would carry them to the outskirts of Khewa, a town of twenty thousand that would look the same today as it did a century and a half ago. Young women wearing chadors stopped farming the fields of wheat, rice, and vegetables lining the roadside to give the trio a cursory glance before quickly resuming their duties. The Marines' disguises were good enough that none of the women bothered with a closer inspection. They had estimated that unless their luck was extremely bad, they could survive twelve hours or so before they were identified by soldiers or one of the villagers.

Way more than enough time.

The men of Mantis Company reached the crumbling clay brick walls of Khewa's borders without incident. The town was defined by its absences—no cars, no electricity, no running water. Evidence of twenty years of war was seen everywhere. Craters left by bombs and land mines made what limited roads there were treacherous to pass even on foot. Bombed-out buildings and homes were in greater number than habitable ones.

The smells of the market guided the men toward their destination. They wandered about casually through shabby stalls built of boards, sheets, and mud and bunched together on each side of a single-lane dirt road. The central market was already bustling despite the newness of the day. In some stalls, slabs of fly-covered meat dangled like macabre wind chimes, while blood-stained butchers called out the day's prices in Pashto. Persian music blasted from cheap radios as the Marines continued their stroll past stalls selling fruit, breads, and rudimentary household supplies.

Two hours had brought a sweltering midmorning before they caught the attention of a town elder.

"Don't look now," Gibson said, his voice hushed, "but it looks like we've been noticed."

The Afghani, with a white beard descending to his chest, carrying a Kalishnikov assault rifle, approached the men the way he might a poisonous snake.

The three Marines turned their backs to the man and moved well away from the women and children in the crowded market. To the extent they could control it, this operation was going to be soldiers only. When they finally stopped, the Afghani took two cautious steps toward them . . . then a third. His dark eyes narrowed. Then he began to shout and point frantically.

His shrill voice rose above the market's din, catching the attention of more men dressed in dirty grey or white robes, each, it seemed, carrying a weapon different in make and age from the others. The commotion rapidly crescendoed, with more Afghani men, some armed, some not, racing up from all directions to surround the intruders. They were screaming, shouting in Pashto, and pointing long, dirt-encrusted fingernails at the three men, now trapped inside the rapidly expanding circle.

"How do you like the show so far, Miller?" the sergeant asked, barely moving his lips.

"Just what you told us, Sarge," Miller said, without a waver in his voice. "Provided they go and get Mr. Big."

He moistened his lips with his tongue.

The Taliban fighters were ten deep now, a hundred and fifty of them at least, many with weapons leveled— PK machine guns, ancient Lee-Enfields, plus a variety of handguns. They were pushing and shoving to get a closer look at the men who had so brazenly strolled into the center of their city.

"Just keep your hands raised," the sergeant said to both his men, "and keep scanning the crowd for Al-Basheer. If our intelligence is correct, none of them will make a move until he gets here."

The closest men in the milling circle were a smothering five or six feet away.

Miller spotted Al-Basheer first. His orange beard and bulbous nose were distinct giveaways.

"That's him, Sergeant," Miller said, as the crowd parted to admit their leader, one of the most powerful and influential fighters in the region.

Al-Basheer strode through the ranks. The sergeant smiled and nodded, and immediately the three Marines formed a tight triangle, facing outward with their shoulders touching. The sudden movement caused some of those surrounding them to step back.

But not Al-Basheer.

"Whatever it takes," the sergeant said.

"Whatever it takes," Miller and Gibson echoed.

In a singular motion, the three men threw off their robes.

The crowd began screaming.

Strapped to each intruder's chest were bricks of explosive, three on the right side and three on the left, with wires connected to a battery hinged to their waists.

"Whatever it takes," the sergeant said again.

The push of a button, a faint click, and in an instant, every man within the warrior circle was vaporized within a white hot ball of carefully concentrated light.

CHAPTER 1

Dr. Louis Francis Welcome could do a lot of things well, but doing nothing was not one of them. His desk at the Washington, D.C. Physician Wellness Office, one of four cubicle work areas jammed inside 850 square feet, had never been so uncluttered. On a typical midafternoon, the voicemail light on Lou's Nortel telephone would be blinking red—a harbinger that one or more of his doctor clients needed advice and support in their recovery from mental illness, behavioral problems, or drug and alcohol abuse. At the moment, that light was dark, as it had been for much of the past several days.

Lou got paid to manage cases and monitor the progress of his assigned physicians, with the expressed goals of guiding them into recovery and eventually getting surrendered licenses reinstated. The holiday season inevitably brought an influx of new docs, often ordered to the PWO by the D.C. Board of Medicine.

But not recently.

He strongly suspected the lack of clients did not indicate a dwindling need for PWO services. On the contrary, as with the general population, the stress accompanying the last six weeks of the year unmasked plenty of physicians in trouble for a variety of reasons. So why in the hell, he mused, absently constructing a chain from the contents of his inlaid mother-of-pearl paper clip box, was he not getting any new cases?

There was, he knew, only one logical explanation for the paucity of referrals—Dr. Walter Filstrup, the director of the program.

Rhythmically compressing a rubber relaxation ball imprinted with *Pfizer Pharmaceuticals*, Lou sauntered over to the reception desk, where Babs Peterbee seemed to be quite busy.

"Hi, there, Dr. Welcome," she said, her round, matronly face radiating a typical mix of caring and concern. "I didn't see you come in."

"Ninja doctor," Lou said, striking a pose. "Any calls?"

"A man who said he wanted to talk to you about the

head of his department drinking too much. I referred him to Dr. Filstrup's voice mail."

"Did you get his name?"

Peterbee forced a smile.

"Not my job."

The woman's favorite phrase.

Lou said the words in unison with her.

The woman definitely knew how to make it through her day unscathed.

Not my job.

"B.P., is Walter in?" Lou asked. "His door's been closed since I got here."

"He's having a telephone meeting right now," Peterbee said, cocking her head to the right, toward the only door in the suite except for the one to the small conference room across from her. The door was also the only one with a name placard, this one bronze and elegantly embossed with Filstrup's name and degree.

"Is this a real meeting, or a Filstrup meeting?"

Peterbee strained to smile.

"How's your daughter?" she asked.

"Emily's doing great, thank you," Lou said shifting his six-foot frame from one foot to the other and switching the Pfizer ball to his left hand. "She's closing in on fourteen going on thirty, and is far more skilled than even our esteemed boss at skirting issues she doesn't want to deal with. So I'll ask again, is Walter *really* busy?"

This time Peterbee glanced down at her phone bank and shook her head, as though she was no longer betraying whatever promise she had made to Filstrup.

"Looks like he's off now."

"When the employee of the year awards come up, B.P., I'm nominating you. Such loyalty."

"You mean poverty."

"That, too. His overall mood?"

"I would say, maybe, Cat-2."

The small staff at the PWO measured the volatile director's demeanor on the Saffir-Simpson scale used by meteorologists to rate the power of hurricanes.

"Cat-2 isn't so bad," Lou said, mostly to himself. "Blustery but not life threatening."

"It won't stay that way if you go barging in there, Dr. Welcome," Peterbee admonished.

Lou blew her a kiss.

"Never fear," he said. "I've got a Kevlar life preserver on under my shirt."

Lou knocked once on Filstrup's door and opened it. The director's office, filled with neatly arranged medical textbooks and bound psychiatric journals, was even less cluttered than Lou's cubicle, a reflection not of the man's thin calendar, but of his overriding need for order. Fit and trim, wearing his invariable dark blue suit, wrinkle-free white dress shirt, and solid-colored tie—this day some shade of gray—Filstrup shot to his feet, his face reddening by the nanosecond.

"Leave immediately, Welcome, then knock and wait."

"And you'll beckon me in?"

"No, I'll tell you I'm expecting an important call, and you should come back in an hour."

Lou pulled back the Aeron chair opposite Filstrup and sat. On the desk to his right was an orderly pile of dictations to review, alongside a stack of client charts. No one could accuse the man of not running a sphincter-tight ship.

"I haven't seen you for most of the week, boss, so I thought I'd stop by and find out how business was."

"Snideness was never one of your most endearing qualities, Welcome, although I'll have to admit that it's not one of your worst, either."

"Who's monitoring all these cases?" Lou asked, gesturing towards the stacks. "Certainly not me."

Filstrup looked down, favoring Lou with an unobstructed view of his bald spot, and theatrically signed a form that Lou suspected might be the equivalent in importance of a follow-up survey from the Census Bureau.

"The Board of Trustees keeps renewing your contract," Filstrup said, "but they don't say how I'm supposed to use you."

"How about some work?" Lou asked, his tone not quite pleading but close. "I'm chomping at the bit."

"You *have* cases to monitor," Filstrup said.

"What I have is a handful of doctors who are in terrific, solid recovery," Lou said. "I'm here to be helpful. I like doing this job, and I've never gone this long without getting a new case to monitor. What gives, Walter?"

"What gives is we have a new hire who's working full-time, and I've got to get him up to speed on what we do around here and the way that we're supposed to do it. You know yourself that the best way to indoctrinate somebody new is to get them huffing and puffing in the field."

"Huffing and puffing," Lou said. "I like the image. Colorful. Asthmatic even."

"Wiseass," Filstrup grumbled.

"So I'm being punished because I'm not full-time, even though I've done more than my share of huffing and puffing?"

Lou had been part-time with the PWO for five years. Five years before that, he was one of their clients, being monitored for amphetamine and alcohol dependence— the former used to cope with a killer moonlighting schedule, and the latter to come down from the speed. It was Lou's belief that having battled his own addiction benefited the docs assigned to him. Filstrup, who was hired by the board well after Lou, would not concur.

"That's not it at all," Filstrup said. "You're working almost full-time in the Eisenhower Memorial emergency room, and twenty hours a week here."

"Can you spell alimony? Listen, Walter, I enjoy both my jobs and I need the income, so I put in a little extra time. Have there been complaints?"

"Since you got moved from the hospital annex back to the big ER, you've seemed stressed."

"Only by my reduced case load. There should be enough work for both Oliver and me."

"I told you," Filstrup said. "Oliver needs to get up to speed."

"This wouldn't have anything to do with him being a psychiatrist like yourself? Would it?"

"Of course not," Filstrup replied, dismissing the statement with a wave.

Lou knew better. He and Filstrup had been at odds

since day one, in large measure over their disagreement as to whether addiction was an illness or a moral issue.

"Does Oliver think every monitoring client should go through extensive psychotherapy?"

"It doesn't always have to be extensive," Filstrup said.

Don't drink, go to meetings, and ask a higher power for help.

Lou knew that the terse, three-pronged instruction manual was all that the majority of addicts and alcoholics involved with AA ever needed. Psychotherapy had its place with some of them, but protracted, expensive treatment was often over the top.

He could sense their exchange was getting out of hand, and kept quiet by reminding himself, as he did from time to time for nearly every one of his docs, that whether the stone hit the vase, or the vase hit the stone, it was going to be bad for the vase.

Filstrup removed his glasses and cleaned the lenses with a cloth from his desk drawer. Lou thought the gray tie would have done just as well.

"Just because you were once a drug addict," Filstrup went on, "doesn't give your opinions greater authority here."

"I can't believe we're going at it like this because I came in here to ask for more work."

The phone rang before Filstrup could retort. He flashed an annoyed look and pushed the intercom button.

"I thought I told you to hold all my calls, Mrs. Peterbee," Filstrup said.

I thought you were expecting one, Lou mused.

"I'm sorry, Dr. Filstrup," the receptionist said. "Actually, this is for Dr. Welcome. I have the caller on hold."

Lou gave Filstrup a bewildered look and shrugged.

"Who is it, Mrs. P?" Lou asked.

"Our client, Dr. Gary McHugh," Peterbee said. "He said it's urgent."

Filstrup reflexively straightened up.

"McHugh, the society doc?" he said. "Put him through." Filstrup allowed the call to click over, then said in an cheery voice, "Gary, it's Walter Filstrup. How are you doing?"

The director's conciliatory tone churned Lou's stomach, but it was not an unexpected reaction given who was on the other line. Gary McHugh tended to the D.C. carriage trade and probably numbered among his patients a significant portion of all three branches of the government. He was renowned for his acumen, loyalty, and discretion, as well as for making house calls. What he was not known for, at least within the confines of the D.C. Physician Wellness Office, was for being one of Lou Welcome's closest friends since their undergraduate days together at Georgetown.

Several years before, McHugh had lost his driver's license for operating under the influence and refusing to take a field sobriety test. The Board of Medicine's knee-jerk policy was to refer such physician offenders to the PWO, and in the absence of another associate director, Lou was placed in charge of his case.

Although McHugh adhered to the letter of his monitoring contract, he regarded the whole business as something of a joke. Lou could not help but enjoy the man's spirit, intelligence, and panache, even though he never had much trust in the strength of McHugh's recovery—too much ego and way too few AA meetings. Still, McHugh, a sportsman and pilot with his own pressurized Cessna, had always been irrepressible, and Lou looked forward to their required monthly progress meetings, as well as any other chance they had to get together.

"Am I on speakerphone?" McHugh barked.

"I was just finishing a meeting with Lou Welcome," Filstrup said, as if the appointment had been on his calendar for weeks.

"Dr. Filstrup, I need to speak with him."

"I'm here," Lou said.

"Dr. Welcome, get me off speaker, please."

Lou stifled a grin at Filstrup's discomfort, and with a what-can-you-do? shrug, took the receiver.

"Hey, Gary," he said, pressing the phone to his ear to seal off as much sound as possible, "what gives?"

"Welcome, thank God you're there. I'm in trouble—really, really big trouble. I need to see you right away."

"Talk to me."

"I can't. Not from where I am."

"Where, then?"

"My house. You have the address?"

"Of course," Lou said.

"When can you get there?"

Filstrup kept quiet and still. Lou forced any urgency from his voice, and pressed the receiver even tighter against his ear. He checked his Mickey Mouse watch, a Father's Day gift from Emily. Nearly four o'clock—eight hours before he was due at the ER for the graveyard shift. McHugh lived in a tony neighborhood, midway between the Capitol and Annapolis.

"I can be there in about forty-five minutes," Lou said.

"Get here in thirty," McHugh urged. "Before too much longer, the police are going to show up here to arrest me."

"For what?"

"For murder."

He hung up without saying good-bye.